CW01647726

For the stars.

Ashen Rose

TABITHA HARDING-CHESTNEY

First published in Great Britain in 2022 by Jawline Productions.

1

Cover design by Stefanie Saw (Seventhstar Art)

Paperback ISBN: 978-1-7397737-0-0
eBook ISBN: 978-1-7397737-1-7

PROLOGUE

Cool air from the open window grazes her cheeks as she dreams happily of flowers and days of blissful sunlight. Not a sound anywhere, not even birds —they haven't yet woken.

She lays in her chambers, breathing softly, occasionally a light snore escaping her lips, sounds whipping between them as they purse. Hair ruffled, strands everywhere, the dark mahogany contrasting against her pale skin.

It's peaceful, blissful. So much so, she doesn't hear the small creak of the floorboards as large black boots carefully step. Hooded faces look directly at her, only jawlines visible. Black, leather clothing, with a simple blue seal on their breastbone; the queen's guard.

Her eyes flicker open. They have already seized her, their hands on her wrists, a cloth gag tight between her teeth. Panic overflows her senses. She screams, cries, only for it to be muffled by the fabric. No matter how hard she kicks, her long nightgown getting caught at her ankles, she can't hit them enough, can't get them to release her.

Her vision spatters, black shadows creeping in, a haze of blue everywhere. Even in the darkness, only with the moon as the light that shines through her tall window, she can slowly see everything fading in front. Consciousness flitting away.

Breath shallow, body limp, the worst going through her mind, she yields, with no fight in her—nothing at all. She wonders what will happen. Who they are. Why her mother's own guards had taken her from her slumber.

She wonders if her mother is injured, if they have rebelled, if they are assassins. Her parents must be dead, and she is next. A princess, the sole heir to the Prithan throne. What will they do to her? She had heard people before, mutters.

What anyone would do to be between the future queen's legs.

As they drag her from her room, limp between their arms, feet dragging along the floor, carpet burns and tender skin already appearing, she can't help but be surprised at the thought she would never finish her book. Never know the ending. She supposed that's what life is like, everyone has an ending, but not everyone knows what theirs is. Was this the end of the Thornton reign? Was this the end of Prithan? Was this the end of her? Would they write about her in storybooks, about the princess taken from her chamber and never seen again? Would she be the victim that starts a war? Would they mourn? Would they carve a statue and place it in the chapel, where people could come and lay apples and wheat and whisper prayers to the Entity?

The corridors, usually bustling, are empty. The only witnesses to her murder, to the brutality, would be the burned-out candles and their holders. The wax drips the only tears that would cry for the blood that would be spilled.

Dark stone walls echo with the wind. She looks at them, trying to figure out where they're going, but only the shadows at the end welcome her. She's known these corridors most of her life. This is her home, yet with all the confusion, nothing makes sense. Her brain is crumbled, her breathing too slow. Her lungs hurt. Panic burns in her bones.

She is taken down a spiral of stairs, the tops of her feet hitting each edge as she's dragged below, pained whimpers escaping her mouth with each impact.

After passing a few corridors, she's greeted by two gargantuan doors she knows well. Carved from oak, a tree of life sculpted in the center, a wooden sun shining down. The thugs clutching her burst through, the chapel opening to them.

The room is large, to say the least. Twenty meters high with wooden beams running across the stone and lines of pews leading to the front. Room for hundreds. At the far end is the pride and joy of the castle. Stained glass windows. A puzzle of color creating an image of animals running from a tree but merging into one cloaked figure, white light shining from their open palms. The Entity. Along one side are statues of Prithan's previous rulers. Queens carrying swords or praying. Watching over the congregation.

She's dragged along the tiled floor, slumped over. Her eye catches her grandmother's statue. A fierce woman, a sword laying in her hands, her wide gown blowing and her stone eyes ferocious—just like she was. The princess's grandmother died when she was young. She doesn't remember much. Only her face and her cold words. The princess was often told she had her hands. A sword maiden's hands. But she had never been able to master the art. Her health didn't permit it when she was younger, and her mother didn't when she was older.

She's slammed onto the ground, her palms stopping her from falling, but not without a slight crunch and a cry of pain. So, this is where she would die? In a place of worship?

The princess had been here only this evening for the winter solstice chapel, bringing fruit for sending to a nearby childrens' home. She had looked up at that statue, run her fingers across the bronze plaque at the bottom and the Ghaldeig words of her mother tongue: Elizabeth Cathryn Thornton, the Ruthless.

She lay on the floor, searching frantically for an exit with only her eyes and keeping her head stationary. Then suddenly shuffles come, boots clapping, and someone else being dragged. But he is not quiet, hasn't stopped fighting. And while they dropped her onto her hands and knees, the queen's guards force him down onto his, keeping a harsh grip on his shoulders.

Out of the corner of her eye, she sees bright blood drip slowly onto the floor, small droplets, one at a time. The princess gently turns her head, looking him over. He only wears his white shirt and casual trousers—the same ones he had on earlier. At least he's wearing proper clothes. She has only a thin nightgown, which causes chills to settle across her skin. She can't help but cross her arms over her chest, worrying that her breasts show through the thin material.

His face is bloody. He has a broken nose and split lip, and even with his hands tied behind his back, he still struggles.

She wishes she was like that, instead of giving up. Her muscles are tired, exhausted in fact. Each toe tingling; she can't decide if it's the panic or the top layer of skin screaming from being dragged across the cold stone floor.

His skin has turned slightly paler since arriving. The sun in Prithan is nothing compared to Turkish Arabia. His hair, usually well-groomed, is all over the place.

Her thoughts wander to why they're there, at night and so suddenly.

She wants to cry, but tears won't come. She'll cry later. The Entity will cry when she is a part of it, when all who had been lost would be together finally.

They come when her mother stands in front of her. Long, honey blonde hair tied up regally, eyes lined with deep blue powder, a matching flowing dress on, pointed leather boots sticking out at the bottom, a gold crown upon her head.

Worst of all is the look on her face. Disappointment, like watching a fawn try and escape a hunting trap, its mother already abandoning it. All that had to happen was the slit across the throat, and she was holding the knife.

There is a gleam in her eye: ambition. The princess had seen it before, many times. But never like this. This is petrifying. This is blood-boiling. Heart-wrenching.

"Màthair?"

The extent of her reply is a displeased grunt.

"*Ana*?" The Prince says, confused.

His own Mother appears next to the princess's, also crowned, dressed in fine clothes, a billowing skirt, beautifully embroidered shirt with various threads and colors. Orange, blue, green, yellow. All of them bright, but nothing to make good of the situation.

"Where's Papa?" the princess asks, her voice shaking and her palms sweaty.

Once again, her mother looks down upon her with disdain. He does appear though, out from the little wooden door at the front.

She had inherited his appearance, dark hair, almost black, like charred bark. Bright eyes, the color of maple tree leaves, and a chiseled face; an Icelandic look that was passed down their family line for generations. But tonight, they both have the same look on their face. An internal pain. Skin, white like a swan. Panic. And his eyes are red, puffy. The tear stains still line his cheeks, the wet trails glimmering in the moonlight.

"Papa!" she squeaks, reaching forward for him.

"It's alright." And then in Icelandic, "*Do not worry.*"

"What is happening?"

"Why have we been taken from our beds like this?" The prince speaks in the common language. It means she knows what he's thinking too. It means she's not alone. She speaks it too instead of Ghaldeig or Cymru or Icelandic.

"Quiet!" his mother snaps, and a guard quickly thumps his head with an elbow. Not enough to knock him out, but to cause pain. He lets out a grunt. But instead of lowering his head, he glares between the two queens, fury racing in his eyes. She just keeps hers down, shaking in fear, because she's realized she will not be dying tonight, but there will be suffering. She still can't understand what, until the priest comes out, the blue leather-bound book in his hand. That book had been the property of Prithan for centuries, since before it was even covered in the dusk. Every regal decision was marked in there. Births, deaths. Her brother's birth. Her brother's death. Her grandmother's birth, her grandmother's death. Her mother's birth, her mother's marriage. And one day... her mother's death. She had peered at the papers in the display some time ago. The ink had cracked slightly, and the old, crisp pages had splintered. Only the priest and the queen are permitted to touch it, and even then, only with fine silk gloves to protect the paper. When she had stood there, slowing reading through the pages, she had wondered when her death date would be written, if her marriage would appear there in a decade.

The realization came then. Her marriage. This was a marriage ceremony. They were going to unionize them.

She begs, "Dim! Dim, I won't do it. Please, don't make me do it."

"Do what?" he gasps beside her, but they still receive no answer. Her mother only orders them up and untied.

The princess's voice takes a grave yet clear tone. "This is our wedding."

He stares at their mothers, betrayal, horror, and perfidy painting his eyes. "No! No! I will not!" He then spits in his language. Angry words she doesn't understand.

The guards hit him again, holding him back as his mother brings out a small vile, a delicate glass bottle with a cork top, pouring the brown liquid into his mouth. He gurgles, fighting, but they hold his nose and lips, not letting him take a breath until he swallows. Almost immediately he goes limp, his eyes wide but... relaxed? Dazed.

"Let it be quick. The drug with wear off soon. We need this done," his mother says, peering at her husband beside her and then at the princess's parents.

The guards force them both up, taking her arms away from her chest, placing them at her sides brutally. Both are standing by the priest, who looks between them with such sadness. An old man with gray hair and a long, wiry beard that goes all the way to his pecks, though it's braided neatly. His clothes are simple, almost as if he too was rushed out of bed. She even notices a bruise appearing on his neck, a sort of red turning purple. He must have refused too. He has always been a good man.

All ties are now off, all restraints, all gags. It's just the two of them, surrounded by guards, their parents, and a terrified priest about to solidify a union that will change their nations.

"Under the moon, we make a union between these two souls. Binding them forevermore."

She starts crying lightly. It doesn't quite seem real.

The priest takes a moment, shutting his eyes, struggling to see the princess he's watched grow up cry in front of him at his words. "With the blood, we bind." He takes out a decorative knife—sharp and small, but beautiful. With sapphires and gold, as well as a matching goblet. Gently, the priest clasps her hand. She hesitates, but her mother clears her throat aggressively, a guard stepping forward. She quickly surrenders her palm, and the priest cuts her ring finger, causing her to wince.

"Why?" she whispers. Of course, no one answers. Only emptiness, a soft wind singing in anguish, fills the room.

Blood drips into the goblet, and the same happens with the prince.

"Please recite what I say," the priest speaks quietly. "I, state your name, vow that under the moon, our blood combined, we are bound by the Entity. Bodies and hearts loyal, souls as one."

The prince goes first, still slightly dazed, but not enough to avoid participating.

"I, Prince Ender Tariq Khan of Turkish Arabia, vow that under the moon, our blood combined, we are bound by the Entity. Bodies and hearts loyal, souls as one." His voice is slurred, but sad. He lowers his head, a scruff of his fringe falling too, hiding his eyes. She thinks she might see a few tears in them. The princess keeps her gaze on him, even as she speaks, her voice shaking. Lost and almost silent, like a long-forgotten wind.

"I, Princess Lorilynn Elizabeth Einarsdottir Thornton of Prithan, vow that under the moon, our blood combined, we are bound by the Entity. Bodies and hearts loyal, souls as one."

The priest places a finger in the blood and traces it across her lips, from just above the top by the cupid's bow to just below the bottom. Metallic liquid seeps through, a headache blooming at her temples. Her chest hurts more, each breath harder. But she can't let herself go, she can't let herself pass out. Entity knows what will happen if she does.

The prince, when the blood is also placed on his lips, makes a face of disgust, his brows furrowing.

"By the joining of the blood, the binding is complete."

Slowly, they turn to face each other. When they had first met, she hadn't looked this far into his appearance. He had always just looked like the people from his country, much like when she looked in the mirror, she only saw another person of Prithan or Icelandic Prithan. But now, she sees him properly. The chocolate tint of his lips, the way his hair curls slightly at the ends, the tightness in his jaw, and brightness of his eyes. They were brown but much lighter than his parents. She wondered what he saw when he looked at her.

Cautiously, they move closer, trying to prolong the inevitable, knowing as soon as they touch, they are married—wife and husband.

She'd always dreamed of something more. A beautiful wedding, someone she loved. The chapel would be covered in flowers and fruits, her dress, long, white, beautiful. An intricate veil placed over her head as she walked with her father by her side. At the end of the aisle would be the man of her dreams. He would grin as he saw her, wiping a tear from his eye. As the veil was pulled back, he would cup her cheek, stroking her cheekbone, telling her she was the most beautiful person he had ever seen.

But this was not that dream. This had her heart hammering—not with love, but with fear and agony.

When their lips touch, it's not gentle, or light, or soft. It is tense, and they don't even part their lips, they just bash them together and move away as soon as they can. No other part of them touches, as though if they do, they will be poisoned.

"The union is complete. You are now wife and husband," the priest says, taking a step back and bowing his head. "I will record it in the book and then come to witness the consummation."

That's when her uncontrolled panic starts. Her eyes go wide as a cry tears from her lips. It hadn't even crossed her mind, the idea of solidifying the marriage.

She screams until her throat is raw, but keeps going, even when they gag her again, and guards drag her through those long corridors back to her chambers, where she has her father gently wipe the blood off her face and hand her a small pill, telling her to swallow it after intercourse to stop her from getting pregnant. She cries when he kisses her forehead, holding her tight, begging for forgiveness before he walks out, leaving only her and two guards.

The silence is ear-splitting, and she can't stay still. She runs her hands gently along her bedsheets. Her father had given them to her for her sixteenth birthday a few months ago. She had seen a seamstress making some when they had visited the National Archives. A shop, a small wooden thing, but these were made from fine cotton, pristine white, and the woman had sewn on silk fabric in the shape of lavender. She couldn't help loving them. When she'd seen them, her grin was gleaming, and when her father had given them to her, wrapped in brown paper and a silk bow, she had almost cried with joy.

The princess thinks of what she'll have to do with them, in a bed that was far too big, in a room much too dark. She can't bear to look. They were her piece of happiness, of what made this chamber home, and soon they would forever be soiled, a haunting reminder of this nightmare.

The princess's chamber doors open, and the priest walks in. He is now dressed in more traditional clothing. A light gown, Prithan's crest on the breast, a cloth belt around his waist. Behind him is the prince. He's been cleaned up, the blood on his face no longer there, but his skin is slightly puffy, swollen. It will bruise badly. The nose seems broken, a lump formed where smooth skin had been a mere hour ago. His split lip is swollen and red, plumping his face slightly.

He's incredibly hesitant as he wanders over, almost as though if he sits on the bed next to her, he will implode. In the twenty minutes since their union, he seems to have gotten more control over himself. Whatever his mother had given him must've worn off slightly.

The prince sits beside her and looks her over. Not in a primal manner, but with wide, fearful eyes, quickly looking away to face the priest and two guards.

"Must you watch?" he spits.

"The ritual must be witnessed for confirmation."

"All of it?"

The priest gives a grave nod but lowers his head. With respect? With revulsion? She couldn't tell. As for the two guards, they turn around, a hint of remorse on their faces. She supposes they're just following orders.

The prince turns back to her—his wife. Her husband. He can't help but look everywhere over her, apart from her eyes. He avoids them, flittering quickly whenever they get close to making contact.

"I never asked. How old are you?" he whispers, his voice tense, uneven.

"I'm sixteen. How about you?"

"I turned twenty just before we left."

"Oh..." That was older than she expected.

"This isn't right..." he murmurs, more to himself, his gaze cast downward, gently pulling a loose thread at the side of his trousers which sticks out between the two pieces of tan cloth.

One of the guards clears his throat. "I've been told to hurry you."

Both glance at him with saddened eyes. He stays still, almost like an ashamed, weeping statue, his head still down. Her heart thuds, her chest tight. She keeps feeling as if she needs to cough, the pressure in her chest building. Her breathing is shallow, and the prince takes her hand, assessing if he is making the right decision. But he does and gives it a small, comforting squeeze.

She peers back at the priest in the corner again. The prince gently takes her head, making her look at him. Even when a few tears come, he passes her a handkerchief, and she dabs the corners of her eyes, not letting the drops fall. Almost as if they were never there. She doesn't want them there, doesn't want the pain.

And that is what she keeps her mind on when she lies down, when he gets on top of her, not letting his weight reach hers. Her tears are gone, leaving only thin trails that quickly disappear, until the only trace of the fear, the pain, the hate, is deep inside her. She will use it every day to stay strong. Because she will never let herself feel like this again.

CHAPTER ONE

Each step in the sand is soft, uncertain. The sea chases and consumes the soles of my shoes for a moment before retreating.

I quickly turn, checking behind me. The castle is up the hill in the distance, surrounded by trees, looking over the forest and sea. Across the sand, inland, I see Castletown, people bustling about and preparing for the celebrations tonight. Summer Solstice. The dusk in the sky hangs low today but light peeks in occasionally, shining over the water.

A stream runs along the beach into the sea, sand frogs hopping about in the water and basking in the sunlight. In the winter when snow falls, the frogs dig into the sandbanks of the stream and hibernate as the water turns freezing, icing over in parts. But they survive. They persist. And then go back to their usual business once the heat returns.

I'm deep in thought as a strip of sunlight graces the ground. I crouch and place my sword down gently, tracing my fingers through the ribbon of light as if I can clasp the sunrise.

Bliss is only ever temporary. The sing of the sword comes first through the air. Too melodic to be the wind. Then the movement of my rapier and hand, sweeping round, clashing. I feel the pull of muscle in my shoulder, the light pound. But I can't let it distract me.

I immediately face him, hair whipping against my cheek as it settles, the plait falling over my shoulder.

Magnús—the most fearsome man in all the Prithan lands. His skin is lined with a sheen of sweat, his shirt sticking to his back. Blond hair spikes out from the bun on his head.

I stare straight into his dark eyes, wrath like war paint. He gives out a low, growling chuckle. Looking right at me, his head tilts to it's side, a smirk on his lips.

"An angry face won't help you." He laughs, keeping his arms strong and his sword straight. Muscles tense and toned. His Icelandic accent is beautiful, like a birdsong. I suppose he was once very attractive.

"You never know," I gasp. Where was he hiding? I quickly skirt my eyes around the beach, but it's bare sand with a few rocks. About a meter behind Magnús there seems a dip where a mound had been. How long was he holding his breath? Specks of grain snows over his head now that I look closely.

"Are we going to stand here until one of us dies of old age? Or will you use your death glare, princess?" His taunt is comical, penalizing. It makes me furious, makes the determination inside me burn more than the aches, the pains, the sweat. He advances, sparing seconds for my mind to calculate his next move. I slam my knee into his stomach, And Magnús reels, allowing me time to position my sword. Then the true fight begins. A ballet of blades. An opera in metal. Light glinting off the steel.

My muscles burn, sharp stabs from using them so much suddenly. But I fight through, determined, not letting him win. If he wins, I will never forgive myself.

His sword catches my arm, then my leg, small drips of blood dribbling down my limbs and into the sand. The sting is intense, almost burning. I want to stop, but I can't. We're face-to-face, so close I can see his pupils adjust to the light, his eyes wide with madness.

"You're making this too easy," he growls, flashing brilliant white teeth, biting the air. My breathing hitches as my chest tightens. I struggle to get my breath. That's all he needs. The weight in his arm changes, knocking the sword out of my hand, out of reach. He pushes me down, catching his weapon along my neck, cutting it, warm blood seeping onto my white shirt.

I'm staring down the blade. One jab forward, it would pierce my heart, blood spurting out, white shirt stained. But today was not the day.

"And you're dead," Magnús spits, his tone harsh. Disappointment veils his face.

"I lost my breath," I argue.

He sets his sword in its sheath and clasps mine from the sand, passing it over.

I weigh it in my hands, carefully running a finger across the blade. So much has changed since he first handed me this sword. I use my sleeve to rub some dirt off. I can feel him watching me, wanting me to face him instead of wallowing in my disappointment.

"Your enemies won't stop to let you breathe. They'll just pierce your body and leave you to bleed on the ground, alone. You'll die. Understood? They'll use it against you. Your only choice is to keep going no matter how much it hurts."

"I'm sorry, Mags."

He examines me. In the two years he's been training me, I've gone from being spindle thin and weak, to who I am today. My muscles have developed, my shoulders and calves are more defined. I feel stronger, as if I can fight back.

"You've still improved," he says.

"But I haven't beaten you."

"Well, I *am* the best."

"Exactly."

That makes him chuckle, and I even see pride in his gaze. "Your faðir would be proud."

"My father would tell me to be careful," I counter and turn to the rising sun. Birds are starting to sing, tweet, and fly between nests in the green treetops. Even the cool autumn wind begins to blow through, causing stray hairs to tickle my cheeks. I can feel them pinking, rouge blooming.

And then everything seems heavy, missing him. My father. My Papa. I think Magnús senses that and places a hand on my arm.

"They'll come," Magnús insists gently, "he promised."

"I'm used to it now. They should have arrived sometime in the past week. And it's not like this is the first time they've sent letters promising to return home yet never arrived." I smile lightly, just enough to stop questions. "We should head back. Someone will soon notice my empty bed and raise questions about what I do with my early mornings."

Magnús gives a low snigger, a small bow of his head. I pass over my sword carefully. In our first session, I had nicked his thumb by accident. He still has the scar, a pale pink line.

"Let's go, Lorilynn."

We wander to the wood line and find our horses happily chewing on the hay we left. I graze my hand over Snowflake's dark mane and then clamber on. We canter towards the path and head through the trees towards Castletown.

Castletown was built at the same time as Prithan castle. Much of it is recycled materials from construction. As time went on, it expanded. What was originally a place for servants to live became a bustling place of life. With farmers, bakers, as well as its own port. Hundreds live there. Bards, beggars, merchants, soldiers, and everyone in-between.

More decorations are up now, bunting across the stone buildings and stalls displaying their colors. As we ride through, a little girl waves happily, grinning and holding up a small daisy towards me. I slow Snowflake to a stop and climb down, crouching in front of her, smiling.

Carefully, she places it behind my ear before giving a small giggle and running off with her friends, her dress trailing behind her. When I was younger, I'd often stare out the window on Solstice, seeing the children happily bound about with flower crowns and sneak sips of apple wine. For years, I longed to join them. Eventually I grew up and there wasn't time.

"Lynn, over here!" a soft voice calls. Lynn. Only here could I be that, just Lynn. They didn't know who I was. And I wouldn't change that.

I turn over to a bakery built into the side of an old house. The top of the building has crumbled, the old roof gone—from charred, sharp edges peering out, it appears from a fire a few decades ago. A new roof was built though, the front beautifully decorated with oak, vines climbing up the side, white roses blooming, mating with the scent of fresh bread.

"Heather! Good morning!" I wave and skip over, beaming. Mags clambers down from his horse, taking Snowflake's reins and following slowly, a shy smile on his face.

Heather is about a decade older than me. A few lines are etched in her skin, but her cheeks are rosy and eyes bright. Her blonde hair is tied up and wrapped in a bandana, a few strands escaping. A smear of flour dusts her cheek. She tries wiping it away only to spread it further. I don't hesitate and wrap my arms around her. We hold a moment before parting.

"How was training?" she asks, quickly peering to where Magnús stands behind me, before returning her gaze to me as if nothing happened.

"Someone—" I cast a glance at Mags, "—knocked me on my arse again."

"What a dick," she jokes, looking at him once more. I give a small smile when she returns her gaze to me, the tip of her nose pinking. "How is her Royal Highness doing?"

I cast my usual sweet smile whenever Heather asks this question. "The princess is well, thank you. She also wants to pass on her adoration for those apple tarts. I have some herbs in exchange for more."

"I'm so glad!" She claps happily.

I peer over at Mags, the corner of his mouth curling upwards.

In the small, silent moment, comes a loud shriek. A pained cry that writhes through my blood. I turn my head to the noise, seeing two villagers walk out of a house, a door between them used as a stretcher, with a sheet covering a still body. My breath hitches, watching a young woman clutch her heavily pregnant stomach, sobs running through her.

Magnús speaks near silently, "That's the fifth this month. It's getting worse."

Heather wipes her eyes and hastily passes over a small paper bag, the scent of sweet butter drifting through my nose. I silently exchange a bag of rosemary and then go back to Snowflake, taking the reins and beginning to walk out of this place.

With the dusk slowly dissipating, particles have begun falling. Those with lung damage are unable to fight infection and our tea stores are gone. There isn't anything to help their bodies fight it. It's an unpreventable epidemic.

I wrote to Mother and Papa two months ago explaining the situation. They said not much longer. Not to worry. But I'm worrying.

"I don't know what I can do," I whisper to Mags as he catches up with me. We both wander through the village, mumbles and murmuring sounding throughout at the death of another. "It feels insulting at this point to send in dried nettles."

"They need tea," he adds.

"They need their queen."

After a few minutes of deafening silence, we approach the castle stables, Castletown in the distance behind us. I put Snowflake into a stall and get him some fresh water. Mags puts his horse away too. Soon I have my tutor session with Adora, and until tomorrow, we're back to being princess and guard.

"If I may, Lorilynn," he says softly, "they have a princess. Hiding behind your illness offers them no hope."

"They already lost their prince. I am not immune to this— far from it. I can't go out there trying to be a white knight only to die too. The tiniest infection could be my end *and* the end to the Thornton bloodline. It would be wrong to potentially put the entire nation through that. Besides, it's Mother's choice. Not mine."

"*You're stronger than you realize*." Then he speaks in Icelandic, "*Stronger than anyone realizes*."

"I'll see you after my tutoring session." I pass one of the pastries Heather had traded to him, then quickly sneak through the garden gate at the side.

Prithan's castle gardens have always been beautiful, green everywhere. Flowers lining every path. Towards the back high hedges dwell, grown over a decade, tall and dark.

When I was younger, I would walk through there, after my return from the Botanical Island. It was a place of sanctuary, where I could have silence and peace.

And even before then, when they were low and growing, I would sit in the library window as Papa read to me when I wasn't allowed outside, the machine by the chair keeping me alive. A maid constantly at my side, pumping it. Mother would often sit on a bench, just at the back by her favorite red rose bush. She would look over the castle, the workers, eyes always watching. Sometimes, when she looked up at the window where I was curled up with a book, I thought I could see a hint of a smile. A hint of joy. A hint of hope—that the woman who bore me, who grew me inside of her, who made up for half of who I am, could possibly be happy.

I walk through now, cool wind in my hair. The sun beams down on the mildew lining petals. I feel a small amount of peace, just before I walk into my room, where I will bathe, dress, eat, spend my day maintaining a castle which no one will ever see, like every other day. It's endless. These mornings are my bliss, a moment for me. Where I feel I have a purpose. And where I feel strong, even if I will never beat Magnús.

I walk along a path to the side door. Old and wooden, a subtle way into the entrance hall. It creaks as I open it, not too much. I creep across the dark wood floor towards the stairs which follow the wall up to the mezzanine and the rest of the castle. At the end of the hall are two heavy doors. In the day, there are four guards in here. At night, only two stand outside, probably breathing into their hands to stay warm. They stop anyone getting in, and luckily don't know about me going out. The castle isn't at risk of attack with the king and queen away, so military presence is a bit more lax than it would be otherwise.

I always disliked the lingering shadows in here before.

Whenever Mother is here, she keeps the curtains shut, letting in little light. I keep them open now, letting sunrise spill inside. It is far happier.

Most noticeable is the tapestry. It hangs opposite the windows, there since before Mother was even born. It's gargantuan, stretching from floor to ceiling, with royal blue silk which ripples like waves whenever the front doors open, a gold embroidery crest sewn in a shimmering thread. A sense of patriotism warms me whenever I see it, a shield with a sword and scroll crossing. Simple, but proud. Whoever sewed it must have gotten infuriated. Sweat, blood, and tears surely went into it. I'm certain they were filled with pride once it was completed.

Slowly, I creep up the grand stairs, stepping only on the tips of my toes. While it is unlikely someone will come, if I'm heard, the supervisor will storm through, thinking I'm a loud servant, and then he'll tell Mother I was caught sneaking through the castle, dressed in the clothes of a guard and covered in blood. I'd get in trouble. So would Mags. I spent so much of my childhood near death, it’s stupid to put myself close to it every morning in her eyes. I know I won't get hurt, but she doesn't.

Every step is carful. One of them squeaks, and I skip over it onto the next one. Reaching the top, I'm taken aback by a mumble of noise I can hear. Voices buzzing. When I realize they're outside my chambers, I stop in my tracks, heart hammering and face pale. I've been caught.

For months, I've been so careful not to be discovered by anyone. Guards, maids, or servants. And now, early in the morning, the entire Prithan council is outside my doors, all dressed, all looking for me apparently in a panic. White faces, none able to stand still, until they see me, then it stops. Instead of watching grown adults panic like toddlers, I'm faced with thirteen people staring at me, all in shock, as if I'd walked in covered in blood. Oh, wait... I look down at the stained red shirt. I know it isn't as bad as it looks, but they stare as if I am dying.

The moment feels like forever. My blood cools and my breathing slows. My chest tightens, and I still don't know what to say. It is just overwhelming.

Adora must notice because he strides over, standing in front, eyeing me over. "Entity have mercy, Lorilynn. What happened to you?" he whispers, fear in his eyes. "Are you hurt badly? Has someone tried to harm you?" He looks at the blood as if a knife is sticking out of my chest, slowly unseaming me.

"I'm unharmed," I insist, keeping my voice low.

"We must speak urgently."

"Can I at least dress first?"

"That... would be best."

I hesitantly walk through the crowd. All watch me, mouths open. They part like the sea. I can feel each of their eyes digging into my back as I shut the door behind me.

My maids have been in. Usually they come at about nine, but everything is neat and tidy. Perfect. I can even hear the tub being filled in my bathroom. A dress has been laid out across my bed. I quickly chuck the bloody shirt off and drop it onto the floor, then begin unbinding my breasts from the cloth strips so I can put some clean ones on. Today's maid, a sweet girl I've seen around but never truly spoken to if I'm honest, wanders over to me with haste. Her uniform is bustled as if it was put on in a rush. I cast her a cautious glance.

"*Do you know what's happened?*" I ask in Ghaldeig.

"*I don't, your highness. But I did hear one of the lords mention their majesties*," she replies, taking the bloody clothes and starting to help me wrap new bandages over my breasts.

"*They're here? Entity have mercy on my soul.*" I tie off the binding and begin dabbing a wound on my arm with a damp cloth, cleaning up blood and sweat. She gently dabs too, and then we hastily slip the dress on and tie my hair up enough that Mother hopefully won't complain.

But a hint of excitement builds up in my chest. I'll get to hold my Papa. I'll get to talk to them about the castle, Prithan, about the crisis and what I think we can do about it. I'll get to apologize. Perhaps I'll get to have breakfast with them. I can have someone run down to Heather's bakery and see if we can get some more pastries. And tonight, we can share wine and watch the clouds, see if we can spot the sun directly and watch moonlight stream through gaps in the dusk. Although I suppose they may wish to rest first or attend business. It's fine though, we have time.

I peek in the mirror. My long hair is messy, dirt and grime camouflaged in the brown. My cheeks have some color. I do, admittedly, look tired but alright. I gleam a quick smile and then storm out the doors to the crowd of lords and ladies in the hallway.

"Where are the king and queen? Are their chambers ready?" I ask. No one replies apart from thirteen pairs of unblinking eyes. I await a few moments before speaking again, "Has the ship docked?"

Adora steps forward hesitantly and holds his hands out to take mine, affectionately grasping them. "Lorilynn..." His voice fades. "Come. Let us talk in private."

I take a moment to look over his face, the desperation in his wide eyes, the lack of chocolate in his skin. How his glasses are even slightly fogged.

My heart sinks.

"No... Just tell me. Please."

The lords and ladies peer around at each other before lowering themselves, all on one knee. Heads down. I feel like a white poppy in a field of red.

"Long live the queen!" one of them declares.

I'm not sure who but they are probably the scariest words ever directed at me. Every spot of color drains from the world and my skirts suddenly feel leaden.

They all chime, "Long may she reign!"

CHAPTER TWO

"Can you explain it again, one more time?" I ask Adora. After the declaration, we returned to my chambers. He's currently pacing the room while I perch on the edge of my bed, leaning forward, with my elbows on my knees.

"And please take a seat", I add. "You're stressing yourself out." He wanders over to my vanity and sits down, running his hands through his cocoa hair, and adjusts the spectacles on the tip of his nose.

"The ship," he begins again, "washed up on the Skye yesterday. The lady of the island rode personally with the news and arrived this morning. About an hour before we found you." His voice shakes. "It looks like the royal vessel was wrecked."

"Wrecked?" I echo. The dusk sea is one of the safest. Besides a storm every few decades that catches a ship or two, there are few casualties. With Prithan on one side and Icelandic Prithan on the other, very few people cross it, and those who do know the waters well.

"I hadn't heard of any storms in the past month," I counter.

"There haven't been any. Perhaps a spot of rain," he replies.

"So how could the biggest ship in Prithan be drowned by some patter of rain?"

"There is evidence of a pirate attack."

"Pirates?" My voice increases in pitch as my eyes widen.

Attacks on ships aren't unheard of. Pirates operate around the East Ocean and Collective Lands, targeting vessels transporting tea to Brigor. But Prithan has no tea or anything of particular value.

None of this makes sense. They're alive. The chaos of the evidence only adds to that. My entire life I have been told to trust what I know. And I know they're alive.

I wander to the table by my bed and gently pour two small goblets of water, passing one to him.

Adora, like Magnús, came with my father when he moved to Prithan to marry Mother. He had been a ward of the late king of Iceland. Originally from Sudan, he relocated in his early teens and became quite a respected academic. Once my brother and I were born, he began tutoring us. At the departing of my parents, he and Mags were tasked with keeping a watchful eye on me. More than that, they both are Papa's dearest friends.

He sips the liquid, and we both take a moment. Whatever happens next will be the epitome of chaos. That is for certain. Until my parents are back, I am the acting monarch. I must keep order while we get to the bottom of this.

In the moment of silence, a fist pounds against the door. I wander over and creak it open. Various officials are still outside but Mags stands there, anxiously waiting. I immediately let him in. He loiters in the center of the room, peering between Adora and me. He has changed his shirt but not much else. His boots are still layered in dirt and sand, with salt streams at the soles. His hair hangs casually around his face.

"Is it true?" he asks, eyes wide.

"Yes," Adora replies.

"Nothing is certain," I counter and peer outside the window. The sun has risen now but the dusk hangs low. Questions stir in my mind. What happened? Why did it happen? And where are my parents?

"Call for a council meeting," I order, surprised at my stern and demanding tone. "Sorry. I don't know what that was."

"It's what the officials need, Lorilynn," Adora says. "They'll use this as a chance to diminish you. Keep that fire."

"They are harmless."

"I don't disagree. But we wouldn't be human if we didn't search for more power."

That makes me nervous, makes the pressure in my chest more

intense.

"I'll get dressed properly and be there in twenty minutes." I carry on.

Mags nods and then leaves, Adora following. There are muffled words before many footsteps wander away. An eerie silence follows. My heartbeat pounds in my head. Each breath is staggered, and I'm aware of every one. The strain in my lungs as oxygen trickles in and out.

I feel that if I stop thinking about it, I'll stop breathing altogether. Fear runs through me. Truth be told, I'm not ready for this snippet of power. It's as if I'm playing crown.

After dressing and tying my hair up, the maid places a little diadem on my head. A symbol of authority. It's silver with little blue gemstones.

The walk to the council chambers is more intense than a stroll should be. Mags and I stride in silence, not stopping, not slowing as we maneuver the council corridors. They're more lavish than the private ones, with paneled walls, golden oil lamps, and thick luxurious red curtains held open with cords.

The servants who maintain them are always at their best. Hair pinned back, white uniforms pristine clean and ironed straight. The guards have their swords polished, each royal blue sash draped perfectly over their chests.

Before any of this, they would all give a small nod of their head as I walked past, but now they bow low, declaring, "your majesty", or "your grace", or "long live the queen". Every time I just look forward, trying to block it out. I can imagine the natter they talk about their new queen, the young naïve girl, the dying princess.

The entire council are already seated when I walk in, silently gawking.

I tread to the other end of the long, old oak table. They might have replaced it years ago if it weren't for the fact that it was so heavy. Not even twenty guards could lift it. It stands out against the rest of the room which has dark wood furnishings, and navy curtains. Most magnificent is the painting of the entire solar system on the ceiling, with gold leaf stars and Sol right in the center.

Twenty-six expectant eyes stare at me as if I have the answers to the universe in my hands. I don't want to speak, I want to curl up into a ball in my favorite chair in the library.

"Let us begin." Adora, sat at my left, pushes a leatherbound folder over. I peer down at the tome, trying to form coherent thoughts.

The daughter of Skye. Maeve Murphey—a woman a few years younger than me, with fiery, coiled, red hair—clears her throat. Her black dress is slightly too large for her. She looks flustered and has bags under her eyes. Maeve and I have met once before. It was a simple, polite exchange when her parents were on business here. Much like me though, she spent her life on an island, just in the north of Prithan.

"Y-your majesty," she begins. Her voice starts shaking and a tear collects at the corner of her eye. The lord beside her places a gentle hand over hers.

"It's alright," Adora says, "Take your time."

"My apologies," she continues, "Yesterday, just before sundown, the queen's ship was discovered washed ashore in ruins on the coast of Skye. Some bodies have been found."

Adora nods at the folder he passed me. I open it again and look through, finding a list with various names. I recognize her handwriting; she often wrote invites to me to her parties as a child. It is delicate and flowing, listing names of guards, maids, and people of station. My eyes hover on two particular names where the water stains are heavy and the writing is far messier.

Lady Catriona Murphey.

Lord Samuel Murphey.

Adora had said the Lady of Skye rode here personally. I had thought it would be her mother, but she is the new Lady of Skye, not its daughter.

It explains her manner, her being here, her nervousness. Suddenly I feel awful for being stern, trying to be strong. It must've come across as mean, the opposite of what she needs.

"Lady Murphey, I am so sorry for the loss of your parents." I motion to a guard at the side. He walks over and lowers so he can hear me speak. "Please escort Lady Murphey to some chambers where she can rest and eat. Get her whatever she requires."

He bows, and then they both leave.

Maeve stifles quiet sobs, and the entire council remains quiet, watching her go.

I have to keep the room though, keep the attention. Talk only when words need saying. I peer over the list of names again. There are about forty. The ship has a capacity of one hundred.

"Where are the names of the king and queen?" I ask, glancing up.

Stirring and chattering begins. They're presumed death but there is hope. Even Adora is silent. I'm asking the correct questions.

"Someone answer me." I try not to smile, but some creeps through. I think of the possibility of holding my father, him kissing my forehead, telling me he is proud. Of my mother keeping the responsibility from me for another thirty years.

Lord Lupin, an old man with balding hair and a large belly, stands next, bowing his head. I've met him many times over the years. His wife had her funeral here in the chapel some months ago. She was a close adviser and friend to my mother.

"Your majesty," he starts and scratches his long beard, "the waters in the dusk sea can be treacherous. They're wide, cold, and filled with the unknown. Even if they survived the attack and ended up swimming, the chances of living this long are minimal."

"But possible," I correct. "I might not yet be queen."

Adora speaks next. Not as a friend this time but as a member of Prithan's council. "But you are. The likelihood of your parents' return is near impossible. Per political law, the Prithan lands must have a queen. You will be crowned as one."

"What if my mother is found, Lord Tersoo?"

"You will still be queen if the coronation has happened."

It all seems very acute. I feel my head clicking, but nothing comes to mind. No idea, no defense, no fantastic plan to solve every problem. Cogs are working but there is no result. The pressure of having the most important women and men in my country staring at me makes it far worse. I want nothing more than a goblet of wine to calm my racing heart.

"What efforts are being made on Skye?"

Lord Lupin speaks again. I should have probably asked for Lady Murphey to stay a bit longer as the island is under her protection, but it's too late now.

"We have forty military personnel there now to search the beaches. About twenty more are on the sea, and a messenger is being sent to Iceland so military there can look that end too."

We're talking about a hundred people. While it is impressive, it's not impressive enough for my liking and the severity of the situation. The water is freezing and wide. No one will survive long without a miracle. We need manpower.

"Send the hundred spare guards here at the castle to assist on land at Skye. And then another hundred military personnel to help at sea," I order and begin to stand. Adora gives a small, warning glare.

An older lady at the back pipes up, "That's two hundred, your majesty."

"Congratulations. You can count."

"My queen," Magnús speaks now and walks forward from his spot behind me. "This, no matter what, is an uncertain time. You need protection. People are going to try and use this as a weakness. Guards will keep you alive. You are the most important person in the dusk lands."

"But why should that be the case? What makes my life more important than my parents? Than any other survivors? Than anyone else at this table?"

"Because you are queen," Adora says, "and Prithan must have a queen."

The room is silent. More eyes are staring at me and thoughts are swindling in my mind. Land is land. That's it. I am one person who lives in a certain spot of the world set in borders made by people of the past. If chaos ensues, there has to be someone to blame. That's what a queen is. A voice who occasionally has a good idea or two.

"I need a moment with Lord Tersoo and my guard," I declare.

Everyone waits a moment before standing, chairs scraping, the occasional voice or chatter. This can't be it. This isn't how we'd end council. They would require more information, but for now, I can't even organize my thoughts clearly. That, or they're too clear. They need a little chaos. I need a little chaos. There cannot be order without chaos.

Once they're out of the room, Mags takes a seat on the other side. I reach for my hair, running my fingers through the strands, taking some breaths.

"They're alive," I say clearly, "I know it."

"Lorilynn..." Adora's voice fades. "Please. Reconsider. Or maybe we can find a compromise?"

"A compromise?" I raise an eyebrow and fiddle with the fabric of my dress, pulling it between my fingers. The candles in the room flicker, hazing us with light.

"Send the personnel to Skye and the sea. While the search continues, we will start preparing for the coronation. Invite allies of Prithan. Start making some agreements."

"Allies?" Mags speaks, blonde eyebrows raised curiously.

"Ptah, Turkish Arabia, the Southern Isle. A few examples."

"Turkish Arabia?"

The small, almost invisible scar on my finger burns hot. My eyes flash visions of memories.

"It'll take weeks for all the guests to arrive. Some countries have been supplied with the equipment for speed and some will receive the news by boat," Adora explains. "We can send out the message but also the men to search. Yes?"

I raise a stern eyebrow. Adora, out of the two, has always been the most straightforward, the most logical. His husband often complains about how he turns cooking into a logistical game.

He and Mags—and Papa—together create the most perfect group. Adora is the brains. Mags has the physical power, the battle strategy. Papa is the leader. I imagine they must have been a handful growing up together.

"Yes," I finish hesitantly. "And I wish to travel to Skye too. At first light." I don't wait for an answer before I leave, my head held high. Determined. I won't give up. I won't accept the responsibility yet. I will not disappoint my country while my mother is missing. I am not a queen yet, but I will be one day, and that day will not be for many years.

I'm walking cautiously along the corridors, coughing as I inhale some dust. I hear footsteps following. Heavy, hard. Running. I peer over and see Mags again. A curious look on his face.

I step aside, close to where a portrait of some old man hangs on the wall. Someone from long ago, significant in history but not much more. Misty light sneaks through an open curtain, dust curling within the beams.

Mags comes to a halt, leaning against the panels with his arms crossed, worry painted on his face. "When I made a vow as your personal guard, I promised to protect you from harm, from worry. To be by your side and do all I can."

"I know," I reply. "You've done very well. Better than any. You're more than just my guard, you're family."

"I feel I have done my duty very well," he begins, "except the day your parents left."

A maid bustles past, carrying a vase of flowers. She bows as she passes, then hurries off.

"I have been training you for two years now. I know every scratch. Every scar. Because I am the cause of them all."

I give a slight chuckle, but his face is stoic.

"Except I did not put the scar on your ring finger."

"I don't know what you're talking about," I reply, hiding my hand behind my back. "I think the morning has got to you. You should rest. We have the festivities tonight and then a long journey tomorrow."

"Entity, Lorilynn," he snaps, rubbing his brow. "It's the prince from Turkish Arabia, isn't it? As soon as it was mentioned, it's like you wanted to burst into flames."

I think back to the emotions, to what was taken, to what I gave. To the recovery and the pure effort it took. To what it takes to not think about it at night. The pain of realizing that I would have agreed to an arranged marriage—it didn't have to be like that.

We're silent for a while when he finally nods, the absence of words being an answer. He begins to turn when I clear my throat, offering a cocky smile.

"I didn't say you could go."

He twists around and chuckles, bowing his head. "Bring an extra sword with you tomorrow. Just because we're at Skye doesn't mean I'm not going to finally beat you." He bares his teeth happily, "Now go find Heather and say goodbye. We might be gone for a few days, and I know you'll secretly miss each other. Or better yet, just get it over with and kiss her. Watching you two attempt to flirt with each other is like watching when Adora tried hiding how drunk he was on his birthday."

He gives a confused look.

"A disaster."

CHAPTER THREE

Solstice was beautiful. The castle became swiftly quiet as it does every year. I peered out the window from my chambers, watching the lights and the dancing, listening to the distant jingle of music. I'd hoped to join this year, but the day's negativities have made a home in my core. I haven't eaten all day. I couldn't stomach anything beside a few sips of warm milk.

Both so much and so little has happened. Council meetings and paperwork. I try to focus, but Turkish Arabia sits at the front of my mind. I know I must face it, but... I don't want to. I have to prepare myself though. For obvious reasons.

It's at the back of my mind whenever I shut my eyes, the feeling of guards' hands holding me down, of harsh breaths, and fear. I've spent two years ignoring it, hiding from it. I hoped to discuss with my parents, with Papa. Talk about what happened. I can't wait to see him, to hold him. To tell him I have missed him.

"Excuse me," I whisper, dabbing my mouth with the napkin and standing from the table slowly. "I'm feeling a little unwell."

This entire thing is awful. I'd woken this morning after sleeping perhaps an hour to be dressed and taken to breakfast in Mother's private dining room, an addition to her quarters. A little blue room with a small fireplace at the end. Mother and the queen of Turkish Arabia sit at each end, the two husbands by their sides. The prince and I are in the other chairs, opposite each other. He's got bruising over his whole face, purple and green. The king of Turkish Arabia looks tired, hair messy. Papa is similar, red eyes with dark circles underneath.

We'd been sitting maybe twenty minutes. Food was brought. Simple, comforting food. The queens casually chatted about the world as if everything is normal and we're a happy family. King Khan, sat at my left, tried to have a conversation. Asking me about my studies. He's kind, that's for sure.

The prince and I, however, haven't made eye contact all morning. The food was starting to make my stomach churn and the little pill had caused my period to start early. That mixed with aching muscles, makes me want to spend the day in the bath.

I bow my head out of respect to everyone before slowly walking towards the door and shutting it behind me. I lean against the wood, my face in my hands, as a sob writhes through my entire body. Once I start it, I can't stop. It's exhausting.

I put weight on my feet again and head down the stone corridor, wiping my cheeks. I'm halfway to the other end when the door opens again. I don't turn, just continue, hoping to reach a corner before they can catch up.

"Blóm," Papa calls, coming after me. "Lorilynn." His voice is soft, like a hug. Warm. Fatherly. I want to hold him. I also want to rip his hair out.

"No," I snap, turning around to see him. "No. Leave me. I don't want any of you to come close."

Tears start pouring from his eyes, down his cheeks. "I just—" he starts, "I want to apologize."

"Fuck your apology."

Papa has never been a fan of cursing, but he doesn't even flinch this time. "I..." he starts then fades. "Your mother and I are sailing to Iceland in a few hours, the royals from Turkish Arabia will be leaving around then as well." He takes a few cautious steps forward, holding his hands out in front of him. He approaches me as if I'm an injured deer.

I take a step forward, wiping my tears, and then run, wrapping my arms around him. It's warm, comforting, but something is different. It no longer feels safe. Nothing feels safe. "I hope you arrive safely," I cry softly. "And I hope it rains the whole way there." I push him away and turn again, walking, not turning back as I snap in Icelandic, "Please wish my husband a safe trip."

That was the last time I saw him, saw any of them. We wrote regularly. It was a bit weird at first, with lots of apologies and going along as if nothing changed. Even Mother wrote a few times, asking me how I was and if I needed anything. But no goodbye, no nothing. The prince didn't reach out, and I didn't send any letters to him, not that I expected to, but perhaps that would have been a good idea? Seems so now. It's too late though.

I stand by the window, looking out at the people. The dancing. This morning I had said they needed medical help, but my mother's absence was doing nothing to aid them. Maybe this is a blessing from the Entity. A gift. Perhaps I can use my temporary power to do good.

There's a light knock on my door. I swish around and wander over, opening it. Adora is on the other side. His husband, Edward, behind him. I've always liked Ed. He works as a gardener. He also makes the best elderflower cordial in all of Prithan.

The two met when Adora came with Papa from Iceland and got married a few years later. They make each other very happy. If Adora and Mags are my uncles, Ed is my aunt. He's bandaged me, cared for me, wiped the mud from my face, and every birthday, he makes me a bottle of rose perfume as a gift.

"Evening," I greet and step out of my room, giving them a warm smile. "Happy Solstice."

"Happy Solstice," they say in unison.

"Is everything alright? I thought you'd be out celebrating."

"Yes." Adora smiles tiredly. "Everything is fine. I just wanted to drop round these for you. We'll do a study session in the carriage tomorrow."

I chuckle and take the books from him. They're all old, the leather cracked and dry. I peer at the spines, the flaked gold letters along them fading.

The Complete Jón Michaelson Written Works.

The Collective: A History.

Molecular Plant Biology: 2140 Aberystwyth University Textbook.

"You certainly like to keep me on my toes." I graze my fingers along the titles and open the biology book to a random page. The paper is bone dry, tainted a kind of brown color from age. There's a circular drink stain from a mug on one side and even faded notes in light pencil. The book was most likely originally printed in paperback in 2140 when it was produced, and then rebound in leather years after. That was an age ago though and it needs more care. Since then, I'm guessing it's been in the castle archive or library.

"The carriage leaves an hour after sunrise. See you in the morning," I finally say and watch them walk down the corridors, Ed hooking his pinkie finger round Adora's. Once they're far gone, I sneak back into my room and find a nightdress, braiding my hair and clambering onto my window seat. I increase the light of the oil lamp and pick up the books again, carefully swiping through the pages. I start on the biology one, and soon time is flying and I'm swimming in the knowledge of the last civilization. I'm lucky to have these materials for my browsing. Prithan has some of the biggest archives in the world—it prides itself on that. A few queens ago, many artifacts were returned to their homelands after being stolen over various years, but all unclaimed or left behind remained. And then, through gifts and trades, more have been added. Prithan is not known for fairy tales. I was never told happy stories of dogs in farmlands, or pirates sailing the high sea. I was taught about engineering, science, old poets, and literature. I don't remember much if any. Ask me about mathematics and I cannot recount a thing. Engineering? I understand the basics. Just enough to occasionally sneak an interesting fact into certain conversations.

While I know the knowledge is of little use to me, I have a sense of nostalgia for learning, of trying to wrap my head around it. A familiarity. A sense of home and comfort. Safety.

After an hour of studying the importance of the mitochondria, I put the book down and pick up *The Complete Jón Michaelson Written Works.* This, I do know. It is one of the few storybooks I was read as a child. Jón Michaelson was a fantasy writer from about four hundred years ago. He commonly is referred to as Iceland's teacher as pretty much every person grew up on *The Hungarian Cordial* and *Economical Allure*. He even wrote a children's book called *Bop the Dragon.*

Bop was a dragon who lived in a cave and loved apples. One day he was feeling very lonely, high in the mountains and had no friends. It was his birthday, and he was sad no one knew until a little girl heard him crying. She ran away, and he thought she was scared until the whole village returned with apple baked goods. Pies and pastries galore. Every year, young children make apple pie for the dragons. It's most certainly a ploy to encourage children to bake, but it's still a sweet story.

I run my hand over the worn cover, the remnants of paint from an illustration nearly gone. I slowly open it and am surprised when something falls out. I pick it up from where it fell on the floor. A small sprig of lavender. Long dried, a hint of scent clinging to it. It's so small, so fragile. I turn the herb over in my fingers, a few dried buds raining to the floor as the memory pours in.

•

Aeron's funeral wasn't far behind us. Papa and I were walking through the gardens. We held hands as a maid carried a tank that was attached to a rubber mask over my face, pushing clean air into my lungs. I still don't know to this day how they put it in there, but I'm a hundred percent sure it is the only reason I'm alive. Particularly then. I couldn't breathe without assistance. I would get sick often. I'd just recovered from the very same infection that had exasperated my brother's dusk lungs, killing him. I'd almost died too.

The walk wasn't long. It couldn't be, my little body was too weak. It was my first time outside in weeks. I'd been so excited. A maid had braided my shoulder-length hair, and I'd put on a new frilly, purple dress which fell to my ankles and had lace sleeves.

The mask was aggravating my skin, blisters popping up on my face. The cool air from the outside was soothing. We came across a purple plant, newly put in the ground. Mother loved roses. They're all over the garden. Often blood-red ones. The purple plant was something different. Peaceful against colored violence. Like the glow of sunrise after a dark night. I'd reached forward and rubbed one flower between my fingers. I could smell something faint through the mask, but not enough.

Papa had kneeled in front of me with kind eyes and gently took it from my face, freeing my nose and mouth.

"I'm sorry, your majesty, she can't have it off for more than a few moments," the maid had said. Her voice was gentle, kind, but sorry. Papa peered up at her and nodded. His eyes had been red from exhaustion, his skin gray with stress. My brother dying had hit him hard.

"Here, quickly have a smell." He held it to my nose. I inhaled the beauty and a cough then rose in my chest. My lungs began aching. He gently placed the mask back on. A small cry escaped me.

Papa stayed kneeled in front of me and placed the lavender in my little hand. I'd clasped my fingers around it and held it tight.

"Blóm," he started saying, his eyes suddenly tearing, "You know you're very poorly, don't you?"

I gave a small nod.

"Your mother and I have decided that you need to go somewhere else where the air is cleaner. There you can grow into a big, healthy girl. You'll leave on a boat tonight,"

he explained.

"Will you come with me?" I squeaked.

"I can't. I need to stay here. I have to keep Prithan safe."

"But..." I started to sob. "I need you to keep me safe."

"I am. This is why you're going somewhere else. To keep you safe and healthy."

"Why can't I do that here?" I continued, tears falling down my cheeks. "Did I do something wrong?"

"No, of course not, Lorilynn. The doctor is very worried about you though; the air isn't clean enough here."

I remember peering round. The air didn't look dirty. I was too young to understand. He then planted a sweet kiss on my forehead and stood, taking my hand again. "Let's go inside. I'll read to you. What book shall we pick?"

"Bop! Bop!" I declared happily, bouncing about. We headed back inside to the library where we sat as he read it together over and over.

•

I had put the lavender, still in my hand, between the pages where it has been for almost fifteen years. Perhaps the Entity brought it to me now for a reason? As a sign to keep going.

"I miss you, Papa," I whisper to the flower. I hope he knows that. I hope he can feel the pain in my heart. I just want to hug him again, hold him tight. Take a walk through the corridors, sit reading in the library together, eat breakfast in the garden every morning discussing how much we both wished to travel to the National Archive and spend hours in the library there. We couldn't though, there was never the interval.

When he's back and well, I'll take him there for a little time. We can have our breakfast looking over the Celtic Sea, spend our days discussing history, nights drinking mead and talking about the stars as we lay in the grass looking up at them.

I would like to keep the lavender out, but I know if I do, it is more likely to not last. Carefully, I place it back between the pages and shut the book.

I haven't been to the chapel for two years now—haven't worshipped for two years. Perhaps it's time. Perhaps this is a sign.

I find my cloak and veil, pinning the lace over my loose hair and put the cloth over my shoulders, covering my body to not notify the whole castle I am in a nightdress. Although the place is pretty empty as solstice worship is at the beach. Inside the large hall is only the statues. I wander down to the front and sit on a bench, just thinking. Feeling. Listening to the wind and basking in the darkness. A few flowers have been placed by my mother's statue but that's all that has changed. I clamber to my knees and pray.

"The Entity who guides us, keeps us warm. I thank you for the gifts you have bestowed upon me. For the trees."

I shut my eyes, clear my mind, and try to let my thoughts leave my body. Colors soon flash, and I feel as if I'm flying through the stars.

"For the sky. For the moon. For the strength. Thank you for keeping me alive. Though I must ask one thing. Please watch over my parents until I get to them. I'll give you anything, just get them back to land safely. Thank you and blessed be."

CHAPTER FOUR

In the morning, after only getting a few hours of sleep at most, I sit on my windowsill and watch light break over the horizon. Hues of orange and pink filter through the dusk.

I'm exhausted, but I've been sitting for so long, I need to move. To get going. A maid will arrive in the next few moments; however, I don't see the point in waiting around for her. I slip off my nightgown and bind my breasts, then put on some brown trousers and a cream, frilly blouse I think was a gift from someone, but it tends to be regal enough that I can greet people with it and maintain the allure of princess-hood. If I find Mother while wearing it, she probably won't box my ears for ruining the family image.

After slipping some boots on and grabbing a jacket, I head downstairs to the entrance hall. It's still quiet, but a few people are loading the last few bits into the carriage. I wander over to a trunk and drag it across the wooden floor, out the front door, and down each of the steps. A maid hurriedly takes it, not noticing me, before carrying it onto the back of the carriage.

Mags hops down the stairs. He's looking tired, hair casually messy and his sword at an angle on his side. He jumps down each step and lands next to me with a slight thud, crossing his arms and looking over the carriage. It's somewhat ridiculous. After a long history of using solid gold carriages, Prithan has admittedly downscaled. Instead, it is carved from fine, dark wood, oiled with metallic paint decorating the sides in the shapes of leaves. Prithan's crest is carved on the front. Dark blue curtains are over the windows, drawn, concealing the inside. Horses will be put on the front to move it along. Usually, dark brown ones because Mother always likes things matching.

"Where's Uncle Adora?" I ask quietly, keeping my eyes on the sky.

"Probably making Ed help him get more books for the journey. He can never have enough." Mags chuckles.

"Don't mock his reading habits because we both know if it came to it, he could hold the information to save both our asses."

"Knowledge *is* power, dear Lorilynn. I cannot argue that." He smiles as there is a clatter behind us. And, as expected, Adora comes bounding down the stairs. Piles of books in his arms, newer bindings that can survive the journey. He drops a few, and Ed follows behind, picking them up. The two share a sweet look that comes from loving someone for so long.

"Their cuteness disgusts me," Mags jokes. "How can two people love each other so unconditionally? Surely they're bored by now."

"You can talk. I see you and Heather making star eyes every morning." I cast him a glance.

He stays looking forward, avoiding my eyes. "I have no idea what you're talking about." His voice is monotone.

I punch his shoulder mockingly and wander towards the stables. I don't want to be in the stuffy carriage when I can ride. Snowflake is awake, chewing away at a sugar cube when I approach. I gently stroke his mane and whisper sweet words as he rests his head on my shoulder, then saddle him and clamber on.

We start going a few moments after. Adora is in the carriage and a few guards are on horses in front and behind us. Magnús has stubbornly chosen to walk. He is a proud hiker and claims he walked around the entirety of Iceland. I don't know if it's true. Papa says it's bullshit, while Adora claims he's telling the truth. Either way, he's insisting on walking the entire two hundred miles.

Sweat is already lining his forehead and the back of his shirt is sticking to his skin. Heat blooms around us, sticky and wet. While the dusk is keeping us somewhat cool, there is still a layer on sweat shining across our foreheads. The horses have had to stop a few times, and I keep giving Snowflake water as we move.

"I've got to ask," Mags huffs after a few hours, "why did you name the horse Snowflake? I thought you'd go with a philosopher or historian. Not a name I'd imagine a fairy being called."

I give Snowflake a quick, albeit loving, pat on his neck. "He's not named after literal snowflakes," I explain, "I read it in a book once."

•

It's after the third day that Magnús realizes that maybe he would like to ride for a little bit of the trek. *Just a little bit.* Prithan castle is far behind us, beyond the horizon, and Skye is nowhere near either. In the distance are capped mountains with rivers running through them. We're surrounded by grasslands, a few birds perching about in trees. When the fourth night approaches, we decide to stop and set up camp. I rest in a tent, and in the morning, Adora awakes to find Mags and me training, much to his shock. He almost passed out. Mostly because he had heard the years of lectures about how I shouldn't be exerting myself. Yet here I am.

After a quick breakfast, we head off again, horses happily trotting along. By the time we get to the boat, it is sunset. Mags then spends the entire trip vomiting over the side, and Adora and I spend it mocking him.

As Lady Murphey is in Prithan, we are seen to by a guard who immediately takes us to the ship. Dusk isn't intense here, and some moonlight shines overhead—enough to make out the shape of the vessel. Soldiers wander the beaches still, torches in their hands.

The great ship has been pretty much broken in half, splintered wood peaking everywhere.

The surface is already dried, pale and cracked. On one side, a dark maroon layer stains messily. Blood. My heart slows at seeing it, the breath knocked out of me.

Sand scopes out for miles, empty and dark. Apart from the ship. I wander away from the group for a moment towards the cool sea, allowing it to ground me.

The water quickly drenches my boots, seeping through to the bottom of my trousers, sticking the fabric to my legs.

So much emptiness. So much nothing.

Adora strides over while Mags examines some of the guards. The shock of seeing the ship has stunned me, anxiety taking over. I cough a little, my lungs hurting.

"Are you alright?" Adora asks softly, pushing his glasses up on his nose. Water starts splashing at his boots as he approaches me. He ignores it even though I see the panic in his eyes.

"I'm uh—" I hesitate, trying to find some words along the lines of 'I'm fine'. Luckily, a loud laugh saves me. I peer over Adora's shoulder at two soldiers who swish their torches about in circles, laughing and skipping.

I stride over, looking between the two. "Stand in line," I order. One looks me up and down. Both giggle. Of course, to them, I don't look queenlike after days of travelling.

"And who are you to tell us what to do?" one mocks.

"That, Private," the commanding officer barks, strolling forward, "is your queen."

The two soldiers stare in disbelief. It is only when the captain bows that the shock paints them. They fall to their knees.

I raise my brows. "Stand in line," I repeat, then raise my voice. "All of you!"

Suddenly, twenty men and women run over. Tall and proud in front of me. Mags remains on my left, looking over them too.

Their uniforms are messy, covered in dried sand and seawater, but buttons are done up and hats are on their heads. Out of respect.

I stroll towards them, looking each up and down, inspecting, every step calculated. I'm in charge. I must be respected. An expectation when officially meeting with soldiers. I've seen my mother do it time and time again.

I meander towards the two who had been messing about and stand close enough for them to see the irises of my eyes. Anger sizzles through me, and they do all they can to avoid eye contact. I stay silent, looking at them, long enough to seem like forever to them.

"Your majesty," they mutter in unison.

"My apologies. I thought you were having a nice day at the beach when I arrived," I spit. Shame veils them, and each lowers their heads. The lack of pride is enough, and an example to the rest not to test me. "All of you!" I bellow, addressing the twenty soldiers. "You are here to search this beach for survivors, for bodies, for evidence. And when you are done here, you will search the next cove, the next beach, the next island. People are dead. People need saving. This place must be treated with respect. If I see you doing otherwise," I point to the blood down the side of the boat, "I will have every drop inside you on the side of that ship like whoever we're too late for."

I cast a glance over my shoulder at Adora and Mags, and both seem surprised at my threat. It must be unnerving to see me act like my mother. Neither are her biggest fans and have only stuck around for my father's sake. They share a quick look between them, only a moment. Sharing pride? Or acceptance?

I turn back to the soldiers. "Thank you for your service. Get to it."

They salute and bustle away, scattering over the beach, seemingly trying to get as far as possible from me, searching over the nooks and rock pools at the edge of the cliffs.

Even I begin walking away, the ship catching my eye in the

distance. My strides are long. I try to maintain composure, but I want to run, search. I want my parents. I want Papa.

Adora doesn't hesitate and jogs to catch up with me, matching my pace, even walking straight through the water as it gallops to our ankles.

"You should have guards with you," he points out.

"I'll be fine. I'm not straying far."

I reach the ship and place my hand gently against the slimy wood. Seaweed and barnacles cover where it has spent years in the water, like little mountains.

The ship has been pretty much broken in half, splintered wood peaking everywhere. The once beautifully crafted windows are gone, only shards left dug into the sides. Little knives. Anyone who caught themselves on one would have a very large, painful gash and a terrible scar to show for it.

Even at half size, it's still titanic. I can see everything throughout as I stand looking in. The bottom is storage, still with a box at the far end. A level up, hammocks are attached to the ceiling, soaking wet and ripped, like fabric ghosts hanging and swaying eerily as a draft blows through the ship. And the top, a separate cabin. Lavish, rich. The edge of a picture hung on the wall, gold frame glimmering. It's starting to rust and the painting itself is destroyed, its canvas rotting and paint blotched. But that's all I see. It's too high, too out of view. I just want to look. I want to see the clues of where my parents might be.

"Has anyone gone up there?" I ask Adora.

He gives an uncertain shrug. A soldier is within calling distance. He gives a quick, nervous peer. I beckon him, he runs over and bows low.

"Your majesty." His voice is low, shaking slightly.

"Was anything found in the ship?"

"Four soldiers and an officer went up but found nothing that could help with the disappearance."

It isn't enough. I look over the fragmented vessel, an ache for answers brewing in my stomach. At the back of the storage area, there's a ladder leading up to the next level. I can get anywhere in the ship using it, except the top cabin.

As soon as I take the first step, I have Adora telling me to stop and soldiers calling that it's not safe. All I focus on is not falling, tripping, or slipping. The wind howls, a high-pitched sound as cold air flies through broken shards, the sea framed perfectly in the distance. Boxes without lids and lids without boxes are scattered everywhere. One still has few contents. Glass bottles. Most of them are smashed, wine stains at the bottom. A dead fish rots there, the skin peeling away. Luckily the alcohol masks most of the smell, so only a small hint of decaying flesh comes through.

A group of soldiers are now gathered, coming through. Even the officer is trying to follow, "The ship isn't safe, your majesty!" he calls.

I ignore him and keep climbing. The slime clings to my hand as I touch the wood, and my shirt hem keeps getting trapped under my palms. I go up to the sailor's level, where everything is empty and it's just hammocks. On the walls are carvings of words, some in Ghaldeig, some in Cymru, Goidelic, Common, and some in Icelandic. Pictures and curses and prayers. One catches my eye, carved deep with stone. Large letters, full of emotion. It must have taken time, done by someone with too much of it, crouched in the corner crying. *I miss my home.*

I haven't been on this ship before, but I know the royal cabin is above. I tap on the wood, trying to find a hollow spot, seeing if I can predict where the furniture is above.

But everything sounds hollow. There are at least two layers of floorboards, most likely privacy for the queen.

The wood seems wet still, moldy and easily breakable. I look around for something, anything, to break through. How did the soldiers get up there?

I hear footsteps, the sound of disgust on that slimy ladder being touched. I expect a soldier, but Adora comes up, his beautifully crafted jacket off somewhere, his hair messy, and a gross look over his face.

"Adora?" He's the last person I expected to see up here.

"I can't let you come up here alone, Lorilynn." He grunts, begrudgingly wiping his hands on his trousers, giving an irritated sigh.

"Then make yourself useful and help me break into the cabin up." I try bashing it with my fist, splitting the knuckles on my hand. The wood doesn't budge.

Adora starts looking around for something. I slam for a time and the wood dents a bit. But he pulls me away.

"Stop it, Lorilynn. You could get at infection."

"How did the soldiers get up here?"

"A ladder. Two of them have gone to get it, but it's in a farm warehouse. Might take a moment to get here."

"I'm not waiting that long," I snap.

"Which is why I'm here with you, stopping you from doing something moronic."

I try again, and he slaps my hand out of the way. "I might be able to lift you. You're small."

"I'm not that small!"

He chuckles and opens his arms. I climb on. I'm not heavy, but I'm not exactly thin or light, so he grunts, holds me in such a way where my feet are raised. I kick the ceiling again and again and again. Splinters of wet wood rain over us, and I continue until there is a hole, and then kick again and again. Adora kneels, and I stand on his hands. He lifts me through the hole. My trousers get caught on a sticking out piece and rip. They're falling open now, my bare leg exposed.

The royal cabin is different from the rest. Expensive furniture is nailed to the walls and floor with brass pieces, and everything is still there, only little decorative items are gone. My mother used to collect perfume bottles and would keep them on her vanity, but there is only an empty surface. Locked drawers line the side of a desk. I walk over before looking at the rest of the broken room and try pulling them out, but they don't budge. I keep pulling and pulling until the whole front drawer comes off and papers fly out. One catches my attention, written in familiar handwriting and language. Ghaldeig. Mother. It's wrinkled like old leather, one half starting to deteriorate in the corner. Ink has streamed down, making it illegible apart from a few words.

Iceland. Elec. Lorliy.

Adora is quickly behind me, looking around the room, great sorrow on his face. This was where his best friend was the last known to be.

"Why were they even in Iceland?" he mutters.

"A diplomatic visit," I reply, reading over the letters, attempting to decipher the mess of wet ink and aged words.

"For two years?"

I peek back at him, his face dejected, filled with genuine sadness and pity. I don't want him to say anything. He must guess that, because he just turns to an unturned chest, one my mother transports clothes in, wood with iron molded on the side, with floral decoration and a large padlock.

I wiggle it around, pulling and tugging, to no avail. Adora tries with a similar fate.

"It's weak from the water. Maybe we can break it?" he suggests and searches around. Nailed on the unit is a candlestick. He forces it up, bits of the wood coming too, then slams it down over and over. It clangs, and soldiers start coming up the ladder; I can hear their footsteps and shouts as Adora continues. He keeps going, a line of sweat beading on his forehead, some of it streaming down his cheeks.

"Let me." I take it from him cautiously and give one, strong thrust down on the lock. It clatters to the ground, and I grin, ecstatic. Together, we open the chest.

Then I scream.

•

Bile coats the inside of my cheeks. Adora is behind the bush, still vomiting. It had been the overwhelming smell first. I feel as if it's in my hair and on my skin.

I know I will forever have what we saw imprinted in my mind. The way his skin had turned wrinkled and blue. The smell, the pained expression forever on his face. The holes where his eyes should have been.

I've seen a dead body before. But that was barely a body.

Captain McKellen. I recognized him from his dinners with my parents. He'd had dark hair and the brightest green eyes. Not anymore.

They'd tied him up, branded his chest, gouged his eyes out, and locked him in that trunk. He probably drowned in the end.

"Entity have mercy..." Magnús curses as we watch the chest being carried down on a makeshift crane. As it is lowered, the smell mists over us again, "And you're sure it's McKellen?"

"Yeah. There is enough to recognize." I feel like being sick again.

"Poor bastard."

A captain hesitantly opens the chest in the distance and looks over the body before shutting the lid respectfully, speaking some orders to the soldiers. One runs over with a white body sheet.

"Is there any good news, Mags? What is the count of people found?" I ask, trying to change my thoughts.

"Forty have been found, Lorilynn."

"That's fantastic! The queen and king?"

"Your parents weren't part of them."

I feel a sad pang in my chest. They're running out of time. "How many survivors?"

Mags peers over at me with a frown, deep depression set in his eyes. "No survivors."

CHAPTER FIVE

I haven't slept. Every time my eyes shut, I see the captain in the shadows of my mind. After a few hours of tossing and turning, I get up and make my way to the beach alone.

We then spend the day searching the island with the soldiers. They take it seriously with me here, but I still catch many glances and glares. By sundown, my feet are burning with blisters, and we decide to return to the Prithan castle. *We* is a word to use lightly. Adora decides.

The ride back is quiet. Neither Adora nor I can bare to shut our eyes, so we mostly read together in the carriage or take a stroll beside the horses. With the captain's body stored behind us, we can't get it from our heads. Neither of us utter a word about it.

In the nights, when we all sit around a campfire, the rest eat while the two of us stare at the flames. We sip water at most.

Now about an hour away from arriving at the castle, we both sit in the carriage, books on our laps. Despite our insistence at the start of the journey to study, not much of it has been happening.

"Do you..." My voice fades as we ride along. "Do you think it was a slow death? A painful one?" My stomach begins to curl.

Adora looks up from the pages, and color fades from his rich cheeks. "I don't wish to think about it."

"I can't stop. I just—I feel the fear. Deep in my bones. As if it has melded into the tissue of my muscle. The fear I imagine Papa and Mother must be feeling right now."

"If they're alive, as you believe they are, fear will be keeping their blood warm. Their bones working. It is what keeps the adrenaline coursing through their bodies and their minds alive." He reopens his book and lets his eyes wander across the pages. A moment later, he shuts it. "To fear is to be human. Often the fear of death prevents it."

"Like fight or flight?" I offer.

"Exactly. As for Captain McKellen..." He pauses. "I do imagine it was slow. All we can do now is return him to the earth and inform his family."

No more words are said. Adora continues to blankly stare at pages and me out the window to the approaching castle. The bustle of Castletown approaches. Normality.

The carriage pulls up outside the main doors. At this point, I've bitten my nails down to the beds to the point where my skin is stinging.

A guard wanders over, declaring, "your majesty" and bowing as I step down. Other guards go towards Captain McKellen, taking the sheet-covered stretcher out and towards a part of the castle where he can be prepared for the pyre.

Magnús, Adora, and I all watch in silence. Soon they are around a corner and gone. My heart hammers; I must write to his family. More, I must meet them, but the idea of seeing them—knowing I'd laid my eyes on the horror—curls my intestines.

After a few minutes, I break out the line we have formed and head inside. A maid comes towards me and bows.

"I'm sorry to ask on my immediate arrival, but could you possibly ready a hot bath and get me something I can scrub every inch of my skin with?"

"Your majesty," the maid begins as we stop in the middle of the foyer. Various guards hang around, standing tall. "Guests are currently in the gardens."

"Guests? Surely the good lord or lady could have waited a week and arrive with international guests?" I tut. Most likely Lord Fredricks and his wife. Not only were they never great fans of the Thornton's, but they loved being inconvenient.

I release the clasp of my cloak and pass it to her. She folds the cloth and leads me to the gardens. Guards open the patio doors with my approach. I quickly peer around, seeing no one, and step onto the grass, looking out for Lord or Lady Fredrick. When I turn another corner towards a small clearing with a fountain, I hear murmurs of voices and see the top of a woman's head as she crouches to smell some of Mother's red roses.

"Lady Fredrick." I turn on my regal voice. "What a pleasure to see you again."

The woman stands. It is not Lady Fredrick. Her hair is still glossy dark, and a cautious smile paints her lips. She doesn't wear her crown, but she doesn't need to.

"Queen Thornton." Her voice is soft. "How lovely to see you again."

My heart starts pounding. Out from behind some bushes, the prince walks slowly, brows furrowed. He's changed a little since I last saw him at that final breakfast. He's taller, and muscles have formed around his shoulders. "Welcome back, Queen Khan," I manage to say. "I apologize for my absence. Have you been here long?"

"Only a few hours."

There are a few beats on silence. Queen Khan straightens her dress and smiles. He wanders over to her and stands tall behind her, keeping his eyes low. I glance over before looking back at Queen Khan, praying she will speak.

"My queen." Mags wanders over, bowing low to me and then the Turkish Arabian royals.

"May I present the head of my personal guard, Magnús."

He bows low. "Have you found the chambers to your liking?"

"They're lovely." The queen offers a smile. "I was about to call for a warm drink for Ender and myself. I would love it if you could join?"

A small hint of panic builds in my chest. I can't hide from them forever. This may be an opportunity to find some answers.

"Let me change and I'll be right there." I swiftly turn around and head back into the castle. Mags follows, saying nothing from a few paces behind me. He is loud with his steps, not enough to be irritating but to let me know he is there.

Once in my room, I change into a summer dress and brush my hair, letting it run loose. Neat and regal but also casual enough for people I have met before. I'm not entirely sure how I'm meant to act around them. Do I treat them as royals of another land, or as my mother-in-law and husband?

I run my finger along the small scar. It's faded, but I still feel a distinct line. I wonder if his has faded too.

After dressing and contemplating running back to Skye in escape, I head down to the terrace. The two are sitting, sipping something warm and talking together.

It's bright and mellow today, light dancing through the dusk onto the grass. Queen Khan looks out, a few strands of hair blowing gently in the wind. She rubs his cheek lovingly. He pushes her away and speaks harsh words but in Turkish, so I can only go from the angry tone.

I stand in the shadows, out of their view. I take a look at the two of them. He's handsome, I'll give him that, but resembles neither his mother nor his father. While his face is sharp, hers is rounder and smoother. His hair is more reddish-brown, while hers is the color of night. He has dark circles under his eyes. She looks well-rested, if not a bit taken aback by the time difference I'm sure both are experiencing.

Why are they here now though? It takes two weeks or so get to Prithan from Turkish Arabia. Unless they've managed to get speed on their vessel through technology. The wind must have been very much on their side.

A maid cruises past me, not noticing as I hide in the shadows, with some warm food for the two. Roasted vegetables. They both take some onto small plates. The scent of the food floats over, and the captain again flashes through my mind. I cover my nose with the skirt of my dress and take a few clean breaths in the corridor.

I planned to wait here until the food was taken away, but Ender catches my eye as he finishes his plate. I bow my head and amble out. He stands from his seat and mirrors me.

Queen Khan nods as I take the spare seat beside her and cautiously flatten my skirts. She starts pushing loose hairs out her face. The silence is like poison seeping into my pores.

Do we make small talk? Do I act like I'm talking to my mother-in-law or an international dignitary and guest of the crown?

I lean back in the chair, keeping my chin down and peer up at the prince—the king. He's looking at me discreetly too, rubbing his scared finger over his forehead.

A maid comes over and bows, thank the Entity, holding three teacups. "Could I interest you in some nettles and hot water, your majesties? Your highness?"

"That would be fantastic."

"What is 'nettles'?" Queen Khan asks as the teacup is placed in front of her. She peers over the green liquid with curiosity. I reach for mine and take a small sip. Ender lifts his and brings it to his lips.

"Stinging nettles stewed in hot water, *Ana. Urtica Dioica.* It's great for kidney function, among other things," he states and peers up at me again for confirmation. He's right. I often struggle to remember the scientific name.

His voice has changed a little, as expected. It's lower, richer, but melodic. It reminds me of red wine.

"That's correct," I confirm.

The Queen picks up the teacup and takes a hesitant drink. After a few moments, she takes another with a positive face. "Impressive. Do you get nettles in Turkish Arabia?"

"No," Ender replies and then turns to me, "I've been studying doctoring. I read a textbook by Doctor Mary Michaels a few months ago. It was good."

"*Herbs of the Hearth*."

He peers up and smiles lightly.

I cautiously smile back before turning to his mother. She is sipping happily, seemingly enjoying the beverage. Again, there is a silence between the three of us. Some birds tweet before I finally muster the courage to speak.

"I think if my mother was here right now, she'd tell me to watch my tongue. However, it's just me."

"You want to know why you were married?"

"Not just that. Why is our marriage so secretive? So..." My words get caught in my throat a moment. "Violent?"

I want to slam her on the table until she cries as I did, but that isn't very regal at all. Another part of me wishes to scream, to run to Adora and Mags and spend an afternoon with them in the library drinking warmed wine and getting the time I thought I'd have before everyone arrived.

"I am very certain you're an intelligent girl," Queen Khan says and offers an uncomfortably kind look. "And with two years to think I'm sure you have some idea."

True.

I think back to every reason and allow logic to select one. But while picking only one is impossible, I recall the very basic idea of the marriage. Why would two royals get married?

"To unite the nations."

"Exactly."

"But, your majesty, why do it in such a way?" I push and sneak another look at Ender. He is upright in his chair, keenly listening, an eyebrow raised. When we last saw each other, I was only sixteen and very much still a child.

They'd been in Prithan a few days before the wedding, perhaps a few weeks? We hadn't spent much time together at all. He had been a twat, if I'm being honest. Nonchalant and seemingly with his head up his backside. He referred to me as 'little princess' many times, which I imagine must have made being forced to marry me even more awful. I may have called him a prick to his face in Icelandic too.

"Look, Lorilynn, Turkish Arabia was having some political disagreements with Sudan and Prithan had just made a big agreement with the Collective. We needed each other. Besides, it has permanent advantages. At my death, Turkish Arabia will join Prithan and create an empire."

An empire?

Entity, I want Mother and Papa back. I'm going to slap them, hug them, and then yell a lot. I'm not sure in which order.

Ender is leaning back in his chair, eyes trained on his mother, then cautiously peers back at me.

I take another sip of the now cool stewed nettles before looking over the grass. A gardener carefully primps a bush at the side. I'm running through every fact about history I can think of without the word 'empire' in it.

"*Ana.*" Ender clears his throat. I turn my head to him and listen. "Why was it done secretly? Why is our marriage not known?"

"Because the power that you two will hold is greatly desired and fragile. With the union, if one of you dies, the other inherits everything. It could be political turmoil."

I feel the entirety of Prithan on our shoulders. I want my parents back, but I do have to trust them and their decision. When they return there will be more questions.

"You look like you're thinking hard, Lorilynn," Queen Khan says. "Here. Let me change the subject. I have a gift for you." She waves over a maid who approaches with a small wooden box.

I take it from her and weigh it in my hands. Carved on the edges is Levantine letters and animals. A symbol is at the center at the top, with a clasp at the front. I flip it open, revealing a necklace. Delicate and gold with a single ruby in the center. It glimmers in the light, shimmering. Beautiful.

"Thank you, Queen Khan." I'm flattered, breathless by its beauty. "I wasn't expecting anything. This is above and beyond."

"Please, call me Azra. And it's a pleasure." She grins.

"Thank you, Azra."

Azra reaches over and takes my hand, squeezing once. I'm surprised by the touch, the warmth. It's nice. Like someone is caring for me. Mothering me. I've needed mothering.

I reach for the necklace and put it around my neck, hooking it securely. While I'm a fan of silver jewelry usually, I can't deny this exception. I want to wear it. Red might not be the usual match to white dresses like the one I'm wearing, but it's such an eyepiece.

She smiles lightly and gives a small applaud. "The necklace was a favorite of my mother's. She wore it at her coronation. She was nervous about becoming queen, and I thought it might offer you some comfort."

"It's beautiful," I add and gently fiddle with the gem around my neck.

"Excuse me, your majesties." Mags comes through. He's wearing his uniform, armor and a dark blue sash. His formal sword is at his side, hanging proudly. He's pulled his light hair back and neatened his beard.

I peer up at him and give a small smile. "Everything alright?"

"Village reports from when we were at Skye. Two more died, one more is not expected to last the night," he informs me, standing straight and keeping his voice monotone. "We probably want to go and see for ourselves."

I stand and bow my head to Azra, then turn to Ender. "You're training to be a doctor, right?"

He nods once.

"Do you know anything about lungs?"

"Yes." He then adds, "I know a bit."

"Then I have something you can assist with."

He scowls before standing and following Mags and me. I pull a cloak on and we begin to walk.

CHAPTER SIX

Ender strides beside me, while Magnús stays somewhat behind us. He has a skip in his step and a gleam in his eyes. I think he's excited to see Heather. His hair is brushed back, and I smell cologne on him. I peer behind and catch his eye, giving him a small smile.

Ender glances curiously between us. "You two seem close," he states as we walk along the dirt path.

"He's my personal guard. Of course, we are."

"His accent. He's not from Prithan?" he asks. He's looking at me as we walk.

"He's from Icelandic Prithan. When my father travelled to the mainland to marry my mother, Magnús came too," I explain. "He became my guard at birth."

Ender nods in understanding and clutches his cloak tighter. The weather here is far cooler than Turkish Arabia. Everything is different, I suppose. I've never travelled out of Prithan, but I've read about lots of places. The jungles of the Collective lands, the sands of Ptah, the fields of Turkish Arabia. I hope to see at least half of them before I die.

Yet, my heart is here in Prithan. Always. Even this single dirt path I have walked thousands of times, where the mud always somehow ends up in my boots and the thistles at the side always catch my skirt. My heart is here, in the vast clouds of dusk and the sea that stretches forever. With each of the people, and every life.

"The dusk is dissipating. Which in itself is good, however, the particles are being breathed in. Some are fine, but many are getting mortally unwell. Fading quickly."

"And you wish for me to examine some of the sick? Have you not got other doctors to look at them?" he says, a hint of judgment deep in his voice.

"Of course. However, I respect that medicine is conducted differently in all parts of the world. There are things you know that doctors here don't," I explain. "Besides, you'll be Prithan's first doctor *and* king." King of Prithan. Apart from some angry words a few years ago, we've barely spoken, and now we run a country together. But I trust Papa. I trust that he put me through this for a reason—a reason which after some rest, he'll explain in extreme detail.

"King?" Ender questions, raising an eyebrow. He stops where he stands and turns to me with determination and anger. "I will never be king of Prithan. Whether your parents are alive or rotting at the bottom of the ocean."

"Don't talk about my parents that way," I hiss. The word 'rotting' causes a deep pit to form in my chest. Again, the images of McKellen fill my mind. Of his skin, his hair, of the dinner with him where he smiled brightly. "We will find them. And I am not happy about being married either, trust me, but there is nothing we can do about it."

"What if there was?" He takes a step closer to me, keeping his voice low so only the two of us can hear. "There was a concept common a few thousand years ago. It died out quickly as it stopped being a priority during the wars."

"And what is this magical concept that no one seems to have ever heard of?" I question, matching his tone. I sneak a look at Mags. He's cautiously watching the two of us, hand carefully reaching for the sword at his side. Ready, just in case.

"It's called divorce," he explains.

"That definitely sounds like you made up a word and are trying to convince me it's a real thing."

"It *is* a real thing," he assures me, "done by millions from all walks of life. Even kings and queens."

"Our parents would never agree to it."

"They don't have to. Yours aren't here, and I wouldn't tell my mother until afterwards."

I raise a cautious brow, "And your father?"

"My father is dead."

Oh.

"I'm sorry to hear that," I say, a heavy feeling in my stomach. "May he be with the Entity."

"Please, your highness, think about it."

Your highness. Not your majesty. For days I've been called queen when it is not my title to have. He still thinks of me as princess. Whether it's to make me more on his side on the matter or actual respect I'm not sure.

"I'll see if I can find anything on divorce in the castle library. Then I'll consider it, Khan."

We carry on to the village. A small patter of rain begins, cooling on my skin and tangling my hair. I raise my face to the sky, letting the water fall down my cheeks. It's harder by the time we get to the village. Many stalls have closed and gone inside. A group of children play in a muddy puddle by the entrance, splashing about. They wave as we approach.

"Lady Lynn! Guard Mags!" They all jump happily.

I wave back gently, as does Magnús, and we follow in. Ender gives a small, kind smile at the children. One little girl shyly wanders over and opens her palm with a small rock. Gray and simple, but a beautiful gesture.

She holds it up to the prince who kneels to the child's height. She passes the stone over, and he takes it, bowing his head.

"What's your name?" she asks him in a squeaky voice.

He peers up at me with confusion. Of course, she asked in Ghaldeig, which he doesn't know. And she doesn't know Common.

"She's asking your name," I tell him.

He turns back to her with a sweet smile. "Tariq."

She gives a little giggle before running past us to her friends, her rosy cheeks blooming in the cool air.

A few of the people come outside and wave, asking for me to send my best wishes to the queen. I nod happily and agree, constantly getting weird looks from Ender, as if he hadn't just told the child his name was Tariq.

Heather runs out from her bakery through the rain. For a second, she falters and almost goes to Mags, but instead comes to me and wraps her arms around my shoulders in a tight hold.

"We've all been worried. Although we guessed you've been assisting the queen!" she says happily. "How is she?"

"She's..." My voice fades, "Struggling." Which is true. This is the first time I've been troubled with the lie of who I am.

"She's in our hearts. You must pass on my best wishes and a rosemary bun or two. A full stomach doesn't solve all problems, but it makes them easier."

"You're too kind," I say and bow my head. "This is a doctor visiting from Turkish Arabia. He and I are going to tend to some patients. Could you keep an eye on Mags while we do so?"

Red rushes to her cheeks, and she gives a sweet nod and roams over without arguing. Magnús immediately starts playing with his hair, a grin on his face. The two share a few quiet words, giggling on his behalf. They lock arms and walk towards the bakery. He catches my eye as he passes, and I give him a joking wink. He rapidly turns his head back to Heather, smiling as they converse.

Ender and I head to a building, which I'm informed houses one of the victims of dusk lung. We knock gently, and an older man opens the door. Short, hunched over, with peppered hair and the greenest eyes. He flashes a mostly toothless grin when he sees me and offers hands out in kindness. I take them and gently squeeze, introducing us and our purpose before heading in.

Gray stone walls are lined with wooden shelves covered in books and plants and trinkets. Things I recognize and things I don't. Statues I believe I've read about perhaps. Religious. On the side of the room is a small table with food laid out. And in color, so much color. Reds and pinks and blues.

"It's stunning," I say to the old man.

He gives a smile again and picks up one of the pieces, showing me. "This is Dhanwantari, a god of healing and medicine," he explains as he places the murti of Dhanwantari carefully down, "My great-granddaughter is in the bedroom. Can I get you a drink? Or some food?"

"Thank you, it's alright," I say as we follow him to a small room at the back. The walls are painted with flowers and stories. In a bed at the center is a small girl, perhaps nine or ten. Her deep hair is splayed out over the pillow as she rests. Her mother sits beside her, holding her hand, tears streaming down her face.

Ender walks over as I explain what's happening. He carefully wakes her up. Her dark lashes flutter open as she sits. He places his hand on her back and rests his ear there too, staying a few moments.

"Can you ask her to breathe normally?" he asks quietly, and I do, keeping my voice calm and gentle. She nods and takes a breath. The sound escaping her is pained, restricted. You don't need to be a doctor to know it is bad. After a few seconds, he guides her down again and pats her arms comfortingly.

"Can you translate for me?" He turns to me. His face is grave, eyes dark. I nod quickly, and he starts, "She has a severe infection which has caused fluid build-up, making it hard to breathe. She probably has brain hypoxia."

I repeat the words back, although I'm not exactly sure how to translate hypoxia. The mother looks at me, more tears falling from her cheeks. The little girl is already back to sleep, hopefully dreaming of happiness and bliss.

"What do we do?" the mother asks.

I repeat it back to Ender, who thinks a moment.

"Keep the room dry and give her any tea you have. She must be warm, and make sure there's no mold in the room. She's young. There's hope she'll heal with the tea."

I stop just before the last sentence. Because we have no tea. At all. Every store across Prithan has been used. And even if by a miracle the Collective arrived early, it might not be enough time. It might be too late now with the damage to her brain.

"I'll talk to the queen about the tea. I'll search every house in Prithan if I must to find some," I explain. The mother wanders over to us and takes Ender's hands, bowing in thanks. In my pocket is a small white handkerchief that Màthair had gifted me some years ago. With lace trimmings and my initials sewn in the corner in sweet cursive. I hold it out to her, and she takes it, wiping her eyes before offering the fabric back, but I just close her fingers around it. "Keep it. It's the least I can do," I say.

Ender and I leave. We go to the next place, then the next, then the next. From old to young, sinners to saints. Fate favors no one, and the dusk is taking those it can. Many will die the coming days.

After the last house, it takes all my strength to hold back the tears. Ender strides to the middle of the town square, stopping by the well, and I follow. The rain is showering now, and we're both soaked to our skin. His hair is dripping, and mine is stuck to the sides of my face.

"How could you let it get like this? How do you have no tea?" he snaps, the pouring water hiding our conversation from everyone.

"It isn't my fault. I tried everything!" I argue back, my spilling eyes camouflaged by the rain. "I wrote to my parents and tried buying tea, but there was nothing I could do as princess!"

"But you've been queen for days now! You've held that power, yet you've done nothing except try and chase after the prospect of not having responsibility."

"My parents are alive!" I spit. "Not searching for them is as bad as committing the ship to the bottom of the sea."

"You're acting like a child. Grow up. Because by doing that you've committed your people here to die." He twists a moment to go, but then turns back. "When life allows us to make the world a better place, we take it. Wholeheartedly. And hope that if we die in the process then it saves lives."

I'm left in the cold as he storms back towards the castle. His shoulders are tense as he walks, kicking the water at his feet.

I'm alone in the space, wanting the ground to swallow me up. Guilt stands beside me in the rain like a hooded figure whose face I can never seem to find.

Thunder booms. There is no lightning. I peer up at the sky, feeling as if I'm floating when first I hear Ender cry my name.

"Lorilynn!" He's running towards me, pounding his fists and arms, screaming Magnús's name. He bounds over, shouting too.

Ender reaches me first. "Entity, you need to apply pressure."

"What are you talking about?" I enquire, then it's as if my legs can't hold me and everything seems to turn slightly blue.

"Quickly!" Mags is now here too, holding me in his arms on the ground. "What's happened? Who did this?"

Ender takes my head in his hands, and I realize there's blood on them. My blood?

Pain. In my shoulder. Stinging and aching. And my head, pounding. Bad. And the world is fading, going dark blue. Stars dance everywhere.

"Get the guards!" Mags screams. "The queen is injured."

I can't see anything anymore. Where has the world gone? There is only the sky and stars.

"Stay with me, Lorilynn," Ender says. "Open your eyes and you can scream at me all you want. About anything. I'll sail the sea myself to find your parents. Just stay awake."

The light is too bright, and then everything goes dark.

•

"When do you think they'll leave?" I turn my head to Adora as we sit on the bench. The wind sweeps through my hair. I peer up at him, and he gives a small glare.

"Be polite, Lorilynn," he reminds me and turns back to the book, making a few notes on the side.

"Mags doesn't like them either. He thinks Mother is ridiculous and indulging them so much," I push further.

Adora again looks down at me from the side and taps on the pages of the book. "Magnús will disagree with anything your mother does. That is no secret. Now keep studying."

I turn back to the book, running my eyes across the words but not actually taking them in. Adora is back to his own studies, writing away. He pushes his specs into his hair and then peers over again at me.

"What issue do you have with the Khans? They have been nothing but kind and generous to you. They brought you that lovely dress."

"The prince called me a child."

"Well, Lorilynn, you are *a child. There is nothing wrong with that. Enjoy being young. The world will slap you in the arse soon and you'll start getting wrinkles."*

"I understand that, but I'm sixteen, not five."

"Sixteen is still young. Twenty is young. One day you'll be my age and your hair will be gray, your eyesight will fail you, and you will wish you could have childhood innocence again. Wish that you could go back to studying Elláden mythology on this

bench with me. Which is what we should be doing now, missy." He chuckles and taps the tip of my nose, then turns back to the pages.

I drag my eyes to my own and read through. Finally beginning to absorb into the information, occasionally jotting things in the notebook beside me. Rough notes, which when completed, I will write neatly and store in the little section of the library I have taken over.

"Princess." I raise my head to find my least favorite prince there. "Queen Thornton said to ask you to show me where the library is."

I peer at Adora who gives a small, teasing smirk and nods towards the prince, telling me to go. So much for his insistence on studying.

"I'm sure any of the servants will be happy to show you where it is," I reply and then quickly return my eyes to the pages. But he doesn't leave.

"Her majesty specifically asked for you *to do it." He's grinning, with his feet firmly planted on the ground.*

"We'll resume later, your highness." Adora bows his head. After realizing I'll receive no support from him, I place the book down and walk towards the castle, making sure to stomp my feet.

The prince follows close behind. Once we're at the door to the library, I look back to see him with a smirk.

"What?"

"You don't like me, do you?" he teases and leans forward, opening the door.

"No. Not particularly," I say honestly. We step through the open door of the

library into the small room, books climbing two stories high on every wall. A large decorative rug is in the middle. Fire blooms in the hearth, a leather armchair neatly at its side. The room smells both of old books and a little of mint.

The prince wanders in, peering over and up at the ceiling, a painting of Persephone there. He sort of seems in awe, eyes wide and sparkling.

"Is there something in particular you are looking for?" I ask him, going to one shelf and running my fingers along the leather spines.

"Not really," he says, "just something to entertain myself with."

"Alright." I point to the other side of the room. "The books on that wall are written in Common. The others are in tongues native to Prithan. There's a section of other languages in the corner." I nod in the direction. "I seem to remember one or two being written in Turkish and Arabic, though I'm not sure if its Levantine or another."

He wanders over and peers at them for a moment before selecting one and perching on the leather chair, glancing over the book in silence.

I wait there for a thank you, an acknowledgement, a goodbye. He just reads as I had wanted to before he'd interrupted.

"You know," I begin as anger bubbles inside me, irritation clutching my chest, "you could thank me. Or at least acknowledge my departure."

He doesn't move a muscle.

"Helvítis tussa," I curse, then turn away and leave.

CHAPTER SEVEN

"She's waking up."

"Thank the Entity."

"Someone get her some water."

"And the other doctors."

"Shhhh," I grumble and peel my eyes open. It's so bright, my head pounds hard. "You're being too loud." My lips are dry and cracked so badly it hurts.

And Entity. My entire shoulder stings and burns. Moving it slightly makes me feel sticky and hot.

Eventually, my eyes adjust to the light. I'm in my chambers, in my bed. The sheets, I don't recognize. Nor the chemise I'm wearing. My hair is braided loosely. I look around. It's night, the moon behind the dusk. Candles light the edges of the room.

Adora, Edward, Mags, a maid, and one of the doctors in –training stand around me. They all look awful. Heaviness is etched on their faces and their jaws are set tight. Eyes wide and red.

Ed runs forward and gently takes my hand in his. "Thank goodness. We've all been worried." He plants a small kiss on my palm and then lowers his voice with a small smirk. "Don't tell them I told you, but both were crying."

A small laugh leaves my lips and an ache goes through my spine. "Can I sit up? Please?" I croak. My throat is raw. Ed nods and slowly supports my back, with the help of the training doctor, while the maid gets cushions ready behind my head. I fall into the fabric and peer over the room more. It's so silent. So still. With eight eyes staring at me, I feel on the spot.

And drained. Incredibly drained.

"What happened?" I question them.

"Something struck you. Your shoulder," Mags explains, his voice shaking. He walks forward and kneels by my side, resting his head on the sheets by my leg. "There was so much blood. You fell asleep, and we were questioning if you'd wake. At some points, you were breathing so slowly..." He starts sobbing. I gently rub his light hair, and he looks up with teared eyes. "It's been days."

"Days?" I quickly peer at Adora, who nods once. Even he's wiping his eyes.

"Eight," he confirms and moves to the other side of the bed, taking my spare hand.

"Eight?" I croak. So much to do, so much done. Guests must have arrived. The tea for the people, the search for my parents.

"I'll fill you in on everything once the doctors have checked you over." He smiles and traces his fingers across my palm. I clutch his hand in mine and peer between my three adopted uncles. All that would make this moment perfect is Papa. And if I could use the toilet.

Three raps sound at the door, and the maid opens it, bowing low at the entry of two people. The first, Doctor Scott who has been at the castle since before I was born. I believe she helped deliver myself and my brother.

Doctor Scott is an older woman, but time has been kind to her. Her red hair is bright with color and her eyes are a vibrant azure like the ocean. She has a cold smile but true care in her eyes.

Behind her is Ender. Looking different from how I saw him earlier—well, a week ago. He wears very official-looking clothing. A dark black coat embroidered with Levantine script in gold thread. And dimije in a pale cream color. He wanders in, looking me over. Doctor Scott takes the side beside Adora, and Ender by Ed and Mags.

"Welcome back, your majesty," Doctor Scott says.

"We're just going to take a look at you. How're you feeling?"

"I'm... fine," I reply.

She gently pulls one shoulder of the chemise down to reveal a white bandage with a small bloom of blood on it. Enough to only be residue. She pulls it away and uncovers the wound. There's a center part, ugly and red, swollen, which has been sewn together, and two cuts above and below. Black thread connects it all, keeping it together.

Now that I've seen it, it feels more tender. Deep and to the bone. I feel it along my spine, my collarbone, my jaw. Even in my teeth. I feel it in my blood, my nails, to the tip of my hair.

"When you first got to the castle, you were speaking gibberish," Doctor Scott says. "Using some choice words. We put you here to rest, but two hours later, we realized something was lodged inside you. Prince Khan and I operated," she explains and then quickly pours clear liquid over the wound, which I'm now realizing is pure alcohol. It burns, making me wish to rip my skin off. Cries of pain leave my mouth, along with curses. I don't mean to, but it pangs to my core. Like fire chewing my skin.

"You were quieter when you were in a coma." Ender chuckles, and I cast him the devil's glare. He lowers his head in apology, but I still see the corners of his lips raised. The uncles all glare, and Mags nudges him in the stomach. He stops chuckling as much.

"Did you find it?" I grit through my teeth as the pain slowly subsides. "Whatever was in me?"

"Yes," Doctor Scott says and turns to the prince, who is now composed and takes a small sewn bag from his pocket and passes it over.

I open it, and a little gold thing comes out onto my palm. Like crumpled metal. Little specks of dark red are in the deep cracks. My blood.

"What exactly is it?" I ask the room. They stand together, leaning close, and shake their heads in confusion.

"I've done some research," Ender continues, "and I have a theory."

"Which is?" I question him, shuffling, and a shiver of pain runs through my body.

"An old weapon that would fire meticulously crafted metal into the victim from a distance."

"So..." I wrack my brain, trying to gather as many thoughts as possible. "This was an assassination attempt?"

"That would be logical," Mags says. "However, we need to verify first if Ender's theory is correct before we can be certain. Until then, you'll have to have guards with you at all times."

"How will guards help if the assassin has a concealed flying weapon?" Ed pipes up and glares at Mags, who shoots a dark look back.

"Stop," I snap at them and then hush my voice. "More importantly, how do we go about verifying the prince's theory? Adora, are there any texts here we can use?"

"If I may," Ender speaks, "while you've been unconscious, more guests of the crown arrived. Among them Princess Chione El Sayed, daughter of the Sultan of Ptah. I've known her for many years."

Ptah. I've never spoken to any of the leaders of Ptah, nor do I know much about it besides what I would consider to be normal knowledge. Ptah is the most northern nation in Africa and has one of the most efficient, honor-bound armies the world has ever seen. The men and women train hard and long, crafting weapons and understanding how they work meticulously.

Doctor Scott finishes up and packs her bag away. Everyone is silent as she does, leaving fresh bandages on the table beside the bed. She doesn't say anything but does bow her head to the room before departing silently. We all stay and listen as her footsteps disappear down the corridor. The maid is in the bathroom, making herself busy.

"How would that help?" Magnús pipes up, crossing his arms.

"My friend, have you learned nothing from years of listening to my ramblings?" Adora chuckles and wanders over.

"My friend," Mags mocks, "have you not learned I've never actually listened?"

Ed and I share a look and chuckle, locking eyes a moment. The both of us are used to this, and it's a refreshing break when all I can think about is how I can't remember the last eight days and the fact that someone might be trying to assassinate me in my own home.

"Then, Prince Khan, would you care to explain to the people in the room who decided to expand muscles rather than IQ?"

Ed and I chuckle more, and pain flares in my shoulder, making me wince. All eyes land on me before I wave it off and Ender speaks. He keeps his voice clear, monotone. "Ptah's royal family are the highest trained people in the world in combat and weaponry."

Including the history of weaponry.

Mags seems to understand and nods, keeping quiet and fiddling with the edge of his sleeve.

"Right, boys," Ed says and stands, tucking the blankets on my bed higher while being careful near my shoulder. "Lorilynn needs rest and having you lot nattering isn't helping."

They all mumble in agreement, and Adora promises to sort out the meeting for breakfast. Ed gives a small wave as he leaves. The last one out is Ender. He lingers, eyes searching over me a moment. I raise an eyebrow before he says to let him know if I have any questions about the injury and then shuts the door. Eventually, the only sound is the birds and the occasional mumble from the guards stationed outside my chambers.

•

I feel exhausted, yet sleep doesn't come. The pain is vibrant, a mixture of aching and stinging. It's as if my shoulder is slowly melting. And it's itching. First, placing my feet on the ground is tough and is weird to move them, pins and needles all over. The maid later informed me when leaving herself that Doctor Scott had applied tight stockings on my legs which is leaving bruises up the sides.

I push myself forward and manage to stand, albeit a bit wobbly but stable enough. I meander over to my wardrobe and grab the lace dressing gown, placing it over my shoulders and putting on some old leather shoes. I try running a brush through my hair but struggle to raise either arm too far. Both feel tight, stiff, pulling at my spine.

When I step out the door, two guards bow low. Despite it being late into the night, they seem wide awake. Eyes bright, perhaps somewhat surprised to see me.

"I'd like to take a stroll through the gardens," I announce. They follow, and as I walk down the corridor, the clang of their armor echoes behind me.

Outside, the wind wisps past. It's cooling. The air is harsh though, and a deep cough runs through me, aching my lungs and shoulder.

My mind is whirling as I walk through the grass. When talking about it earlier, it was just words, theories in a confused brain. But lying in bed for four hours with only myself for company has set everything in stone.

Of the fact that I just, again, faced death— and it may have been an assassination attempt. If it had succeeded, then the only way the Thornton line would continue is if my parents returned and had another child. Which is hard to imagine when they can hardly stand to be in a room with each other for more than a few moments.

There's a small stone bench by Mother's rose bushes. I take a seat, and the guards stand a few feet away, keeping a watchful eye out.

"May I join you?"

I whip my head around to see Azra, also dressed in a nightgown, standing by me. She's brushed her hair but left it loose down her back. A kind, motherly smile lines her lips, warming the cockles of my heart. I slide aside on the bench giving her room.

She gracefully sits and peers over the darkness of the gardens, from the grass to the sky. "It's beautiful. I'd always expected less because of the dusk, but the extravagance and color amaze me," she explains softly.

"They're my mother's pride and joy. She chose plants that didn't require as much light and they thrive here," I reply and pick a red rose at my side, brushing my fingers along the silky petals as if it were her hair.

"I'm glad I've caught you, Lorilynn. I wish to talk to you... about your parents." She swallows nervously and takes my hands gently in hers. I sense the conversation, her trying to convince me they're gone. That it's going to be okay. Then she'll use the phrase 'it's alright to cry' and offer her shoulder to me.

"Many of us have different beliefs about their fate. That is no secret. However, you believe they're alive."

I know it.

"Yes."

"I hope you don't mind but I sent my own ship and crew in the search for them, alive or dead. I would have asked first, but you were unwell and no one would allow anyone to visit you, so I went ahead."

I glance over her face, over the pinkness of her cheeks, the small signs of age appearing at her forehead and sides of her lips. The signs of humanness I've never seen in my mother.

At her words, at what she's done, it brings a sense of warmth into my chest, of hope. As if the Entity is embracing me.

There is still a sense of uncertainty in Queen Khan's face, a fear deep in her wide eyes and fluttering lashes.

My mind wanders to seeing her two years ago. How harsh and scary of a woman she was, what she had done. Put Ender and me through.

"Why?" I whisper. "Why do this? Why help me when it favors you for them to stay gone?"

She lifts a hand, placing it on my cheek. Warmth spreads through my skin. "Because two years ago, I did something terrible to you and my son. Something which can't be undone. Nevertheless, it has connected us as a family. And as family, it is in my interests to keep us strong. Particularly when our business is ruling queendoms."

Ruling queendoms. One day, when Azra herself joins the Entity, it'll be an empire. My empire.

Damn.

My shoulder shudders, twinges. A reminder that I should be resting. A week of deep sleep only disturbed by the nightmare of reality is enough to keep me alive. Now I must become strong.

My departure from Queen Khan is simple, official. As it were the middle of the day and we were clothed in finery, not nightgowns. Our heads bow slightly and we separate. My guards stay close, heads lowered.

As I make my way towards the door, hand poised on the cold iron handle, Azra speaks one more time behind me, and I turn.

"Queen Thornton, one piece of advice."

She's standing tall, strong, a fear deep in her eyes, but queenly, regal. She's demanding to be listened to. Once she sees my attention is on her, she continues, "My son has his father's ambition and my determination. He is not to be trusted."

•

He is not to be trusted. Her words linger in my mind, echoing around my skull. He is not to be trusted.

Trust.

Trust is in the bones, in the blood. Does he have my trust?

I'm not sure. He saved my life, that is certainly true. If anything, he at least has my thanks.

I lie on my bedsheets, my back aching with exhaustion but also tingling with the itch to move. After everything I've experienced this past week, I should rest, I should be *able* to rest. I should sleep like the dead. Yet my eyes can only shut a moment before they fly open again.

Soon, I'm up and out of my chambers. This time, only followed by one guard. A young boy who I'm pretty sure I could kill myself in my current condition. However, a guard it is. Enough to satisfy Adora.

We traverse straight to the library. Inside the double doors, the cold pricks at our skin. Ash is all that remains of the fire, wind singing through the stone. I'm regretting only wearing a nightgown.

The smell is still distinct and crisp. Old pages mixed with the scent of peppermint that is often thrown into the flame to give the room a fresh smell.

I wander to the far section with foreign languages and trace my fingers along the Arabic shelf until I stop on a beautiful one with a fine cover and gold embossed letters. I'm not sure who it is by or what the title even is, but it feels warm under my touch, as if it's the one I'm meant to pick. Carefully, I slide it from its space, running my fingers along the spine.

I reach for the cupboard door and take out a pen and ink, along with a sheet of paper, writing away. At the back is also a roll of black string. I try breaking it with my teeth, but it doesn't budge. I end up using the tip of the guard's sword, much to both our amusement, and then wrap it around the note and book.

It takes a few minutes for us to reach Ender's door. I close my hand into a fist to knock but think otherwise, resting it again instead on the floor. I peer one final time at the note before wandering away.

Thank you.

L. Thornton

CHAPTER EIGHT

Sleep does not come in the end. I simply stay in bed, staring at the ceiling. Soon, light trickles in and maids slowly file through the doors, along with Doctor Scott who checks my bandages and lectures me for not resting.

After she leaves, I am bathed and dressed, brushing out my tangled hair.

I am joined by Adora in the dining room for breakfast. The long table separates us— apparently, it is protocol. And protocol must be followed, even if it requires me raising my voice for him to even hear me.

"I've set the meeting up," he calls as I dig into some toast. "Princess Chione is most keen to be introduced."

"When will it be?"

"Pardon?" He stuffs some fruit into his mouth, turning his ear towards me.

I sigh, forcing myself out of my chair. My shoulder pangs hot, and I wince, but get myself up and go over to him, perching on the table in front of him.

"When," I repeat, "is the meeting?"

"Ah!" He tosses one more slice of apple into his mouth. "Prince Khan will fetch us when the princess and her guards have finished praying."

"I see." I stride to an open window where, right on cue, I see who I presume to be Princess Chione wander through the gardens with guards, prayer mats tucked under their arms.

To call her beautiful is an understatement. Even from the distance, she might be the most stunning person I've ever laid eyes on. Her skin is slightly lighter than Adora's, and her hair is tucked into a hijab the color of a sunset. Her cheekbones are sharp, jaw precise, and she walks with a grace and determination I can only hope to have one day.

"Did you ever meet the Ptah royal family before becoming a ward?" I ask Adora, keeping my eyes on the princess. Nerves slither through me at the prospect of the meeting; she's an accomplished royal with a far better reputation than I have.

"I did, however, I was very young. I don't remember anything. Even then, Princess Chione hadn't been born yet, so I wouldn't be able to tell you anything about her," he explains. His chair scrapes across the floor as he stands and wanders over to me. "Can I give you some advice? Not as a member of your court, but as your uncle?"

I turn to him and give a small nod.

"Remember, you're amazing. Don't let self-doubt hold you back."

I embrace him hard. So much so, my wounds throb, but I ignore it and just hold him as his warm arms surround me. I rest my head in the dip of his shoulder, listening to his calm breathing, matching my breaths to his.

"You can do this, Lorilynn," he whispers. "You have control."

I have control.

As he holds me, a guard hesitantly walks in.

We unarm each other, turning to the man. He bows once before informing us, "Your majesty, your grace. Prince Khan of Turkish Arabia has requested an audience."

Adora quickly squeezes my hand once before we step apart from each other.

"Please, welcome the prince in," Adora says for me. He then goes and sits on his seat again while I go back to the spot of the table and steal his glass of apple juice, sipping happily. He casts a warning glance at me as I stick my tongue out at him as the *clop* of Ender's boots sound. He bows his head as he sees us, stopping by the wall as we finish up. He looks well rested today, and there's even a gleam in his eyes. I'm sure he's excited to see the princess, a friend in this unfamiliar world.

"Princess Chione is in the council chambers," he explains, then tuns to Adora. "Lord Tersoo, would I be able to have a moment with

Queen Thornton?"

Adora casts an unnerving glance towards me. Asking permission. I give him a quick nod. He wanders out the door, bowing once as he passes Ender, leaving the silence as our company.

"Would you like something to eat?" I motion to the table of food. He shakes his head, taking a few steps closer. He's about a meter away, his hands behind his back like the proper prince he is.

The scent of citrus fills my nose again as I notice the little changes to his appearance. He doesn't look like Prince Khan, but instead Ender. His hair is neat but loose and he's wearing a crisp white shirt under his jacket. And the scent, more than his natural scent, something more. Aftershave.

"I just — " he begins, nerves lining his voice, "the book."

"The book?" I raise an eyebrow.

"Thank you."

"You kept me alive," I explain. "The least I can do is give you a gift in appreciation."

"Being able to help operate on the new queen of Prithan is a gift enough."

The two of us walk from the dining room, down the corridors, my guards not too far behind.

"In your professional opinion then, does my skeleton look normal?" I joke, turning to give him a comical grin.

"I wouldn't know. I've never operated on anyone before you."

My chest tightens at that. He'd never operated on anyone before and chose a royal of a different nation as his first? What if it had gone wrong? The chaos...

"That's a very dangerous game, Prince Khan."

As we approach the door of the council chambers, Mags is waiting outside. I give a small smile and wave. After Ender has gone in, I embrace him a little when a small mark on his neck, almost hidden by his armor, catches my attention. Blush floods his cheeks as my eyes linger on the purple and red bruise.

Then it drops.

"Mags," I teasingly lecture, "is that a hickey?"

"No," he replies too fast and starts pulling his leather collar up, trying to cover it.

"Well, that explains why you missed breakfast." I frown. I had almost died last week, and he's found time to frolic with someone. I storm into the council room last. Everyone else is already there, waiting.

I take a seat at the end of the table, the princess at the opposite end, her guards spread throughout the room. Ender is on one side of the table near the middle. Disappointment lines his face. Before, his wide eyes filled with excitement had searched the room. Now, they seem sad, like the color of the sea on a cold day, a mist hovering over the water.

Adora stands beside me, as does Mags. Enough to offer support as my lords, but also close enough for me to feel their presence, to know I'm safe.

Sitting even closer to the princess, I can see her beauty even clearer.

Her lips are a light pink, like blooming rosebuds, contrasting perfectly with the warm green of her eyes. I think perhaps I'm staring as she gently clears her throat, casting a glance at Ender.

"Queen Thornton, may I present Princess Chione El Sayed of Ptah," Ender announces.

"It's a pleasure to meet you," I dictate clearly with what I intend as a warm smile, "I hope you're finding your stay here pleasant."

The room all feels very official. Everyone here stands straight and tall, in uniform. Even if that uniform is a title. A servant knocks gently on the door and comes in with a tray of hot water. Everyone is silent as she places the delicate cups down, one in front of princess, one in front of the prince, and one in front of me. I take a small sip to keep my hands busy. Nerves line my stomach, and under the table, my leg bounces rapidly.

"So..." I begin, every head snapping towards me, "Prince Khan said you may be able to assist me with something."

She quickly looks at Ender before returning her eyes to me. "What can I do for you?"

"A member of my court was stabbed by some sort of phantom.

They were operated on." Adora steps forward and pulls a small glass box out from his jacket. Inside is the little piece of metal, still crumpled. "This was found inside them, and Ender wondered if it was from an old weapon."

Princess Chione leans over, and I pass the box over across the table. Long, feminine fingers inspect the glass before sliding it open and taking the segment out. As she inspects it, I notice she wears no rings and callouses line the palms of her hands. A hard-working woman, ready to fight. The kind of woman I've always wanted to be. Her lashes flutter as she motions one of her guards over who also peers with curious eyes. They mutter near silently between themselves before he nods, then resumes his previous position.

"I'm sorry for your court's loss, your majesty." Chione lowers her head in respect, placing the metal back in the box.

"What do you mean?" I reply, keeping my face still and calm.

Control.

Ender's eyes trail between the two of us, as does most of the room.

There's something about Chione that demands respect. She holds the room. Perhaps it's the beauty or her clear maturity for someone who must be my age or the fact she seems to think before moving and speaking. Everything calculated. Yet, there's warmth, kindness.

"You said that a member of your court had it embedded in them." She takes a careful sip of her water, swirling the cup in her hand.

"It..." I wasn't planning on revealing my absence was caused by my near–death, yet the words leave my mouth. "It was me."

Her eyes shoot up, a smile curling her lips and amazement lining her cheeks. "When was this?" she asks.

"Days ago," I reply, smiling back. "It was kept quiet."

"May I say you're looking very well considering you were shot not too long ago."

"On the contrary," I say with a chuckle, "It hurts like a bitch."

The room goes silent a moment, most likely at the fact I swore in an official meeting with one of the most respected royals in the world. I can feel Adora and Mags sharing a worried look behind me. Guards peer nervously at each other, and Ender's mouth is slightly agape in shock.

There are no lies in my words. I am in rather a lot of pain, and there's a secret flask in my dress pocket for when it gets so severe I need a little help.

Princess Chione's face stays still as she appears to register what I said, until she grins bright. "I once got accidentally impaled by a loose sword in my calf when I was a young child. I screamed the entire palace down for days on end after. We'll have to compare battle scars. I have this particular one that I find looks sort of like a horse from tripping over my skirts last year."

"It's ironic, Chione," Ender adds, "that you train five hours a day yet the worst scar you get is from tripping over your skirts."

She laughs in response and suddenly the tension-filled room feels more relaxed and calmer. My shoulders no longer reside by my ears and my chest no longer feels as if it'll implode.

All my years of hiding, of stories and stereotypes, hasn't held me back, luckily. Perhaps Princess Chione and I can become friends. I think I'd like that.

"As for the metal, I can confirm Ender's theory. What you have here is a bullet, which is a small canister fired at high speed towards a person, lodging it in their body," she explains. "The victim loses blood fast if death isn't immediate. These devices—guns—haven't been known to exist for the past few hundred years."

"Which is seemingly no longer the case," I add politely. My brain starts whirling again. Gun. I recognized the word, most likely from studying the history of war.

But the fact is, they haven't been manufactured for long, so the weapon must be an antique. It's a miracle it still works—and unfortunate for my shoulder.

"My guess is that it's also the incorrect bullet for the gun. Meaning that if I was the one firing it, I'd stand close. I wouldn't risk being more than ten meters away." They were there, maybe watching me bleed in the rain.

Watching blood bloom on my white dress like the Grim Reaper's rose. And no one noticed.

The remainder of the meeting is less business, more casual conversation between the princess and Adora, talking about the differences between Africa now and years ago when Adora still lived there. After an hour, we decide to finish the meeting as I've learned all I need and now need silence to think. While the conversation with Chione is wonderful, it is time for business.

Everyone stands, all bowing. I lower my head out of respect, and we leave, Chione and I beside each other, muttering words of friendship.

"You definitely must try the pear jam," I say to her. "Over breakfast in the next few days, on the terrace?" I suggest.

She nods and smiles, squeezing my hand. "I would love to, your majesty." She grins, then her head turns to the side where Ender leans against the wall, arms crossed and disappointment lining his face. Her features sink, eyes sad. "He won't be coming," she says to him.

His eyes flick up at her a second before dropping to the floor. "I know," he replies. "I should have known."

Without another word, he steals down the corridor, away from us both. Chione eyes follow him, as do mine.

I wonder who Ender was waiting for and if it had something to do with his preened appearance and eager eyes. A small hint of my heart sinks for him. For the fact my husband is apparently in love with someone else? Perhaps. Someone Chione knows. It's illogical to feel strongly about it when both of us never agreed to the marriage.

What's more illogical is that I'm thinking about that instead of the information I just learned. First, I was shot with a gun. Second, I probably should be rotting in the ground. Last, is that all these facts go to show that someone tried to murder me.

"I, um," I say to Chione, "I have some thinking to do. If you'll excuse me." I bow my head once more, her doing the same.

As I begin walking away, feeling her eyes trail behind, I wave some guards over, including Mags, who is quietly sharing words with Adora.

We stride down the corridor, Mags at my side. I want to ask who they are, if its Heather, if he loves them, but he is in too much of a happy place I don't wish to ruin his moment. I suppose after my near-death he needed to blow off some steam. Gross. Although I'd argue he should have waited until at least twenty-four hours after my awakening.

We ride to the village. I want to return though, connect the dots a little. All signs of my assassination attempt are gone, although as Snowflake trots through, there are stares. Of course, the village people now know who I am who I am, and my anonymity is gone.

I suddenly feel as if everything is closing in, the wind compressing me into a prison. Their eyes burn through my skin with disappointment.

Surprise? Both?

Heather is outside the bakery. She's staring too, but not at me. She and Mags beam at each other.

Ah.

Well at least they finally admitted their feelings for each other.

He hops off, and they embrace as I clamber down too, giving Heather a small nod as I wait at the side for Mags to detach himself from her. Thank the Entity she doesn't bow.

After a while, I clear my throat. "I'm going to the beach."

He turns to face me and nods with a smile.

"Shall we go?"

He casts a glance at Heather. "I'll keep an eye on you from here."

I peer through the thick trees where the sea is just in sight. I want to argue, worried about being alone, but he looks happy, at peace. I'm anxious he'll be annoyed if I do.

Once I reach the sand, I plop down with my hands on my knees, letting my hair waft in the wind.

My shoulder aches, but it's manageable. I rested through most of the pain. Small blessings, I suppose.

I just... I want answers. I want to be at peace. I want to know where my parents are, who is trying to kill me, why I'm married to Ender. I run my thumb across the scar. It's faded, only a pale, pink line left.

"Penny for your thoughts?" The voice, smooth like melted chocolate, sounds. He speaks Cymru.

I whip my head around to find a farmer boy, his face imprinting on my mind. Blond hair smothered in muck; hands calloused.

Plus, he didn't call me *your majesty*.

"Or I can go?" he offers, flashing a charming smile, the kind that could make any girl's heart melt.

I pat the sand next to me, and he collapses after a day in the fields.

It's only then I notice the thing attached to his belt. Wooden and metal, but clear.

I don't have time to run before he grabs my mouth so I can't scream and has a knife at my neck.

CHAPTER NINE

The knife digs in, blood blooming with the sting of his blade. Warm. I try screaming, but it is muffled by his palm. Where is Mags? Where are the guards? Where is *anyone*?

My heart pounds deep in my chest, my shoulder pain increasing, the skin feeling as if it's stretching. His breath is in my ear, deafened by my heartbeat.

"Please," I beg under his hand, the taste of dirt and oil covering my tongue.

"Hush, my queen," he says gently. "This will only take a moment, and then you'll be with the Entity, with your parents."

I struggle, pant, try biting his hands. He holds me tighter so I can't move, can't breathe. My lungs scream, demanding oxygen. Like they did when I was younger, when there was so little air going to them that darkness peaked the edge of my vision. I keep moving, making sure he doesn't even have a second to strike, to drag the blade across the smooth skin of my throat.

Where is Mags? Where is he?

I'm alone in this. No one is coming, no one can hear my squeals under his hand or see the tears streaming down my cheeks. Blood is running from my shoulder and down my dress. Another one ruined.

"Stay still," he hisses in my ear, but I move more in any way I can until I manage to catch his nose while slamming his head back, knocking me forward, my palms colliding with the edge of the water, saltiness splashing in my face. I cast a look back where he's recovering, blood staining his hand and chin.

I scramble into the water, screaming for help, for anyone until my throat is hoarse. My drenched hair slaps against my face, and I keep going, pebbles and sand scratching my palms and knees. I'm almost fully submerged, but then he grabs my skirt, tugging it so my face splashes in the water. Grains of sand seep between my teeth, falling down my throat. I try to get up, but before reaching the surface, he holds my head down, pushing it into the rocks. Seaweed tangles in my hair, my eyelashes, even up my nose.

I fight to swim, trying to get away, clawing at the water. He steps on my upper back, keeping me down no matter how much I scramble.

It's been minutes. I'm only seconds away from swallowing that deadly gulp of water.

I do all I can do—I pray.

Entity watching over me, guide me to you in peace so that I might join you and watch over the world. Watch over those I leave until I can be with you.

I start to exhort myself, accept the fate, allow a slither of water into my lungs to burn, and it does. Badly.

Well, at least I'll be able to guide my parents home, find out where they are.

But then, as I go still, he lifts his foot, turns me over. I keep still, keep my eyes open, keep my breath held no matter how much my lungs scream for air.

He picks me up and examines my face, placing two fingers in the crook between my neck and jaw. Checking for a pulse. But then his eyes bulge with realization that there is one. He is too late. I grab the gun at his belt, slamming the hilt against his temple and swaying my body so he's now underwater.

And I then hold him, taking breaths finally and keeping him under by his neck, looking directly into his brown eyes. They beg, plead. His hands reach for me, scratching to be released.

If I do, he'll kill me. Only one of us can survive this, and it will be me. After an eternity, he stops moving. I do not make the mistake he does. I keep him under until I see light fade from his eyes and bubbles rise from his open lips.

Then it hits me like a cannon.

I killed him.

I feel as if night is floating down to me, cloaking me. Like I can't escape, night merged with wrath. A part of me just died too, always to remain here in the sand and sea.

"Lorilynn?"

Ah. Now he arrives.

I don't cast Mags a glance as I haul the body from the water, picking the gun and flinging it to the ground as I climb up the beach, soaked through. My hair sticks to the side of my face, the heavy skirts of my dress flying about my ankles. I storm past him to Snowflake, clambering on and galloping back to the castle, not glancing at anyone as I do.

I go to my chambers, dismissing all staff in there, and curl up in the window seat, clutching my knees to my body, rocking myself as his dead eyes blind my thoughts. Brown, like Ender's. A shiver runs through my spine.

I feel water in my lungs—*hear* it. I force a cough, but my hand is dry. The rest of me is a mess, shivers running through me as cold pricks my skin. My knee pounds.

A knock sounds, thrice. Gentle. Unwanted.

"Leave," I snap and turn to face the window again, looking at a group of soldiers marching outside, probably to secure the castle. Which means Mags is back. Probably at my door now. The knock sounds again.

"I said, *leave*!" I shout this time.

Instead of a knock, it’s a voice. "It's me," Ender says through the door. "There was word you might be injured."

I remain on the windowsill a little longer, debating if it's too late to pretend I'm not here when another cough escapes me. And... I don't want to be alone.

I head to the door, open it, and look at him. He gives me a light smile, a warm one. I allow him in before firmly shutting it.

Immediately, he goes into medical mode and searches my body for marks. I sit on my chair in a corner and slump as he crouches in front of me.

"We should wash your eyes first. You have sand in your eyelashes."

I don't speak, don't argue, and make my way to the bathroom, perching on the floor as he kneels, gently taking my face in his hand. He supports my head, tipping it back and pouring a little water in from a small glass.

I flinch a little, but he traces a finger across my cheekbone, whispering soft words of encouragement. Afterwards, he passes a white handkerchief, and I dab my eyes.

"Better?" He sits opposite me on the tiles. I give a slight nod before he reaches for some clean towels. "I need to check your wound. Doctor Scott isn't available. Would you be alright with that?"

I do not answer, only begin undoing what I can, allowing the wet dress to fall to my waist, revealing the wound which has bloodied the binding around my breasts, white fabric drenched in ruby staining. I can't quite see the mark, but he places the towel against it, pressing hard.

"Good news is, you don't need new stitches," he explains, moving closer. "It's just a big bleeder." He keeps his hand on my shoulder, tight. Maybe not as tight as need be.

"Who is he?" I whisper, my memory returning to this morning, to the words shared between him and Chione. "He means a lot to you." Not a question.

Ender seems to retract a bit, his dark eyes finding the floor. I stepped on a nerve. But his hand remains on my shoulder, a finger tracing my skin.

"He… he is a prince of Ptah. Chione's brother," he begins to explain. "I haven't seen him since I came back from Prithan two years ago."

Two years ago. Our wedding.

"We..." His voice fades and his eyes glaze over. "The end of our relationship was abrupt and filled with questions I knew I couldn't answer or else I'd put our countries at risk."

"I'm sorry," I apologize, "I never realized you were gay and had to go through the consummation."

"You need not apologize," he says. "I'm not gay. I don't have a preference. I'm attracted to all manner of people."

"But you loved him." Love. He'd experienced the beauty of it and had to rip it away from himself for the sake of Turkish Arabia, Prithan, and me. I am not the one he should have married.

"I did." He lowers the towel and leans forward, examining the wound a little before raising the cloth again. "I hoped to be able to offer an explanation, a goodbye. A... anything."

"Goodbyes are only for the fortunate." My parents' eyes flash in my mind. Of the abrupt confrontation I had with Papa before he sailed. And no matter how much I scamper through my brain, I can't remember the words I last spoke to Mother.

And the assassin, the man I killed. He won't get a goodbye. I know nothing about him, if he has a mother or father waiting at home for him. A spouse? Children? They'll never get a goodbye. Even if there isn't someone, he'll never get to say farewell to the moon or the stars or the morning dew.

I feel it in the deep pit of my stomach, heavy and thick. Guilt, like a swamp. Thick and gloopy and dark. Ender stays silent, placing a hand gently over my own.

Calming. I squeeze once, interlocking my fingers with his.

The doors in the main room of my chamber fly open, cracking

against the walls. I can't see them, but I know the footsteps.

"Lorilynn?" Adora calls.

"Lorilynn, where are you?" Mags follows him, panic laced in the cracks of his tone.

I peer at Ender before standing, putting my dress back on properly and striding out, the anger I feel clear in my eyes.

When I turn that corner, relief shrouds them both as they run to me, embracing me with tight arms around my shoulders. I hold them a moment before pushing them away, not able to meet my eyes with Mags.

He was meant to be there. He should have been the one to take the life, not me. He should have made sure I would never be put in a situation like this.

"Are you alright? Are you hurt?" Mags questions rapidly, both their eyes going over my wet hair, clothes, my skin and bruised neck.

"She's alright." Ender's voice comes from behind me. He's there, leaning against the bathroom doorframe, his arms crossed. Something tugs in my chest. "I want to do a few more checks, but she'll live. Albeit perhaps with some bruises."

Adora has his eyes on Ender, while Mags's gaze is glued to me, and I finally look at him properly. "I'm so sor—" He starts before I interrupt him.

"Save it," I hiss in Icelandic. I won't shame him in front of Ender.

"I could have died while you were too busy flirting."

"Please..." he tries.

"No." I hold up a finger. "I woke two days ago. The assassin was still out there, but you are too worried about screwing Heather."

"But—"

"The crown always comes first."

The two of them stay silent before bowing their heads in respect of a queen. Entity, I'm turning into Mother. She'd be proud.

"You are dismissed." My final words.

They leave, heads hung low, and guilt stirs in me again. But then I remember what it was like with the sand and water in my mouth, and it disappears rather quickly.

•

Ender ends up checking my chest, listening to it from my back as I breathe. After a few moments, he happily declares that he thinks I've coughed the water out, but that I need to keep warm so I avoid infection which with my history could provide an issue. With that, I start a fire, and we sit in front of it on blankets, one wrapped around each of our shoulders.

"Didn't you say your leg hurt?" he asks quietly, breaking the silence.

I pause a moment, the pain tingling. It's not terrible, doesn't even cause me to limp, but I suppose it's worth checking. I lower the blanket and lift my skirts, revealing my bare calf, where a few purple bruises are beginning to flower.

His calloused hands run up my skin, gently feeling the bone and muscle. Our heavy breathing is the only sound. My heart hammers in my chest as I watch his nimble fingers halt on my knee, pausing as his eyes flick up, the deepness meeting with mine.

Neither of us says anything, we just look at each other as his hand still touches my bare skin, warmth seeping through his palm like water flowing down a river.

"Any pain?" he questions, his breathing quiet. Whisps of sound at most.

"No, thank you." Despite this, his hand remains there, the amber light from the fire dancing on his tanned, chiseled skin. Glowing.

That heartbeat of mine quickens, my skin warming up. My breath hitches in my chest. His eyes are still matched with mine, his own breath slow as intensity paints his skin.

"So..." I murmur, needing to change my thoughts. "Do you want to end our marriage because you want to marry Chione's brother?"

His face drops.

Great job, Lorilynn.

Then he looks at the floor, pulling my skirts down and kneeling back in the blanket again.

"No. Maybe it once was, but not anymore." He doesn't meet my gaze. "It's more about..."

"Reclaiming. Deciding?" I suggest cautiously.

"Yes."

I understand that. But our parents are right, this brings strength for them, strength for me, for Prithan's future. I can't go against their wishes and do an anti-marriage ceremony that hasn't been done for years. We're royals. Servants of our nations. Our lives must be lives of sacrifice for them.

Every one of the people, every soul, holds a place in my heart. And I must do all I can to keep them safe. It is how it is.

I think Ender knows that, knows it's the result of my choice. He deserves the stars and universe, to find love and have beautiful children. I expect him to have lovers. I do wish I could give him the happiness he deserves, but something in my soul tells me it's a sacrifice to make. Because there is no room for selfishness as princess.

The energy that had been there only moments ago when his hand was on my skin has dissipated into shadows and nothingness.

"Apart from your studies, what have you been doing these past two years then?" I finally ask, moving completely away from our nuptials and parents.

He starts to smile, reminiscing about his training, healing and various balls and holidays. He also tells me about his father and described Turkish Arabia to me: golden suns, great, vast ocean, and history embedded in every city. His favorite is Damascus, which also happens to be the world's longest surviving city and where the palace is.

I then talk about Prithan, the Botanical Island, my illness. And Aeron, what it was like losing a brother. I clarified that there is very little I remember of it, of funerals or tears or getting used to playing alone.

"I—um... I don't remember much being young either," he says, "I was in an orphanage until I was four."

That comes as a surprise, hitting me deep in my chest like a bat. I hadn't known that.

"An orphanage?" What would the son of the queen and king of Turkish Arabia be doing in an orphanage?

"My parents couldn't conceive. They took me in as their son, but everything before then, I don't remember it." I'd never known that never heard about it. "I got a name, an opportunity. Love. A home. They're my world—Turkish Arabia is my world. Whether I grew in my mother's stomach or her heart."

"Do people know?" I question next. Just because I hadn't heard, doesn't mean it isn't common knowledge.

"It's no secret. No one really cares. On the contrary, I think they love me for it. A commoner prince. One of the people."

"You'll make a great king."

"One day." Not soon. I hope so too. I hope that I go back to princess and the world to make sense.

The moon rises and the room turns darker. We end up staying there for hours, sipping on wine and eating food brought to us. We talk, we laugh. Just about *stuff*.

Nothing of any importance or value but it means the world.

Because I've never had a conversation like this, never let myself laugh, found myself listening intently.

Eventually, the time comes for rest. I need to recover, and he needs to return to his chambers.

"Ender." I smile, leaning against my bedpost, the blanket still around my shoulders. "I'll see you tomorrow."

He pauses a moment. "Tariq. My friends call me Tariq." And then he's out the door.

I smile softly as I remember his laughter. But then his mother's voice comes into my head.

Do not trust my son.

CHAPTER TEN

The next morning, Chione and Ender—*Tariq*—join me for an early breakfast on the terrace. I'm still not sleeping well, and both were up quite early. Chione to train and Tariq to study. I'd sat in my bedroom window watching the princess as she battled like a dance, swift and beautiful. Gracious but with mercy. Any blow delivered by her is done to be quick, simple, and painless. She's an angel—made from the stars and core of the universe. Her guards, while also very good, never beat her. They always seem to yield or be caught out by something, and they've been training with her for years.

The only person I imagine to be a potential match is Mags. Maybe. They both have different styles, an unpredictability about them.

Afterwards, I go down and ask her to join, Tariq finding us soon after.

It's blissful to be out before the rest of the castle has woken, a little disheveled. As maids hadn't risen yet, my usually pristine locks are running loose. Even the prince is the same, hair a mess and dressed similar to yesterday. As if he hasn't gone to bed yet. Someone mentioned he's in the library most days. Dedicated to his work. It's admirable.

Attractive.

I quickly swipe the thought away, realizing that my eyes have maybe lingered on him too long.

I swirl the cup of warm water that's in my hand a moment, raising it to my lips and keeping my eyes away from him. I instead try to focus on Chione, on her gentleness and caution. In everything but him. From even the way she butters bread to placing the knife down.

"So, Princess El Sayed, tell me about Ptah. I find I don't know much about it," I say. She peers up happily, and I take a bite of toast.

"Just Chione is fine," she says with a chuckle, chewing some bread herself. "And... it's hot. Beautiful."

"You miss it?"

"Immensely. Although I'm sure that's normal. I mean, Tariq—you miss Turkish Arabia?" Tariq. She calls him by his casual name too. Of course, they must be close.

"So much, but I know I'll be home soon," he explains.

"Is Prithan that bad?" I tease.

He meets my eyes a moment with a smirk. "Prithan isn't bad," he defends. "Its queen is a little irritating. Stubborn."

I chuckle and raise my eyebrows mockingly before turning back to Chione, who smiles sweetly between the two of us. A knowing look paints her cheeks.

"Tell me about your countries. I'm serious. I want to know," I push, truth in my words. I do want to know. There's little I'm aware of about their lands beside the fact that they're hot and on the other side of the world.

"Ptah is..." Chione starts, and a haze covers her eyes as if she's there again. Back in the sand. "It's home. The center of the world. In each hard moment, I shut my eyes and think of there, of the sunrise, and I know everything will be alright. I know I'll be home again, and that patience is all I need, that everything will make sense soon."

Bliss. A dream. Home. Like the Botanical Island. I'd never found myself aching to be back before, but listening to her talk like that blooms a gentle yearning in my soul. A desire to be home. My true home. A need for the sunrise which I'd looked upon in my worst time, the sunset that had kept guard of me.

At that moment, Mags comes out, dressed in his armor. I haven't spoken to him since yesterday, since the lecture. I had hoped to today, to ask to start training, apologize for my manner which was fueled by stress and fear, but seeing him... I can't face my mistake. Can't admit I was wrong when I remember my heart hammering with the water seeping through my teeth. Because yes, I was harsh. But he wasn't there, and it had almost cost me my life.

He takes a spot a few meters away, eyes carefully watching, standing back. He looks professional, hair pinned down and face clean. His sword is at his side, ready. The mark on his neck gone, covered by an undershirt.

The thought of him and Heather makes me happy. Entity knows they both deserve it—but not at the cost of the crown. If I must bear its burden, so must everyone else who claims its benefits.

"What was it like growing up here?" The question is asked of me by Tariq. I snap my head away from my watchful guard and back at the table. What was it like growing up here? Quiet. Dark and cold. But not on the Botanical Island.

"I spent a lot of my childhood on an island far south of here," I explain. "It was different. Beautiful."

"Home," Tariq says, finishing the thought I couldn't bear to say. Because he's right. It is home.

"Yes..." Under the table, hidden from sight, his leg gently touches me, his knee against mine. At first, I'm surprised, but I lean into it, the solidity.

Suddenly, above us comes a deep sound, breaking the silence like a thread through the eye of a needle. Booming and deep. A shadow forms in the sky, flying over when the screams start.

Cries of "Bomb!" and horrifying noises. Some run inside, but I remain. Chione and Tariq too. Mags pounds forward, armor clanking.

"Protect the queen!" he bellows, grasping my arm.

"Wait! Wait! Stop!" I shout over the noise and stand. I'd never heard the sound in real life, not for years, and excitement builds inside me. "Everyone, stop!" A gleam starts on my face.

"Lorilynn, what is it?" Tariq asks curiously and takes a place beside me. Chione also rises, sheathing a weapon I hadn't realized she'd raised.

"That's not a bomb..." Chione begins and then it flies over, zooming through the clouds, it's red nose exactly how I remember. Mags remains at our side, his hand clenched around my arm, ready to take me away. But he doesn't need to.

I gasp, joyous. "It's an airplane!"

•

Chione, Tariq, Mags, and myself go through the castle to the front lawn where the giant metal bird is perched on the grass, denting the turf, but I can forgive that.

A gathering of people, royals, officials, and servants find themselves all on the steps. Adora, Mags, and I are positioned at the front.

Wind gently blows, spinning the front propeller of the silver machine. It's stunning. Long with red stars and windows along the side. A ray of sunlight seeps through the dusk, glinting off the shiny side.

While we watch, there is audible silence. The flag on the side is the one of the Southern Isle. I have met a few members of the family in the past, but my guess is one of the older siblings was sent, if not a customary official. That is usual.

When the door opens, the little girl in me, that we all have no matter how old we grow, sparks up again.

His stride is longer, although he's always been tall. He clambers out clumsily, dark hair long and at his chin. He always kept it up, but not anymore. As he opens the door and steps out, his light eyes peer around at a land he hasn't seen for years.

My feet pound the ground as I rush into a sprint, leaving everyone behind. At first, he doesn't notice me, but then he too is running until our bodies crash and my arms are around him in a warm, very unroyal embrace. He rests his chin on my head, wrapping his arms around my shoulders.

"You've grown," I whisper into his chest.

"You haven't." He chuckles.

"I've missed you, Koen." I chuckle too. "Why are you here? I thought they would have sent one of your siblings or that uptight advisor your mother always had around."

"In the schmoozing of a new queen, it is always best to send someone the queen favors," he explains, and we part. He still holds hands around my waist, keeping me close as we have been before. "And on that note..." He lowers himself to a knee in the grass, placing a lingering warm kiss on my knuckles. "Queen Thornton, a pleasure."

"Stop, or I'll start referring to you as prince of the Southern Isle," I tease him, pulling him up so he towers over me and again places his arms around me.

"Everyone is watching," he murmurs into my hair. After a moment, I sneak a look back to see my breakfast guests and my uncles watching, all with various looks of confusion or disdain on their faces. I let my arms fall a moment.

"Everyone can screw themselves." I laugh, turning back to him. "Entity, you're different."

"You haven't changed a bit, Lori."

"Come inside. I'll introduce you to everyone, and we can get you a warm drink. Then you can show me your airplane," I say excitedly, keen to see the device I've heard so much about in books I'd spent my childhood reading. It made a big difference from the flying devices we'd made from paper in the drawing room when rain had kept us inside, throwing them across the room and seeing who could get them the farthest.

"I figured that would get you excited. They're a beauty, aren't they?" Eagerness is thick in his tone as his eyes dart to the great metal bird—like they used to at his toys when we first met those many years ago. No, he hadn't changed. Just become more beautiful and golden. His skin still resembles hazelnuts, smooth and dark and warm. Like the sun gifted him its rays at birth. Even when we were children, I thought he was son of the sun.

"Stunning..." I find myself looking at the features of the face I so dearly treasure. He stares at the airplane with adoration in his eyes. As if it's both his best friend and his child. "How did you get an airplane?"

"The internal parts are original. We built the outside around it—with some help."

"Help?" I push, and he stiffens a moment, just a second and so little. A minuscule hesitation before we're interrupted.

A warm hand touches my arm and then a soft yet regal voice says, "Prince Koen, I feel like I only saw you six months ago." Chione's tone is warm, happy. They move together and shake hands before both steps back. I wasn't aware they knew each other, that Ptah and the Southern Isle had relations, but they seem professionally familiar. He smiles politely as does she with their interaction.

The hand is still on my arm, holding loosely but closely. I peer at him over my shoulder, a hint of something in his eyes I can't quite place.

"This is Prince Khan of Turkish Arabia," I introduce. Tariq bows gently as does Koen before the two shake hands, exchanging pleasantries.

"While we're on introductions," Koen says after the two have stepped away from each other, "I have some people you must meet too."

I open my mouth to ask who, to ask why he smiled so excitedly when he said that, even more so than when he stared at the airplane, but he's already walking back towards it, striding happily, swaying his arms side to side.

"How do you know Prince Koen so well?" Chione pipes up, watching him stride away.

"We spent a lot of our childhood together," I explain, eyes catching Tariq's a moment. He still has that look, a coolness I can't place.

"Sweet," Chione says. "We'll see you inside?"

"Yes. At the ball tonight?" I raise a brow at her, at the quick roll of her eyes followed by a nod and a smile.

I imagine the clothes she'll wear. They'll be beautiful.

Chione offers a small wave at her waist before turning inside. After a pace, she twists her head to Tariq who still stands by me with his hand on my arm. He squeezes once before turning and following her. The two of them head inside once they reach the castle doors, sharing inaudible words.

As I wander to the plane, Koen stands at the bottom on some stairs made from an old ladder with a hand out. A slender woman with sleek black hair takes a gracious step out. At first, I think he's married, but then I come closer, seeing the fine details of her cheongsam. Red fabric, gold veining up to birds carefully embroidered in the fabric. A metallic chain around her neck, glistening even in the shadow, and the triangle crest that hangs from it.

My feet stop moving. My heart beats faster.

As she steps onto the grass, she peers round. At the sky, the ground, the castle, and me. After her comes a gentleman with the same crest hanging from his neck, like a noose of wealth.

Together they stand tall, strong. Unbeatable. A reminder of who they are.

In my years as princess, Màthair had kept me out of politics. My father had always encouraged she give me a childhood, particularly after my brother's passing and my illness appeared so unbearably.

When I was coming back from the island, a few days in, they explained they wanted me to have some years to get to know them, the staff, the castle, and the dynamics of how it all worked. When I was to turn twenty-one, I would begin taking an active role. Of course, no one ever anticipated this would happen. Perhaps they would rethink it if they could see what the future would hold. Wherever they are, they probably regret it now.

However, when I was newly sixteen—just before the visit from the Khan royals—there was one occasion when they couldn't hide the politics, no matter how tightly the door was shut.

"I will not *be doing such a thing!" Màthair snaps, the sound muffled by the*

thick wood of the door. "You may think you're almighty, but I am sovereign on Prithan land, not you." Her voice strains, breaking. As if her throat is giving up and dry. They'd entered the meeting some time ago when light was high in the sky. Now the moon sits on the dark blanket of velvet above us, shadows creeping up the wooden floor.

I've been sitting outside the dining room door for an hour now. There is something about them, their demeanor. The woman seems young yet wise. Beyond her years. That medallion crest that hangs around her neck fascinates me. The triangle in the center glinting against the candlelight when they had arrived last night. She had let me hold it a moment, even promised she'd bring me one next time if I wanted.

This afternoon when they had gone in, she had waved once, and Màthair had caught it, casting me a glare before closing the door sternly.

I hadn't listened in at first. Adora had lectured me on it before. But soon he, I, and Mags all crouched outside the doors listening in on our queen and king and their discussion. Discussion is a strange choice of word admittedly. It's more the woman calmly talking too low for us to hear, and Mother snapping a response. Papa is seemingly silent.

"Who is she, Adora?" I ask in a whisper, listening to footsteps that could be approaching from the other side of the wood.

He and Mags share a look, a quick moment before he speaks. "Do you remember when you were sick, we would give you tea sometimes? When it was really bad?"

I nod.

"That woman is a part of the 'Collective' who grow the only tea in the world."

I peer again at the door, listening to the familiar sound of my mother's angry voice behind it. We have a whiskey glass between us on the floor. I gently put the cool crystal in my hand, raising it to the door, placing it against the wood and putting the bottom to my ear.

"We don't need your blood-tea. We don't need anything from you." I hear Màthair spit at the woman. "You will not hold Prithan as long as I breathe." There's a beat of silence. "I think you should make your way home in the morning."

That is Papa. I've never heard him talk in such a way.

Then comes the footsteps, wide strides. The three of us don't have time to move, so the door opens to us standing, listening. I await the lecture, the stern words, but Màthair doesn't even make eye contact with me. Only Adora.

"Adora, will you see to it that there are no issues with our guest's departure in the morning."

Adora pops his hands behind his back and bows low. "Of course, your majesty."

Then I feel a hand on my upper back. I expect it to be Papa, but then I realize he's still in the room. Màthair. I peer behind me as the hand guides me along the corridor protectively.

"Queen Thornton." We're halfway down the corridor when the woman calls to Màthair. Everything stops, including us, and she turns slowly, precisely. "Prithan will give us what we need, mark my words. Even if we have to pry it from your hands."

"As long as I reign, you will never hold this country." She turns, keeping that

hand on my back and leading me away.

"Your majesty?"

I'd been in a daze, staring at those triangles around their necks, my heart still hammering at the memory. At the exchange, the woman had had with Màthair. These may not be the same people, but it's the same chain, the same triangle, the same mindset.

Even if we have to pry it from your hands.

You will not hold Prithan as long as I breathe.

As long as I breathe.

"Are you alright?" the male with the triangle says.

"Lorilynn?" Koen asks, placing a hand on my shoulder.

"Sorry," I apologize. "Welcome to Prithan."

"Thank you," the woman pipes up and bows her head, offering a hand to shake. Not a usual greeting to a royal. "I am Hui San, and this is Björn. It is a pleasure to meet you, Queen Thornton."

"And you." I offer the best smile I can, "You must be tired. Please, let me show you to your rooms."

As long as I breathe.

As long as I breathe.

As long as I breathe.

Two years ago, my mother said they would only get what they needed when she was dead. She is now missing after her ship was destroyed. And the very same Collective is here.

I'm letting them straight into my home.

I spend the next hour vomiting in my room.

CHAPTER ELEVEN

Preparations for the ball have been drowning the usual peace of the castle for hours. Maids setting up the ballroom, caterers getting food ready. I tried getting some quiet in my chambers, tried reading and walking and thinking.

The words haunt me still.

As long as I breathe.

Maids kept coming in and out. Eventually I started getting in the way and decided to get my veil and go to the chapel where silence may find me.

A pew at the front is where I've remained for some hours now. Soon the dancing will begin, the sun will set, and night will intoxicate everyone. Tomorrow all will wake with a headache, nausea, and complaints to go around.

People, royals from Europa, and servants come in occasionally to pray and give offerings, but they leave after a time. Now as the ball approaches, everyone is getting ready. Leaving only me, the statues, and the Entity.

Candles flicker as darkness creeps in, and soon, light music starts far away, seeping through the walls. A maid will surely be panicking to find me. I need to get ready and put on clothes made from fine fabrics that could pay for the tea we so desperately need.

Màthair would be angered if I traded with those who potentially planned her demise. Yet they are the only people who can give me what the nation needs. Those people's faces are imprinted on the back of my skull, their desperation. Some will be dead by now. I have a responsibility to them, and to those alive to keep them well. That is my role as ruler. That is the vow I take as this country's princess.

"You look deep in thought," Koen says as he creeps up, taking the seat on the pew next to me. "Not that that's new."

I bump his shoulder with mine. "Fuck off, Koen. That almost sounded like a compliment," I tease with a smirk.

"It was. I've always liked your thinking face. It reminds me I'm fortunate to be so handsome."

A joint chuckle escapes us. He hasn't changed, not really. He never took anything seriously when we were young, perhaps apart from our farewell.

He's ready for the ball, wearing his military jacket and polished medals. His hands rest on his knees. Slowly, one moves across onto my lap, grasping my fingers and squeezing once.

"How are you, Lori?" he whispers.

I want to tell him everything, from the wedding to the lies to the secrets to the fact I believe he just flew attempted murderers into my home. I sigh, pausing a moment. "I'm alright."

He raises an eyebrow. "You sure?"

"I'll be fine. I've survived worse."

"I heard you were stabbed by a phantom."

"I was shot, and the assassin was no phantom, although he is now. May he rest with the Entity."

"May he rest with the Entity," he repeats, stroking my cheek. "You're healed?"

I pull down the shoulder of my dress, revealing the mark. Rough around the edges but healing well. The bruising has faded somewhat, only patches of green and yellow and purple blooming in a light color, almost hidden among my pale skin.

His hand traces down my neck to the wound, gently touching the outline of bruising. His fingers are warm and soothing against my skin. I lean into them. Him. Resting my head on his shoulder.

"Do you remember when you slipped on the rock by the sea?" he asks. "I rescued you, and you got blood all over my white trousers."

The sea had been wild that day. We'd snuck away from lessons and gone to the beach cliffs, as rock pooling was best there. I'd slipped as the waves splattered, cut my knee, and ripped my dress. The maid was furious—about the dress and the risk of us going towards the stormy ocean.

"I didn't ask to be rescued. That was your choice."

"You still ruined my trousers." Koen grins.

"Not on purpose," I shoot back.

Soon silence takes over again and we find peace in each other's company, in the occasional comment or laugh, all with our fingers clasped together watching the wax drip down statues, the veil on my hair softy flowing in a breeze. Soon, rather scandalously, I take it off and fiddle with the soft lace between my fingers.

Perhaps if we had more time, we could be here all evening, but the ball is waiting, as is Tariq by the door. He clears his throat, causing Koen and I to snap our heads around to him.

He's ready for the ball too, wearing smart clothes and a jacket that falls to his knees, with black with gold embroidery delicately sewn in all over in the shape of flowers and vines. It's beautiful. Very much something I could imagine him wearing.

Tariq holds himself nervously, leaning from one foot onto another, watching the two of us. His eyes drift between Koen and me. Suddenly I feel the depth of him being my husband, that I can't be like this with

Koen—it isn't appropriate. I must leave that part of my life in the past. The memories. The history.

It's what Màthair would have expected, what Papa would have wanted. I can't let myself get whisked away and forget that. I can't be selfish.

"Your maids are looking for you, your majesty," Tariq says in a monotone voice of formality. Of a prince who has clearly interrupted something.

"Yes. Thank you." I stand slowly, casting a smile at Koen before placing the veil back over my head and striding down the aisle, Tariq's gaze harsh on me while I do, his head turning to face me as I pass him and go through the doors.

In my chambers, they've run a bath and readied a dress, one that I haven't seen yet. Everyone is waiting for me. As soon as I enter, I mutter apologies for my absence, which they politely accept before ushering me to the bath and stripping clothes from me.

"We've got to hurry you, your majesty," one maid, Efa, says. "Everyone else is already there. You don't want to miss out on the fun."

I sink into the warm water, hiding under the bubbles they kindly put in. "Both of us know this ball was not my idea," I state, twirling a finger in the water. "Traditions must be upheld and such. I'm sure my mother complained lots at her coronation balls."

Efa is an older woman. Age has greeted her as a friend, wrinkles lining her smile and silken spiders' web for hair. While she has been in the castle for years, she only joined my maid personnel after they redistributed Màthair's servants in her absence.

"She did, you're right," Efa confirms as she gets a towel ready for me, holding it up while I clamber out. "Almost as much as Magnús did."

"Considering how much the two of them utterly despised each other, they were both very similar," I comment.

She gives a small chuckle and an understanding smile, nodding in agreement but says nothing in return.

In my bedroom, Efa reaches for the rather large rectangular wrapped box that has been placed on my bed. Around it is a red ribbon tied in a bow.

"I had this brought from the stores. I thought you might like to wear it tonight," she explains and turns her back to fiddle with something on the vanity, seemingly giving me a moment to myself to remove the packing around whatever gown this is.

I reach for it, tugging the ribbon off and pulling the top of the box back, revealing a deep red gown with little roses sewn into the fabric, gold thread etched at the sides, and tight sleeves that go to the wrists. I haven't seen this dress myself. That's a lie—I haven't seen it since I was a young child, but I have seen the coronation portrait of my mother hundreds of times, in which she wears it. I reach down and touch the velvet, tracing my finger across the folded fabric. A little bit of her to have with me tonight, until she can be here herself.

"Thank you," I say to Efa, "it's perfect."

She turns and smiles, helping me dress, then adding finishing touches. Placing the jewels Azra gave me on my throat, rubies on my earlobes, and fingers.

"Don't look too down, your majesty," she says after a time as I sit on the vanity while she places my hair in a style. I hadn't even realized I had been seeming so glum. "Isn't the prince from the Southern Isle there? Weren't you too close? I'm sure he'll keep a watchful eye on you."

Koen brushes the tears from my cheek with his thumb, and I wipe those falling from his eyes. He looks over my face with such sadness, such wishing and hope. The servants walk past us from the front door to the carriage with all the bags, maids waiting in the carriage for him.

"They can't just make you go. Please, write to them and say you're staying. Please, Koen..." I beg, sobbing. "I don't want to be without you."

Koen leans forward, placing his forehead on mine as we shut our eyes. "You'll always be my best friend, Lorilynn. No matter how far apart we are," he whispers before stepping away, taking my happiness with him. He doesn't look back as he climbs into his carriage, shuts the door, and starts to move. The horses trot away, my only friend with them. I didn't get to hold him one last time, didn't tell him my feelings. We should be climbing trees and swimming in the sea, not seeing each other for what could be the last time.

I'm sobbing, my shoulders shaking as I watch him go, my companion, going back across the oceans to a home that hasn't been home for the past nine months.

We're each other's family.

Adora steps from the house, hands in his pockets, Mags behind him with a look of sadness too.

"Lorilynn," Adora says softly, "come inside. Let's get you ready for the evening."

"I think the cook is making your favorite for dessert tonight," Magnús follows up.

I turn away from the open road to face them when their attention shifts back to the carriage, and I look too. It's stopped and a figure is stepping out, running back.

It's Koen. He's running back.

I'm run to him as fast as I can. Until our bodies slam together and I'm holding him and he's holding me, then his hands are on my cheeks, and he presses his lips against mine.

We were thirteen, and it was a crush, but... yes, we were close. However, he seems pretty chummy with his new friends now.

Not too long after, she has finished and I'm ready. I straighten the last of the floor-length gown, swirl it around once and feel it as it moves at my ankles. I exit my chambers, turn the corner into the corridor, and am immediately greeted by Tariq, leaning against the wall with his arms crossed.

I keep walking.

"What is it, Tariq?" I ask, somewhat breathless, striding through the corridors, his footsteps following just as fast.

"We need to talk." He voice is monotone.

"About what? Can this not wait until later?" We approach the ballroom, music building, people starting to come into view through the open archway leading to the marble floor. I see Azra with a glass of wine, talking to a representative from Congo.

"Our divorce," he replies rather loudly, so anyone close could hear. Which happens to be half the political influences of the world.

Beside us is a door—I'm not sure to where, however, I open it and rush through, revealing the old music room that no one uses because none of us Thorntons know how to play anything.

A pianoforte sits in the center on a small platform to act as a stage. The rest of the room is empty aside from the portraits on the walls with white sheets over them to protect from age and dust. I promptly shut the door behind us as he steps in, leaning against it to trap him from escaping. He takes position against the piano, crossing his arms over his chest, creasing his tailored jacket.

"Watch your volume," I lecture him angrily. "Every political influence in the world is currently in the next room. Any of them could hear you."

"How else was I going to get you to talk to me, Lorilynn?" he says and takes a step forward. "I gave you time to recover, but we can't spend forever avoiding this conversation."

"My opinion on the matter hasn't changed, Tariq. Getting shot changes nothing," I explain as the music starts increasing in the next room.

"But the prince does," Tariq says, following it with, "There's something between you two. If we're married, you can't be with him."

A pang hits my heart as he says that, guilt of the truth, but also, it was one kiss. A kiss fueled by sadness and hormones and a teenage crush. By a desire for the world to seem perfect for a little bit. At the time I'd thought about it for days after, remembering the feeling of his lips on mine. But now, it just seems like a clumsy first kiss.

"You're thinking there is more than there actually is," I respond, not quite able to meet his dark eyes.

"But there is something. Isn't that right?" he pushes. "He could be your king one day, your marriage could be in love, not fear. You would create a strong alliance for your countries."

"I said no, Tariq," I snap, perhaps too loudly. "I trust our parents; I trust this alliance. Accept it and move on. I'm not expecting you to care about me. Fuck who you want, love who you want—just sacrifice marrying them for the sake of our countries."

"But we shouldn't have to, Lorilynn," he urges, moving to stand in front of me, only inches away. His scent fills my nose, rushing the blood around my body.

"Just *stop*," I snap again. "Stop being selfish."

"*I'm* being selfish?" he replies, then mutters a word in what I believe is Turkish and sounds a lot like he's cursing at me.

"You're a prince. It is your responsibility to do what is best for your people."

"You talk to me about responsibility when you won't even wholeheartedly accept you're queen. Your parents are dead, Lorilynn. You are going to be crowned and we both know it'll be too late to divorce then. Either way—they're at the bottom of the ocean somewhere, and you're wasting the power you have because you're scared your mother will return and punish you."

Tears well in my eyes, the captain's body cursing the back of my mind again; his murderers could be in the next room.

"You're wrong," I whisper. "They're alive. I know it in my blood."

"Then you're fucking stupid."

I can't find the words to respond to that, so we just end up staring at each other in silence. If it weren't for the door opening, we might have remained there for hours.

"What are you two doing?"

Tariq's gaze breaks from mine and shifts to where his mother stands behind us, a confused looking lining her features.

"Just talking, *Ana*," Tariq says.

She raises an eyebrow, casting a concerned glance at me and the tears forming in my eyes. "About what, Ender?"

His words echo in my mind, anger bubbling deep inside me. I want to hurt him back.

"We've decided to announce our marriage tonight at the ball."

"No, we haven't," Tariq immediately counters, panic lacing his voice. "We haven't decided that at all."

Azra takes a moment to peer between the two of us with no less confusion than before. The only noise is the music in the following room.

"Well..." Her voice fades with hesitation. "I'll see you two in there. Don't take too long. People are starting to look for you both." She turns around, leaving the room, looking back a single time before rejoining the ball, leaving the two of us alone again.

"Lorilynn... Please, you can't be serious," he begs, the intimidation gone from him and instead replaced with desperation.

I could give in to his sad eyes, his begging. At least grant him more time to figure out how to convince me—not that he will. But as soon as it's announced there will be no turning back. We both know that. But that is the strength we need—that Prithan needs—particularly with the Collective here. Establishing the union between our countries will provide power and mean that if they go after me next, there will be still a king.

I don't look at him and grasp the handle, leaving the room and making sure the door slams behind me.

CHAPTER TWELVE

The ball is in full swing at my arrival. I sneak through the open double doors, avoiding the official announcement and peer around. The room is large, and most of the time these doors are kept shut as it is only used for entertaining. Tonight, the grand space is filled with perhaps a hundred people—guests and servants alike. Everyone at their best. In a far corner is a string quartet playing a sweet melody which couples dance to in the center of the room, servants gliding between them with trays of sparkling wine and food.

One servant passes me with a tray of lovely, little bits of bread and some sort of fish paste. It smells divine, but they are gone before I can grab one, going to the far side of the room where Koen talks with the Collective members, clutching his own glass of bubbles.

For a moment I think of going there, of saying hello or how are you or teasing him about his haircut, but then I remember who he is with, who his friends are. Who stands next to him.

Another waiter wanders past with a silver tray glinting in the light, holding glasses of sparkling wine. At noticing me, he bows his head, offering one, which I promptly take and pour down my throat—perhaps too rapidly—then place back on the tray as he stares at me with a look of disbelief, a comical smirk at the side of his mouth.

"Your majesty." He bows again before continuing, and I am left alone in the vast room of royal protocol. I may have ended up standing there all evening if it weren't for the savior of Princess Chione waving me over.

She has positioned herself at the side of the room, her guards standing around her, dressed impeccably. She chose not to wear a dress, but trousers and a shirt, which is a part of her hijab in flowing white silk, adorned with sapphires on her fingers and dramatic makeup. Her guards have the same color and blue sashes, but each also has their own style or addition such as a jeweled badge or headscarf or ring.

I saunter over and join her in glancing over the ballroom and the dancing. The food, the drinks, the music is all magnificent, yet our attention doesn't move from Koen and his friends.

"You dislike them as much as I do?" she asks as she sips a glass of orange juice, keeping her eyes on them. Hui San is gently biting into a particularly lovely looking canapé, smiling as she eats and tapping her foot along to the music. The gentleman, Björn, is talking with Koen, seemingly agreeing on something as they nod together and chuckle, then asking Hui San, who starts nodding too, and their eyes glance around.

"What do you know about them?" I ask. I'm not denying her statement.

"I haven't met those ones before, but last year they took a 'diplomatic' visit to Ptah. All in all, they were only there for perhaps a week or so. Ptah hasn't purchased tea leaves for years, decades even. Not in the years I can recall. My father dislikes them, always has. We use different methods medically, so we haven't needed to trade with them.

"They wanted to sell us a new blend," she explains, "one made from jasmine as well as the usual plant. My father debated it."

"Debated it? He didn't make the deal?" I push and finally look at her, at the grave face she holds and the way her little finger taps on the edge of her glass.

"They used to ask for jewels, fine things—perhaps metals, but they don't want that anymore."

"What do they want?" I ask cautiously.

"They phrased it as 'prisoners and persons of low value' to have work for them in tea fields."

"Slaves?" I gasp, uncertain if I perhaps misunderstood. I had to have misunderstood.

"I didn't believe it at first either," she replies, casting a glance at me.

"That's disgusting..." But as she said, she didn't have an epidemic. She *could* say no. They are the only hope for my people, the only ones to provide the medicine and care they need to survive whatever is happening to their lungs. To fight off the infection that could be their downfall.

Do I choose to take the tea in exchange for people, or do I say no and let more die? Someone loses their life one way or another. Someone I am meant to protect.

"I think they attacked the ship my parents were on," I admit.

She turns her head to me, mouth agape in disbelief. "Do you have any proof?" she pushes, but I shake my head rather sadly.

"It's just speculation. I'm certain my mother had many enemies in and out of Prithan. That is what it means to be queen."

The two of us remain standing there for a while, speculating and discussing discreetly. She is polite but open about her beliefs. Ones which I wholeheartedly agree with.

Despite meeting the princess so recently, I find myself talking to her as if she is a friend of years. We joke, we tease, we discuss and disagree occasionally.

After perhaps twenty minutes of us laughing and talking, a light tap on my shoulder makes me turn, leaving the conversation and seeing Adora. He's also in his best clothes but his face is his concentrating one. His 'work face' as I used to call it as a child. He'd wear it when he was about to try and convince the ladies and lords to do something.

"Can I have a moment, Lorilynn?" he says, raising his voice over the music.

I nod, casting a glance at Chione in apology for leaving as I am led by him to a quiet corridor away from guests which turns to the kitchen. Servants wander up and down, bustling and busy. They don't notice us standing there, too focused on fetching food or drinks.

"I won't keep you long," he says, "but I promised Magnús I would talk to you."

"I'm not doing this, Adora," I scold immediately and go to leave, him catching my arm as I turn, gently pulling me back. Not painfully, but firmly.

"Lorilynn," he tries lecturing.

"No," I firmly reply, snatching my arm away. "If he wants to speak to me, he can do so himself."

"You won't give him the chance. Just—train tomorrow. He can talk to you, and you can get some strength back. Please." Adora eyes widen, and he pushes out his bottom lip. His begging face that he knows I can't say no to, no matter how much I don't wish to talk to Magnús.

"I'll think about it," I say and begin walking away to hear him call my name one more time.

"Lorilynn!"

"I'll think about it!"

•

The ball continues and soon it's pitch-black outside, only the light of the candles and chandeliers hanging from the ceiling illuminating the room, the dancing. The bottoms of my feet pound from waltzing with so many people for so long now. Alcohol has warmed my blood and food sits in my stomach happily. Exhaustion is deep in my bones. I've laughed at so many not funny jokes that my cheeks hurt and shaken so many hands I want to scrub them with soap and hot water.

The music is at its peak and shows no sign of mellowing. People still ball and laugh, wide awake. At this moment, I wish for nothing more than to go to bed and sleep for hours. Maybe even some warmed apple juice with a nip of whiskey too. Alas, I must stay here and entertain guests until sunrise. With a room full of people with different time zones, someone is always awake. Which means the ball will still be in full swing when the sun rises.

I'm taking a rest on a chair at the side after a particularly long dance with the representative from Vatican. They were excitable, to say the least, and waltzed me around for what must have been at least ten minutes non-stop. This beautiful dress is now seeming heavy, and being able to take the weight off my feet for a few minutes is bliss.

As I perch in the chair, I carefully sip a glass of juice —I've had enough to drink for one night—and Azra carefully glides over with a smile on her face and a glass of something red in her hand. She perches next to me, looking out over the dancers beside me.

"I remember my coronation balls," she says. "I wasn't married yet—in fact, I met Taylan that night," she explains, staring into the distance with fondness in her eyes.

"I'm sorry for his passing," I say softly.

She peers down at me with a gentle smile and takes my hand, squeezing once and taking it to her mouth for a sweet kiss, like I'd expect my mother to give me if she ever showed any affection. "And how're you?" she asks, placing my hand back on the chair and taking the one beside me, straightening her skirts.

"Tired," I reply, taking a sip of my drink.

"You can rest shortly. Everyone soon will be too drunk to even realize who they are."

I chuckle, knowing it to be true. One of the royals from Europa then reenforces her point by stumbling slightly with a servant, both then profusely apologizing to one another.

"Point proven." She chuckles before taking a more serious tone. "Your parents would be proud of you. You know that, don't you?" she says softly.

I'm surprised by her words, more so by the truth. I do think they would be proud. I hope they would.

Azra reaches in a pocket hidden in her skirt and brings out a small handkerchief, passing it over. I dab my eyes gently, not even realizing tears had formed there, the wetness on my cheeks a surprise.

"I'm proud of you too," she says. "I know my country is in good hands when I pass."

"You think so?" I ask, giving her back the handkerchief which she pushes back for me to keep.

"I know so," she replies before turning her head to the ballroom where Tariq glides towards us.

He bows as he approaches and holds a hand out to me, one placed behind his back. "May I have this dance, your majesty?" He says clearly, matter-of-factly. Like the masked voice he used when he first arrived. The voice of a prince, not a friend. The voice people listening would expect. A voice which doesn't indicate the argument we had hours ago, or the feeling in my stomach I get when I take his hand, standing and letting him guide me to the dance floor, peering at Azra before looking at the ground, unable to make eye contact with him. Particularly when he places a hand on my waist and I one on his shoulder. His scent wafts into my nostrils, making my head spin and my legs weak.

As we start dancing, we stay silent, my eyes firmly on his chest. He lets go of my hand, keeping the other on my waist, and lifts my chin so I look at him, into the eyes I've been avoiding for the past minute.

"Look at me," he says quietly, just loud enough for me to hear him over the music. "Please."

I finally lift my gaze to his face. They are gloomy but bright. I stare in silence while he leads the dance I'd forgotten about.

"What is it?" I ask sharply.

"I want to say I'm sorry."

"Wha—?" My voice fades. Sorry? He's sorry? "Is this some last ploy to try and get me to change my mind?"

He shakes his head, dipping me slightly as the dance requires then bringing me back up to face him. "It's not a ploy, just an apology," he explains as we sway in time with a crescendo in the music, stepping to the side to match the other couples. "For what I said and how I acted."

"Well..." I say, not sure how to respond. I hadn't expected this, hadn't expected for him to apologize. "I apologize too. For shouting. But I'm not changing my mind."

"I'm not apologizing to get you to change your mind, Lorilynn," he states. "I'm apologizing because that's what husbands and wives do when they're wrong."

"Husbands and wives? You mean to say..." Husbands and wives. Husband and wife. Married. He's apologizing because he is my husband and accepts that.

"Prithan and Turkish Arabia are what matters. Our lives are not our own. That is what we take on when we have the title. Having an alliance through marriage is what is best for them. I was too driven by my own feelings to see that." The music ends and everyone applauds, including us. While before I couldn't meet his eyes, now I can't stop looking at them. He is peering around at everyone. Clapping dies down as music starts again. Couples rejoin and start dancing. I just stand next to him in the center of them all. He finally faces me and offers his hand again for another dance. I don't take it, just remain looking at him confused over his sudden change of heart. I'd lay bleeding on the ground not long ago, and that hadn't altered his mind.

"What changed?" I blurt, now having to raise my voice above the music.

He pulls back his hand after realizing I'm not going to take it and moves closer to me to avoid being danced into by someone. "I'm not sure. But we can be happy, right? We can make the best of this situation?"

"I meant what I said about you having a relationship with someone perfect. I'm not going to stop you from having children or living with them. Perhaps my choice of words was harsh, but I genuinely mean it."

"I know you did." He's calm and offers his arm again as people begin staring at us as we stand in the middle. "You're going to make an amazing queen one day. It'll be an honor to be your king."

I take his hand and place the other back on his shoulder. We start twirling again, appearing as the happy couple but both our faces are grave. I thought I'd be happy. I should be happy. Màthair will be pleased, Papa will be pleased, Prithan is protected. I may have to deal with the Collective and somehow selling slaves for tea, but I have his guidance now and Azra's support officially. He spins me in his hand during the dance, and I slam back into his chest, taken aback by the sudden wall of him. His hand falls back to my waist once more as we dance slowly, merging with the others around us and suddenly we're one of many again.

"Does this mean I start referring to you as Tariq Thornton?" I ask him gently, a hint of a smile in the corner of my lips.

"I think I'm going to keep my name." He chuckles. "I've had it for twenty-two years after all. Ender Khan works. But you can still just call me Tariq," he teases on that last bit, and I blush. It feels strange now, like a string of awkward is between us. The banter we had before seems gone, replaced with formality I would expect between my parents who were very much not in love with each other.

I take my hand from his shoulder, snatching my other back. This feels wrong, so very wrong. Realizing I'm moving away, he releases his grip from my waist and looks my face over a moment. Then again, I'm staring at the floor, my thoughts racing over every word he said.

Our lives are not our own.

I don't want that though.

I want to choose him, not because a wedding two years ago says I should, but because I like the way he makes me feel, and I want him to feel the same way.

He's looking my face over with pure confusion, brows furrowed and his eyes searching over my features.

Azra is on the far side of the room, now sitting in the chair I left, searching. I remember her standing at the ceremony, cold and hard.

I want to choose Tariq, not because his mother was watching. I want to choose him, not because my own watches or my father stands crying in the corner, but because when he touches me, I melt.

He's still there silently, and I take his face in my hands, crushing my lips on his for a moment. He quickly wraps his arms around my waist, holding me tight. My heart implodes in my chest as I feel his lashes on my cheeks, fluttering shut. Every part of my skin is set alight, red blooming on my face.

And then it's over, and I am shuffling my way through the dancers to get out the room, out his sight as soon as possible.

Because most importantly, I want him to choose me, not because of a wedding, but because he feels the same way about me that I feel about him.

CHAPTER THIRTEEN

I grasp the front of the skirts, quickly escaping down the corridor to my chambers. But Koen seemingly saw me leave and has followed, repeatedly calling my name as we both stride down the stone floors. Eventually, I can't pretend I don't hear him.

I stop and turn to where he meets me, a grave look of concern over his face. "Lori, are you alright?"

Maybe he saw the kiss. Should I feel guilty about that? I'm not sure how this is meant to work.

"I'm fine." I swallow, my heart still hammering from the thought of Tariq's lips on mine and the warmth in my stomach.

Koen takes a step forward, holding his hands out. I can't read his face, it's blank. Nothing like what it was when we were younger.

"It's just all a bit much," I explain.

"I can't do much there," he says and opens his arms, "but would a hug help?"

A hug. To feel the warmth of another person, a friend, would be amazing. To be held and have my hair stroked and be told that everything is alright. Yes, that would be perfect. To feel safe.

I step forward, opening my arms and stepping towards him. I anticipate his warmth, but then there's a golden glint and I'm stopped in my tracks, my heartbeat pounding in my ears.

"What is it, Lori?" he asks, looking my face over. I can't help staring at his chest and the gold glinting in the candlelight. The chain swings from his neck perfectly, as if it was made for him. The triangle hangs there, shining bright as it reflects the candlelight behind me, flickering light in my face. He must have put it on after we had been in the chapel. I know what that triangle means—he's one of them.

"Lori?" Koen inquires again, lowering his arms to match mine, which had dropped to my sides.

I peer up at his face, shaking in my bones. Does he know? Does he know what they might have done? Was he behind it? Did he sit at a long table in a meeting with them, putting forward the idea? Remembering the friend he had, and how they could make her queen and conform her to their needs so they can get the deal they want.

I never thought he could be one of them. It had been bad enough to think he brought them, but what if he brought them because he was one of them?

My eyes are locked on the triangle. He notices, offering a hand out to me, but I step away from his reach, my breath ragged and chest heaving. I feel as if I'm going to be sick.

"Lorilynn..." His voice trails off as I turn and start walking away. He snags my wrist, yanking me back towards him, eyes filled with concern, yet he just left a bruise.

"Let go of me," I hiss, snatching the hand back, rubbing my arm.

"I'm sorry, I didn't mean to hurt—"

"What's going on?" Tariq comes around the corner, eyes darting between us, harsh lines on his face.

I peer at him over Koen's shoulder, blood rushing to my cheeks at the memory of the kiss we shared moments ago and how his hands felt around my waist. "Nothing," I reply, turning around so I don't have to look at him and start striding down the corridor, his footsteps chasing me. From the corner of my eye, I see Koen stand there a moment before turning back into the ballroom. Tariq, on the other hand, follows after me.

"Lorilynn, wait!" he calls as I clamber up the stairs in the gallery, clutching the side to make sure the dress doesn't topple me over. I keep striding though, not daring to look back. Part of me wished Koen had followed too so I don't have the prospect of being alone with Tariq.

Eventually I make it to my chambers, opening the double doors and hurrying in, slamming them behind me. His footsteps sound on the floor outside, stopping. His shadow creeps through the crack between the stone floor and the bottom of the door. I lean against the wood, sinking to the floor in a mound of fabric and feelings.

There are two gentle taps on the other side.

"Lorilynn?" he says softly, muffled by the wall between us. "Talk to me."

I'm silent for a bit, praying he'll leave, but he doesn't. I lean my head against the surface behind me, hoping his footsteps start and fade into the distance soon.

"I'm, uh, tired. I'm going to sleep," I finally reply, my voice coming out a higher pitch than I intended.

"Please..." he says. I almost don't hear him as he speaks no more than a mumble.

"Night, Tariq."

There's a pause, and then finally, his footsteps fade into the distance, leaving my heart hammering against my ribcage.

•

He'd only those said two words, over and over.

"I'm sorry..." He does up his trousers, quickly standing from the bed in the darkness. The two guards turn around, paleness on their faces. One of them looks as if they're going to be sick. I think I'm *going to be sick. I reach for the lavender bed sheet,*

bring it up to cover myself.

The priest finally lifts his head, coming forward and saying a light prayer in a language even I don't know. Then he bows and silently leaves the room, only the guards, prince and I remaining. It seems eerily silent for so many people.

An ache blooms between my legs, and I quickly peek under the sheets as a hint of blood stains the white of the under sheet.

"We're instructed to take you back to your chambers," one of the guards says to the prince.

He slowly turns to them, nodding silently and going towards them, placing a hand on the door and pausing, seemingly thinking to himself before he pushes it open and leaves. The two guards follow, leaving me alone. The air suddenly feels cold, nipping at the bare skin of my neck and shoulder where my night chemise has fallen slightly. A sob escapes me.

My body is starting to hurt now from being dragged and beaten and battered. Breathing starts to become hard from the burning in my lungs, my throat hoarse from crying and my eyes stinging.

I need to get out of here, out of this bed, out of this room. I clamber down onto the cold floor, my grazed feet stinging with the movement. After a few seconds, it subsides, and I patter to my wardrobe, taking out an old, hooded, cloak that had belonged to Papa's stepsister. She had left it when visiting once, and Papa said there was no point sending it back and to just keep it.

I grab some boots, sliding one on my foot only for the grazing to sting again, making me wince. I search through to the back of the cupboard, finding some long socks, placing them over my feet and trying the boots again to no avail. Even with the extra layer of fabric, they are overly tender.

I don't fret too much or waste time, slinging the cloak over my back, clasping it at the neck and creeping out the doors, hoping anyone near is asleep. I slip into an alcove as two guards pass on a patrol, quickly disappearing down the corridor, mumbling about something that happened in the public house.

Once they're out of sight, I carry on, avoiding various people, and sneak out the kitchen.

Outside is prickly cold. Frost has started dancing on the grass, wetness seeping into the socks. I can't be out for long, but I need the time. The freedom to not think about what just happened on that bed, in the chapel.

I start walking through the roses, clutching the cloak tighter around me as the wind howls.

Apparently, I wasn't the only one who needed air. On a bench, staring at the ground is the prince, shivering in the coolness. He hasn't even got a jacket on. At least he has shoes.

I stay statue-still when I see him, trying to think of what to say. But after a few moments, I realize he hasn't seen me.

I creep back, careful not to make a noise. However, a rock I hadn't noticed before decides to be the spot where my foot lands, and I let out a small yelp as the sharp edge digs into the unprotected sole of my heel.

I think about running, but it's too late. His head whips towards me, his eyes shocked at my presence.

"Are you alright, princess?" he asks, standing and looking me up and down. He hasn't changed clothes. In fact, I question if he has even been back to his chambers yet after all.

"Uh, yes." I swallow. "I'm sorry to have disturbed you. I'll just be on my way, your highness."

"No, please." He motions to the bench. "I was just leaving anyway." The prince pauses before walking past, but waits a few meters away, keeping his distance but peering at my wet feet.

"Your shoes?" he asks with a raised eyebrow.

"My feet got hurt in the... process of events tonight. Shoes were too painful," I explain, giving a somewhat nervous smile. To complain about grazes is comical in comparison to him. His nose still has a trail of blood leading from it and his eye is starting to darken around the edges.

"Well... you should be careful. You'll catch a cold," he replies rather quietly, slipping his hands into his pockets and shuffling from one foot to the other. Eyes trail up and down me.

I tighten the cloak around my shoulders, hiding the nightgown I'm wearing. Not that it matters. He's my husband—we've consummated. We're married.

For the next few moments, both of us shuffle on our feet, whisps of cold air floating from our lips in the briskness. I'm waiting for him to speak and I think he is waiting for me.

"Well, um... Goodnight." I turn around, walking back inside as I start to shiver.

"Princess?" he calls after me, quiet enough no one could hear but me. I turn to face him where he's taken a hand out from his pocket and holds it out for me to shake. "My name is Ender."

I step forward and take his fingers in mine. "Lorilynn."

•

I awake the next morning, still in the dress. After Tariq left in the night, I stayed against the door for some time until my back ached, eventually wandering over to the window seat and watching people pour into the gardens to sit on the grass as the sun rose, a group of them sharing a bottle of wine. I must have fallen asleep before getting to my bed.

My back aches and my shoulder is stiff. The wound has closed well, and I remember what Adora had said last night about training. I need to train. I need to move.

I wrap my shoulder in new bandages, a clean scar forming, and grab the training sword, strapping it around my waist.

As I step out, instinct tells me to watch out, but I realize I don't have to hide anymore. Truth be told, I expect most of the guests are still asleep or nursing hangovers, but a few nod or bow as I pass them, eyes darting over the weapon at my waist. No one says anything though, and I slip through the corridors to Mags's door, my fist poised over the wood. Ready to knock.

I never do.

I can't stop remembering the feeling of the water in my lungs, the bullet in my shoulder. The warmth of my blood down my dress, and the absence of his aid that he promised. The fact he could have stopped it before it had even started if he hadn't been so distracted by Heather.

I choose instead another door on the far side of the castle. Chione is surprised to see me when she opens it, yet she still greets me with a smile, particularly when her eyes flit to my sword.

It only takes her and her personal guards two minutes to get ready, and soon enough, we're in the bitter cold, battling and clashing our weapons together.

I train with Chione first, and she is a master. Beautiful and merciful and refined. If I were to choose someone to remove my head, it would be her, and I'd even say thank you afterwards.

I end up sparing with one of her guards as she watches, giving out orders in Masri occasionally and advice to me.

"You're treating your legs and arms as if they're not connected," she says from the side as I swipe my sword forward, the guard jumping above it, the blade only reaching the air. "They should move together as one."

The guard and I move apart, bowing our heads as both of us breathe. My lungs are burning, sweat dripping down my forehead and back. I can feel a bruise already blooming on my stomach from a particular blow, and there is a new cut on my arm. Yet, I'm thrilled. I feel alive, free. My mind is somewhere else, not focusing on how it felt to have my lips on Tariq's, or the memories of when we were first joined.

"I can't even pretend I know what you mean," I say jokingly. "Don't they move together anyway?"

Chione steps forward, grinning, shaking her head. "Try again. This time, tune in to your breaths. And move your whole body as one."

The guard and I get into position once more, then I take a strike at him. He catches my leg with his, almost knocking me to the ground. I grasp his hand and use it to propel myself behind him, kicking his legs out from under him. He falls to the floor, grunting as he looks up, cheeks pinking.

I hadn't realized the audience we'd built. Koen and the Collective, Tariq, and... Mags. A look of hurt crosses his face, a deep sadness. I'd trained without him. I quickly look away, not able to meet his eyes as we all disperse, shaking hands with the guard before striding away.

With Mags towards the castle, I don't want to go that way, and with Tariq towards the garden, I can't face going that way either. So, I turn towards the woods, quickly losing myself in the trees, grass fading to dirt and hedges, roses becoming nothing more than a blanket of amber debris on the soil. After a minute, I feel I'm far enough in I'm safe in the quiet. Neither of them would have followed me that far. Or so I thought. Because as soon as I sit on a fallen tree, resting my head in my hands, Tariq appears.

"Were you running away from me?" he questions with a raised brow.

"Of course not," I pant, "I was *walking.*"

He pushes his hands into his pockets, slowly ambling over to sit opposite me on the log, kicking the dead leaves with his foot.

"I see. I thought you might be avoiding me after yesterday."

"Yesterday?" I feign ignorance. "What about yesterday?" The kiss? The fact I stormed off?

"At the ball," he begins, my heart beginning to beat even faster in my chest. "You never announced the marriage."

A small sigh of relief escapes me. It's quickly replaced by the realization that I think he's right. I can't imagine spending my life loveless, where the only kisses I get are the ones from a man who doesn't want to be with me. How can I put that in words?

"No, I didn't." I'm not entirely sure what to say next.

"Does..." He hesitates. "Does that mean you've changed your mind?"

Yes. It does.

Cautiously, keeping space between us I stand from the log, leaning on a nearby tree instead. "Are you able to make the arrangements?" I ask him, crossing my arms and peering to the ground.

He nods slowly.

"For tonight?"

"Tonight?"

I lift my gaze to where he stares at me with wide eyes, arms by his sides. I wonder what he expected to come from this conversation, for me to say I just had a bad moment? That I was weak, but nothing has changed?

"I'll let you know when and where," he confirms and offers a curt nod, finally turning to leave, taking a few steps towards the castle before looking back, glancing over me a moment before speaking again. "Are we going to talk about the kiss?"

There it is. My heart beats faster again and my feet start moving past him. I don't cast a glance in his direction as I pass, but I do mutter something along the lines of "See you later" and quickly make a break for it back to the gardens. I'm acting like a child, this is ridiculous. But whenever I think about the kiss or how my heart beats faster when we're close, I'm reminded of how I'll never truly have him.

I shouldn't want him though. The only reason this happened is because of a horrible night and having choice taken away. Now I have that choice. I have the freedom, and for that I am thankful. Yet I can imagine what it would be like to stay together, to smile at each other, perhaps renew vows so we can do it our own way. One day in the far distant future, perhaps we would have a child. Or we could adopt one like his parents did. But it's not going to happen because I would spend forever also watching him love someone else, being tied to duty. While he could love another, I never could. If it were discovered, the marriage contract would break, putting our countries in jeopardy. Marriage law states that the first child must be of the spouse. It's unfair. He could love, but until we had a child, I could never be physical with anyone but him. I'm certain that's partly why my parents hated each other so much. Because they each deserved better. I don't ever want that.

I keep walking into the clearing of the garden, checking behind me to see Tariq isn't following, and walk straight into Magnús.

CHAPTER FOURTEEN

Walking into him actually hurts a little. He's still choosing to wear his chest plate, so my jaw meets with a metal wall. I might even have a bruise later.

"What were you doing in the woods?" Magnús asks, raising an eyebrow just as Tariq meanders out too, hands in his pockets, probably making it seem as if we were doing something highly inappropriate.

"I was on a walk," I reply, rubbing my jaw. I finally cast my eyes up at him. He looks sad, regretful. Young. I think about what Adora said. That I should give him a chance, yet I can't stop remembering the water in my lungs, the blood on my dress...

"I was hoping to talk to you," he says, "Please, your majesty."

He called me your majesty. He's never called me anything other than Lorilynn. It sets nausea inside my stomach. I wonder if I can ever get past it, past the water or the pain or the anger. I hope so. It's exhausting. I'm just not ready yet.

I want to walk away, because I know he'll say he's sorry. And I truly know that, but sorry doesn't stop the fact it happened. It doesn't magically mean the memory vanishes or the scars fade to nothing.

But I owe him this conversation; he's family. And anger doesn't stop love. I think the reason the anger is so deep is that my love for him runs deeper.

I don't reply, just give a slight nod and take a bench at the side, looking over the deep red of my mother's roses. She loved them so much. The sweet scent reminds me of her now. He looks over them too, something on his face I can't quite place.

He touches one petal with his fingers, stroking it as if it is the cheek of a long-dead lover.

Neither of us make eye contact. I wonder if I should say something, break the silence.

"How're you feeling? You look as if you've healed well," he says.

"I'm alright, thanks," I reply, fiddling with a loose thread on my trousers.

"Listen..." he begins, "I wanted to say I'm sorry— *truly sorry* for what happened. What could have happened."

I can't think of any words, can't respond as memories flood back. The feeling of his hands, the pain that speared through my whole body. The desperation for oxygen.

"I—" he starts to say, but I hold up a hand, not able to hear the word sorry again.

"Please... stop apologizing," I breathe. We're silent again.

"Alright," he says, "but just so you know, I've taken a step back from Heather." There is a twang in his voice as he says her name, "I'm your uncle. I love you. You're my queen. I shouldn't have let something else become more important than that. More important than duty."

"Duty?" I breathe, fire igniting in my stomach. "Duty is in the bowing and the primping."

He leans forward where we're sitting, peering over to me as his blond hair falls over his eyes that search my face, resting his elbows on his knees.

"Duty is a façade of rules and stupid expectations that is required of every soul in this castle, in this family. Duty is wearing a crown and the dresses, wearing the armor and waving the flag." I carry on, tears pooling in my eyes. "Being my guard, keeping me safe is more than *duty*," I spit the final word, my tears pooling on the dirt bellow. "It's a vow. A vow you made to me, a vow you made to my father."

I shuffle slightly where I am sitting, taking my eyes away from him to the sky. The crowd that had gathered is now long gone. The gardens are peaceful. One gardener, eyes on the ground, focusing on one of Màthair's roses, readying it for the spring. Apart from that, the area is bare. Chione and her guards have gone, perhaps to breakfast or prayer.

It is just us and the Entity.

"The vow was broken when that assassin clasped his hands around me. That vow broke when the first breath of water entered my lungs."

"Lorilynn..." His pained expression peers over my face as he reaches for my hand, twisting my insides, but I move it away onto my lap. I don't want sympathy or sorrow. That wasn't the point of this. "You are stronger than you know," he finally says. "Stronger than anyone I know."

"But I don't want to be strong, Magnús. I never wanted to be strong," I say, standing from the bench. "I wanted to be safe."

•

My mother's study is a room I have never actually been in before. It is situated in her chambers, through a small door. It is surprisingly large with a grand mahogany desk, two armchairs at the sides, and a roaring fireplace.

In Mother's absence, paperwork has piled high.

After this morning, I returned to my chambers where a servant informed me of the work and helped me dress before bringing me here. It was strange walking through her chambers, the ghost of memories lingering like the sheets hanging over furniture. To be sitting finally was a relief. Wine was brought, the fire started. Warmth filled the room, the alcohol calming my soul. It helps me review the papers, review the news that more have fallen to sickness. That it wasn't just the villages here, but also towns and cities from the north of Prithan to the island west. Death takes many, any it can. Clutching them in its unyielding grasp.

Their names in lists forever imprinted on my brain, always to be remembered, the guilt of it hanging over me. It seems unfair I should survive dusk lung while they painfully perish. That I survive while my brother didn't even make it long enough to grow tall. Perhaps if he had lived it would be different, I wouldn't be alone with ruling.

I can't dwell on that though, can't focus on the past, not when I need to fix the present. Starting with the tea—the hope I can give Prithan. Perhaps we can agree on a different payment. Perhaps Chione was wrong.

I press the bell above the fireplace, a maid shuffling in after a few moments, asking if I would like anything. I simply request her to fetch the prince of the Southern Isle and his two *guests*.

I expected they would be at least an hour, but no. Ten minutes later, the three of them are here. Hui San and Koen on the two chairs, Björn at the side, leaning against the fireplace, looking over the room and out the window, gazing at something I can't see far in the distance.

"Are any of you thirsty?" I offer, tidying up the desk, shuffling loose papers into piles. They shake their heads, eyes instead on me.

"No, thanks." Koen clears his throat.

"What is it we can do for you?" Hui San says. Her voice is sweet, angelic, her brown eyes lined in white, making them bigger and brighter. Her dark hair is pulled back neatly, putting the focus on the beautiful orange of her satin dress. I've never seen a color like that before, radiant and beautiful. Glowing in the hue of candlelight.

"I'm sure you've heard the rumors—that Prithan is in a crisis," I begin. This isn't going to be easy. It was simple to blame Màthair in her absence, but I could have done more, perhaps this is me admitting that. But now the Entity has blessed me with unlimited power, nothing to stop me. I can give Prithan what it needs in time for Màthair's return. She and Papa can recover, and everything will be handled.

"The epidemic?" Hui San says in reply, eyes searching my face.

"It is often referred to as an epidemic," I begin, "but it isn't infectious. For hundreds of years, Prithan has been cloaked by clouds of pollution left from the Fourth War."

"It is where the name *dusk lands* comes from," Koen says.

"Yes, that's right," I confirm, casting a glance towards him as he peers at me with curious eyes. Björn still looks outside the window, seemingly uninterested. But I know his ears are listening. He is just waiting for the moment to speak. "And while the clouds have covered the nation for so long, as the phrase goes: what goes up, must come down. We have been blessed with pockets of light—but at a cost.

"It started just over twenty years ago," I continue. "Some would develop breathing problems, chest infections. Death follows. Their lungs fill with fluid or they tighten, not letting air in. It has taken many. Too many."

"That is what your brother died from, is it not?" Björn finally pipes up. Hearing others talk of Aeron always surprises me. No one speaks of him. Apart from occasionally Magnús and Papa. I wonder if he exists sometimes for all I can remember is holding Papa's hand as the rain fell and the small coffin was lowered into the ground, a single, blood-red rose on top. Is he just a figment of my imagination to help ease the loneliness?

"You also had it," he says, "but you survived because your parents sent you to the botanical island, to where there is no dusk."

My time on the island wasn't strictly secret, however, my illness' severity was as the sole heir of the crown, greatly suffering from the same condition that killed my brother. If it was knowledge that it was killing me, the crown would have been questioned. Unrest would have followed. However, as my friend, Koen was someone I trusted with that information. He was someone I trusted with my fears and my feelings. With the all-consuming calm that took over the time I could feel my body shutting down. It was him I trusted with what it was like to be old enough to understand that the reason I was sent to the botanical island and my brother was not—because I was the female child that was to be queen. He would have always been a prince and it wasn't worth the risk of sending him away, so he died and I lived. Sometimes I wish it were the other way around.

"Yes," I say, my voice coming out higher pitched than I had intended. "That's right." I cast a glance at Koen, who lowers his head, his eyes not reaching mine. "I survived though, became stronger. I am blessed. Lucky. Others are not, which is why it is time for us to talk."

Hui San gives a light smile, nodding, and reaches for something at her feet. She brings up paperwork. More damn paperwork. It is pushed forward on the table, letting me peruse my eyes over neat handwriting. Numbers and weights and calculations.

"These are estimates based on previous transactions and taking into account your current situation," Hui San says.

"Take a look and tell us what you think," Koen adds.

I scan the document, looking over the neat writing and numbers. The previous transactions and circumstance changes. The total suggested amount in the transaction is ninety-two metirico. "What is a metirico worth?" I question.

"One metirico is forty-two kilograms, your majesty," Koen says, which receives a slight nod from Hui San, a proud gleam spreading across his face like a young child being told they got a math question right.

"So, you're proposing an exchange of four thousand kilos?" I clarify.

"Just under, actually," Hui San corrects, sending a shock of unease through me as her voice seems to hiss. There is something about Hui San and Björn that unsettles me. The two seem to know each other well, occasionally sharing secret looks and little expressions that work as their own language. Koen doesn't fit in between them, sticking out like a white poppy in a trough of red.

"So..." I place the paper on the desk between us. "What would this amount cost Prithan?" I raise an eyebrow. What would they demand? The answer was at the tip of my tongue. I wanted to say the words, surprise them somewhat—partly because I want to see the shock on their faces when they realize I have been talking about them to others, and partly because I'm not sure I can bear to hear the word slave.

Hui San and Koen remain quiet now, Björn answering my question. "You know what we want," he says, and for the first time, stops leaning on the side, reverting his eyes to mine. "Don't you, my queen?" he says in Icelandic. With the name Björn, I presumed he was from one of the Scandinavian lands – Nordia perhaps - but I never realized it was the one I am currently queen of.

There is something intimidating about us talking in a language that only the two of us know. It is like being in a room alone with him, where no one can hear me scream. While Hui San seems bright like the sunrise, he is dark and intimidating like the dusk that haunts the sky.

"Should we not talk in a language that everyone can understand?" I ask, albeit quieter than my intention. "I don't want to seem rude."

Björn grumbles slightly, wandering to the window and looking straight out. "I would argue trying to undermine us is ruder, Queen Thornton."

"Undermine you?" I repeat, unsure of what he is talking about.

"You thought we wouldn't find out?" he says. "You thought our eyes didn't extend this far?" Björn turns back to me, gaze piercing my own as if they are rays of sun and I am ice that needs to melt.

"I wish I knew what you were talking about, but I truly have no idea." Insistence comes from me, and I honestly mean it. I have no clue what he is accusing me of. I cast a glance at Koen. His face is unreadable. He warily peers between Hui San and Björn, occasionally even glancing at me, seemingly as much in the dark about this as I am.

"Don't lie," he hisses. "We want it. Give it to us, and we will give you the tea and forget this whole thing happened."

"Look." I stand in the chair, matching Björn's height across the table. "There must be something going one that I am not part of because I haven't the faintest idea what you're talking about."

Suddenly, Björn slides his hand across the table, dragging the contract, an oil lamp crashing to the ground, glass shattering and papers burning fireplace. Thank the Entity there is no oil in it, or half the room would be up in flames. I watch the paper turn to ash, engulfed into nothing more than specks of dust.

Hui San and Koen sit in silence, still as stone, eyes darting between Björn and me. I could have him arrested for that, I could have him removed from the castle, from Prithan. But if I do that, the offer of tea goes with them.

"Björn," Hui San warns quietly.

He casts a glance to the two before wandering again to the window, gazing out at the distant fields.

"We'll give you the tea—if you hand over the electricity," he says after moments of silence.

"What in the name of the Entity is *electricity*?" I hiss, finally taking the seat at the desk again. "And why would I have it?"

The word doesn't seem new, but it is not one I recognize. I'm sure I've heard it somewhere over the past eighteen years, but it's not something I understand. So why is it so valuable to them? "Just—" Björn snaps, taking a few heavy breaths, still looking out the window. "The electricity for the tea. Of course, you can keep your electricity, but then you will have to watch thousands more of your people die, knowing that you could have done something about it."

I swallow nervously, glancing between Hui San and Koen, both of whom seem slightly shocked by the occurrence of the meeting, yet it wasn't Björn's behavior that shocked them. That's for sure. They seemed surprised that I insist I don't know what they're talking about. About whatever this electricity thing is.

I ask them to leave, and the three file out, Björn first, casting a glance of ice at me. Hui San then follows, bowing her head slightly as she sashays away. Last through the door is Koen. He walks after them, hand resting on the pendant around his neck. He glances at me as he leaves, sorrow and apology on his face with silent departure.

Now alone, I scramble my hands through the gray dust on the floor, trying to recover what I can. There are only snippets of paper, charred at the edges. The important parts are long gone, forever lost in the amber glow.

I curse under my breath, sighing audibly, a cloud of dust billowing. I pick up pieces of broken glass, placing them on the side of the fire in a neat pile, along with the other parts of the oil lamp.

I press the bell for the maid, trying to pick up the smaller pieces before she arrives but not a minute later there is a knock at my door, and it opens slightly.

"That was quick!" I comment, reaching through the ash as I find a ruffled piece of paper that has survived the flames. Mostly.

"What in the Entity's name are you doing?" the voice says.

I turn from where I'm sitting on the ground to see Tariq looking down at me with raised eyebrows. "I thought you were the maid," I clarify, turning back to the fireplace.

"Is this a bad time? I just wanted to talk about tonight."

"Tonight?" I turn back to him.

"Yes, uh, everything is in order. We'll be divorced by sunrise."

CHAPTER FIFTEEN

"That fast?" I say, standing and brushing the powder from my skirts.

He nods once, looking at the broken oil lamp. I just pray he didn't see the Collective members leave or put two and two together.

"Yes. I think the priest was happily surprised for me to ask," he explains.

I go back to my seat, sitting and peering over him. He moves from one foot to the other, perhaps even a little excited by the prospect of marital freedom. I am too.

"He will be waiting for us in the chapel at the high moon. The proceedings will take only a few moments. You have nothing to worry about."

"I'm not worried," I say, playing with a patch of ash on my skirt.

"You seem agitated, princess." My chest flips a little when he refers to me as 'princess'. Perhaps because it helps me cling to knowing my parents are alive, or perhaps because he is the only one who calls me that now. "I just presumed it was to do with the divorce. Or the kiss."

My cheeks heat, eyes looking anywhere that isn't him. "What kiss?" I say after a few moments of silence.

"Lorilynn," he says, his voice like honey, "you know what kiss."

I remember how it felt, how my heart hammered in my chest. "Fine." I give in. "I know the kiss. If you can call it that."

He smiles broadly. "Am I really that bad of a kisser?"

I blush more, a small laugh that sounds more like a giggle escaping me. "It was fine," I say, "Just fine. As fine as a kiss that is forced can be."

He suddenly stops smiling and raises an eyebrow.

"Forced?"

"You thought our marriage was to be announced. Of course, you kissed me."

"Lorilynn..." He shakes his head. "You think the reason I kissed you back is because of the marriage? Is that why you agreed to the divorce?"

"Is it wrong for me to not wish to spend my life being kissed by someone who doesn't want to kiss me?" I finally say, making eye contact with him.

He peers over my face before turning towards the door, pausing as his hand reaches the knob. "See you at high moon," he says before leaving me with paperwork and a racing heartbeat.

•

The castle is quiet tonight. After a few more hours in the office, I go to my chambers, changing into a clean dress before veiling my hair and walking to the chapel. I'm not exactly sure what to expect.

I open the doors, immediately greeted by the amber flames of candles and silver moonlight streaming through the windows. The priest and Tariq are already at the front, talking in hushed tones. When I step inside, both cast glances toward me, watching as I walk down the aisle to the front where they are.

"Your majesty," the priest greets, bowing his head.

"Good evening, your excellence," I say in return, bowing in return and taking his hand in mine, squeezing once. "Alright, let's do this," I say softly, keeping my voice low in fear that someone is just outside the door.

"Face each other and hold hands, palm on palm," the priest says quietly.

We shuffle slightly, turning to each other as we did two years ago, and take each other's hands. His is calloused, warm. It feels nice to hold.

The priest takes a deep blue ribbon, tying it around our wrists in a casual bow loosely, connecting us. And then it begins.

After a few words and moments, he cuts it, the silk fabric swaying to the floor, landing on the ground in a small pile. I feel an urge to kick it, incinerate it, throw it into the ocean. That ribbon is a symbol of undoing what was done to us. And I feel proud of that, but for some reason, also a little upset. A part of me feels sad that this ever happened. Any of this. The trauma took months to recover from, and I would have done anything to get to this point. It isn't fair it happened in the first place.

"Is that it?" Tariq asks the priest. "It is done?"

The priest gives a single nod. "It is done." He smiles a little, taking a step back to give us privacy, going to deal with something in the far corner of the room.

Tariq turns back to me, now with both hands in his pockets, a small grin on his face. He peers me over, kicking the dirt with his shoe.

"I should get going..." I whisper. "I have to try and figure something out in the library. See you tomorrow, Prince Khan."

"See you tomorrow, princess."

I don't focus too much as I turn away and walk down the center, back from where I came and out the doors, finding myself leaning against the doors on the other side, taking a moment. I take the lace veil off, then quickly get away before anyone can find me or think to ask what is wrong.

•

Considering the hour, the library is empty when I arrive. The librarian has gone home and only a chill sits in the air. After putting the fire on and wrapping a blanket around myself, I start prowling through the books on the shelves, trying to find at least one mention of electricity. So far, history books from the last two hundred years and journals of recent travelers from Prithan are empty.

I give a frustrated sigh, wishing Papa was here to offer a helping hand. Perhaps he knows what the fuck they were talking about.

The silence is broken by a light knock at the door. My head shoots up, the later hour having me wonder who it could be.

"Come in?" I call lightly, not moving from the rug. I'm perched at on the floor, a sea of open pages around me.

"Am I disturbing you?" Tariq asks as he wanders in, looking over the books on the floor, then me in a blanket cocoon. He steps carefully, holding a glass bottle with a honey-colored liquid inside and two glasses in the other hand. "What are you doing?" he raises a brow.

"Research," I say, folding the architecture book on my lap. "Don't suppose you know what electricity is?"

Tariq shakes his head and steps forward. I motion to the chair at the side, but to my surprise, he takes a seat on the carpet near me, popping the cork on the bottle. A strong smell of alcohol fills the room. He pours the liquid in the two glasses, only a small amount, and passes one to me.

Hesitantly I pick the glass, sipping a small hint. It burns as it goes down my throat, soon being replaced with a warm feeling, like honey and wine. I feel my nose relax—I hadn't even realized I'd been scrunching it up.

"What is this?" I ask. "It burns," I joke. The taste is pleasant, the alcohol heating my stomach.

"It's just whiskey," he says, taking a sip himself.

"So, what can I do for you? Or are you just here to poison me?" I tease him.

"Well, I was hoping to talk to you about something," he says.

"About the divorce?" I raise a brow. "You know there is no going back."

He chuckles, taking a sip himself. "It was about something you said today in your study—about the kiss."

That stupid kiss.

"Why are you so obsessed with that?" I roll my eyes, hoping it hides the blush ever blooming at my cheeks, taking another sip of the fire liquid, using the glass to conceal my face.

He swirls his own a little, meeting my eyes. My heart hammers in my chest, my blood pulsing. I take another sip, my whole body warming as it slides down my throat.

"You said that you thought I kissed you back because of the marriage..." He places the glass down.

"Please..." I breathe, embarrassment building up further inside me. "Just let it go." It comes out as a beg. I want to stop thinking about it, want to stop the feelings that are inside of and pretend it never happened.

"Lorilynn..." he says softly, his voice like red wine. "Come here."

His eyes are deep and swirling in the light, beckoning me to him like a star in the sky.

I glance up at him, wondering what he is planning. I pause a moment before hesitantly moving across to him, ending up opposite, books surrounding us. I straighten my skirt slightly, perching. Our faces are only inches away, his knees touching mine.

"I kissed you," he says almost silently, his voice smooth and rich, "because I wanted to." He peers over my face, the candlelight dancing across his tanned skin, warmth radiating from him.

"What?" I breathe, my heart racing as blood heats in my veins. Every inch of my body waking up at his words.

"You heard me," he says back in a hushed tone, a smirk teasing his lips.

I stay there, unable to move. He places his palm across my cheek. His warm, calloused fingers against soft skin. They brush my cheekbone, softly moving to my hair, stroking my skin. A shiver runs down my spine. I shut my eyes, welcoming his touch.

"I want to do it again," he finally says.

I flick my eyes open to see him looking directly at me. Intense brown mixed with hints of amber I hadn't noticed before.

The only sounds are the crackling fire and our breathing.

"Then do it..." I finally say and I almost don't believe I said it, but then his lips crash against mine, his hands in my hair. A soft moan—an actual *moan*—escapes me, seemingly setting off a fire inside him.

He wraps both his arms around me, pulling me onto his lap, both of my legs on either side as I straddle him, our lips moving together. His hands travel up and down my back, tugging me so close our chests are pressed together.

I run my tongue against his lower lip, causing him to shudder, pulling me in tighter. Not a single inch is between us. He leans back a moment, pressing kisses to my neck, lips light and delicate, tongue grazing my skin, planting soft kisses on my throat, traveling to my lips before meeting them again. The kiss consumes me, the feeling of his body under me, the heat that travels through me. It's a fire I want to burn in, a flame I want to caress my bare skin.

I reach down his back, keeping my mouth on his, tugging at the base of his shirt. At the first touch of the skin of his back, my body fills with more warmth, as much as the drink. I keep tugging, pulling it up, more and more skin appearing. He parts from my lips a moment, enough for me to remove his shirt over his head and fling it somewhere in the room.

My eyes gaze down his body, down hard muscle and toned shapes I didn't know he had the time to perfect. I want to touch every part of him—kiss every part of him. I place a peck on his collarbone, tugging lightly at his skin between my teeth. He leans his head back, letting me reach his neck as

I plant more kisses and nips.

His hands travel down my back, fiddling with the ribbons before finally undoing it, pulling it down, helping me hurriedly unhook the sleeves, leaving the mass of fabric at my waist. His eyes gaze over me, the skin on show, the binding of my breasts around my chest.

"You're perfect," he whispers, taking a moment and resting his forehead on mine.

"Piss off," I whisper back with a smirk.

He gives a low chuckle, gently tracing my bottom lip with his thumb. I'm lost in his eyes, heat coming from every inch of me, heart pumping. I feel him beneath me, feel the firmness. I want more. He does too. I want to reclaim what was taken from us. I want to enjoy my body, his body. Our bodies.

"Don't stop." It comes out as a whimper. "Keep going."

"Lorilynn, princess..." My name on his lips is like the birds' first song at sunrise. "Are you saying...?"

I nod, letting my fingers run across his shoulders and down his arms, taking his hands and pulling him to the ground on top of me. We lie facing each other there. He balances on his elbows, hovering above me a moment before grabbing my dress that is still around my waist and dragging it over my legs, letting it fly across the room, discarded in a corner. I use the moment to undo the bandages around my chest, unwrapping them from around me and discarding them too, bearing all to him.

My hair hangs loose, the fire beside us crackling. His eyes wander over me, all of me. His lips crash down on mine again, hand grazing the edge of my breast, teasing like fireworks across my skin.

Without leaving his lips, I struggle with his belt buckle, finally removing it and throwing it aside, rapidly lowering his trousers and watching him as he takes them off fully, leaving the two of us bare. Completely. My eyes trail over him—all of him.

Tariq returns to how he was, leaning on his forearms, kissing me again, planting them over each cheek briefly before moving to my lips deeply, sliding his tongue against mine. He positions himself and then starts pushing inside me slowly. I wince a little, but then the pain completely disappears, replaced with ecstasy.

He's careful, slow at first. I think he is worried he'll hurt me. His kisses become more intense, and I can see the focus in his furrowed brows as he moves. My hips grind against him, my hands running up his back, nails digging into his skin.

It feels good, really good. But I want more. The pressure in my soul builds, not enough though. I move with him, faster, urging him deeper. He lets out a small chuckle against my lips. I can feel the smile too. That damned smile.

"More," I gasp as he takes a break from my lips, looking my face over with the most beautiful grin.

"Patience," he says and kisses the tip of my nose as he slows even more.

"Fuck patience." I smirk and hook my legs around him, urging him in further. And he listens, thrusting into me at quicker pace. Over and over. Something inside him lets loose, a growl escaping him. That fire inside me burns bright, and I roll us so I straddle him, controlling the movements. He looks up at me, eyes tracing every curve and peak of my body. I rock forwards and backwards, the bliss building up inside me. I shut my eyes, my head going back as the fire burns brighter, almost exploding.

I lose focus, and he rolls back, the flames inside me taking over everything. And then it happens, like a star exploding. My breath escapes me, a shiver writhing to my fingertips. He slows too, his own release burning deep within him.

And we lie there, glowing in the remnants of our shared supernova. Only our breathing fills the room. He wraps his arm around me, sweat beading on our backs. I roll into him, resting my head in the crook of his neck, breathing his scent. He plants a simple kiss on my forehead before looking up at the high ceiling, a small smile playing on his lips. A dimple appearing by his eye.

I trace my fingers along his chest, along the curves and tones of his skin, gently kissing his pectoral muscle.

"Are you alright?" he asks after a while. "Did I hurt you?"

I shake my head. "You didn't hurt me," I assure him, "I'm alright."

We lie there for some time in each other's arms, talking, drinking. Eventually, I fetch the blanket from the chair and lay it over us as we rest. Soon enough, our bodies find each other again. This time slower. We move together until the sun rises, whispering sweet nothings and when we aren't connected, we hold each other.

Finally, the fire dies down to nothing more than embers, and I watch as Tariq's eyelashes flutter closed and he drifts into a deep sleep, his arm still around my bare waist.

I lie there a while, watching him dream peacefully, as if the world around us doesn't exist. He doesn't stir, doesn't mumble, doesn't snore—just holds me.

I find myself thinking about what we have just done, and how different it had been to the first time. I'd felt as if something was taken away from me then. But now I have it back. I'd chosen and reclaimed it. I hope he reclaimed it too. It was so different. There was no fear, no tears. I wasn't afraid to touch him, to take control. It was just the two of us enjoying ourselves and each other. It was kisses and forbidden words and privacy. Most importantly, it was choice. We did it because we wanted to.

Soon these thoughts fade, and my own eyes shut, the safety of his arms around me giving me comfort and warmth. And I welcome sleep as if it is an old friend.

CHAPTER SIXTEEN

Waking up, our bodies still together and his arms around me, is like being at home. Sleep lasted for a few hours. When I flutter my eyes open, the sun is fully in the sky, the painting of sunrise replaced with blue.

I roll onto my back, bones aching slightly from sleeping on the floor. I sit up, realizing that something else is aching too. It is a good ache.

Tariq is still asleep, thick lashes on his cheeks, arm is still over me. My lips feel swollen, the lingering memory of his kisses like butterflies on my skin.

The memories of the night before wash over me. How we had moved together, the kisses we shared. A blush blooms across my cheeks.

For the first time, I can see the room properly. Discarded glasses and the half-empty bottle sit in the middle of the floor. Tariq's shirt is beside me. My dress and chest binding are on the other side.

I must get up. Anyone could come in and see us wrapped in each other's arms, naked.

I gently lift Tariq's arm, placing it on his abdomen as I don't want to wake him, and quietly go to my dress, beginning to put it on enough that I can go to my chambers and get ready for the day. My maids have probably already gone in and seen the bed bare—I just hope they don't put two and two together. Not that anyone knows or will know this happened.

Once I've tied the ribbons, I go to the chest binding at the other side of the room, reaching down to pick it up when a book catches my eye, a book that ticks a clock inside me. The green leather is embossed with gold lettering, the words shining like the golden piece of the puzzle. *An Introduction to the Physical Sciences*, written by Doctor Mary Wellton PhD. It is one I haven't read and only briefly looked through. But there was something about it that I remember. There was this fascinating chapter about energy and power. I hadn't realized there were so many options. One stuck out to me, this web of light and heat that moved fast and couldn't be controlled.

I reach for the book, perching on the ground against the bookshelf, and open the pages, dust blowing in the air as I scour through it. And there it is, plain as day.

Electricity.

My breath turns somewhat ragged as I plough over the pages. But where could they make such a thing? Where could this come from? Where could this so-called power source be? Nowhere in the castle or on Prithan that I know of. Wait.

I stop, letting my eyes remain on the page. I relive every memory I have of my parents and those last few hours with them. It might be a piece of the puzzle. The puzzle I've been trying to solve for two years.

Iceland.

They went to Iceland to produce electricity.

"Entity have mercy..." I say to myself, eyes still pouring over the pages.

"What're you doing?" Tariq tiredly mumbles. I peer over to where he sits upon the ground, the sheet we had used falling to his hips, revealing the toned skin that glows in the light. My eyes linger on his abdomen perhaps a second too long before I return them to the pages.

"Just reading," I reply and sneak another look at him. He runs a hand through his hair and reaches for his trousers, slipping them on loosely. I won't admit it, but my eye watches him a moment as the sheet falls, a blush warming my cheeks as I divert back to the page.

"Reading?" he questions as he wanders over and sits on the ground next to me, so close I feel the warmth radiate off him. "What are you reading?"

I peer up at his face finally, properly. At his dark eyes that I had stared at for quite some time as he moved over me last night. And there's that blush again. I'm not entirely sure how to talk to him. Do we address the previous evening? Do we talk about how we had kissed and laid together? Do we do it again? Or do we pretend it never happened? Aside from our wedding night and my teenage kiss with Koen, nothing like that has ever occurred to me before. My heart pounds just thinking about it.

But this isn't his first experience at romance. He's been in love. Perhaps that is why he's so comfortable with me now, not worrying about how all he wears are trousers. I have a spike of jealousy at the thought of him being intimate with someone else. It is ridiculous. I shouldn't be thinking like this—it can't happen again.

"A physics book," I say, showing him the cover. "Yesterday before you came into the study, I was meeting with the Collective. They mentioned this thing—this power source—called electricity." I pass him over the open page, our fingers touching a moment as he takes it.

"Well, biology is more my thing." He turns to me a moment and grins. "But this looks powerful, really powerful."

"It could revolutionize the world, even out the scales," I say. "It isn't new technology. It disappeared a few thousand years ago."

"Why?" he asked curiously.

"I'm not sure. I suppose the means of producing it couldn't adapt and was lost."

"Until now."

"Yes. Until now."

There's another moment of silence between us as we both sit there. I'm suddenly aware of how close we are, of our bare arms touching and the golden skin of his chest. I want to make him get dressed, but I also want to kiss him.

That cannot happen. We're divorced. It would be scandalous if someone walked in now.

Apparently, he's thinking about it too, because he clears his throat before speaking. "So... should we talk about what happened?"

I take a breath, keeping my eyes locked on the window out the library. We *should* talk about what happened. We need to talk about how this changes nothing, how it was just our emotions. "It was just... hormones and alcohol getting the best of us," I explain, fiddling with the hem of my dress. "And the excitement of the divorce."

"Yes, I agree," he says, "but it was more than just sex. It was taking our bodies back."

"Choosing to be intimate because we wanted to, not because of a religious ritual," I finish.

"Exactly," he says, perhaps somewhat too enthusiastically. Then comes more silence between us. "It was just a one-time thing."

"Yes, one time. We're friends. Nothing more, nothing less."

"Friends who just happen to have seen each other naked." He

smirks. "My favorite type of friends."

I mock punch his arm, casting him a warning glare but end up laughing. He joins in, and we sit there in a fit of mirth.

"Is that you trying to flirt?" I say, raising a brow when I can finally control the laughter.

"Depends. Is it working?" he replies comically.

Definitely flirting.

I roll my eyes and shut the book, reaching around and putting it back on the shelf. I stand, tying the back of my dress better and throwing Tariq his shirt. He slips it on, concealing his bare skin. A small part of me regrets not looking one last time.

I grab my shoes and put them on, tying my hair up with a strap of leather, stopping when I catch my reflection in the mirror above the fireplace. A purple bruise sits on my collar bone, a bruise very obviously caused by someone intimately. Hair has to go down then. I cast Tariq a small glance. He smirks slightly at the bloom before fixing his shirt and shoes. I can't judge too much, admittedly we both marked each other during the previous night's events. I rather enjoyed doing it, if I'm honest. But we're friends now. Just friends.

"I should go," I say softly. "I have to figure this mess out."

"Well, let me know if there is anything I can do," he replies, holding his hand out to me to shake. "Friends?"

I take it in mine, shaking. "Friends." I look up at his face, deep into his eyes, and the string in my gut tightens again. We slam into each other, lips on lips. He pushes himself into me so I'm against his hard body and the bookshelves. Our mouths work in tandem.

Shit.

Alright, we're friends. Special friends.

His hands are on my hips again, lips pressed into my neck. "I want to kiss every inch of you," he mumbles against my skin. "I want to feel you again."

My cheeks blush at the memory from last night. "We can't, Tariq," I breathe as he caresses my collarbone. "This has already gone too far."

"Hmm," he mumbles against my skin. "I want you to be my undoing, princess."

"I'm serious, Tariq," I say again and manage to push him away even though I want nothing more than to pull him closer. "I have to go. This can't happen ever again."

He reluctantly pulls away, his hand lingering on my cheek a moment before leaving a foot of space between us. "I know you're right..." he says sadly, looking at the floor. It takes every bit of energy within me to walk to the door and leave, heading towards my chambers.

Luckily, the maids have already been and gone. I grab a clean shirt and trousers, putting them on, tying up my leather boots and heading to the study. Now, away from Tariq and his very convincing words, my mind is clear.

Electricity. Prithan must have electricity.

And I bet it is what my parents were overseeing in Iceland.

I send a message to Mags and Adora, requesting them in the study as soon as possible. The two arrive before I do, sitting and looking out the window as I stride in, the fire alight, warmth holding me, hopefully concealing the pink of my cheeks. I can't stop thinking about what happened last night and this morning. I need to stop and focus on my duties.

Both my uncles cast me glances as I enter, giving polite smiles. Their eyes gaze up and down me as I take a seat. Adora is himself, giving a slight smile. Mags and I don't quite make eye contact yet. It still feels strange. It's as if when I look at him the water fills my lungs again and I'm back on that beach.

"Sometimes I wonder if you two follow me around." I chuckle. "You're always everywhere we meet before I am."

Adora gives a light snicker in return. Magnús stays silent, his eyes darting over me with care.

"It is our jobs to be at your beckoned call, Lorilynn," Adora says, "and to know where you are, with whom, and for what reason."

Red blooms on my cheeks again—they couldn't know. For all they are aware of, I was reading in the library. I'm not going to push my luck and test the waters. If I'm being honest, I was in the library reading... for some of the time.

"That does sound somewhat threatening, Adora." I smile, but then remember why I called them. "I have some questions regarding my parent's departure."

Magnús and Adora, for the first time since I came here, now share a look before their eyes find me again and they both nod, awaiting whatever I'm about to say.

"Fire away," Adora says and leans back in his chair casually, crossing on leg over the other.

"They left to go produce electricity, didn't they?" I ask. Straight to the point. I expect Adora and Mags to react or raise brows, but—nothing. No recognition at all.

Interesting.

"Alright, let me rephrase." I sigh. "In your own words, why did my parents go to Icelandic Prithan?" I again look between the two of them to see no reaction. No raised brows or uncertain shuffling. However, there is something— confusion.

"Well?" I push.

Adora peers over at Mags, who is staring at something on the table, thought tracing across the front of his expression. For years I have seen the duo laughing together, sharing words and advice and quiet whispers. Yet this is haunting them. They genuinely know as much as I do—nothing.

"Did Papa seriously not tell you anything?" I mutter. "You were his advisors—his brothers. He told you everything."

"Your father was... different when we last saw him,"

Magnús explains. "He..." Magnús waves his hand around a moment, seemingly searching for the words in the common tongue. "He was lost on the moon. Metaphorically," he finally says in Icelandic.

I cast a glance to Mags. Lost on the moon? It's a poetic phrase for sure, and I understand.

"It started a few days before the Turkish Arabian royal family arrived," Adora adds. "He began missing breakfast, then he would be seen wandering around the corridors at night. Always wishing to be alone."

"That sounds like he had depression. Not that he was farming a power source in secrecy," I point out, raising a brow.

"Or perhaps guilt?" Magnús suggests. "He had to put someone he loved through something terrible and it was eating him up inside."

For the first time, Mags and I make eye contact. We both know what he's referencing... the marriage. The marriage that no longer exists. Perhaps father was consumed by guilt. I knew I would be if I put my child through that.

Adora is silent but peers between the two of us. Now would be the time to tell him. But there is no need. It's over, there is no point in putting him through the trauma too.

"I have heard of no terrible thing, Magnús," I say calmly, keeping my eyes locked on his. "And if a terrible thing *did* happen, it would have been dealt with by now."

There is a pinch of silence as we stare at each other intently, minds whirling. I made careful choosing with my words, hoping the secret meaning carries through. After a moment, he nods once and drops his eyes back on his lap, breaking the tension. Message received; problem solved.

"He began acting strange around the arrival of Queen and King Khan? And their son?" I clarify.

The two peer between each other and give a curt nod. Then the idea sparks inside me. How ironic that it sparks only when we are divorced. What if Tariq and the marriage are tied to this somehow?

My heart starts hammering deep in my chest again, memories pouring through like a waterfall. A part of my stomach tightens at thinking of him, his name. No, I cannot be distracted. I can't let this change anything.

"This electricity." Adora tests the word on his tongue. "Do you think it has something to do with the visit those years ago? And your parent's departure?"

"Perhaps. But there are too many pieces to a puzzle that isn't quite fitting together yet," I say.

"Wait," Magnús says, his eyes darting across the space, "maybe not."

Adora clears this throat as Mags keeps on thinking. I take the opportunity to lean back in the chair, to take some breaths and allow the words to weigh on my shoulders. Of course, the marriage happened and then they left. But what does this have to do with Turkish Arabia? How does it connect to electricity?

"Are you going to share with the room?" Adora says looking at Magnús. "Or will you keep us on our toes?" Magnús glares a moment at Adora, giving a brief friendly chuckle.

"A few weeks before Catriona and Einar left," he begins, shock running through me. I haven't heard anyone call my parents by their names in years. It's always your majesty or king or queen. Adora notices too, raising eyebrows at how *human* their names sound. "Einar was in his chambers, and I went in. He was looking over these blueprints with machines on them. He rolled them up quickly, but I caught a peek. Perhaps they may have some answers? However, I'm pretty sure he took them with him to Iceland."

"So, we only have some random blueprints that are most likely across the dusk sea to go on?" Adora raises a brow.

"This is Papa we're talking about," I contemplate aloud. "Knowing him, he would keep copies somewhere. Copies that are probably still in Prithan Castle."

"That isn't exactly much, your majesty," Mags pipes up. I shoot him a momentary glare, however, truth be known, he is right. It isn't much to go on. But it is all we have to offer. It means doing something I don't particularly want to do.

"If he made copies—*if*—they would be in his chambers. Correct?"

The two give small nods in agreement.

I search my mind, the memories of Papa's room in my head. I'm not sure where in his chambers he would keep them. Perhaps in the chest or under the bed. I suppose there is one way to find out. I have to go search them myself. A small part of my chest curls at that. It'll be like kicking up sand at the bottom of the ocean, facing that he isn't here right now. No one has been in those rooms for years. With his absence, sheets were laid over the furniture and the rest left to be.

"Would you like us to come with you?" Mags offers, placing a sympathetic hand over the desk between us.

"It's not a big deal," I reply, "I'll be fine."

"Are you certain? We don't mind," Adora offers.

"I'm certain. I stand by what I've said. He will be back soon. But I need to find these plans if I can, or at least *something*."

"Well, at least let us walk you to the door," Mags insists.

I hesitate a moment. "Fine."

CHAPTER SEVENTEEN

The three of us stand looking at the large double doors perhaps for too long. No one has stepped foot in this room for two years. We have been silently looking at it for... I'm not even sure. The doors match the rest in the corridor, were it not for the two leaves carved into the front. A small touch father had added when he first came to Prithan.

I reach for the brass handle, the metal cool under my touch. I push down, wood creaking low as it seeps open. I nudge both doors, revealing the chambers to us. The curtains are shut, white sheets draped over the furniture, ghosts like the memories that linger.

A musty smell pours out, clouds of dust running for freedom. Adora places his hand on my shoulder. "You sure you can do this alone?" he murmurs low.

I peer up at him and give a single nod. "It's fine. He'll be back soon," I speak. He and Mags share a quick look of raised brows between them before I knock his hand off my shoulder. "I won't be long anyway." I step into the room before they can argue and shut the doors, not daring to see the looks on their faces. And then it is just me and the shadows of memories. The first step in immediately takes me back to running in as a small child, a maid struggling to catch up after me as she holds the machine. To when I was fifteen and Papa got sick—just a minor illness—and I brought him soup in bed and placed cool cloths on his forehead, to the two of us sat by the window sneaking glasses of whiskey after Mother had gone to bed.

It's too dark to see anything, so I stride over to the curtain and swipe them open. I take a moment to peer over the room. The blue walls, the wood floor. I go to where a portrait is covered by a white sheet and pull the fabric off, revealing an old painting. Of me and my brother before he died. Us neatly next to each other, dressed in fine clothes and false smiles. My dark hair harsh against his blond curls. He was always far more of a looker than I was. If he had survived, I'm sure he would have caught the eye of many. I'm also sure he would have been a shit too, but we'll never know.

I end up removing all the sheets, collecting them in a pile in the center of the floor. The furniture seems bright now, and the room almost normal. His bedsheets need a wash, and a candle wouldn't go amiss, but it's as if he never left. Little trinkets of his still lie on the side, clothes still folded neatly in drawers. I carefully remove one of his shirts, feeling the cotton under my fingers. I hold the fabric close, breathing it in, hoping to catch the scent of safety and home I always got but... nothing. It's faded. My heart sinks. Only dust and wood clings to the cotton. What if it never smells like him again? I stop myself. I cannot let myself think like that. I quickly take a deep breath, folding the shirt and putting it back neatly.

At the end of his bed is a trunk. A wooden cube with a latch at the front. I slowly step over to it, lifting the metal and heaving the top open so it falls back, revealing mounds and mounds of paper. I let out an exasperated sigh. This is going to take forever. And whatever it is I'm searching for may not actually be here.

I grab a cushion from his chair and plop it on the floor by the chest, slowly taking out the first chunk of papers. A leather binding wraps around the yellowed pages, keeping them all together in a roll. I untie and flatten it out, revealing lots of pencil drawings rolled together. They spring out in a pile, raining down like snowflakes. I pick the nearest one up, a small portrait of a woman smiling. Simple, done in pencil. I don't know who she is, yet there's a story. There's a story in every drawing, and there are hundreds. Piles and piles. Some portraits, some designs, some botanical studies. Everything. I've never seen Papa draw, yet they must be his. I always thought of him as a king and nothing more, but this is a side of him I never saw.

After perhaps two hundred various drawings and explorations, I find something. Unlike the rest of the scribbles, this is printed in dark black ink and shines like satin on the parchment.

Thick lines form this structure of wheels and cogs and metal. A weird device seemingly driven by someone across fields. As it moves, it churns up dirt, placing things on the ground and then spurting water from the back. The machine is curious. A design of perhaps Papa's? Certainly plausible. The only aspect about it I can't quite understand is how it would be powered... oh.

The penny drops—like a boulder.

Machinery. Electricity.

Fields.

That isn't too much to go on. Apart from the timing.

All this happened around the marriage. Yet it still doesn't quite make sense. I dig my hand further into the pile of papers, pulling out the first thing that clutches in my fist. I bring my hand out where a tiny notebook bound by a thick card cover pressed with small flowers and rose petals. I glide my hand across the front before prying it open, taking a look at the first page.

Another pencil sketch of a young girl, maybe three or four, with long hair tied up and a sweet dress to her ankles. She jumps about, a grin on her face. She's there on the next page too, this time crawling happily along the ground. The whole notebook is filled with sketches or her. Some laughing, some she doesn't look at the artist. Then there's the second to last page, and the realization hits me. *I* am the child.

My heart aches as the little drawing shows me sitting on the ground, mask on, playing with a toy of some description. Some blocks that I forgot existed, that had different letters painted on them. They were probably in an attic somewhere now. I hadn't seen them since I left to go to the botanical island.

I turn the page once more to the final one and tears start flowing from my eyes uncontrollably.

It's a sketch, the same as the others, but this time it has a title written in Papa's flowing writing. *Peace.*

We sit on the ground, legs crossed and me on his lap. Still small, still slightly chubby but smiling. Both of us are. He reads to me, apparent laughter escaping us both. I'm not sure if this is a memory or just a dream of his, but it is beautiful.

I try using my sleeve to wipe some of the waterfalls flowing from my cheeks, but it is useless. They keep flowing like heavy rain.

What if... what if he is gone?

No.

There's a gentle knock on the door a few moments before it opens, and Magnús's blond locks peek through the gap.

"Entity, what're you doing? It's been hours," he teases before noticing I'm crying and his face drops. He comes in fully, quietly shutting the large door behind him and stepping over, crouching in front of me. "Hey, don't cry," he says. "What is it?"

I could show Mags, but it sort of feels like a secret between Papa and me. I discreetly slip the notebook into the back pocket of my trousers and try wiping the tears from my eyes.

"I miss him immensely," I reply.

Mags peers over my face with deep sadness and places a hand on my shoulder, sitting on the wooden floor to my left. "Sometimes when someone is gone, it feels like the world can never make sense again. Soon, the chaos begins to map itself out, and you'll begin to understand how to live with the hole in your heart."

I frown at his words. Wise as they may be, I still feel the water fill my lungs when he touches me, the feeling of life slowly fading from my body with every ounce of absent oxygen, of every drop of lost blood. I shrug his hand off.

"I think I found something." I quickly change the subject and push forward the ink prints. "I think it's some sort of machinery," I offer.

His eyes fall over them, wandering over analytically. He takes the plans and turns them, looking from different angles, as if that'll help. "And what exactly are these?" he questions with a raised brow.

"I believe they're farming vehicles. They seem to be adapted for fieldwork and run on electricity," I explain, pointing at various parts, "But then I got thinking. This all happened around the time Tariq—" I cough. "Around the time the prince and I married."

Mags slowly turns to me again. "Tariq?" he says. "You're on nicknames now?"

Heat flowers on my cheeks. I ignore his question, peering over the plans. "I'm wondering if it is all connected."

Magnús looks me over. "Earlier, you mentioned that if a terrible thing had happened it would have been dealt with. What did you mean by that?"

"The prince and I are no longer husband and wife," I say simply. "The situation was dealt with. As I said."

His eyes dart over my face. "How?"

"He was as unhappy with the union as I was," I reply carefully. "It was finalized last night. We no longer have to worry about the matter."

"I've never heard of such a thing." He frowns.

The situation is too complex to explain to him, partly because I don't want to risk having to mention the intimacy between us this past evening.

Before heat can befall my cheeks, I turn back to the plans. "It has to be connected, but how?"

"Well..." Magnús pauses a moment. "What does a marriage with

Turkish Arabia give you?"

"I'm not sure." I sigh uncertainly. "Turkish Arabia?"

"And what does Turkish Arabia have that Prithan doesn't?"

A spark alights in my brain. "Turkish Arabia is clear of dusk."

"Which means...?" he pushes.

"Turkish Arabia is better for farming."

Fuck.

"Tea," I breathe. "My parents were trying to grow tea. They were trying to produce tea faster than the Collective."

A grave shadow casts his face. "Entity..." he murmurs. "What if they catch wind of this?"

"What if they already did?" I point out. "What if they sent pirates to destroy the ship?"

"This isn't enough proof to accuse them," he says, "and if you do accuse them and you're wrong, it will mean war. A war that Prithan might not win."

"I know..." I take another look at the pages. All of it was for wealth. To bring more power. To topple the Collective and even out the weighing scales that have plagued the world for too long. And the cost was forcing their children to marry, secretly so no one would catch wind and try assassinate them before the lands were joined.

I stand, rolling the paper plans and taking grasp of them carefully in my fist. Mags stands too, watching intently. For a moment, we look at each other before he holds his arms out.

"Would you like me to hold you a moment?" he asks. It's inviting, an embrace would be a warm comfort. It is also tempting. I even take a small step forward but then the water pours in and I feel the oxygen leave me, the blood pool down my dress. I wonder how long it'll take for everything to be the same as it once was. Or if it ever will.

I swallow. "I should go find the prince... share what I have learned."

Magnús drops his arms and looks sadly at the ground. "Yes, of course."

I stroll past him and rest my hand on the door handle. More tears fall. Tears that I can only explain as nostalgia eating my insides like a disease of light burning through me. Desperate for the past to be present, for more time. For Papa to be back, for Mother to keep frowning, but be here. To be able to hold Mags without remembering what happened, without blaming him for it.

I turn back to him. "I am trying, Uncle Mags," I say delicately before leaving, shutting the doors behind me and turning my back on the snippet of the past that remained. My feet quicken their pace as more tears fall, sobs shaking through to my core. I want to disappear, to hide. I sneak into an alcove at the side, swiping the curtain so that I am hidden, and lean against the wall, gathering myself as much as I can. I can't do this, not now. There will be a time to mourn the girl I once was, but it is not now. One day, soon, I will be able to cry and scream and run away. Now I must do what is best for Prithan—for my people.

It takes a few moments to collect myself, to wipe my eyes and peer out. Tariq is wandering up slowly, an open book in his palm, eyes scanning the pages as he bites his bottom lip with intent fascination. Something deep within me clenches.

I remain at the side, waiting until he's close. Then I grab him by the arm, dragging him into the alcove, pressing myself against him immediately, our lips already joining.

He is a fire I long to burn in, a river I beg to drown in, a desert I search to get lost in.

Eventually, reluctantly, we part. His dark eyes glance over my face, thumb brushing away a train of tears from my cheek.

"You've been crying, princess," he whispers, tenderly cupping my face, brows furrowing with concern.

I place my free hand over his, letting my eyes shut a moment at the warmth, the feeling of being held. One of his arms rests around my waist, holding me close to him.

"It's nothing." I try to conjure a smile. "I need to talk to you in private."

He hesitates a moment before peering around the small alcove comically. "Is this not private enough?" he asks with a small smirk, brushing a lock of hair from my face. He pauses a moment before letting the smirk disappear, the face of a prince overtaking. "This is serious, isn't it?"

I give a small nod, and he takes a step out into the corridor, as do I and make sure to fix my shirt, straightening it out and running a hand through my hair. And then we stride along, my mind dashing chaotically.

The fire has been settling for a while now. A few embers still burn, some warmth radiating as we lie down. Tariq traces a finger in soft circles along my bare hip, my ear pressed against his hammering heartbeat.

"Is that what it's meant to be like?" I ask him tenderly.

He peers at me, the corner of his lips raising slightly.

"Yes, princess," he replies just as peacefully. "Like voluntarily gifting the other person a piece of your soul."

I breathe softly, planting small kisses on his toned pectoral. "Perhaps heaven does exist then."

A low rumble escapes him as he chuckles. "If heaven is this, then I hope death finds me soon and swiftly."

"I believe that is all many of us can hope for." I smile, my eyelashes fluttering as tiredness creeps through me. His hand runs through the locks of my hair, the careful movement lulling me closer to sleep. I peer up, his own eyes shutting too, lashes softly fanning his cheeks. Soon his breathing dies to slow sweeps, his chest rising and falling

steadily.

There is a strange power in the intimacy of the moment. In the vulnerability of us both. We bared all, moved together and shone. We whispered forbidden words in each other's ears and touched parts that few had touched before. Secrets have been shared, pain put out in the open, yet peace finds me at this moment like a blanket or the many stories in this library. He could ruin me now. He could have me declared a used-queen. But I know he won't. Deep down, I trust this man with every inch of me, every cell inside me. I want to stay like this forever.

Soon, it is certain he is asleep. He still holds me, slightly looser than before, but his arm hangs over my back. I slowly sit up, leaning and planting a simple kiss on his lips. He doesn't move, just stays sleeping.

"I kissed you," I whisper, knowing he can't hear, and he isn't awake, "because I wanted to too." I carefully place my head back on his chest and lazily draw circles on his collarbone before my own eyes shut and I greet the darkness of sleep. Falling through a dreamless night of bliss.

CHAPTER EIGHTEEN

We fall into a side room, shutting the door behind us and turning to face each other. He cautiously reaches to my side, taking my hand in his and running his fingers across each knuckle tenderly.

"You're sure you're alright, princess?" he asks. My heart beats faster at his soft words. He pulls me close, wrapping strong arms around my waist, burying his head in the crook of my shoulder. The embrace feels intimate, not romantic. It's supportive. "You're doing brilliantly," he murmurs and plants a kiss on my cheek. "Keep going. You've got this is hand."

I shut my eyes as we breathe together, silence overtaking us. It's just us and our entwined heartbeats. I finally part after a few moments. "Thank you." I offer a small smile, keeping his hand in mine. Not quite ready to let go.

"Always," he says and returns the smile. "Life will do all it can to break you, and no matter how fragile you may be, you can't let it. You fight."

I give a curt nod. I know he's right; this can't finish me. I cannot give in to the tears, the heartache, the possibility that I'm wrong and my parents aren't coming back.

Back to business.

I roll the plans out on the table in front of us, peering over them once more.

Tariq wanders and focuses too, his brows raised. "I'm not sure what we're looking at here," he says, glancing over the paper.

"I believe it's designs for farming equipment. For tea."

He frowns. "For tea? What has this got to do with me and Turkish Arabia?"

"Hypothetically, Prithan has everything it needs to efficiently grow it. The plant saplings on the botanical island, machinery to make production more efficient and faster, and the electricity to power said machinery." He raises a brow as I continue. "What *doesn't* it have?"

"Uh..." He hesitates, eyes darting across the room. "I feel as if this is a trap to insult your country."

"I promise this isn't a trap." I sigh. "Prithan is also known as the dusk lands," I say. "It has struggled with producing certain plants because we have no land for farming that is bright enough. Plants need sunlight, and we don't have that."

He nods, beginning to understand. "But Turkish Arabia does."

"Exactly," I breathe. "It's why we were married. Because the only thing that could break the bond is our deaths. And if no one knew about the marriage, why would we be assassinated?"

"So perhaps someone tried to have you killed because they found out we were married? And they either want to break the union or have Prithan under Turkish Arabian rule."

"Potentially."

"But we are no longer married," he says, "which means the alliance doesn't hold the same strength."

"Which means I can't uphold whatever bargain my parents had with your mother. When they return, they can figure it out, but as long as I rule over Prithan, it is over," I explain. "I need the tea for the sickness. I'll be giving the electricity to the Collective. I must put the lives of my people above the power Prithan holds and could gain. We need that tea as soon as possible. I can't let another soul die waiting for this plan to come together."

"Have you spoken to my mother?" he asks.

"No. I came straight to you first," I say.

He takes a seat across the small room, placing the book he had been reading before we'd met up on the table and running his hands through his hair as he thinks, eyes darting across the room.

Do I go over and comfort him, or does he need space?

"A part of me is devastated that we were put through that for fucking *tea*," he spits, "but somehow... it's brilliant. It would change everything."

"But it's not going to happen," I snap. "I've already almost lost my life because of it once. I don't think it's unreasonable for me to want this all to stop." More tears roll down my face and my chest tightens. Each breath begins to burn, my diaphragm slowly collapsing in on itself. Every inhale demands to be pushed out at once, as if too much air and not enough is inside me all at once. I can't feel the tips of my fingers or toes anymore, only the pounding inside my chest, in my neck, in my head.

"Lorilynn?" Tariq questions, though it becomes noise puzzled between ragged breaths and the blood pumping around my body.

I yearn to run, to move. Breaths come in and out of me fast, as if I'm sprinting across the sea trying the float on the water while it just swallows me whole and tries dragging me to its dark depths.

"Hey, hey, hey." Tariq jumps up and strides to me, taking my face in his hands. "It's alright. I've got you."

I'm not sure what happens after that, but we end up sitting on the floor together, my head resting on his shoulder as he strokes my hair. My lungs don't burn now. My body doesn't want to run, my heart has slowed. Everything is alright.

The embrace isn't sexual, but it is beautiful. Even with our clothes on, I feel as close to him as I did when we were together last night.

As his hands run through my hair, my ear rests against his heartbeat. Things are complicated, things are hard. There is no denying that, but it doesn't mean things won't be alright in the end.

"Don't tell anyone about this," I mumble into his chest. "About all my crying and panicking and doubts."

His chest vibrates as he chuckles. "Out of all the secrets we share, surely this is the least of your worries, princess." he says delicately. "But no one outside this room will ever know it happened. I promise."

I sigh deeply. "I should probably go and sort this mess out." Yet I don't move, and he doesn't stop running his fingers through my hair. Staying with him truly is like heaven. I feel... safe in his arms. At peace.

"Tariq?" I say quietly.

"Yes, Lorilynn?"

"Will you come to my chambers tonight?" My heart hammers deep in my chest as I wait for him to answer. I didn't exactly know the words were leaving my mouth, but they were. We had said we were friends, and we are, but his company is like soaring through the galaxy of stars, pretending the world below doesn't exist. And when he holds me, it doesn't. It is just us, two people. We aren't princess or prince, queen or king. We're just *us*. Two people, not bound by vows or duty, only a connection of trust and affection.

Tariq plants a kiss on my hair and stops running his hands through it. He takes a breath. "I would like that very much."

My breath turns shallow as my heart squeezes in my chest. Anticipation lights like a match inside me. "Great. Good. Good," I babble and sit up fully from where we had been leaning against the wall. I push myself up into standing, offering a hand down to help him up. He grasps it and pulls, coming to his own feet.

We stand inches away, fingers still clasped together. "We're not very good at being just friends, are we?" He grins lopsidedly.

I blush slightly. "No, we aren't." I smile. "We can never be anything more. But I intend to enjoy this friendship as much as possible before you sail back to Turkish Arabia."

"Oh, do you now?" he teases. "Well then," he pauses a moment, "I'll be there just after nightfall."

A small curve creeps at the corners of my lips. "I'll see you at nightfall."

"Nightfall," he repeats one more time before leaning down and planting a simple kiss on my lips, slowly leaving the room, myself following a few moments later after my heart has stopped racing.

•

Azra is in the garden stroking a blood-red rose when I find her. She is tracing the petal as if it were the silken cheek of a young child. I still hold the plans in my palm, rolled up once again.

My approach is slow. I stand a few feet away from her before she peers up, immediately greeting me with a grin.

"Queen Thornton," she says. "I haven't seen you for a few days, child. How have you been?"

"It's over, Azra," I announce, keeping a small distance between us.

Her face goes cold. "What's over?" she hisses.

"The marriage, the tea. *Everything*," I say. "Did you really think we wouldn't figure it out eventually?"

Blood rushes from her skin, and she tries approaching, a hand out to reach me, but I take a step back. My parent's betrayal is also hers. Fortunately for them, they aren't here right now, and Taylan Khan is dead, so he will never have to have this conversation. She, however, is right in front of me—the symbol of broken trust, of betrayal. She was meant to love her son, yet she still put him through that. Still put *us* through that.

"Don't touch me," I snap and snatch my hand away. Then more tears fall. "Tariq and I... Ender and I got a divorce."

"Tariq?" She glares. "You call him Tariq?"

"This has nothing to do with him and me. This is to do with the plan you had to grow tea. To overpower the Collective."

"Watch your volume, Lorilynn," she hisses. "Anyone could hear you."

"Let them," I shout, but then withhold myself. She is right. I take a breath, wipe my cheeks, and compose myself. "Did we matter to you? Or were we just a ploy for wealth and power?"

"Of course, you mattered," she says, her eyes welling. "I love my son. Your parents loved you." She tries taking a step forward. "We had to be cruel to be kind. We had to protect you." She holds her hand out again. "It was all for you two. We wanted to give you the world."

"We don't want the world," I say, still ignoring her hand. "It's not happening. It's over, alright? When my parents return, you can try to sort it out between you." I take another step back, peering around.

Luckily, apart from some gardeners, there aren't many people around. Koen is across the green lands though, his eyes watching us curiously. Out of earshot. He is slowly moving forward though, keen to find out whatever this heated conversation is about between us.

"Lorilynn, please. I'm sorry that you found out that way. We were planning on telling you. Ender and I were on our way when we received news of your parents' death," Azra explains. "That is why we arrived so soon, because we were coming. We aimed to tell you everything. I vow it on the Entity."

"Enough," I spit. "I will only repeat myself one more time. Unless my parents waltz through the castle doors in the next twenty-four hours, I will be giving the rights to the electricity to the Collective and there is nothing you can do." I take a breath, my heart hammering in my chest.

Azra's face softens, the rage in her eyes dying down. Her hand is still there out to me, eyes darting over my face, her own soft and motherly. She swallows. "Alright." Azra meets my eyes. "Is there nothing I can do to change your mind?"

"No. Just please—*please*—let me stay away from this."

Azra gives a small nod and takes a bolder step forward, wrapping her arms around me in an embrace. Openly accepting me and my choices. My eyes catch Adora's, who is on a bench in a corner I hadn't noticed before.

Gently, she combs my hair with her fingers. "Your mother would be proud," she whispers in my ear. "It's alright, child. I understand. And I'm sorry for all the pain we caused you."

I find myself wrapping my own arms around her, resting a head on her shoulder. Her hair smells fresh and warm. I want to drink the scent, bathe in it. It's beautiful.

"You've grown into a radiant, brave, intelligent girl. And while you've certainly caused me a boatload of inconvenience, I'm so proud of who you've become." We part and she looks my face over, placing a soft hand on my cheek. "You were the perfect daughter-in-law, and you would have made a marvelous queen of Turkish Arabia."

I place my hand over hers, years of longing for my mother's affection building inside me. Tariq is lucky to have someone so caring and kind to guide him. I'm lucky to have had her as a maternal figure.

I expected the queen to be angered by the news of the divorce, of my refusal to carry on with this plan. But she still welcomes me with open arms, still holds me while the world crumbles and my hope trickles between the rubble like water soaking into the dirt and lost forever.

"Please, dear child," she whispers, "I know your mind is made up, but do not let my son win you over. Do not trust him. He will stop at nothing."

I move my head away so I can see her face, her wide, begging eyes and desperation laced into the lines of her skin. "What do you mean?" I ask her firmly. "If there is something I need to know about the prince, you must tell me now."

"He will do whatever he can to get it," she replies in hushed tones.

"Get *what*? The electricity?" I keep pushing her to clarify. What does she mean? Is she implying he knew the entire time? Is she implying that it is all a lie? "He won't get it. The electricity is going to the Collective, and that's final." I raise my voice perhaps too loudly now, and curious Koen stops in his place behind Azra, eyes wide. He heard, he definitely heard.

Azra frowns, worry crossing her glance before taking a step back. "Watch your back, Queen Thornton. Trust is often broken by those you hold closest." She picks up her skirts and quickly stalks off, leaving me alone. I take a deep breath, concealing all sign of tears from my face. I am so tired of crying.

"Lori?"

I turn and come face-to-face with Koen. "Yeah— yes?" I say, correcting myself from the slang. I'm a queen, he is a prince. He shouldn't be addressing me as he does, yet there is something beautiful and sweet in his words, in the casualness. In the way he says Lori, as if I am made of china so delicate it'll shatter at the next rush of wind.

"So, you found it? You found the electricity?"

"Technically."

"Technically?"

I sigh begrudgingly. I don't have the bloody energy for this. "Yes, technically. I know where it is. But that's all," I say. "It might not even be ready, or able to be moved."

He peers to where Azra has left to go back inside the castle. "Prithan has the technology?"

"I believe so. However, I haven't seen it myself, and it is all just theoretical." I pause a moment, trying to gather my thoughts. "I can't give you the electricity now, but I have something else that might be of interest."

He raises a brow. "Something else?"

"Yes. They're these plans, like engineering blueprints. I can explain it better and show you during a meeting."

"Wait, so you have the electricity but you're not giving it to us?"

I groan in annoyance. "I don't even know if Prithan has it. It is just *theoretical.* I can explain everything later."

Annoyance builds inside me. Entity have mercy, I just want to sit down and not be hounded with questions I don't know the answers to.

"These plans... Why would they interest us?"

"I believe that there's a way to more efficiently plant, grow, and harvest tea," I explain, "without the use of slavery."

Suddenly the blood runs from his face, paleness creeping up from his cheeks, coolness radiating from him. His eyes are a painting of shame and anger. I wonder if he knows. He's too blinded by the power to care, but still a small part of him seems ashamed to be profiting from a company that treats humans as objects that can be owned.

"Now he's silent," I mutter. "Set up a meeting tomorrow. We can discuss matters then, see if we can come to a conclusion." I take a step back. "And maybe you can think of an explanation to joining the Collective and using their slaves." I take another step away. "I for one can't wait to hear it."

"Lorilynn..."

"Ah, it speaks."

Koen keeps where he is, lowering his head, eyes on the ground.

"There is always more to any story than the eye sees."

"That is true," I say harshly. "Stories always are more than just the surface, but it doesn't justify the villain. And you are most definitely the villain."

"Many villains are the heroes of their own story," he calls after me as I walk away.

"And many heroes are the villains of others," I call back and stop, turning around to look at him. "Just think to yourself, Koen. Which are you? Will the history books write you as a hero or a villain? Or worse, will you just become a part of the Collective? Your name forever lost. A nothing."

"Surely that is better than being remembered as the villain?" he says.

I shrug. "What are we if we are not remembered?" I start walking again, looking forward as I stride across the garden. "I'll leave those thoughts to you, Koen. Would you rather be the villain or a nothing?"

CHAPTER NINTEEN

A smile lines my lips. It probably shouldn't. I'm in a corner of the gardens, a small patio area that sometimes holds an open fire. Right now, however, it is just empty. Moss and weeds begin to grow through the cracks. There used to be a bench here, but it must have been taken away after the wood rotted. Little patches where the legs stood stain the stone. I slowly sit, hoping for a few moments to myself. To breathe.

My mind wanders over every part of the past few hours. It's been a whirlwind. It started with the divorce, then the night in the library. Then the plans, the figuring it out. And Azra's words. What secret does Tariq hold? Why shouldn't I trust him? And why, despite his mother's warning, do I want to give myself to him?

"You seem deep in thought, your majesty." Adora walks slowly towards me, his hands behind his back and hair ruffled. He appears casual, his shirt untucked at the top, buttons loose. A relaxed demine covers him.

He crouches, taking a seat next to me on the pavement, smiling at the sun.

"I'm just thinking," I say.

"Anything I can help with?" I shake my head, and Adora carries on looking out. I do too. The light is shimmering against the castle windows, reflecting softly in our eyes. It's so rare for the sun to shine like this in Prithan, but it's happening more and more often. The dusk is at its end. A new age has begun.

"This is your country, Lorilynn." He sighs, turns to me, a smile on his lips. "I have faith you'll make it the best it's ever been." I feel the impact of what he's saying in my soul, knowing he thinks that I'll be a ruler worth working for. "I've stayed on this council, waiting for the day when you'll rule, knowing I want to be here to watch it happen and be a part of it."

"I feel like it's not my time to be queen yet." And I don't. I still feel they'll be found. They *have* to be found.

Please.

"There's no sign of anything anymore, Lorilynn. The generals are wanting to start pulling out, get the soldiers back to usual duties."

"I won't give up. You know Papa wouldn't give up on me, why should I give up on him?"

A longing, remembering smile covers Adora's face, and he gives a single sigh, twiddling thumbs slightly on his lap. I've taken to playing with a bit of moss on the pavement between us.

"Thank the Entity you've always been more like him than your mother." He places a hand over mine and squeezes once. Something Papa did. Mags and my mother didn't get on well, it was common knowledge, but he was father's friend. Adora never shared his opinion of my mother but he was loyal to the crown. Never before has he spoken an ill word against her. "You got his best qualities."

"Really? Like what?" I got his hair, that's for sure. There are portraits of him younger with dark mahogany curls down to his shoulders. I inherited the color. All the girls dyed theirs with flowers and oils, hues of pink and blue and yellow and red. I tried countless times, but it never stuck, never held. I was just left with oily locks that took weeks to get back to normal. I suppose now I'm grateful for his hair. Because Adora's right, I am more my father's daughter than my mother's.

"You got his kindness." And here I was thinking he was talking about my hair.

"Was he happy? You knew him better than anyone."

"He..." Adora's voice fades away. "As you know, your parents didn't have the happiest marriage. When I first saw him at the wedding, he looked sad, but your father was always about sacrifice for Icelandic Prithan—which was just Iceland at the time. He would do anything for his country. It was his greatest love, until you and your brother.

"After your brother died, he... he told me you were the only reason for him to remain here. He loved you both so dearly. It broke him utterly. And when you got sick, he was so scared of losing you too. He wanted to spend every moment by your side but—"

"But Mother told him no."

The heaviness that had disappeared for a bit comes back, and I feel so selfish suddenly for being happy when there is still so much pain and loss in this world.

"I want to show you something. A gift."

He leads me deep inside the castle, to a room I've never been in before. It's below ground, the only light coming in through a slit at the top of the wall. Stone lines everything. There is no furniture, only a velvet cloth over something. It's my height, and weirdly human-like. I don't know if I should be nervous, but excitement stirs inside me.

"I was going to wait for your coronation, but I'm hoping that this will show you. Your reign has come, Lorilynn."

I pace around the item slowly, looking it up and down for any indication of what it is. But I honestly don't know. It looks sort of like a headless person.

I glance over at Adora, but he just stands there, grinning and nodding me forwards. The material feels heavy under my touch and soft. Underneath is hard and cold. I think it's metal. I tug, and the fabric slips to the floor. I can't help but physically lose my breath at what's underneath.

Silver, shining like water reflecting moonlight. Smooth and strong and oiled. Fit to support woman's form. Prithan's emblem on the front of the center breast. Twining metal runs all over like vines, and the bottom matches with pads for knees and elbows. Armor. A queen's armor.

"This must have taken months... How did you know about my training? Mags and I were so careful to be discreet." I can barely make out the words in my awe. This armor is not for show.

"I didn't. This was from your father. He had it made for your nineteenth birthday. I've kept it a secret for some time now."

"But... how did *he* know I was training? He was across the ocean in Iceland. Did Magnús tell him?"

"That I cannot answer. But it's been here, waiting. Your father asked me to keep it for your birthday in case he couldn't make it. He didn't want you to be forgotten." He smiles to himself for a moment as if somewhere else. "He'd never forget you."

The armor gleams like a star. It seemingly will fit perfectly, and black leather underneath will protect my skin. I can't help but feel as if I recognize it, the design, the way to metal is shaped.

It takes a moment, looking back over life, to realize I've stared at the stone version of this armor so often in my life.

"This is a replica of my grandmother's armor. The one she wears on the statue in the chapel."

"No." He walks forwards, each step echoing in the room, the sound bouncing across the stone. Cautiously, he takes my hand, places it over the emblem on the chest, coolness climbing through my fingers. "This *was* your grandmother's armor. And now it is yours."

My breath hitches and my pulse slows. It's armor for a queen. A warrior queen who I hope to be one day.

"Your mother had it archived after the late queen's passing. About a year ago, Einar ordered it restored and brought here. And this is where it has stayed. Under my protection."

Two raps sound at the door, and in comes one of my maids, bowing low. Official manners, official protocol. The official way to greet the queen of Prithan.

As soon as that armor is over my shoulders, my hair tied up, and I leave this room, they will think of me as queen—as a woman. I'm not that yet. Eighteen is too young for this. I just want to live. Be free. I want to be a princess, not a queen. That selfishness should be proof enough.

I look between the maid and Adora. She waits at the side to help me undress, and he looks keenly, hoping that I'm overjoyed, ready to accept the role of ruler. One day I will be ready to place the armor on, but it is not today.

I want to disappear, vanish. I want to be gone. Sail away, maybe to Ptah, or to the Wastelands, and find somewhere to live, a recovery spot until my insides melt away into nothing. At least I'll be free. It's better to be free and in pain than captured and numb. I long for that pain. I just feel nothing. Not even nothing. Just *not*.

I will not give in. I will not stop searching until that crown is forcefully placed upon my head. Soon, I'll return to Skye. Then Icelandic Prithan. Tonight, I am going to lay with a man, a man who makes me feel something. Gives me normality. A man who has freed me and I have freed him. And tonight, we will free each other again and again.

"Lorilynn?" Adora clears his throat. I've been staring at the armor for a few moments now, silence veiling the room.

"Uncle Adora..." I whisper. "I-I can't."

His face crumples and his whole body slumps. "It's time, Lorilynn. I'm sorry, but they're gone."

"No," I snap back.

"Lorilynn," he says carefully and reaches forward, placing a firm hand on my shoulder. "I'm sorry, but..." Tears build in his eyes, but he rapidly blinks them away. "They're gone. It's time."

"No," I spit again. "It isn't time. They're alive."

"Lorilynn—"

"No!" I shout, my voice cracking, and turn. I storm out of the room, slamming the doors behind me. Five minutes, I want *five minutes* to myself. Five minutes where no one talks about electricity or being queen or responsibility. Five minutes where I can sit and think about stupid things like what I want for dinner and what book to start this evening before bed.

I find myself in the chapel with the hope that I can have a moment between only myself and the Entity. Luckily, the Entity has no questions. The priest is working at the front, dressed in pearl white robes as he lights some candles and burns incense. A green candle is today's choice, for the earth. Perhaps he casts a spell for a farmer or the woods? It isn't my business, only his and the Entity's.

When I first came in, he cast me a small bow, but let me be. And he is a blessing for that.

The floral scent of incense hugs me, relaxing every muscle in my body. Like I so wished, I get those five minutes—I get ten. I think about silly things. I've decided to scour over some old religious texts before bed, that I'm going to see if I can just have a light stew for dinner in my room. I've also decided I'm going to have a warm bath after dinner, time to wash my hair and clean myself. Apply some perfume. Because I'm going to enjoy myself tonight, and I'm going to make sure Tariq enjoys himself too.

The priest finishes the spell, sealing the small jar with the green wax and placing it in a silken white pouch embroidered with his crest. I've received many of those small spell jars over the years, mostly healing spells that have been sealed with wax blue like the sky.

I haven't truly spoken to him for some time. I stand, wandering over, and wait for him to finish. He relights the incense before turning gracefully, offering a kind smile.

"My queen." He bows, planting a wet kiss on my hand. "I'm glad you've come to see me. I must speak with you, but you seemed so deep in thought I didn't want to disturb you."

This man truly a gift from the Entity.

"Thank you," I say. "I just needed some peace."

"Then you certainly came to the right place. I aim for this to be a sanctuary of calm and harmony." He gestures to the room, a small smile lining his lips. "I am glad you can find tranquility here. Anything I can help with?"

I shake my head. "That is kind, but I doubt there is little you could do. Unless you wish to swap places?" I chuckle.

He gives a slight jitter in response. "Fancy yourself priesthood, eh? You would be a marvelous priestess. I, however, think my hair wouldn't look very good in the crown. So, sadly, I'm going to have to pass."

I smile, finding myself laughing a little. The man is bald, his head shiny like a torch. "Shame." I chuckle. "You needed to speak with me? What can I do for you?"

"Well, I'm afraid it won't help with the tranquility aspect of this room," he says and wanders behind the table, pulling cotton white gloves on and taking out the book of records. I haven't laid my eyes on it since my wedding two years ago. He waves me over, and I take careful steps, scared that one wrong move will somehow damage the pages. I peer close to it, looking it over.

The priest looks up before peering around the room, making sure we're alone. He then opens it, crisp pages flicking wide, a soft wind that carries the scent of the paper lightly kissing my cheek.

"Last night, after the divorcing ceremony, I came here to note it down," he begins to explain, "but... well, you can see."

He stops flicking through, stopping at my mother's name and... the rip where mine should be. Instead of the gilded page is a blank one, ready for my own daughter. A jagged edge, a hint of splattered ink and a few flakes of gold are the only proof that anything was ever there.

Someone else has touched the book, someone has damaged the book. Someone has the page. My page.

"Fucking hell," I mutter, then quickly raise my hand to my mouth. "My apologies for the language, your excellence."

"Worry not. I said the same thing when I saw." He gives me a half-smile, but worry lines his eyes. "I've never had this happen before. Nor has any priest before who has manned this chapel."

"Why would someone do this? Who would do this?"

"I have no idea who, but perhaps I know the why," he explains, closing the book and tracing it with a gloved finger. "Under the eyes of the

Entity, you are divorced, but until it is marked on that page, there is no proof of it."

I look his face over with furrowed brows. "Meaning that on paper we are legally still married?"

"No," he says, and I give a sigh of relief. "However, if something were to happen to you and me, that piece of paper would say that you're still married, meaning that he has the potential to rule Prithan in your absence."

"Fuck," I breathe, but this time take no care to apologize.

"Fuck indeed," he says in agreement. "Under Prithan law, I need an official witness from convent to be here for the making of a new page. A message has been sent, and she will arrive tomorrow afternoon. It'll stop being a problem by this time tomorrow, but I wished to warn you for obvious reasons."

"Who else knows?" I question.

"No one."

"Let's keep it that way."

"Agreed. Just... be careful, my queen. You're too high to survive the fall now."

"I'll simply have to learn to fly," I reply. "It wouldn't be the first time a queen of Prithan had to grow wings."

I lift my gaze from him to the statues lining the walls, to the queens forever remembered and solidified in marble stone. Poised ready to rule, guide through hardship. Many had been killed, many had died of old age, but all overcame problems. All overcame issues and defied death, defied destiny, defied the Entity. I would become one of them. One day. This little taster is just the first lesson.

"You're far to wise for your age," the priest says. "When the time comes to crown you, I will do it with confidence and pride."

"I've had to face things most eighteen-year-olds never have," I reply, not quite able to meet his eye.

"Life has been unkind to you. Even before the marriage, you lost your childhood to sickness and death's lingering shadow."

"I suppose it is both a blessing and a curse," I say. "I have been on the cusp of the reapers scythe. But they let me go. I hope when it is my time, I can greet death as a lost lover."

I take a deep breath, inhaling as much of the incense as I can, letting it relax my bones. "I should go, your excellence," I say and begin walking away. "Thank you for informing me."

"Of course." He bows. "Please, take care. Keep a dagger on hand at all times. You never know who may be behind this."

"I will, I promise." I pause from my steps and turn back to him. “Keep me in your prayers tonight."

CHAPTER TWENTY

The bath has begun to cool. I gently make swirls in the chilled water with the tips of my fingers, droplets of lavender oil dancing between the motions, dissipating eventually into tiny stars on the surface.

I've been here for perhaps an hour, letting every inch of my skin relax in the gradually disappearing heat. I decided to keep my hair dry, tied up messily above my head, tendrils falling along the side of my cheeks.

"I've placed a towel on the side, your majesty," Efa says, her brow lowered as she peeks around the door, still trying to give me privacy.

"Thank you." I smile. "I'll be out in a moment."

"Take your time, my queen." She returns to the main bedchambers, leaving me to get out.

I lift myself slowly, careful not to glide on the stone floor, and grab the towel, wrapping it around my body and drying off before slipping on a lace, floor-length robe, tying the front in place. My dark hair falls past my shoulders, the curls beginning to peak at my ears. I stand in front of the mirror, looking myself over. My lips, my eyes, the way my jaw sinks in and my cheekbones poke out. I haven't been eating enough. My skin is pale, eyes shadowed. Does Tariq think I'm attractive? Does he like this? I gently trace over my collarbone with the tip of my finger, much like how he did last night. The memory blooms and a blush rushes to my cheeks. I feel as if I need a cold bath.

I step into the main chambers. Efa has placed a nightgown on my bed, a pitcher of water at the side. I peer at the chemise, white and simple, with little flowers embroidered at the hem. It isn't what I would consider attractive. I'm not even sure what I consider attractive. If I were to have sex with someone, what would I find alluring? My mind whirls as I overthink. It shouldn't be this hard, particularly when I hope that neither of us will be wearing *anything* eventually.

"Can I get you anything else?" Efa asks, straightening the corners of my bedsheets.

"This is perfect. Thank you." I smile sweetly and go sit at the vanity, beginning to run a brush through my hair.

"Goodnight, your majesty." She bows.

"Goodnight." I grin back. "Efa, would it be possible to sleep in tomorrow? I can get myself ready. Have the morning to yourself."

Efa pauses and turns back, hand poised on the handle. "Of course.

Sweet dreams." We share another small, pleasant gaze before she leaves the room, the door clicking shut.

The glow of orange on the horizon slowly disappears. I brush my hair through, letting it fall over my shoulder loosely. I even dab some light rouge onto my cheeks and lips. Only a little to make me not look like I'm half dead. As the sun goes down, my heart beats more and more until eventually, darkness takes over and stars dot the sky, dusk clouds letting one occasionally shine through.

I've begun pacing the room, my bare feet padding along the oak. My chest thumps and this strange yearning sits in my lower abdomen. I feel nervous. I feel excited.

Then the knock sounds, just twice. Light but clear. I opted to keep the silken robe and put the nightgown away. It dances at my feet as I wander over and pull the handle down, opening the door.

"It's me," Tariq says, his voice low.

My insides curl in on themselves. I open the door fully and he slips into the room, locking it shut behind him.

We're inches from each other, silence shrouding all but our heavy breathing.

"Evening," Tariq says softly and looks me up and down, lingering on the opening of my dressing gown.

"You found your way here, alright?" I inquire.

What a stupid question.

I assess him. He's changed. He wears dark trousers and a shirt the color of midnight. Different than usual. Still, it makes me swoon.

Tariq chuckles lightly, but there is a small fault in his eyes. "Yes." His voice cuts through the quiet. And then there's silence again. I'm not entirely sure what to do now. I take a step back and try giving a smile despite my rapidly beating heart. But he grabs my hand, pulling me into him so I drown in the scent of spice. Our chests are pressed together, hands entwined.

"Can I kiss you?" he whispers, eyes flickering to my mouth a moment. I give a small nod and he moves forward, placing his lips delicately on mine. I shut my eyes, melting into his arms.

After a swooping moment, we part and he places our foreheads together, softly breathing. He delicately grazes my cheek with his hand, keeping a firm arm around my waist.

"Are you feeling better?" he asks in a low voice.

"Please, let's not talk about that," I reply quietly. "Let's not talk about anything." I run a hand through his soft hair. He shivers, shutting his eyes and leaning into my touch. "I want to just be us. Two people. Just for tonight. Please."

Tariq meets my eyes, placing a hand on my cheek, gently running his thumb across my lower lip. "You're beautiful. You know that, don't you?"

My face flushes. I lower my eyes, a nervous giggle escaping me. "Don't be ridiculous, Tariq."

"I'm serious." He places a hand under my chin and raises my eyes to him. "Take the compliment, princess."

I look his face over and give a small nod. "Thank you." A nervous laugh escapes me, and I finally manage to take a step back, swinging my arms in anticipation, going and sitting on the edge of my bed.

He stalks over, perching beside me about a foot away. His eyes trail across the room, from the window shrouded in darkness to the bed.

"Is something wrong?" I ask him with furrowed brows.

"It's different from how I remember." He swallows, still gazing at the bed. Of course, the last time he was here was two years ago.

I peer around myself. "It's a different bed," I explain. "Different sheets."

"Different time," he finishes and places a hand on my thigh over the fabric.

I reach down, putting mine over his, but use my fingers to open the front of my nightgown, the material falling to the side, his knuckles brush the skin of my leg.

Warmth surrounds me, blood pumping around my body, heat beginning to radiate intimately in anticipation. Our eyes lock again, and suddenly we're a knot of limbs and tongues and yearning. His hand remains on my thigh, while mine tangle in his hair as our mouths still work with each other.

He pushes me onto the bed, gripping my skin that sends a shiver through me. I start trying to unhook his shirt from his trousers, but he catches my hand.

"You are the most impatient woman I've ever met," he mumbles between kisses, his touch gliding along the crook of my neck.

I look up at him with wide eyes. "I haven't done this often. It's still new to me," I reply.

He looks down and plants a kiss on my neck, featherlight. Fireworks explode over my skin. He moves his lips to my earlobe, gently nibbling a little before whispering softly, the air from his mouth tickling the skin of my lobe. "Shut your eyes, princess."

Excitement explodes over me, and I do as he asks, closing my lids as more kisses are planted on my throat. My hips lift, moving over his leg as he continues to press his mouth to my skin. But then the warmth disappears, replaced my coolness to my throat.

I flash my eyes open. He straddles me, making sure I can't get away. And where his lips had been only moments ago, he now holds a dagger. I can't quite see it, but I feel it dig into my skin, the gleam refracting against the candlelight.

Every moment we shared, every secret flashes before me. Those eyes I lost myself in now stand over with determination.

It's him.

He sent the assassin, took me to the village to make sure I was there. He knew about the marriage and knew that the page would be proof of the union. He wants my crown. Prince Khan is going to kill me.

•

The carriage draws into the distance, quickly disappearing. I sit on the stone stairs out front of the castle entrance, not caring for the rain that is pouring down heavily, sticking my hair and clothes to skin.

After the confrontation with Papa this morning, our parting hadn't been more than a brief embrace and words that would be expected. Màthair, however, did grace my cheek with her hand and inform me they wouldn't be long. Then the two got in the carriage and disappeared.

The Turkish Arabian royals are long gone too. The queen and king both bowed as they left. The prince and I had sort of stared at each other a time before stiffly shaking hands. He had looked back as he climbed into the carriage.

"You should come inside, Lorilynn," Adora says as he clambers out with an umbrella. "You'll catch a cold, and the doctor has warned it won't be good for your lungs."

I don't respond but reluctantly stand. He holds out a hand for me, and I take it, ducking under the umbrella with him. Adora leads me inside, a maid quickly coming over and wrapping a towel around my shoulders and patting my hair lightly with a cloth, as if that is going to take the shiver from my bones.

"You seem sad," Adora says, shaking the umbrella, "They'll be back soon. Don't fret."

"I'm alright, Uncle Adora," I say, "I'm just tired."

"Did you not sleep well?" he pushes.

I run my thumb along the cut on my fourth finger, the wound stinging. A permanent reminder of the night's events. "Not really."

"I'll ask for some chamomile to be sent to your room tonight," he says happily, none the wiser to the bruises that mark my skin, or the nightmare imprinted on my mind.

"That would be nice, thank you." I give a small smile. "I'm going to go to the library. Catch up on some reading."

I take a few steps away as he gives a small nod of acknowledgement, beginning talking to a maid. I silently make my way upstairs, slipping into the library and taking a seat, wincing as a cramp ripples through me.

My period is particularly violent this time, and early. It arrived not long after I took that small pill. In all honesty, every part of me aches. I feel battered and wounded. And exhausted.

Slowly, I roll up each sleeve, an array of bruises painting my usually pale skin. Finger marks from where the guards gripped me tightly, dragging me. I lift my skirts to above my knees, and sure enough, deep purple blooms on each one from being slammed down on the stone.

A sob writhes through me. I bring my hand to my mouth and bite down to try and stop noise coming out. Tears stream heavily down my cheeks as my whole body shakes. How could this happen? Why did this happen? I don't want it to happen again. It shouldn't have happened in the first place. I was completely defenseless, completely vulnerable.

A small knock sounds on the door. I rapidly push my skirt down, pull the sleeves back, and scrub away the tears. "Come in!" I call, perhaps overenthusiastically, and quickly grab the closest book, bringing it to my lap.

Uncle Mags opens the door, a mug of something steaming in his hand. "Adora sent me," he explains and sets the mug down on the side table. He peers at the book, raising a brow.

I look at him, confused, before finally looking at what I have open on my lap.

The Kama Sutra.

I look up at him with a panicked expression. "I can explain."

He holds his hands up in mock defense. "I'm not going to judge, Lorilynn. You do you."

I roll my eyes, a genuine smile flaring over my cheeks. Even a small laugh escapes me. I shut the Entity damned book and place it back on the shelf. I then reach and clasp the mug in my hands, the heat seeping in through my skin. I bring it to my lips, and warmed apple juice coats on my tongue.

Magnús pulls a seat up opposite me, leaning forward with his elbows rested on his knees, looking directly into my eyes. He knows that my lies glow in my eyes.

"Adora thinks you're upset about your parents leaving," he says. "I think you're upset about something, but not that."

I take another deep glug of the juice, using the mug to hide my face, not caring about the heat burning my tongue. I'm under strict instructions to tell no one. Including him. I stay silent, and when there is no more apple juice, I keep my eyes averted away at the floor, or the shelves, or the window.

Anywhere but him.

"Alright, you don't have to tell me," he eventually says, "but if I can help, let me."

I finally meet his eyes. Memories of the guards, of their hands on me and the pain and force and blood. I never want it to happen again. I never want my life to be out of my own grasp again.

"How long did you train to become a guard?" I ask him quietly.

He blows out a puff of air. "I joined when I was fifteen, spent fourteen years in the military, and then retired to the Icelandic Overseers. From there, I worked my way up to my current position. Why? You plan on becoming a personal guard?"

I chuckle again. "I'd just like to be able to protect myself somewhat."

"Want to put me out a job, eh?" he teases with a fatherly smirk, pinching my cheek with a careful hand. "I think it is a wise idea. One your mother will put to an end as soon as she finds out. And she will find out."

"Unless she doesn't," I say.

"You'd have to find a fifl to train you."

I meet his eyes again, batting my lashes. "Well, I see a fífl."

He gives a bellowing laugh. "I'm not training you. Do you know how much trouble I'd get if you got even the tiniest scratch?"

"We can be discreet, Uncle Mags. I promise I won't tell."

"Lorilynn, I can't." He stands from his chair and begins walking away, my chance of self-protection going with him. I jump up, grabbing his sleeve. He stops when I do, turning to face me with a concerned look.

I'm not sure when the tears started, but they fall heavy, seeping down my neck and to the wooden floor. My chest aches, my bones hurt. I keep my grip on his arm as the tears turn to cries and a sob takes over my whole body.

"Please," I manage to say. "Please, train me. I'll work harder than any soldier you've ever taught. I promise."

His eyes flit over my face and a caring hand lands on my shoulder. "What happened, Lorilynn?"

I shake my head. "Please. Don't let me be this vulnerable."

My memories pour back in waves, the feeling of the floor under my feet, the blood on my tongue, the pinch in my hips.

Magnús's face is grave as he peers over mine, keeping his hand on his shoulder a moment. He crouches in front of me looking up, making himself smaller, less threatening. "Lorilynn, did someone hurt you?" he asks softly in Icelandic. He's gentle, keeping a firm hand on my arm, but the grip loose so that I can pull away without a moment notice. "Talk to me, it's alright."

I squeeze my eyes shut, urging the images out my head, the feelings on the guard's grip on my wrist. I'm thankful they've all left with Mother and Papa. I don't have to see them anytime soon.

"Would you like me to hold you?" he says softly.

I open my eyes and nod.

He cautiously stands and wraps his arms around me. I hold him tight, resting my head on his chest, sobbing, tears running down my cheeks. And he just holds me, keeps his arms wrapped around me as I cry, letting the betrayal, the fear, and the pain leave my body. I cling to him, scrunching the fabric of his jacket in my fist, soaking his white shirt.

Magnús strokes my hair, hushing my cries.

"Tomorrow morning, I'll meet you by the stables at sunrise."

I stop crying and move my head so I can see him but still keep my arms wrapped around him. "What?" I murmur.

"Don't be late. And wear clothes you don't mind getting dirty or ripped," he says.

I let go of him, take a step away, and look him over. "Are you saying you'll train me?" I ask skeptically.

"If your mother finds out, we'll be locked in the cells for a year," he sternly replies.

"So that's a yes?"

He gives me a small smile. "It's a yes."

CHAPTER TWENTY-ONE

The room is cold. Freezing. It chills my bones, yet I just sit shivering against a stone. I have been for hours perhaps. Without sun, there is so little light, only a faint glow from the moon.

But it doesn't stop the armor's glimmer. Its beauty. Magnificence. A queen's armor. The metal as it was mere hours ago, the fallen fabric still on the floor in a crumpled heap.

I've been sitting here for so long my limbs have got holly prickles. The stone has numbed my back; fabric doesn't protect skin against the cold.

Earlier, I had known as soon as I put that armor on, I'd be accepting my fate.

My fists are clenched, knuckles white. I could remain here as long as I want and nothing will change.

It is only when the sun rises, and amber light seeps into the stone, that I finally stand and trace my fingers over the metal.

Prithan's greatest ruler wore these, fought with her men in these, was expected to die in these. A warrior queen. She had laid down the path for Màthair to rule, and she had laid it out for me. The best I can do is lay it out for my children one day. So they can guide my countries into a utopia that'll I'll never see, and one day, Prithan's people will always be safe, fed, and happy.

When I was four, I once found my mother crying privately in her chambers. I'd gone to see if Father was there, but instead found her as human as I've ever seen her. For years, she'd been flawless, alien. A crown on her head, dress always pristine. But she just sat on her bed, stray hair escaping—the always perfect queen not so perfect. And she only wore her underclothes. Her petticoat and chemise. She was raw, thin. Broken maybe.

"Màthair?" I hesitate but walk closer slowly, making sure I look collected. She doesn't like me looking messy. Even though she does herself now.

The tears stream down her face. She turns. I think she's going to hit me. But she doesn't, instead holding me close, kissing the hair on my head.

"What's wrong?" I squeak, but she just strokes the hair on my head, over and over. I can feel my forehead getting wet from her tears. And she keeps doing that. Eventually, I melt into her hold and wrap my arms around her too. But it just makes her cry harder.

"Our lives are not our own, Lorilynn," she whispers, just between us, "and you have to wear the crown, stand strong. You have to be perfect, otherwise, they'll tear you

apart piece by piece."

I hadn't said anything after that, just let her hold me for a time until her maid came in to help her dress. She appeared later in the throne room like she was before. With her head even higher, eyes brewing with determination as she sat and looked over her people. For a moment, we had kept eye contact—she even gave me a nod before becoming what she had always been. And I never forgot those words, never forgot what it was like when she was at her weakest, but also honest and strong.

Màthair, I will wear this crown, I promise. But I will wear armor first.

My parents are dead. I will never see them again, never hold my father or bow to her. I accept it. Accept what I am. Queen. I am the queen of Prithan. I will not let anyone tear me down, I will wear the crown. I will be perfect.

I will never let my guard down, never let anyone hold a knife to me again. I was Princess Lorilynn Thornton. I will be Queen Lorilynn Elizabeth Einarsdottir Thornton.

I carefully undo the dressing gown, letting it shimmer to the floor, leaving me completely bare. And then, slowly, I remove the metal, the undershirt, the leathers, and place them on myself. The fit is like it was made for me, formed around my body. It's lightweight and easy to move in. I feel protected. I am strong.

Like a second skin. I don't feel drowned, or held down, or slow.

Every curve and peak matches my body. I angle myself, a mirror in the corner of the room catching my eye. Despite my hair down loose and red surrounding my eyes, I look like a queen.

Even with the cut on the right side of my neck, and the dried blood dripping down. I'm a queen, especially now. I hope it scars. I hope that every time anyone sees it, they feel a coolness deep inside them, knowing that someone tried to take my life—tried and failed. I hope they wonder what happened to the assailant, what punishment they faced.

My armor clinks as I stride through the corridors. Occasionally, a maid or servant bows low as I pass. Usually, it would make me cringe, but now I don't mind it so much. A guard waits by the doors to the gardens, his eyes wide as I stroll past him into the sunlight.

Chione and her guards are already out, training together. Sweat beads on her face as she pauses her fight, turning to face me as I walk out. A smile spreads over her face.

"Your majesty." She beams, bowing low for a moment before taking my hand and planting a kiss on my knuckles. "I must say, even I'm jealous." She looks the armor up and down, eyes lingering over the gleaming metal. She invites me to train with her and her guards. We do, swords clash. They teach me new ways to fight. I even manage to teach them a few things.

I hold my sword at the edge of one of Chione's guard's chins, fire burning in his eyes as he tries looking me over, assessing if he can win. He can't. And all of us know it. He raises both hands, yielding. Delight shines through me. I just defeated one of the world's best-trained guards in combat.

I lower my sword, shake his hand, and cast a glance at Chione. A grin is spread across her hazel cheeks as she claps. Her guards also join in. A small audience has built, some officials, Azra, and Adora. His eyes are filled with pride and a sense of deep sadness. I meet them with my own for a moment, giving him a single nod.

I'm ready.

He carefully steps forward toward me, gazing up and down the gleaming armor I wear. "It really does fit you perfectly," he says. "You look magnificent, my queen." He gives a small bow of his head, and my chest swells with sadness. Because I am queen, his queen. I push it aside, gently wrapping my arms around him, resting my head on his shoulder. He gives a surprised chuckle, but quickly wraps his arms around me, planting a kiss on my hair.

"This is very unregal." He chuckles lightly.

"I'm queen, I can do what I want," I reply with a small smile.

A laugh rumbles through him as he keeps his protective arms around me. I suddenly don't care who sees. Let them know the trust I have in Uncle Adora, let them know I am not alone.

"I'll start having your things brought to the queen's chambers," he says once his laughter has died down.

"Thank you, I'd appreciate that."

Adora takes a step back eventually and clears his throat. "I'm afraid I have some bad news."

I give an exasperated sigh. "Can I have at least one morning?" I complain. "Certainly I've earned it. I mean, we were just having a moment and everything."

"You've earned an entire year off, Lorilynn. But I'm afraid this is serious." He sobers up and nods towards the side. I suppose whatever this is would be better told without half the court staring at us.

I take a few steps as the crowd disperses and we lean against the fountain, keeping close and our words quiet. Concern crosses Adora's face, a frown lining his cheeks. My chest tightens, more anxiety filling me.

"What's happened?" I ask gently.

"The priest—someone attacked him in the night," Adora says gravely.

"Shit, is he alright?"

"He'll survive. He has a broken jaw though, among other things."

"Among other things?" I question.

"They tried to cut out his tongue."

•

The wind kisses my cheeks and hair, a small shiver running through me as the cold bites at the bare skin of my face. I made sure to choose a dress with sleeves, knowing that nights are starting to get darker and winter is creeping in.

The sea crashes into the sand, droplets of water spraying onto my tongue, salt exploding like fireworks on my tastebuds.

I sit, my dress laid over my knees, water soaking the hem and my feet, coolness grounding me. Reminding me this is real.

Adora informed me the priest had been rushed to a hospital a thirty-minute carriage ride away. He's stable, just in pain. Aside from having a large gash on his tongue, he also has broken ribs and a dislocated shoulder.

My memory led to the conversation we had had just last night. He had warned me, and I'd been so driven by lust that I hadn't paid attention and almost lost my life because of it. He almost lost his tongue, and it is all my fault.

I now wear a dagger, strapped to my thigh, hidden under my skirt.

"Lorilynn..." His voice is shaking, quiet.

I turn my head quickly to find him standing a distance away, wearing the same clothes he was last night. Darkness hangs from his eyes, a lack of sleep paling his skin. His boots are speckled in mud, trousers caked in dirt. He's been wandering through the night.

I stand, my hand reaching for the dagger concealed in the fabric. I keep it poised there, ready.

Tariq.

Ender.

Prince Khan.

The man, who for a time, held my heart. And then a knife at my throat.

"You have lost the right to call me that," I snap, trying to withhold the despair dancing inside of me, but tears are falling. I opened myself up, let myself feel human, let myself feel good. I let him inside me. "I am a queen, and you will address me as such." My voice is filled with hatred, anger, weaved with threads of crimson and darkness. It is raw and harsh.

The prince opens his mouth to speak, searching my face, but he quickly shuts it, straightening as if someone is tugging strings above him. "Your majesty." The words come out from him in a struggle. "Why am I still alive?" he asks. "Why have you not had me imprisoned or beheaded or hanging from a rope?"

"Because I cannot be fucking bothered," I spit. "You are scum. It is not worth going to war over *you*." A flash of hurt crosses his face, and it only fuels my rage. I hope my words feel like the knife he held to my throat, stabbing him repetitively in the chest.

I take a step towards him, getting so close my heart hammers, his scent taking over. He could slash my throat, he could choke me, he could grab my hair and drown me. Part of me hopes he tries.

"Just... kill me, please," he begs in a whisper, a glaze hazing over his eyes. "Your majesty," he quickly adds, the words hesitating on his tongue. As if they're uncomfortable.

"You are a liar, a betrayer, and while I would take great pleasure in knowing you were rotting at the bottom of the ocean with my parents, I will take even more pleasure in watching you spend a long, miserable life, knowing that you failed while I carry on. Until one day, I don't even remember what you look like, and you will be just one man from my past. One pathetic man."

He doesn't respond, just stands straight, hurt flashing over his brown eyes as he looks over my face. Until it becomes too much, and then he looks anywhere but.

I step back so there's space between. So that I won't strangle him with my bare hands. "Did you send the assassin?" I ask.

"Yes," he replies without missing a beat, then reaches into his pocket, pulling out a crumpled page. "I also have this..."

I step forward, snatching the paper from him and unfolding it. It's the missing page, the very one the priest told me was missing last night.

Lorilynn Elizabeth Einarsdottir Thornton

Born on the waxing moon of the twelve month, the 417th year of dusk. Married on the full moon of the fifth month, the 433rd year of dusk.

"The priest?" I ask, "that was you also?" The prince gravely nods.

Tears prick my eyes again as I turn away, walking in the other direction. The priest has a family, people he loves. He is hurt because of this bastard. It isn't fair to the man, who did nothing but treat the prince with kindness and all he could to repent. It isn't fair, because I opened myself up to him—body, mind, soul, and heart.

I turn around, my anger running through me like liquid fire, and storm back to him, slamming my fists into his shoulder, causing him to stumble backward. "Fuck you," I hiss, spitting at his feet. "Why? Why did you do it all?"

He swallows nervously, putting his hands in his trouser pockets. "For my home, my country. For Turkish Arabia. For the tea."

What else? I've been so blinded by keeping Prithan safe that I forgot other royals will do whatever it takes to bring their country out on top. And why would romance or friendship stop that? Azra was right. She warned me not to trust the prince, yet I gave him everything.

"Was having sex with me part of the plan?" I snap, "or was that just some fun game for you to play? You wanted to brag about how you managed to get your cock in the queen of Prithan? How you managed to get her to whisper sweet words in your ear and cry on your shoulder?"

Pain flashes across his face a moment. I'm beginning to hit nerves.

"Sex had nothing to do with it, Lorilynn..." His voice fades. "Your majesty."

More tears sting my eyes, falling down my cheeks. Every kiss, every touch. Every divine and wicked thing was all a lie. Every firework, every moment of bliss. When I thought I made him feel how he made me feel. All lies. I am such an idiot.

"Once I am crowned, you will leave my country. If you ever set foot upon Prithan land or enter my sight again, I will remove your head *myself.* Understood?"

For a moment our eyes meet, and darkness swirls in his, the memory of last night flashing in mine.

"Tariq...?" My voice squeaks, his blade pressing against the dip in my throat. A sting writhes through me, warm blood beginning to seep down my skin. Sweat immediately builds down my back, the blood rushing through my veins, but not in the way it was before. "W-what are you doing?"

"I said shut your eyes." His voice is low, soft, as if he's lulling a child to sleep. "It'll be over soon, princess."

It could be over, all of it. I can escape this life, this burden. I can just shut my eyes and join the Entity's welcome arms, join my parents, my brother. Let Adora rule Prithan until the next in line is found. It isn't my problem anymore; all I can do is shut my eyes. I can be selfish and let go.

No.

The voice in my head is loud.

No. Don't give in.

You are the queen of Prithan, and you will not give in.

His knees are on my shoulder, my arms are at my sides. But if I can hook my legs around him, somehow get the knife away from my neck, then I have a chance of beating him.

I thrust my hips up, managing to get my knee to land in the center of his back. And it works. He jumps, the knife becoming loose in his hand. With his movement, my hand wriggles from his grasp and I sneak it through, grabbing the front of his shirt, slamming him down on the bed, switching positions so now I'm on top, his fearful eyes staring up at me as I hold the very same knife to his throat.

My eyes burn bright, my heart hammering in my chest. It's him, it has always been him.

He tips his neck back. He's ready, he wants me to do it. I could, I could slice the skin, or call for him to be arrested. Azra might understand, but she would feel pressure to go to war. Her only son may be a murderer, but he's her only son, and only heir to Turkish Arabia until he remarries.

My breathing becomes harsh. I urge myself to try, to slide the knife across his skin, but I can't. Only frustrated tears come out.

I jump off him, stabbing the knife into the frame of my bed instead, the metal singing. The prince stares at me, sitting up on his elbows, confusion flashing across his face. His eyes flicker with realization? Remorse? Both?

"I trusted you..." The words come out more like a pained whisper. I don't want to cry, but my cheeks are wet. My heart aches so much I feel as if my chest can't take it anymore, as if I'm going to implode. My sobs tear through me, my body aching, my heart bleeding.

I can't stay here, can't look at him. I quickly turn, running before he can even say another word.

"You know..." I start taking steps away, hoping my words will break his heart like his actions broke mine. "Your parents deserve a better son than you."

He shudders, a faulting expression cast across his face. I scoop down and grab my boots, lifting my skirts, and storm off, leaving him with only the sea, the sand, and the dusk as company.

In the distance, Magnús is slowly stalking from where he has been watching, close enough to see me and check I am safe, far enough to not hear. He watches with a keen eye as the prince sulks away, giving me a small nod of acknowledgment before allowing me my space once again.

CHAPTER TWENTY-TWO

Björn has taken the chair across from me in the study, a pipe between his lips that he inhales lightly, blowing out some smoke now and again. His eyes are locked on me opposite him, the desk and papers between us. I cough as some of it wafts over to me, swatting the mist as my lungs contract at the scent. It's floral, ashy. I think he's smoking tea leaves.

Hui San is on a chair beside him. She looks marvelous as always, her hair pulled back, youth lining her cheeks. Koen leans on the windowsill, occasionally peering over my study before his eyes find me again.

When he first stepped into the room, his eyes had fallen to the bandage on the side of my neck. For a moment, he had reached for it, but quickly took his hand back, exchanging regular greetings with me instead before taking his place.

Hui San's eyes had fallen to it. Björn chose not to acknowledge, which I was thankful for.

"So, let me get this straight." Björn clears his throat, taking another drag from his pipe before blowing the smoke out into the room. "You *think* you've got the electricity?"

I sigh. *Entity give me strength.* "As I said," I begin, irritated, "I think Prithan has electricity, but it will take some time to confirm."

Björn gives off a small groan of annoyance, casting a glare to Koen that I don't exactly understand.

"Koen, will you leave us?" Björn finally remarks, a panicked look crossing the prince's face before he stands from his perch, hesitantly leaving, casting a look that sends an icy shiver down my spine—a warning. He bows his head before shutting the door behind him, the lock clicking in the strange emptiness of the room.

"You two are close friends, are you not?" Björn begins. "Koen speaks very highly of you."

I frown at the question. It feels strangely intimate. "Uh, yes." I swallow. "We grew up together for a time. On an island south of the mainland."

"The botanical island?" Björn raises a brow. A small stake goes through my chest, a pang of anxiety. Not many people know the island well enough to call it by name. It's a small paradise, a hidden heaven.

I nod once, keeping my eyes locked on him. The hairs on my arm begin to rise.

"A beautiful place, I imagine," Hui San says, leaning forwards and giving a small smile, one that feels comforting – not as threatening as Björn's demeanor.

"Yes," I answer, looking at her directly so I don't have to peer at Björn much longer. It feels as if his eyes will burn into my skin. "It's home to me."

"Now, tell me, Queen Thornton," Björn interrupts, his voice booming. He leans forward, taking another puff from that bloody pipe. "Is it true you have some Camellia Sinensis saplings there?"

Camella Sinensis, commonly known as the plant that grows tea. Collective territory.

"Yes," I say, trying to remain professional. "The Eden archives have an array of plant matter and saplings. I believe Camella Sinensis is included in that," I say lightly. "I'd have to contact the supervising officer of the project to be sure." I know the plant is there. My conversation with Azra basically confirmed it.

I just need the tea, more than the Eden Project has. I need the Collective's tea. I need to help my people.

"Interesting." Björn leans back in his chair.

He casts a glance at Hui San before turning back to me with his sharp eyes. "Our deal was plain. No electricity, no tea."

"I know. However—" I reach down to my desk for the designs my papa had stored in his chest. "I have these."

Björn holds his hand up flat to stop me. "No."

I raise a brow, "Excuse me?"

"The Collective wants electricity. That is the only way you will be getting your hands on the tea, your majesty."

"Electricity is powerful, it is unknown," I breathe, frustration building inside me. "I don't know how it could be transported or produced. I can't trade it yet because I don't know *how*." I take a breath. "I will as soon as I can. I promise."

"No electricity now, no tea now," Hui San repeats from beside Björn. At least she has some guilt in her eyes. He just keeps his glare keen. With the lack of sleep and the heartache, it is hard not to cry. I just want a break. Two minutes alone to cry.

"Please, just listen." I bring the plans out, spreading the paper across the desk in front of me. It piques their attention, and both lean forward, sharing a look. "As a promise of my good intention, take these. I believe they can help make farming more effective," I explain. "I want this to be our first trade, just to tide us over with enough tea until I can safely and effectively get the electricity to you." My voice shakes. I'm desperate. I just want my people safe, happy, healthy. I want them to not just survive, but live. They're not even surviving at the moment. Not without that tea.

Hui San reaches in the pocket of her white dress, bringing out a small pair of glasses, holding them to her eyes as she peers over the paper. Even Björn has stopped glaring at me to look at the fine lines, the images and notes of the scroll.

My hands shake in the silence. Maybe they are thinking about it, perhaps they're going to accept.

"How is it powered?" Hui San asks.

"Electricity, I believe. Which I would transfer to you as soon as possible," I reply, not missing a beat. My heart hammers as sweat builds on my back. I feel both shrouded in heat and cold at the same time, a small sickness building in the pit of my stomach.

Björn finally looks up, raising a brow, "How long have you had these?" he asks sternly, leaning back in his chair, crossing one leg over the other as he takes another puff from his pipe.

"I only recently found out about them," I say, and it's the truth.

"One might interpret this as Prithan trying to take over our business," he continues. A shiver runs down my spine like ice. "A threat," he then says.

Björn quickly nods towards the bandage around my neck. I resist the urge to reach for it self-consciously. My skin stings where the cut is, heart aching with the memory.

"Seems like someone wants you dead, Queen Thornton," he states, then smiles. A crooked smile with sin and murder hiding there. "And you seem to only want to make that list longer."

Suddenly the room feels far smaller, the walls slowly moving in and crushing each of my bones at a time, the cracking ringing in my ears. Each breath becomes haggard, labored. I slowly guide my hand between my skirts, clutching the handle of the dagger on my thigh, the metal warm from being on my skin for hours. I grasp it tight until my knuckles ache, ready to unsheathe it at any moment.

"I only found out about it mere hours ago. I vow upon the Entity, I'm not lying," I speak. I have to breathe. I have to keep the room. I cannot let them take the high ground. I cannot let them take the power. I try to keep my voice steady, sit up straight. Mother would tell me to not let them win, to not let them take control. I can almost hear her voice now, ordering me to raise myself above them. "Look, I've told you what I know. I'm offering you something that could revolutionize your business. Take it or leave it. But I will get that tea, mark my words."

Björn rises to his feet, his fist reaching across the table, grasping me by my neck, his fingers digging into the already tender flesh. "We will give you the benefit of the doubt. Perhaps your parents are behind these things. These plans will be leaving with us. The electricity will be leaving with us. If I get even the hint of intention from you to produce tea, I will bathe in your blood, your majesty," he whispers, those icy eyes alight with fire and rage.

"I could have you executed for this," I reply in a whisper, letting my eyes trail over his features.

"But you won't. Because if you do that, you can kiss the tea goodbye. And watch your people die. First of disease, and then through war."

"Björn," Hui San says sternly, then speaks some words in a language I can't place. As if it gathers words from various nations, putting them together into a new tongue. Whatever she says makes him stiffen, loosen on his grip around my throat, and sit back in his seat, continuing to smoke his pipe.

I rise fully, standing over them. The pain in my throat a fuel for the anguish within me. I feel like a ball of fire is growing inside my chest, ready to explode at any moment. All it'll take is a little more fuel.

"Lay your hands on me again," I say boldly, "and you won't have hands. Cer i grafu."

The two stare at me, clueless by my words.

"Get out," I translate. It comes out as an order. Back straight, looking down at them. I'm in charge. I rule this queendom, this room. They may have an empire, but they're on *my* land.

Both stand, filing out the room in silence, the final waft of smoke trailing after them. The door shuts, and

I'm left alone. What just happened? Oh Entity, what have I done? There's no way I'm getting the tea now.

And I also think Björn just threatened my life. I reach for my throat, carefully rubbing the skin. It feels hot, sore. I don't think it is infected, simply abused.

I find myself in the ballroom, this time enjoying the emptiness and hollowness of the room. I sit on the floor at the far side, clutching a bottle of brandy in my grasp, sipping it. The fiery liquid slides down my throat and warms the cockles of my soul.

Entity, what am I going to do? How am I going to get tea?

I lift the bottle, taking another swig. Truth be told, I'd meant to grab the whiskey when I'd snuck into the kitchen, but in a panic of the cook coming around the corner, I'd grabbed whatever was closest and ran. Which is stupid. I'm queen—it's not as if she would have said anything. She probably would have passed me a glass and some cheese to go with it.

The ballroom, without all the people and music and food, is surprisingly blissful. Simple. I'd chosen the room because I figured it would be quiet. And it has delivered, plus more. My little corner is comfortable, warm. The perfect place to realize I fucked up.

The doors open, Chione striding in. Like a goddess. It isn't fair. How could the Entity make someone so beautiful and leave the rest of us to suffer? She's chosen to wear simple clothes, as she normally does, her hijab matching.

"Someone said you were in here." She smiles as she wanders in, a slight skip in her step. She sits beside me, looking over the emptiness of the ballroom.

"What can I do for you, princess?" I ask, motioning towards the bottle, offering her some.

"I can't, but thank you." She smiles. "I came to tell you how good you were this morning in training."

I offer her a shy smile, a blush rushing to my cheeks. "Really? Thank you." A warm feeling runs through me. It could be the alcohol or the compliment. Or both. I'm not going to complain.

Chione nods at the brandy. "You alright?" she asks with a quizzical brow.

I move my gaze back to the bottle, taking another glug, resting my head against the wall behind me and shutting my eyes. "Are you asking as a princess of a fellow nation, or as a friend?" I glance over at her.

Chione casts me a small smile, placing her hand over mine. "Which would you prefer?"

I lean my head over, resting it on her shoulder. "A friend would be nice." I sigh. "I've never had a friend, well, not a female one."

Chione chuckles lightly, resting her head on mine.

"Tell me then, friend. What bothers you?"

Again, maybe it's because of the alcohol, or maybe it's because of the day, or maybe because I feel safe in the arms of Princess El Sayed. I tell her everything. I tell her about being dragged from my bed at sixteen, about the marriage, about saying goodbye to Papa, about the assassin and Magnús, about my shared intimacies with the prince, about what it was like having his blade to my throat. About what our parents were doing, about the electricity, the machinery, how Björn just had his hands clasped around my neck.

She says nothing, listens to each word carefully, occasionally nodding or squeezing my hand, just letting me talk. It feels like hours. My jaw hurts from my words, my heart aches, and my cheeks are streaked with yet more damned tears.

Eventually, when I feel there is nothing more I can say, no more strokes of the brush I can use to paint my story, Chione finally speaks. Her mother tongue, words I don't know. I peer up, wondering what she said.

A small smile dances on her lips. "Trusting men, dear Lorilynn, is like trusting water in a sieve."

I peer up at her a moment and let out the clearest laugh I have in days, one that is as crisp as water, and as fresh as the greenest grass on the botanical island. Suddenly, the tears and heartache don't matter. Just for a moment, they mean nothing. Chione laughs too, still resting her head on mine as I lay on her shoulder. It's nice.

"Have you thought about forming an alliance?" she asks gently. "Getting support in this situation? Having a relationship with a country based solely around the situation Prithan is in?"

I sigh heavily. "I mean, Prithan has alliances. It's why you're all here." I swallow the lump in my throat. "If I'm being honest, I don't know what I'm doing. I never anticipated being queen this young. I never received the training. I'm not sure how it works."

"Asking for help is alright. You're no less strong for doing so," she says. "Have you ever heard of a union of allegiance?" She keeps her voice gentle.

I shake my head.

"It's somewhat like a marriage..." she begins.

I raise a brow. "I've only just gotten divorced."

Chione chuckles. "I said *somewhat* like a marriage. It's a platonic union between two royals to join their countries in an alliance. Unlike marriage, the countries remain as separate states, however. They wouldn't become an empire, just stay connected. It is only broken by the death of a participant."

"Is this you proposing then?" I ask.

She smiles and gives a small nod. "You have Ptah as a friend—you have *me* as a friend. If you wish."

I finally turn to her, look her face over. "I'd like that." I smile. "What now? Do I kiss you or give you a ring or something?" I joke.

Chione laughs. "I don't think my wife would be too pleased about that. A hug is just fine."

"Do you wish to talk to the sultan first? Check if he is alright with it?"

"My father trusts me," she says. "He knows I always do what is best for Ptah... for the world. Which is why I have a condition to our allegiance."

I peer up at her, frowning. What could Prithan have that Ptah could possibly need?

"You have the means to take power away from the Collective," she says. "If you do it, Ptah will be right beside you," she promises.

"I told Queen Khan I was giving the technology to the Collective," I say. "We might not have Turkish Arabia's support."

Chione listens. "Perhaps, but if years of work have gone into it, I doubt Queen Khan would argue too much. She'd probably be overjoyed."

I take a deep breath, then another swig of the brandy. "Would you be able to share your tea supply stores with Prithan until we're producing enough? I have an epidemic on my hands, an issue I have to deal with now."

"Of course. I will write to my father tonight." She pauses a moment. "Does that mean you accept the proposal?"

I peer up at her with a smirk. "Do I have to wear white?"

Chione laughs a beautiful laugh, her head falling backwards. "Only if you want to, Thornton."

•

The ceremony is not what I expect it to be. We go to the beach with her guards and stand by the sea, using a knife to slice across our palms, grasping each other's hands so we become one unit. We speak together, a vow that doesn't marry us, but our countries.

"I vow, as long as I live, to be the voice of our nations as they are unified as one. To fight under your flag, to protect our lands, to work as one, to be allies until my last breath." For the last line, we speak different things. I say, "This I vow upon the Entity." She says something I don't know the translation for. We smile, our eyes going to the horizon, and suddenly the world doesn't seem so lonely.

CHAPTER TWENTY-THREE

The sun begins setting. We sit with bandages carefully wrapped around our palms as hues of orange seep through the cracks of dusk. Her guards sit with us, breaking bread and smiling. We talk, and she tells me about Ptah. About her father, the sultan, her mother, and her siblings. The brother who held Prince Khan's heart.

She tells me of her wife, Amna. They met when Chione was my age, five years ago. Amna was working as a cook, and the two fell in love. Despite the backlash of her not being of noble birth, they got married. The two were meant to come to Prithan together, but she chose to stay after a friend fell ill.

"You must be excited to see each other again," I say. "Do you miss her?"

Chione smiles sadly out to the ocean, a deep sigh leaving her. "I miss her so much it's as if my body has no heart when we are apart."

A small spike of jealousy fills me. I wonder what it's like to love someone like that, to give someone your soul fully without fear. To love someone so much you never want to be apart from them.

I look out at the sea, the calm. I wonder if that is was love is like—tranquility. I wonder if that is what Adora feels when he looks at Ed, or what Mags feels when he looks at Heather. I wonder if I'll ever feel like that again.

"I should go find Queen Khan," I say, standing from the sand. "See if she's interested in reuniting our ideas despite the fact I divorced her son and threatened to kill him."

Chione looks up at me with careful eyes. "Are you going to tell her what he did?" she asks.

I nod. "Azra will keep him in check and me safe," I say. "I trust her."

"Let me know if I can do anything," she replies, and I walk back to Snowflake, climbing on his back and trotting to the castle, enjoying the quiet. I don't feel the alcohol anymore, only the cold pinching my skin.

Once inside, it takes twenty minutes to find the queen. I search her chambers, the gardens, then a maid tells me she's in the music room. What would have been nice is if she'd mentioned the prince was there too.

I step in, greeted by the sweeping sound of violin strings dancing through the air. I peer around. Azra sits relaxed on a chair as he stands a few feet away, playing a melody I don't recognize. It's beautiful. He looks tired still, his skin a tinge of gray. The usual shine his hair has is gone. When I step in, his eyes meet mine a moment, before quickly flicking away, fingers continuing to work the strings of the instrument.

Azra casts me a smile, patting the seat beside her.

"Lorilynn," she says calmly. "Come, sit. Enjoy the music."

"Actually..." I begin, nervously flattening my skirts, wanting to get this over with, but I cannot quite find the words just yet. I swallow the scattered thoughts of my brain and take the seat, my eyes falling to the prince as he continues to play.

I would never admit it, but there is a tug at my heart at hearing the music. I have to blink away some tears. Apparently, the prince doctor also spared time to master music.

"When he first came home, he felt shy. Wouldn't speak a word to us," she starts, keeping her eyes locked on him with motherly admiration. "Until one day, Taylan and I heard the most beautiful sound. We followed it to the music room, and there he was, playing away on this violin that was far too big for him." She smiles softly to herself. "We spent the next nine hours watching him. After that, he began opening up to us." A longing sigh escapes her. "Every time I hear him work the strings, I'm taken back to those happy memories."

Azra's love for her son shines bright in her like the sun must shine in her lands. It's admirable. She warned me about him, warned me not to trust him, so she knows he could have hurt me, yet she loves him anyway. Perhaps so much the flaws don't matter. I wonder if I could love a child like that— wonder if Mother loved *me* like that.

Eventually the song finishes, and for a moment, silence blankets us again. I take it as my opportunity to finally speak, get back to business.

"Azra, can I speak with you privately?" I ask, leaning over to her and keeping my voice down, as if that'll stop the prince from listening.

She casts a glance between the two of us, nodding. The prince waits a moment as we both peer at him before realizing he needs to leave, then places the violin down and wanders out. Except as his hand reaches for the door, landing on the gold knob, we are all stunned by the echo of ringing bells.

Bells only chime on two occasions. Weddings and danger.

There is no wedding today.

•

"Any estimate on the current number of dead?"

We storm down the castle halls, Mags, myself, and the castle head of guards, Joan. Adora also keeps in stride behind us, taking in every piece of information being exchanged between the three of us. Maids and servants and guards bustle around. Suddenly the demeanor they have upheld for weeks has vanished, replaced the hurrying and fear.

I hadn't believed it when they told me.

A boy from the village had sprinted to the castle with the news, blood soaking his shirt, tears streaming down his rosy cheeks. He'd stormed into the entrance of the castle, declaring loudly that there was an invasion, pirates were in the village. Adora had heard, and while many had hesitated, he immediately rang the bell, bringing us all together. And then things havn't stopped. The first company of guards have already been sent out—another is about to go with Joan. A third will be leaving soon after. But that is all we have. Guards. The soldiers are on Skye, my decision is biting me in the ass as I was warned it would. Except my people are dying because of it.

"We can't be sure yet," Mags answers, "but expect the casualty list to be high."

I give a stern nod, regret and fear rippling through me like a snake. We keep moving—now isn't the time to stop. Now is time to protect my castle, my people, and the guests of the crown.

"Set up a pop-up medical station in the ballroom to treat who we can until they're stable enough to be transferred to a hospital," I order. "Get whatever you need. Rip up bedsheets, open the bottles of my father's antique spirits. Anything we can spare to help."

Adora nods from behind us. "I'll deal with that after escorting you to your chambers."

I stop in my tracks, the small group stopping with me. I turn to him, a frown shrouding my features. "I won't be hiding in my chambers, Adora," I explain. "I intend to fight alongside my people."

"You cannot be serious." He scoffs, eyes looking over my face. "You're queen."

I stare deeply into his eyes. "Exactly. I'm queen."

For a moment, the four of us stand still as statues, waiting for Adora to continue his argument. But after a moment, he gives a small nod.

He swallows. "I'm going to be furious if you die," he murmurs. "I'll resurrect you to kill you myself."

"I'd expect nothing less." I shoot him a small smile.

He wraps his arms around me a moment in front of everyone. While it is no secret I am close to my adoptive uncles, it generally is frowned upon showing said affection. But fuck that now. I hold him tight as he plants a tender kiss on my forehead. Then he whispers words softly in his mother tongue. I've never heard him speak Nilo-Saharan. In fact, I had suspected he'd forgotten it. Yet the words leave his mouth like a blessing. Before I can ask what the meaning is, he's away in the other direction, already ordering maids for preparations. He'll sort things out, and every inch of worry I have about leaving the castle vanishes. Adora will handle it, no matter what.

Joan clears her throat, saying, "I'll ride with the second company. We'll work on helping remove the injured and innocent, taking them to safety."

Joan and I haven't truly ever spoken. She's always been present in my life. Age lines her face, her blonde is beginning to gray, yet her eyes are young and filled with a strength I can only hope to possess.

I hold out my hand which she firmly shakes in hers. "Thank you," I speak.

"Your majesty." She gives a quick nod. "You have my sword until my dying day." A vow, a promise that knights usually made to their queen at coronation. One that we haven't had yet. I look her over, squeezing her hand a moment before she quickly runs, a guard meeting the woman and passing her a sword as they head to the armory. Next time I see her will be in battle. My first battle.

My heart begins hammering in my chest, fear rushing through me. I could die, I could get hurt. People *will* die. I'll probably kill again.

"Go get your armor on," Magnús says to me, taking my head in his hands. "We have to hurry."

It is ready in my chambers when I run in. Efa hurriedly helps remove my dress, slipping the under leathers and clothes on, quickly placing the armor overtop. She runs a brush through my hair, rapidly braiding it so it isn't in my face, pinning a bun at the base of my head so it doesn't hang loose down my back.

I look in the mirror a moment, at who I am. And despite the fear that pools like blood in my stomach, or the clammy sweat that already builds on my palms, I know this is where I want to be. And if I die, I die. I would be proud to fall among these men and women, to protect what I love.

Efa places a hand on my shoulder. "Entity guide you," she says softly in Ghaldeig. "There is one final thing." The maid retrieves a small box wrapped with black ribbon. She opens it, revealing a simple silver headband, a single sapphire positioned to sit in the center of my forehead. She raises it, resting it on my head. It fits perfectly like a halo, snug and secure but not tight. I feel complete, like a queen. A queen fighting with her country.

Magnús smiles as he sees me, handing over a great sword of glinting silver, gold inlays in the handle. My father's sword.

I balance the blade in my hand, getting used to the feel in my grip before sheathing it. And then we begin the walk, each step of my shoes echoing along the stone floor as he follows behind. As we stride, everyone we pass stops, bowing their heads, mouths forming an 'O' shape.

I've gone from being a sickly princess to a queen walking to potentially die for her people.

Magnús takes his place beside me, and my other side is soon occupied by Chione, who only hours ago had vowed to protect my country as her own. She has her armor on, a curved sword at her side and a hijab the color of Prithan's flag tied around her hair. My heart warms at the companionship.

I give each of them a nod before striding through the lobby, both at my sides. A small group of people have gathered. Maids, servants. The prince. He pauses as he sees us, and for a moment, our eyes meet. And then he falls to a knee, bowing his head low. Soon enough, others do too, and I lift my gaze forward, walking out into the hammering rain to where Snowflake waits, saddled and ready. I climb onto him in one swoop, grasping the reins. The last squad of guards rides up. I urge Snowflake forward, encouraging him to build speed as we race across the roads I have walked many times. Perhaps that'll be my final time seeing them. Again, I won't regret that.

Wind sweeps through my hair, strays flaying as they escape my braid. My heart thumps with every gallop, teeth chattering. Fear writhes through me. This is what sacrifice is. Understanding you could pay the ultimate price but still go forth. My death would mean a new age for Prithan completely. In all honesty, it won't bother me if I'm rotting in the ground or ash in the wind. Another person's problem. My burdens currently are the invaders, shielding my people, and defending the guests who are under my protection.

As we approach the village, screams, cries, and the clash of swords are already audible as well as the rich, copper stench of blood consuming my senses. I clamber down off Snowflake, immediately propelling myself into the town square.

My heart drops, breathing coming to a sudden halt. On the ground, my soldiers fight and clash with these pirates. There are so many of the enemy alive. And so many Prithan soldier's dead. Streams of blood snake into the dirt, mangled bodies lie disfigured among the rubble of this village I so cared for. Blue Prithan cloth mixed with the liquid red.

One of their heads—*a head*—rolls forward. He's a guard I've often seen around the castle. A young man, maybe twenty or twenty-one, with hair like midnight sky and eyes gray as the moon. A smiler. Someone who would always try to make everyone happy. Even me. He would grin until his bright eyes crinkled at the corners, saying hello to everyone. But now those bright eyes stare at me, empty. Dead. Nothing. Just nothingness.

"I-I can't do this, Mags. We can't win. Too many are dead," I breathe. My hands have turned numb with fear. I can't even feel the cold nipping the ends of my fingers anymore. The third and final group of guards gallantly ride out, screaming battle cries, fearlessly defending their queen and country. Brave. And I just sit on my horse, watching pirates cut them down, destroy them, ruin them. Turn them from people into mounds of flesh, bone, and sinew.

Every time I see one of them die, I feel more stuck where I am. Like wax is keeping us where we are. I need to die today. I need to die with these people, my people. It's time I accept that.

Magnús clambers down from his own horse, placing a supportive hand on my shoulder. "You are queen of Prithan, Lorilynn," he says. "You are untouchable. This is your land, your people. Not theirs." He places a single hand on my cheek, fingers already cold against the warmth of my skin. "You have my sword until my dying day."

I take his hand in mine, giving it one single squeeze before clasping my father's blade in my grip and ploughing towards a group of pirates tormenting a female villager. There is a particularly tall, burly one and I don't think twice as I slice my sword across his back, metal crunching against bone. His blood showers as he cries out, splattering on my skin, the armor. The villager is covered in it has it pours from him like forbidden wine. Soon enough, he falls to his knees, color having left his skin and flesh raw and gaping. I offer a bloodied hand to the villager and help them to their feet, watching them look at me a moment with wide eyes before running towards the castle.

I don't have the time to check if they make it before a hand grasps my waist, flinging me into the mud. I land in a heap with a thud, a split of pain shooting up my side at the collision with the ground, the impact compressing the air from my lungs.

Breathe, Lorilynn. Breathe, I urge myself, just managing to get oxygen into me in time to roll away and avoid a sword to the face. My assailant is raising their blade, ready to plunge it into my side when I just about grasp my own, blocking their attack. The woman lets out an angered scream, her tangled hair flying through the air as she attempts again, but I'm quick. She falters. I'm on my feet, keeping my weapon in my grip as she clashes yellow teeth as if she can scare me away. Soon our swords are together, faces inches apart as she attempts to overpower and knock the weapon from my hand. I stand my ground, putting all I can into keeping balance and strong.

"I will be the last thing you see, princess," she spits in an accent I can't place. Her anger and determination are focused on my face, so she isn't prepared when I kick one of the feet from under her, knocking her to the ground. I raise my sword, casting it into the soft flesh of her stomach.

Blood oozes, pained screams leaving her as crazed eyes search my face, trying to undo time, her mistake. I take my sword from where it protrudes from her body.

"It's queen," I say down to her as the last whisp of life leaves her body and she falls limp. I stare down at her lifeless corpse for a moment, waiting for the regret, remorse, horror I felt when I first killed that assassin. But there is nothing. I suppose it gets easier each time.

•

Time stops existing after a while. No longer do I feel the hours, but rather the ache in my arms. I'm not dead... yet. Many are though. And we are not done. Considering these raiders came in on a ship there seems to be an endless supply.

Sunset has begun, the familiar orange hue starting to shroud the dusk, glimmering over the ocean in the distance. Chione found me eventually, battling a particularly large man. She beheaded him swiftly. I can still taste his blood on my tongue. The two of us crouch behind a cart of hay, hiding to catch our breath while a small group of the invaders stalk around a courtyard. Both of us are exhausted. The ache in our muscles burns and my lungs feel tight. And my soul... my soul is bruised. I can feel it beginning to crack. I have watched too many of my people fade away, their guts laid out in front of them.

I look Chione's face over. She looks mine, and for the first time, I see her falter. We don't know if we're going to make it out of this alive.

Voices slowly come closer. Perhaps we have about thirty seconds until they find us. We might win, we might not. No one else is in sight. Chione's men are helping get survivors to safety, Magnús is cutting down a group of them attempting to break into a house last I saw him. I wish I could say goodbye.

It is just us, just two tired women with a smidge of hope and some spare prayers. What a waste; we could have had an amazing future. Our nations could have had amazing prospects. I painfully shut my eyes, tears falling for the future this world might never get. I'm surprised to see Chione crying too, streams forming down the blood sprays on her cheeks.

"For Ptah," I whisper to her, taking her hand in mine for a moment and squeezing once.

"For Prithan," she whispers back, and then we stand. Ready to fall for what is right. Ready to fall. I'm going to see my parents... my brother.

Except as we do, three figures appear from the shadows. Three faces. First is Mags, his eyes alight. Then Koen, dressed in armor, his hair a mess, blood and dirt across half his face. And then the prince, armored, the seal of Prithan on his breastplate. The three of them are like fire consuming wood, painlessly ending the pirates' lives before they realize the queen of Prithan and a princess of Ptah were near them.

I shut my eyes as rain patters on my face. My knees give way with the relief, and I fall into the dirt, letting the mud soak my leathers and cool the blisters on my palms.

It isn't over.

The prince approaches, blood from his sword pooling in a puddle. I look up at him, much like I looked up at him when he held a knife to my throat, but now he holds a hand out instead.

"It isn't over yet, princess," he says, the rain becoming heavier around us. I want it to be over, I want it to be finished. But I can't give in yet.

I reach up, taking his palm in mine, and he pulls me to my feet. I shoot him one single nod as I stride to Mags.

"Have we got as many out as we can?" I ask him.

He swallows. "I can't find her," he says so quietly, so fearfully. "I can't find Heather."

I look my uncle's face over, the soft lines of his usual frown, desperation that leeches from his features. I have been so angered by my selfishness, I never thought of him. He deserves love, happiness. He has fought hard.

I reach for the undershirt I have on, grasping a scrap of it and ripping the fabric into a strip, taking it and wrapping the cloth around the harsh blisters on my palm. Then I take my sword, ignoring the stinging as I grasp it tight.

I catch his gaze. "Then let's go get her."

CHAPTER TWENTY-FOUR

Koen and Chione are tasked with going to the beach to see who is left, to try and figure out where the boat is that they arrived on. Mags, the prince, and I stalk towards the bakery, taking out a few stray invaders as we do.

The chaos has died down now. No one moves but us. Anybody that lies on the ground is just that, a body. A shell. May they be with their Gods.

We prowl silently through the raw graveyard. My eyes wander over the ground, the blood, the barbaric nature of everything. I hope I never see a sight like this again. Never see my people dead, their memories lost forever. Some I recognize, faces forever imprinted on my brain. Other's I don't. Guilt consumes me. Who were they? Were they my people? Even when I feast my eyes upon the deceased pirates, shame swirls inside me. Was I the cause of their last moment of agony?

Perhaps not, but I killed many. There is no denying that.

Soon, the bakery comes into view. The windows have been smashed and there is a dismembered arm hanging from the broken glass.

Fuck.

My heart drops at the sight of it. I peer at Magnús's face, the horror painting it. We're too far to see if the arm is possibly Heather's. Fear radiates like heat from him. His eyes are filled only with desperate determination, the hope that his love still breathes.

The three of us crouch on the ground as we make our approach, peering to see through the shattered window. The bakery features a congregation of pirates and captured villagers. They are huddled in the center, mouths gagged and hands tied behind their backs. The captors tower above, taunting them. One particularly large man with a pipe between his teeth traces the tip of his sword across the tanned throat of a woman I recognize, one I haven't seen for a time.

Tears streak down Heather's cheeks, blood matted in her hair as she lets out a muffled cry. But then it is as if the Entity guides her, and she goes still as her eyes meet my uncle's as we poke our heads out. Her features relax slightly at the sight of him.

At seeing her, a small sob escapes Mags, his sword beginning to shake in his hand. I gently place my own on his arm. "Be strong, Uncle," I say in Icelandic and place my hand over his heart. "Be fierce and strong and love will protect her."

"And who will protect me?" he asks with a small, scared, smile.

"I will," I murmur with a tight smile. "I'll protect you."

Magnús gives a strained chuckle and leans forward, planting a quick kiss on my forehead. He is tense, sweat collecting at his brow. I don't think I've ever seen him like this before, so scared to lose something. And I know it isn't his own life he fears losing—it's Heather's. He loves her. With a kind of love I so wished my parents shared. With a love that Adora has for Ed. With a love I thought maybe I could share with the prince in due time. But now it is not the moment to dwell on that. It is a love that I have wrongfully restricted,

"How are we doing this?" the prince quietly from where he is crouched behind us. We both analyze the situation, counting the various pirates and exits.

"Alright, how about her majesty and I go straight in," Mags starts. "Your highness," he says and turns to the prince, "go through the back, just in case we need you. That way if it goes tits up you can help get the villagers out."

I nod in agreement, as does the prince. Magnús begins moving carefully, and just as I am about to join him, the prince's hand grasps my wrist.

I turn to face him, still keeping out of sight.

"Be careful, your majesty," he says, his deep eyes searching my face with wide desperation.

"And you too, Prince Khan," I reply, standing up with Mags as the two of us walk towards the bakery.

The captured villagers vocalize with relived sighs at the sight of us. Many are injured. And I'm also pretty sure one of them is dead—the man's skin is a greenish color, his eyes glazed over, and the gag in his mouth somewhat slipping.

I'm sorry. Another one I failed.

At the sight of us, the pirates raise their swords until a crooked old man limps forward. His voice is rough like charcoal, a deep throaty sound that makes me think he desperately needs a doctor.

"Let them in," he croaks, and the two of us step into the disheveled bakery. Broken glass cracks underfoot with each step. The usual joy of the establishment has been replaced with pure chaos. Counters are a mess, instead of delicate loaves of bread and pastries and cakes, there are empty baskets and flour poured over. Years of building warmth, gone in a matter of seconds.

The man who spoke perches on a chair at the side. He looks well into age, perhaps his sixties. His skin is wrinkled, eyes dark, light hair matted. He has a cigar between his teeth, the smoke billowing out, replacing the usual smell of fresh cinnamon rolls with tobacco.

"If it isn't the queen of Prithan herself," he says, teasing layering his voice as he leans back in his chair, resting his head against the wall. "We figured that this might get your attention. Although, I half-expected you to send your best guards." The pirate stands and gives a small bow, somewhat mockingly. When he peers up at the rest of his crew who just stare at me, he sends them a sharp glare. "Bow, everyone. Bow. We are in the presence of a queen."

There is a small grumble from the crew, but they all lower themselves somewhat. It feels embarrassing, humiliating. A mockery of my title, my land, of my people who lay dying around us.

"My name is Captain Francois." He holds a wrinkled hand out. "But you can call me Jacob."

I will *not* be calling him Jacob.

I hesitate before taking the hand and giving it a shake. He grins a mouth of white teeth, offering a cigar from his jacket. I firmly shake my head to which he then offers Magnús one. He too denies the captain's offer.

Captain Francois saunters back to his little chair and sits, picking up a half-eaten loaf of bread, and bites into it. Heather cringes a little at the sight of the last piece being demolished by a man with blood in his eyebrow. She has watched her entire life being destroyed in front of her eyes.

"Your quarrel is with me, captain," I say, making sure I do not let the exhaustion shine through my voice. "Not my people. Let them leave so that we can sort this misunderstanding out between the two of us. No one else has to die."

Captain Francois takes a deep drag from his cigar, flicking the ash onto the ground. "Says the woman with my crew's blood on her face," he says, eyeing me up. I don't even know how I look, how much blood is on me, how much of it is mine, and how much is others. The captain flicks his half-burned cigar to the ground, pushing the browned stick under his heavy boot. "So you're here in good nature?"

"I'm here for my people. To end their suffering. No tricks. I just want them safe and healing."

I am exhausted enough to give him what he wants in exchange, but I don't mutter those words. I will at least pretend I have some strength, even if it is a lie.

"No tricks?" he says, a smirk appearing on his lips.

"No tricks," I repeat.

There is a pause of silence, where for a moment it feels as if only the captain and I are in the room.

"A lesson, dear queen..." the captain begins, "pirates are all about trickery. We make no promises of honor." He gives a single nod, and then the blow comes.

I don't see who it does, but the impact is bright on the back of my head. I feel it vibrate through my neck, my spine. My knees crumple under me as warm blood trickles from my hairline.

And then the sound starts, like a ringing that is both deafening and silent. I can't focus as it chimes so loudly in my skull, as if someone is shaking a bell only some centimeters away. Yet there is no one.

Everything seems so bright, and nausea hits me like a violent wave. If I had something in my stomach, I would be vomiting, but I haven't had anything except the brandy, which I am very much regretting now.

I blink as the pain takes over, the entire left side of my body aching. Luckily the sound dies down into a hum, and I realize that apart from it, I can hear nothing from that ear.

My heart hammers and the pain only intensifies. Heather moves forward in a bid to help me, only to have a pirate grab her wrist and lift her in a way that makes my bones ache. Then the *pop* sounds as her shoulder slips out of its socket, and she cries out, a pained sound that chills my blood.

I can feel Magnús's rage. The sound of his sword being unsheathed rings through the air as he goes to drive it through the pirate.

But then it happens, and I don't know where from.

A small dagger flies through the air, landing in his neck.

He is on the ground.

The cries shrieking through the air are mine.

I scurry over to him, ignoring how the ringing gets louder and the brightness increases as I do. I just need to be with him, to make sure he is alright. I promised to protect him. I will protect him.

I press my hands into the wound, but blood is already seeping through and bubbling between his lips. He tries speaking but only pained gurgles come out.

"Hush," I say, hands shaking as I try and control the flow of blood, tears blurring my vision. However, I see his eyes begin to flutter shut, his blond lashes resting on his cheeks.

"Open your eyes, Mags," I say, but it comes out more as a sob. "Open your eyes, and I'll train every day with you. I promise." I watch his chest rise, fall, rise, fall, rise.

"Magnús, open your eyes," I demand, more tears falling.

Rise.

Fall.

Rise.

Fall.

Nothing.

•

I'm lying down on something soft. There's that ringing noise. There are also careful voices. Hushed tones.

My head pounds. My tongue feels dry. Every part of my body aches.

Sound is still absent on one side.

Everything feels bright.

My chest feels heavy.

Magnús is dead.

"Lay still, Lynn," the voice says, feminine and hushed. A cool cloth is on my forehead. "You're in the castle," the voice continues—*she* continues.

I peel my eyes open, the light pouring in, the ceiling of the ballroom above me.

"Her head injury. She may be delirious," another voice says. Ed. It's Ed.

"Someone help her sit up." Adora. That voice belongs to Adora. He sounds scared.

Arms reach down, supporting the back of my head as I strain to reach up, peering around the room for the first time. I was right—this is the ballroom. The makeshift hospital I asked Adora to prepare. For a matter of hours, they did well. Very well. Along the wall are chairs, from plush to simple wooden ones. Most of them are taken by villages and soldiers. The ones who can sit up for themselves. The severely injured are in beds made of anything, from boxes and piled up books to sheets on the floor. People patrol with aprons and leather gloves, carrying trays and warm drinks and bandages.

The cries of the injured sound through, although, other than that, the room is quiet. Some sleep. But no one who is here is dead? I don't know where the dead are.

I finally take my gaze to myself. My armor has been removed, the bloody metal resting on the floor beside the bed. A lot of that blood belongs on Magnús. More has soaked through the clothes that I still wear, the white shirt. Even my leather trousers have stained patches.

Various eye stare at me. Adora. Ed. Someone I believe to be a medical assistant. And Heather. Her eyes are rimmed with red, skin tarnished with scarlet and bruises beginning to appear. Yet she still offers a kind smile, still holds the damp cloth to my forehead.

"How... I don't remember what happened," I say, words wisping out my throat.

"Rest, my dear." Ed crouches beside me so he is level with the makeshift bed I'm on. "Don't fret. Prithan is safe." He keeps his voice quiet, but now that my eyes are open, I struggle to piece together what has happened.

I was in the village—in the bakery.

Magnús was dying.

Now, I'm in the ballroom.

I feel as if my head is going to explode. And my heart—my heart aches.

"Perhaps I should tell her majesty what happened?" Heather says as she turns to the group. "Then she can rest without worrying."

Adora and Ed peer between themselves before nodding, assuring me they're close if I need them and heading in their own direction. There is much to be done and no point in them waiting around in my despair when there is plenty of heartache to go around.

Once it is only Heather and me, my mistakes and guilt run through my mind.

"Where is he?" I ask in a whisper.

Heather's eyes meet mine as she dips the cloth in a bowl of water, bringing it again to my head but instead of placing it against my forehead, she begins wiping away my cheeks, blood and grime soiling the white cloth, dissipating into the water as she dips again, bringing it to my cheeks once more.

"On the beach," she says simply, "for the count, and then the pyres."

So, he is dead. Magnús is definitely gone.

Another sob takes over my body. An ugly, raw sound. Tears stream down both mine and Heather's cheeks. I peer up at her with wet eyes. Her shoulder is bandaged, her arm back in place now.

I took their time away. They loved each other, and I stole their last weeks through my own pure selfishness and fear. I can never make it up to them. That love is as cold as he is. Heather is crying too, silently and far more dignified than I am, but her tears fall freely.

Why does she tend to me with such care and compassion?

"After Magnús joined the Entity, the captain took his sword and held it at me. He said he was going to paint the floor with my blood. You entered a rage—like something took over your body." Heather keeps her voice low, her eyes searching nothingness in front of her. She pauses to dip the cloth once more, but instead of bringing it to my face again, she holds in clasped in her hand, stained pink water dripping onto her skirts. "You were quick. The captain didn't see it coming. His head rolled onto the floor. You grasped it by the hair and carried with you here."

"I carried a severed head?" I barely breathe, staring at my hands.

"You threatened anyone who asked to move it." Her eyes peer over to the side of the bed. My heart starts pounding as mine follow her to where a bloodied brown sack sits beside the bed.

Fuck.

Entity forgive me.

Fuck.

"The captain's second just dropped her sword and surrendered. When we got here, you collapsed in the corridors, managed to vomit too. A doctor is on his way from the hospital, but with everything, there's a delay. You'll be seen first, as queen."

As queen. I was her queen, and I was her princess before that. But I never told her. She chose to be my friend because she wanted to be. Because she liked me, not because I was a ruler—and I've taken all that trust and turned it into heartbreak. Yet she still sits here and fills my memory.

I let my teared eyes wander the room again. Chione is across. She's alive. Good. Her hijab is smothered in blood but still so perfectly on her head. Her armor has been removed but red soaks through the underclothes as she sits at the foot of a bed, helping bandage a guard's arm. For a moment, she peers up, our eyes meeting. We share a small nod before I turn back to Heather, groaning as I move my legs to the side and try to sit up.

Where are Koen and Tariq? I hope they're unhurt. I hope they're alive. Please, Entity, let them be alive.

I hesitantly place my feet on the floor, feeling the cool stone.

"Woah, Lynn. Don't rush," Heather warns gently, holding her arms out. "There's no rush. Rest."

"The second-in-command. The new captain. Where are they?" I ask, keeping my voice low as I reach for the bloody bag with the pet head. It's heavier than I expect.

"I believe she's in the cells now," Heather says. "I think you should lie down a while longer."

"I can't just stay here when I could be so close to finding out the truth." I groan as I stand, a little wobbly on my feet at first. It's as if my balance is off, and I find myself having to take a moment before taking my first step. With the head in my hand, I ignore the outburst and arguments from Adora and Ed as I make my way through the room and out the door, stumbling over the carpeted floor to the corner of the castle I haven't been in, to the dark basement where horrors lurk, where the truth might be hiding.

CHAPTER TWENTY-FIVE

My walk to the prison is long, and my head pounds with each step. But I make it, being guided to the cell where the new captain lies unconscious. She is younger than I expected, perhaps maybe even eighteen like me. Her fire-red hair is cropped short by her ears. Her skin is rich and dark, making the fire bright.

I sit with her on the other side of the bars, still bloody, still in armor under clothes. Slowly she begins to regain consciousness. Her eyes flutter before they go wide. She tries moving, but the chains around her ankle stop it. Her face slowly trails upwards, onto me, the blood, the armor.

"Queen Lorilynn Thornton," she says, grunting as she pushes herself up, tracing a hand along the bandages up her arms and head. At some point, she took an injury too.

"Captain." I give her one nod. I reach for the bag beside me, grab onto the slimy hair, and lift the head out. Just long enough for her eyes to graze over it, for the impact to sink in. She says nothing though, does nothing, just stays still like ice in a winter's morning. I place it back in the bag and kick it away.

There's a pause as her eyes meet mine, "Burn it," she says. "I'm Captain now?"

"Not for long. You're now the leader of an invading entity. I'm going to have to have you publicly executed."

"How?"

"Hanging or beheading, depending on if you answer my questions in a way that is a benefit to me."

"And my surviving crew?"

"I'll think about that."

There are a few moments of silence. Uncomfortable, occasionally filled with a mumble, or footsteps from above, shouts or cries of men and women being treated in the hospital. The wind howls through the cells, sending a cold breeze. Despite the chill, the girl doesn't move, shudder, or shiver. Just stares at a spot on the wall behind me.

"I-I'm ready to talk. To negotiate. Please let my crew live. Take what you want from the ship, just let them live freely," she speaks. "My name is Oni."

It gives me honor; she is a good woman. A good captain. While the last had sat in his throne on high, hiding from the blood, she had wanted to die with her people. We're alike in that way. She is a queen in her own right, her queendom is just smaller. Yet it still means the world to her.

"I'll honor it if you give me what I'm due," I reply, matter of fact, plain, simple. And true.

"What do you wish to know first?"

"Why you tried to invade?"

Oni nods and readjusts herself. She sits cross-legged, running her hands through her red hair. "To kill you. But first... we were told to kill your parents on their planned sail back from Icelandic Prithan."

"Tell me what happened. Every detail," I order, my voice shaking. To know the truth, to find out what happened, is the key to everything. I need to know if there's a chance I can hold my father again.

"We waited and followed the coastline, then appeared and stalked the royal vessel over the ocean between the two pieces of land. They knew something was wrong. Took a different route, towards a northern island of Prithan."

"Skye."

"Our original plan had been to kill your parents at the docks then take the castle immediately, but we ended up having to act about two miles offshore. Going aboard, doing what needed to be done, and then heading back on our boats, cannoning the royal ship to the ocean floor.

"We then sailed around the coast, far enough for no one to see, hiding behind an island in the north until we received information to storm the castle. And that brings us here."

There is a shuffle. A guard comes down the stairs, along with a nurse. The guard carries a jug of water and a metal goblet. The nurse has more bandages. Mine are soaked in blood; they need changing. She kneels in front of me as I sit on a wooden stool, unpeeling the cloth, beginning to bind new strips around the wound. After she's done, she looks at the bruise that's forming on my head. I peer at my reflection in a bucket of water, seeing the dark and green blooming from my hairline.

The guard pours a goblet of water, then passes it to me. I'm parched, incredibly parched. There is nothing more appealing than the idea of this water. I peer up at Oni and see the way she looks at the jug. The crisp skin on her lips, the dryness in her eyes. I slip my hand through the iron bars, holding the goblet out. She cautiously reaches and takes it, her fingers grazing mine. Oni sluggishly brings it to her lips, dragging down large gulps.

"Thank you, your majesty," Oni mumbles, downing every drop. Slowly, she passes the empty goblet through the bars again. I refill it and give it to her one more time. I've told her she is to die, yet she is honest. She has earned the water that is between her lips.

"My parents... was it kind?" I whisper.

She casts a wary glance at the guard, at the nurse. They both remain silent, pretending they aren't listening.

"We stormed in. Your mother was in her bed. We grabbed her out, still in her nightgown, and hanged her. It was reasonably quick. Her body was discarded into the sea," she explains in a heavy tone.

I imagine her limp body suspended, white nightgown blowing in the breeze, that perfect hair in dishevels. The screams and cries of fear, watching it happen. My father's eyes widening as he watches his wife float away—the wife he hated. The woman who had been the bearer of his children become nothing more than a dead carcass alone in the cold ocean.

Knowing what happened to my mother quakes a deep crevice in my soul. Knowing she had died in pain.

"What about my father?" It comes out as a feared whisper. I don't even know if I want to find out the truth of my papa.

"We cut his throat and threw him over."

I think of the blood that layered the side of the boat. How many people must have been laid over there and had their throats sliced, had been hauled over the side and left to fade in the freezing water? The ice sinking into their bones as everything turned black and then were no more.

"Did he scream?" I quiver. Tears start sliding down my cheeks, making rivers in the fields of dirt on my skin. "Did he cry?"

"He was dignified," Oni says calmly, her head lowered. She fiddles with the rim of the glass as she speaks. "Shut his eyes and let it happen. He also went first. Showed no fear, just whispered under his breath in his mother tongue. A prayer maybe? One of the crew understands a bit of Icelandic. He said he thought he was talking about flowers."

Blóm.

The nurse discreetly hands me a handkerchief. I dab my eyes, covering the delicate white fabric in dirt and blood. I wonder if that's what his shirt looked like. White smothered with red and grime. I'm just staring at the cloth, clutching it in my hand. The nurse doesn't demand it back, just finishes a bandage on my leg and leaves, the guard following. Then it's just us again. Oni and me.

"Why?" One word. One question. Probably about four thousand answers.

"Why does anyone do anything, Queen Thornton? Power."

There is immense truth in her words. Everything is about power. Power is why so many are dead. Why my parents are dead. Why my guards are dead. Why Mags is dead.

"Who is to blame? Who is the reason for so much death?"

"The royal from Turkish Arabia."

Tariq. Prince Ender Khan. All along. He battled wearing false colors. He probably knew he would live no matter what.

"Prince Khan," I mutter, wallowing in my stupidity.

But she doesn't say what I think she'll say.

"No, your majesty. His mother, Queen Azra Khan."

•

The sun shines down, just in the height before the moon will creep up to its place. Orange lights the sky, soothing the woes of the day as the sun starts to set, pink crashing over the sea. The sand will be cleaned by morning, the bodies laid to rest, the injured cared for.

I'm not with the injured, not with my soldiers. I am in the gardens, in a clearing which is perfectly viewed from the chambers of Azra. Her lights are low, but I can see her wondering around, preparing herself to bed as if no one died today.

She is clean, bloodless. I'm still armed, bodily fluids coating me. Dry and caked on my skin. My hair flies everywhere, messed and curled from the sea, but that band still sits upon my head. The band of a queen, of a Prithan queen. It's time she realized that.

I reach for the spike—a stick I collected myself and sharpened with a dagger. I plunge it into the ground and reach for the burlap sack, the captain's head inside. It's cold and beginning to carry the scent of death. Something that lives deep in the pit of your stomach, always lingering, always making it feel heavy. The flesh has started to gray, his skin unnaturally soft and waxy. His cheekbones have begun to hollow out, eyes crinkled.

I plunge his head onto the pike, through the neck. It makes a squelched sound, putrid smell escaping. And then I lace it in alcohol. Clear and strong-smelling. Finally, I wait. Wait those moments for Queen Khan to look out her window, to see me. We make eye contact, just as I strike a match, and throw it onto his head. And it burns, bright. Hot.

When Azra looks at the flames leaping over him, flesh melting, she can see me right behind. The fire dancing in my eyes. And I want the message to be clear.

I know. I know everything.

It ends now.

Because I am Queen Lorilynn Thornton of Prithan. And this country is mine.

If you try and take it, I will destroy you. Because here, I am the Entity made in flesh. I am a God.

•

After talking with Oni, my heart still rapidly beating at the conversation, I limp to my chambers. Efa is already there and helps me remove the bloody clothes, carefully lifts the warband from my hair and brushes through it. We're silent the entire time, my thoughts racing to my parents.

I'll never get a goodbye. Never watch them on my pyre.

Never know where they rest.

I push through the pounding pain, through the ringing, through the emptiness on one side where sound is all but absent. Even as she insists on brushing my hair and braiding it before I go back to the ballroom, I find it strange at the sudden absence of all noise. It's not quiet, it's just... not.

As soon as Efa frees me and I feel settled on my feet again, I stand and stride to the ballroom. My balance is still uncertain. Occasionally, my footing wobbles, but I stay upright. I must, particularly when I enter the ballroom. Doctors are still held up, and there is so much to do.

I'm immediately handed an apron by a servant who is too busy to realize it's their queen. Not that I'm complaining; they are so focused on helping with the healing of soldiers. Which I then focus on, jumping into the action.

A maid bustles by me carrying a basin of steaming water towards a man who is lying on a bed. His leg broken, white bone piercing the skin. His screams are raw and crazed.

I don't think, just rush over. They need to reset the leg before cleaning the wound, but it'll be agonizing. He's sobbing, kicking as they try holding him down. Tears stain his cheeks and his knuckles are white.

I approach his head and take it in my hands. Bright blue eyes search until they find me, peering wide. And then he's silent for a moment.

"Y-your m-majesty," he stutters in Ghaldeig, "I'm s-s-sorry f-for my m-manners."

"Shhhh." I gently graze his cheek with my thumbs, keeping his eyes at mine. "You fought so well. You're so strong. You just need to be strong one last time. Then you can rest." I speak in a hushed tone, keeping calm. He needs calm.

"I-I'm s-s-scar-r-ed..." he trails off.

"I'm right here. It's just you and me, soldier." I offer my hands, and he takes them. "Squeeze as hard as you need to. Don't worry about hurting me."

He nods quickly. Beads of sweat form on his forehead, slipping down to his cheeks. I don't look anywhere, don't check with the nurses, just stare deep into his eyes, showing him I'm here for him.

The sound of bone going back into place is vulgar, like a clap of hands. It stiffens my neck. He cries out, squeezing so hard on my hands they pound with my heart. More tears stain his cheeks.

Immediately after, he calms. The breathing in his chest reduces to a normal pace and his long lashes flutter, his grip loosening. Eventually, his eyes close, sleep consuming him. He needs rest, but he's alive.

There's a sheet folded at the side. I blanket him with it. Keeping him warm, keeping him comfortable. Volunteer nurses have already finished and are off scattered with the next people. I should be too.

I help others any way I can. Bandaging wounds, hydrating, looking at various cuts, serving nettle tea.

Soon the sun begins to rise, and night comes to an end. For the first time, there is more light than dusk. A quiet settles over the ballroom as an orange hue shines down across us with heat like an embrace from the Entity themselves—from Papa.

The silence is cast away by the sound of the main doors opening, two bloody men walking in, their heads hanging as sea and blood and grime coats their hair.

Tariq and Koen.

My heart settles seeing them. I hadn't realized the worry that had been eating away at my stomach until suddenly it's gone. And they're right here, they're safe, uninjured. Mostly. The prince has a large, deep gash along his neck. Not enough to cut his throat, but enough that it has bled a lot and will get infected if it isn't cleaned soon.

For a moment, the two of us join eyes, our chests heaving. But soon enough, he walks towards a seat. I move my eyes to Koen who looks so... fragile. I walk over to him, holding out a small cup of warmed nettles for sipping.

"Koen... take a seat," I say, placing my hand on his back and guide him to a spare bed, helping him sit. He shakes, his skin is ashy and pale. The scent of death lingers in his hair.

"We've been collecting the dead, taking them to the beach," he mumbles, his eyes a little dazed, as if he's reliving the horror. He probably is. Has he battled before? Is it his first time as well as mine?

I place my hand on his cheek as I crouch in front of him, keeping my voice low and quiet. "Thank you, my friend, thank you." I stroke his cheek a moment before reaching for a cloth, dipping it in water and beginning to clean the blood.

For the first time, his eyes snap to mine. "I never took you for the caring type, Lori." He chuckles.

I cast him a small, encouraging smile. "I can be kind when I want to."

He grins back, teeth shining against the dirt of his skin. It's nice to see him smile. It means he's still there, that he can heal. We can heal.

Koen's eyes travel to the prince across the room before flicking up at me. I don't need to look to know he's watching us.

"The prince of Turkish Arabia is not what I expected," he states as I dip the cloth in the water and lift it to his forehead again.

"What did you expect?" I ask emotionlessly, my mind whirling from the words Captain Oni said of the Turkish Arabia royal.

Koen gives a small shrug. "I didn't expect him to be so... empowering. I always heard he studied a lot, trained a lot. I expected a soldier, but he is so much more than that."

I keep wiping a spot on his head, going across the same clean line over and over as my mind whirls. It wasn't him—he wasn't behind it all. But he still held a knife to my throat. Koen notices, gently taking my hand in his carefully, looking my face over.

"He cares for you deeply," he states, and I can't quite make eye contact with him, "Is there something between the two of you?"

I give my head a small shake. "No, there isn't. We used to be friends."

"It isn't my business, Lori," he begins, still holding my hand, not letting me wipe the dirt, "but whatever he did, he's gone above and beyond to make it up to you. I think you should listen. Give him a second chance."

I look Koen over. I think about Mags, how I didn't give him a second chance, and now the opportunity is gone. But he still held a knife to my throat. While he didn't kill me, he did destroy my trust. I subtly reach for the dagger on my thigh under my skirts, feeling it tight against my skin, a reminder that I am not unarmed.

"You're right," I say and begin lacing a bandage over a small wound on his forearm. "It isn't any of your business."

Yet I still peer back to the prince, and when Koen is clean and resting, I start walking over to him. Because I didn't listen to Mags, and now he's dead. The least I can do is listen.

CHAPTER TWENTY-SIX

He's sitting on one of the chairs, head leaning against the wall, eyes shut as the gash on his neck bleeds a little down his stained shirt. I don't think he's sleeping. I had laid on his sleeping chest for a night, enough to know the movements and count them. No—he's just resting.

"You should bandage your wound, Prince Khan," I say, and his eyes snap open, his head straining from where it rests on the wall to look at me. He winces. It must hurt. "You're a doctor. Surely you are aware of the chance of infection on a wound of that magnitude."

The prince sighs, moving his head back again. "I don't have the energy, your majesty. A maid is not available to help me yet, so I will wait."

"I do not know anything about stitching wounds, but if you tell me what to do, I'll do it," I say, and his eyes flash to me again, surprised and wide. He shuffles on his chair before nodding slightly. I take that as acceptance and fetch what I believe I'll need. Hot water, alcohol, a needle and thread. Cloth to clean and a dressing for when it is done. I also get him a hot drink to help with the pain, not that it'll do much, but it is something.

First, we need to take the armor off. He's managed to get the small pieces removed, but I catch his limbs shaking from exhaustion and pain. So, when I begin unclipping the chest plate, he doesn't argue.

Much like everyone here, his underclothes are also caked in blood, some of it dry, some of it still wet. He'll need something clean to wear after.

First, I douse the needle, thread, and my hands in alcohol before using the water and a rag to wipe away the dirt that surrounds the wound. Luckily, it's a clean slice so it should be easy to stitch.

As the dirt washes away, and even though I am gentle, he grips the edge of the chair, knuckles turning white.

"I'm sorry, but I need to clean it," I apologize softly. "Almost done and then I can start stitching."

"It's fine, you're doing a good job, your majesty." He swallows, keeping his neck stretched as I dab the last bit, dousing my hands in alcohol again before threading the needle.

"Have you ever stitched someone?" I ask him, my hands shaking a little as I raise it to the wound.

"A few times," he says. "Start by securing the thread. Don't stitch too tight, but not too loose either," he directs as I pierce his skin, bringing the strand through. He winces. Even his eyes water a little. But the prince stays still, breathing steadily as I focus on each stitch.

After moments of silence, I finally speak as I do the last few ones before gently tying it off. "I know the truth," I say, and he moves to look at me. "Stay still, I'm not done." I keep my voice low. He moves his head back, again gripping the seat, but not through pain. "Your mother wants Prithan for the tea, so she asked you to seduce and kill me."

As I finish and secure the bandage, he moves his head so he can look at me. "She never asked me to seduce you," he admits. "That was of my own accord."

"Were you to kill me the entire time? Did you lay with me knowing what you had to do?" I ask, using the cloth and water to wipe the new blood that has seeped from the wounds.

"She asked me to do it the morning you told her of the divorce, after our night in the library."

So, he hadn't laid with me knowing he would be my death. The feelings we shared were genuine. He had wanted to have sex with me, so he did.

Entity. Alright.

"Thank you for today."

His dark eyes flick to mine a second. "Of course, your majesty. It is the least I can do after everything."

"You should have just hidden and stayed back," I say softly. "You wouldn't be hurt now if that were the case."

"And you'd be dead. As would Princess El Sayed," he states. It's true, not that I'd let him know that.

I start packing up the materials and soiled cloth, being careful not to accidentally stab myself with the bloody needle. "I should go. I have other soldiers to care for," I try explaining, going to stand when his hand lands on my hip—in a way a lover would, not a prince to a queen. A pained ripple flows through me. The prince quickly retracts his hand when he realized what he's done and groans as he goes to stand, eyes looking at the gash on my head.

"Has a doctor seen to you, your majesty?" he asks.

I shake my head, a pang of pain flowing through my spine at the sudden movement, nausea building inside me, the ringing in my ears sounding again.

"You should let one see to you. That head wound looks bad," he says and guides me to the seat he was just in. I expect him to fetch someone, but instead, he leans in front of me and kneels, carefully looking over my face and gently touching the skin around the wound.

"I thought you were exhausted," I point out as he gets too close, causing me to wince a little.

"I have a little energy to spare for the queen of Prithan." He swallows. "Do you feel sick?"

"Yes," I reply, "I haven't vomited for some hours though."

He nods, his eyes continuing to look, gently pinching the skin along one of my arms, along my leg. "You can feel this all?"

"Yes?" I question as his hands move to my face, fingers touching along each side.

"Any numbness in your face?" he questions.

"No numbness," I confirm.

Then he snaps his fingers by my ears, and there's nothing on one side. I only hear it quieter from my other ear.

"Can you hear that alright?" he questions, brows furrowing. "From that ear specifically."

"I, uh." I swallow nervously. "I can't hear anything from that ear." My heart hammers as a grave look falls over his features.

"Do you have tinnitus too?" he pushes.

"Tinnitus?" I raise a brow, unsure of the word. "A phantom ringing in your ears."

Ah.

"Yes, I have a phantom ringing," I confirm.

He offers a hand and helps me up on my feet, motioning for me to walk over to the wall and back again, which I do. My knees wobble under me as I walk, my vision a little blotchy. Without my mind set on helping someone or something to get, it seems harder. By the time I'm within reach of him, he holds a hand out and helps me sit again.

"Look, Queen Thornton," he begins, "I believe some of your nerves are damaged in your brain." He swallows. "As swelling decreases, you'll stop feeling so sick and be steadier on your feet, but..."

I frown. "But what?"

"I don't think your hearing is going to come back, princess." He looks my face over. "And I think you're going to have tinnitus forever."

My breath hitches in my chest. That isn't exactly the worst news. It isn't exactly the best either.

"I could be wrong, your majesty," he says, perching in front of me with sorrow and pity in his eyes.

"Yes, but you could be right." I stand, running my hands up my arms. "Would you consider meeting me in the chapel after dinner? I'd like to talk to you," I say simply, raising my chin. Trying to look like how my mother would in this situation. She wouldn't acknowledge the heartache or the physical pain. She'd remember that she was queen, that she had to move on for Prithan.

The prince gives a small nod. "You need rest."

"You aren't my doctor." I scowl. "Chapel? After dinner?"

"Chapel. After dinner." He bows his head a little.

"Queen Thornton."

"Prince Khan." I bow back before stepping away, using the wall to lean on as a guide as I make my way around again, helping who I can.

More hours pass, and eventually, those who are destined to die have passed, and those who will live are beginning to get about. Some have been taken to their homes, villagers are beginning to get rest in a camp that has been set up.

Rebuilding will take time, but it will be done. By the next solstice, they will be home and they will be healing. From both this and the illness. Because I'm getting the tea.

Heather is crying softly in an alcove when I find her. Her eyes are rimmed red. When she sees me, she quickly wipes them as if the tears will disappear.

There are occasions where words need to be said, and occasions where words cannot be enough. This is one of them. I don't speak, don't say anything, just take her in my arms. I stroke her hair and let her sob into my neck.

Both of us have lost Magnús. But Heather has also lost her livelihood. Her bakery is in ruins. Sure, it can be repaired, blood can be washed away and bread can be baked again, but... she will never walk in and not remember the trauma of what happened, the pain of watching the man she loved die and the queen she trusted letting it happen.

I let it happen.

After what seems like seconds but also hours, her sobs die down into small sniffles, and she takes a step back.

"I'm sorry, your majesty." She wipes her eyes.

"Lynn is fine. Please," I practically beg. "Call me Lynn."

She gives a small nod. "Lynn. As in Lorilynn?" She pauses a moment. "Why didn't you tell us you were our princess?"

"As in Lorilynn," I confirm, and there's a moment of silence between us. "I wanted to be your friend before I was your ruler. I'm sorry." I pause a moment. "Anything you need, I will arrange it. Anywhere you want to go, anything you require. Money, a carriage, somewhere to live," I babble a little.

Heather just gives her head a small shake. "I grew up here—this place is my entire life. I could never imagine leaving. I don't know where I would go," she cries.

"Then don't. Stay. As my ladies' maid," I blurt, and perhaps it is out of place or insulting. But I owe her. "You can stay in the castle, and you'll be paid. Then when you're ready—if you choose to—you can rebuild the bakery."

Heather looks my face over, her features crumbling as she nods, taking me in her arms again. I thought she'd be angered or insulted, but she just needs time and healing. Magnús would want her safe. I want her safe. I want them all safe.

•

My head continues to pound throughout the day. The ringing—tinnitus—might be my least favorite thing in the world. Sometimes it feels so loud it's deafening. So after shoving some food down my throat, I finally make my way to the chapel.

Sitting on the bench is a blessing. And I feel as if I could topple over and sleep forever, but there is too much on my mind. Far too much. Particularly if I can pull off what I believe I'm going to pull off.

"Azra Khan? She's the reason for all of this?" I ask. I'd been so wrong and naïve throughout it all. Right from the start.

"We've been in waiting for six months. Waiting for the right time." Oni runs a hand through her short hair, the other rubbing the back of her neck nervously.

"What did she pay you?" I ask.

"A promise," she announces. "With a small taste upfront."

"Tea. She promised tea. Didn't she?"

Oni nods, gently but clearly. It's simple—get Prithan to marry off their daughter in secret and create a union. Wait until that side of the bargain is complete on their end, then kill them. Daughter becomes queen, your son becomes king. Kill the queen, keep the proof of the marriage, gain control. Act as queen. Create profit and tea. All under the nose of the Collective.

I could have saved so many lives if I had just realized. If I had used my brain. If I'd had not been so trusting. And Tariq had done what was ordered, was doing what he was told was right for his country. Now I must think of mine.

"How old are you?" I ask her.

"Seventeen."

"We both hold so much power for such a young age." I stare at the iron bars, a droplet of water sliding down one, clinging onto the metal. "And we both rule our queendoms, no matter how big or small, in a world filled with so much darkness. I just want to leave Prithan a better place than I found it, live a long life, and be happy."

She looks down, the weight of her forthcoming death lingering. Her eyes sad and watering. She's accepted it. She's accepted the role. To be a sacrifice for her crew, her people.

"I've changed my mind." I make my voice clear, straightforward. "I won't be killing you. There is no point. I beheaded your predecessor. That's enough for me now. The first step to peace is letting you live, to sail the sea."

Oni's eyes immediately brighten, eyebrows raised. She seems understandably hesitant. "Really?"

"I will let your whole crew and you leave here without a fight, without injury. You will all be treated in the hospital. I will help you. In a few days, you can sail away."

"Alright..." Her voice fades, and she creeps forwards and clutches the bars, looking between them. Her face is pressed against the metal. "There's a 'but'. I can feel it."

"There's always a 'but' in politics."

Everything I do now I must do for my country, for my people. I must do everything for what's best.

I start, keeping my voice calm as my brain works like clockwork. "I need you to sail under my name. I need you to sail under the flag of Prithan."

"Your Majesty?"

I blink my eyes open, the light pouring into my vision. I must have dozed off, because the prince is standing in front of me with a worried look.

"Are you alright?"

I rub my eyes, my head pounding. "I'm fine." I wince, holding my head a little as I sit up. "Exhausted."

The prince gives a small nod and takes the seat next to me. He's changed clothes now and his hair is washed. He has also removed the bandage. The stitches look decent, though I do say so myself, and the wound is clean. I doubt he'll get an infection. Though never speak so soon.

"Your stitches look good," I say and shoot him a small, shy smile. "Whoever did them has a steady hand."

The prince chuckles in agreement. And then we sit beside each other a while in the silence. Just for a while. Even the tinnitus begins to settle.

"My mother received your message loud and clear, by the way," he says. "The flaming severed head was a nice touch. She certainly won't forget it."

"I was angry. Looking back, that may not have been the most... *regal* way of dealing with my feelings."

"On the contrary, I wasn't lecturing you on your decision, Queen Thornton. I think she certainly got the shock she deserved." He looks over at me and casts a small smile. "You said you wished to talk?"

"Yes," I confirm and take a breath. Where do I start? "The Collective," I say, "threatened me, my crown. And I'm beginning to think our parents were right in trying to find a way to even out the scales."

The prince keeps his eyes on me as I speak, talking about how I believe that we should go forward with the plans, even though my parents are dead, and his mother is a murdering bitch. When I finish, he takes a moment to continue looking at me.

"*Ana* will be hard to convince," he finally says. "After your fire show, she'll most likely be scared to talk to you."

"Which is why I'm asking you. How would you go about doing such a thing? How would you get her to trust me and renew the agreement she had with my parents?"

The prince breathes deeply as he thinks, his eyes wandering over a window at the side. "My mother is a complex woman, but she likes to think she is in charge. Let her think she still is. Allow her to steer the ship—but you own it, so it doesn't matter how she directs it."

I don't answer him, instead thinking about his words, about the power. There is no denying our parents were right in joining the countries. The Collective think they can break Prithan, but Prithan is strong.

"Chione and I entered a union of allegiance," I say, then pause a moment. "I told her everything."

"Everything?" He raises a brow.

"Everything."

Yes, Prince Khan, I told her you held a knife to my throat.

His eyes move forward again, his Adam's apple bobbing as my words settle in.

"Have I apologized yet? For what I did?" he asks carefully.

"I'm not sure," I admit. All his words since have been muddled in my head, and truth be told, I can't quite form sentences properly. Honestly, I'm struggling to form most words at the moment. Ruling a country and trying to change the face of the world is hard on a good day, let alone with your brain screaming in your skull and a constant pounding in your temples.

"I'm sorry," he says softly, his voice shaking a little. "I truly am sorry."

I peer over at him, my eyes searching his features. He's looking at me now, his brown eyes wide and begging, darkness swirling inside them. "There's a way you can start making it up to me," I murmur.

"Tell me, please," he practically begs.

I rise to my feet, a little uncertain at first, but stable enough to walk in front of where he is sitting. I'm not sure how such things are meant to go in situations as this, but this time I want to do it properly. The prince watches me curiously as I lower myself to my knee in front of him. He raises a brow curiously.

"Prince Ender Tariq Khan of Turkish Arabia," I begin, my words trembling, heart hammering.

"Yes...?" he whispers nervously.

"Will you marry me?"

CHAPTER TWENTY-SEVEN

That night was the worst of my life. Climbing into my sheets, bathed and brushed, I thought I would be asleep until sunrise. But while sleep had found me at first, after only two hours, I wake to my eyes feeling as if they are being crushed, my head pounding to a point where I can't bear to open them, and nothing will stay in my stomach.

I feel death lingering in the corner, preparing to take me. Through all the pain, I am calm and at peace, ready to take her hand, if only to stop the agony.

But morning comes, and the pain begins to subside. When the sun shines through the window, I wake—exhausted. I almost wish death had taken me. Because fuck, my head hurts.

Everything hurts.

As my eyes flicker open, a careful hand supports my head, holding a cup to my lips, and I drink it down.

"You scared us there, Lynn," Heather's soft voice sounds.

"Thank goodness," Chione then says.

I turn my head to the side, seeing her stand by the wall, exhaustion hanging under her own eyes. I carefully sip the water, my lips cracked and dry, managing to get the strength to sit up. My head immediately feels better than it did, although my throat burns with bile and my back aches.

Efa steps forward. "He's on his way," she says and curtsies, bringing forward a clean nightgown. While I don't exactly want to address it, there is the lingering scent of sweat and vomit in my chambers. It's almost enough to make me gag again, but I don't think I have anything left to bring up.

"None of the doctors were available," Chione says, plodding towards me and taking a seat on the spot beside me. "So when your maid notified Heather of your condition, she came to me and I fetched Prince Khan straight away."

My heart drops.

My memory of the conversation a mere few hours ago.

My proposal. His response.

"What happened?" I croak, managing to sit fully so I can drink the water properly. My hands shake a little as I lift it to my lips. I notice how bruised my knuckles are now that the battle has set into my skin. I peer at myself in the mirror, and my face is an array of purple and blue. The injury on my head has seeped bruising down to my jaw, and there is a purple flower forming around an eye.

Entity, I look awful.

My doors creak open and the prince strides in, exhaustion hanging on his features. His stitches are still holding strong. He's changed back into clothes befitting a prince, but his sleeves are rolled up, concern lining his face with furrowed brows.

"Your majesty," he greets and immediately walks to the bed and leans over me. "How're you feeling?"

"Confused mostly..." I swallow as he gently uses his hands to turn my head to inspect the wound. "I'm not entirely sure what's happening... or what happened in the night."

"Your injury swelled, increasing the pressure in your skull. Or you got acute hydrocephalus. I couldn't be sure without looking at your brain. However, you still need it," he explains. "Luckily the swelling has gone down, and your wound isn't leaking spinal fluid anymore, so I can safely say that the worst is over, whatever it was." Never do his eyes meet mine.

"Am I going to die?" I ask carefully as he steps away, fear twirling inside me. I don't want to die—I'm not ready.

"No, I don't believe so. Although you were close. If I hadn't performed a lumbar puncture, it's possible you would have."

"Lumbar puncture?" I question with a raised brow.

"I drained some of your brain fluid through your spine." He

swallows. "You need to take it easy today. No fighting, no running. Nothing strenuous. And lots of food and drink." Watching the prince is strange as he paces and explains things. It is cool between us, tendrils of tension stretched out. He is acting as my doctor, nothing more. He *is* nothing more. I must not forget that, and I must forget everything that happened between us.

"Is such a thing possible?" I raise my brows.

"It is," Heather confirms, looking queasy, "I watched. Biggest needle I've seen in my life."

The prince gives a small chuckle before looking me over once more. "Notify me immediately if you start vomiting again or any concerns, your majesty. I would tell you to stay on bedrest, however I know you aren't going to do that, so please be careful." He looks me straight in the eyes a moment. "Please." And for that single moment, I feel as if it's only the two of us in the room, only his words and mine.

I swallow and give a single nod. "I promise." I say, peering across into the mirror and seeing myself before I strain and start to push up from the bed and to my feet, head twinging, muscles crying, but I'm standing. Instead of the nightgown I was wearing the before, which I presume is covered in various bodily fluids, I wear just a shirt, my bare legs on display for the world. I would shy away, however, much like my face, bruises line them. My knees are practically purple, my shins covered too. "Thank you, Prince Khan. You are dismissed."

The prince bows his head before swiftly leaving. I turn to the three other women, expecting concern, but instead I am greeted with raised brows. I stare at them a moment, hoping for an answer to their looks.

After a painfully long moment, Heather goes to the wardrobe. "I will fetch you something to wear," she declares, turning and sifting through the fabric.

"And I will get your breakfast brought up, your majesty," Efa says, quickly leaving my chambers, the doors shutting behind her.

I look at Chione, a single brow raised in question. She crosses her arm and sits in the chair Heather had been in beside my bed. I lean back, sitting cross-legged.

"Did you and Tariq... make up?" she asks, wiggling her brows a little.

"Make up?" I question, then lower my voice. "Are you asking if I had sex with him?"

"I mean... if we're going the direct route. Yes. I'm asking if you had sex with him after the battle yesterday."

"He tried to *kill* me, Chione," I say, keeping my voice clear, not minding that Heather is here. She even casts a frown over when I say that, but quickly snaps her head back to my clothes. "Why do you think I'd let him in my bed again?"

Chione looks at me with a raised brow, and even Heather turns to us with the exact same expression. I look between them as my ladies' maid speaks. "Were you not in the room just now?"

"Yes. He checked up on me and then left," I speak. It was only a few minutes ago at most. I don't see what the big deal is.

"The way you looked at each other. The way he said 'please'." Chione continues, "Not to mention what happened in the night."

"What about me almost dying suggests the two of us had sex?" I frown, but there is a hint of a smile. This is rather amusing.

"As soon as I went to him, he was practically running through the corridors to get to you," Chione says.

"He's training to be a doctor. If anyone was dying, I'm certain he'd run," I say in his defense. "I think the two of you are wishing for something that isn't possible now."

"So, you're saying that nothing happened between the two of you?" Chione asks skeptically.

"Nothing happened." *Apart from me proposing to him.*

"If you're sure," she says, giving me the side-eye.

"I promise I will tell you if Prince Khan and I have sex. I vow it on Prithan." I manage to chuckle, and Chione bellows back. Even Heather smiles as she picks out a black dress and hangs it up, moving to the vanity and beginning to prepare the things I need for my hair to be done.

Considering this is her first day as my ladies' maid, she is already doing a fantastic job. But then my eyes fall on the deep black of the dress.

She's keeping herself busy. Because today Mags's pyre is being lit on the beach, as is everyone else's who passed.

The dread of the day settles in my stomach as Efa comes back in, holding a tray with fresh bread and butter. And while originally my empty stomach was begging for food—now... not so much.

I carefully pick up a piece, nibbling the corner as Chione talks about the day, telling me how her injured guard is doing at retraining using his hurt arm. Heather even speaks about her first night. She compliments her rooms, talks about how she and the cook are already friends and exchanging recipes.

I arranged for some new dresses to be brought to her. Just some clean things that I hope she'll like. She's even wearing one today, a cotton gown that is a deep green, a gold pin on the breast in the shape of a crown, an indication of being a lady of the queen. Seeing her wear it brings a small smile to my lips, knowing that I can keep an eye on her and hopefully soon she will be happy and at home. And when she meets Mags again as the Entity, she can tell him of life in the castle.

She helps me get into the black dress, a floor-length simple gown, and then runs a brush through my hair, Efa styling it simply in a braid. Today is not a day for finery.

The ride to the beach seems both too long and too short. The entire time my heart hammers in my chest, particularly as Snowflake trots through the ruins of the village. There are no bodies anymore, but stains of blood still litter the ground. The scent of death lingers in the air, only thinning out as we approach the sea and it begins to dissipate to the igniting smell of ash and flesh, fiery heat beginning to burn on my cheeks even before we make it through the treeline. But when we do, it is ablaze, a city of fire. Tens of pyres built of wood line along the shore, some already burning, some waiting to be lit, bodies wrapped in white material.

Heather is beside me, and while her eyes are dry, I see her hand shake a little as she bites her nails. A guard captain spots us and walks over, removing his helmet and bowing at our presence before motioning his hand, leading us past flames and smoke until we reach a pyre that is a little away from the rest. Adora is already there. His cheeks are not dry.

Immediately, we take each other in a tight embrace. He buries his head in my neck, and I hold him tight as my eyes shift over the pyre. The wrapped body that lies on top. Silently looking up at the disappearing dusk clouds, forever gone. My heart aches at seeing him, seeing the shell that was him.

Heather has her eyes glued on the corpse. I peer at her a moment, Adora too with a look of confusion. I link my arm through Heather's, hoping to distract her a moment as I guide her to Uncle Adora. "Heather, may I introduce my other uncle, Adora. Adora, this is Heather. Heather is Mags's other half."

Adora looks less surprised than I expected. Although, thanks to

Magnús's neck those weeks ago, the entire castle knew he was sharing his bed with someone. I think Adora's surprise is because he never realized love was a part of it.

Adora gives Heather a warm smile. She holds out a hand for him to shake, but he ignores it and brings her into an embrace. Her eyes widen a moment before shutting and she wraps her arms around him too.

"Welcome to the family," he mumbles, still keeping her close. Ed comes and hugs me too, kissing my hair. After the tears and the embraces, we all finally part and turn to the wood. A guard comes over with a lit torch, bowing. I expect him to light the pyre, but Adora holds up a hand to stop him, and the man pauses.

I peer at my uncle, confused when he goes to his bag and pulls out two of my mother's roses. They're bright and red like blood, their stems still layered in sharp thorns. He holds them both out to me. "You will never get to place your parents on the pyre," he says softly. "I thought maybe these roses could be a symbol, so you can spread the ashes of them in the name of your parents. Perhaps it can help you find some closure."

My breath hitches as I take the flowers, carefully sliding my fingers over the soft petals. My parents are dead. Magnús is dead. Their bodies will never be found, most likely lost forever in the dusk sea.

I slowly walk over to the pyre, my boots seeping into the sand with each step. When I'm close enough, I carefully place the two roses beside

Magnús. A soft wind sings, hair blowing in my face. I hesitantly reach for the wrapped sheet and place it over Magnús's arm. He feels cold and hard. And where I always felt life, there is nothing. It isn't him anymore.

A single tear falls down my cheek. "I'm sorry, Uncle Mags," I say, too low for anyone to hear. "Thank you for everything." I pause a moment as more tears fall. "I love you. I love you, Magnús. Tell Papa I miss him too. And I promise I'll keep Heather safe. Always."

There is no response, obviously, but I do feel the wind blow a little harder, and the hair on the back of my neck stand. I think he hears me. I step back, turning to the guard with the torch and give a single nod. He goes forward, bowing his head at me as he places the torch beneath the wood, going down to his knee and lowering his head as the fire grows, consuming the wood and becoming a blazing sun.

I step back and rejoin Adora and Heather, holding both their hands as we watch the smoke rise and Magnús's body be returned to the earth along with the other departed. The only sounds are the sea and the lapping of the flame at wood and flesh. It is agonizing.

I've never heard Adora sing, but his voice breaks the deafening silence, a deep sound filled with texture and life as he sings a song of Iceland, a song that I heard Papa sing when he thought he was alone.

"Moon-rise, sun-down,

Watch the waterfall,"

My mouth opens, joining him. I've never sang before, but I'll sing for the dead today.

"Wind, trees,

Rock, Mountain,

Land and sky,

I let my sword fall, I let my sword protect,

For home is my blood,

And blood is my home."

It takes hours for the embers to glow, and the ash to drain into the sea, back to the earth. Afterwards, everyone makes their way home, and all those who need to be returned to the Entity are. I allow everyone to go ahead, riding on Snowflake some hundred meters behind as I let my mind think about the days. Sun is beginning to set as I return him to the stables, planting a kiss on his neck and gently stroking his black mane, even sparing a carrot. I know I must retire, I know that Prince Khan would tell me to rest but I don't feel ready.

I miss Magnús. I miss Papa.

I miss my mother.

The garden welcomes me at the hour. Thanks to everyone retiring to dinner and to wash their skin of ash, it is empty. I wander through, my fingers grazing over the various plants and roses like she always did. Only now, when she is gone, do I see the love my mother had for this garden. I always despised it, but it was somewhere for her to be happy, somewhere for her to be herself.

While my mother and I rarely saw eye to eye, I still love her. And I believe she loved me too, which is why she was always so strict, so harsh. She just wanted me to be the best I could, wanted me to be strong. And I believe I am strong now; I won't lie that a part of that is because of her.

I'm uncertain how much time passes. I find a bench near the tree line of the woods that surround the castle and sit, resting my eyes as I allow nature to surround me. For the first time, I feel my heart slow, feel my body relax. My mind slows and clears, and I feel as if everything will be alright. That I can get used to this life, I can be a good queen for Prithan, for the world.

I feel as if it'll be worth the pain for a better world, and I don't mind it so much.

Then a hand covers my mouth and I'm pulled into the woods.

CHAPTER TWENTY-EIGHT

I kick. I scream, even though the hand is still clasped over my mouth. The grip is tight, wrapped in my hair and pulling me into the deep abyss of trees, the castle rapidly moving into the distance as we move further away from the gardens, from the people.

"Let me go, you bastards!" I curse, scratching at them as best I can to no avail. They placed a blindfold over my eyes. All I manage to see is one of them is male and white, but not so pale that they grew up without the sunlight like Prithan citizens.

I believe there are two of them because of the footsteps, but neither has spoken. The blindfold has risen only a little, enough for me to see with one eye that we're moving deeper into the woods.

"Fuck you both," I spit, kicking and trying to get them to let go of my hair. My scalp has already been abused enough. "Entity curse you. Waste of oxygen scumbags." I keep screeching and eventually, when my ass has been dragged across the dead leaves enough, we come to a stop and they slam me down on the ground. I feel blood begin to ooze from the wound on my head.

Sorry, Prince Khan. In my defense, this isn't my fault.

The assailants speak for the first time. And while I don't recognize their words, I recognize their voices.

Björn.

Hui San.

I shouldn't be surprised.

They let my arms go, and I quickly lower the blindfold, seeing the two of them lean over me, a rope between them. Are they going to hang me? Like my mother was hanged? My eyes dart over to the tree, and I kick, trying to get up, but Björn slams me back on the ground, grunting as I do, but he rests his knees on my shoulders, beginning to tie a noose.

"Tie this to the tree," he orders Hui San, who shakes a little as she fiddles, trying to string it up on a branch beside us.

"No one will question why you decided to kill yourself," Björn practically growls. "Your parents are dead, one of your uncles is dead. It all just got too much for you," he taunts, keeping me down while Hui San finishes.

I manage to spit on his face. "Fuck you." I curse in Icelandic. "You are a coward."

"Fret not, Lorilynn. You'll never have to worry again soon." He smiles, even sparing a moment to stroke my cheek as if we were lovers in bed. "You'll see your parents. Isn't that what you want?"

"It's ready," Hui San pipes up as our eyes flit to where the noose now hangs. Björn stands, lifting me by my shoulders and pulling me over, forcefully putting the hoop over my neck, tightening it.

Again, he gently traces his thumb over my cheek, eyes dancing over my face.

"Don't touch me," I snap.

He sighs sadly. "Such a waste." Björn steps away, talking with Hui San in the language I don't know. While he is calm and calculated, her face is filled with emotions and loud words. She's scared, shaking. Sweat lines her forehead. She doesn't want to do this, yet she still does. She still begins lifting the rope, so it pulls me high. My toes go to their tips as I try and struggle as the noose tightens around my throat.

Björn notices her struggling, strides over, and takes the rope in his fists, hoisting it up. My feet no longer touch the ground, my face screams as blood rushes to my brain.

I shouldn't be this calm. Why am I this calm?

I have perhaps forty seconds until I lose consciousness.

Fuck.

Forty seconds. Thirty-five now.

My legs kick, struggling to reach the ground. My eyes feel as if they're about to be compressed from my skull as the blood increases the pressure in my brain. I gurgle, scratching at my neck to try and let a slither of oxygen in. The panic has now settled deep in my bones. I think back to a lesson Magnús taught me. *Don't panic. Panic kills faster than anything they can do to you.*

I have not survived this long to die now. Mags did not die for this.

Think, Lorilynn, think.

Think.

Think.

Twenty seconds.

The dagger. The dagger on my thigh. I can cut the rope.

I swipe my hand at my skirts, lifting them and risking my neck for a second as I grasp at the fabric until the cool hilt is in my palm.

Five seconds.

I quickly unsheathe the blade, chaotically swiping it in the space above my head until the rope is sliced, the threads breaking at the touch of the blade. I fall to the ground in a heap, coughs convulsing through my whole body as I inhale as much air as I can.

"Fuck, get her!" Björn shouts, pointing at me. I don't bother staying. I sprint, the knife still in my hand. Leaping over the creak, bounding as fast my exhausted feet will let me, my neck crying in agony as I do. Their footsteps and panicked cries are behind me, but I refuse to listen and go until I jump, leaves and branches snatching at my skin, and fall on the grassy ground at the feet of someone. Of Chione, thank the Entity.

"Lorilynn? What's happened?" she breathes, crouching on the ground, offering me a hand as I gasp for breath, my lungs still not recovered from the rope, tendrils of it still hanging from my neck.

Björn and Hui San run through the shrubbery, breathless, panicked eyes looking at me. While I cannot speak just yet, my throat already swelling, I raise a pointed finger to the two, my arm quivering as the last smidge of strength leaves my body. They both stare at me, the blood leaving their cheeks, hands shaking as they raise their them in defense. But there is none.

Chione turns to her guards, ordering something in her tongue with harsh words. They storm forwards, securing the two Collective members' hands behind their backs, marching them inside the castle. I watch, finally the feeling of safety settling into my bones.

I want a day. One day where someone doesn't try to kill me.

One. Fucking. Day.

Chione offers a hand, placing the other supportively on my back as she helps me stand, eyes looking over my neck, which will most likely also be bruised soon too. I'm meant to be having a coronation in two weeks. Chances are, I'll look like a rainbow if I keep this up.

"Lorilynn, are you hurt?" Chione asks carefully, keeping a hand on my arm. "Shall I get Tariq?"

At this point, my arm could be hanging by a thread and I'd say no. I need space from him.

"No, I'm fine," I say, my harsh voice coming out as a strained croak.

Chione doesn't seem convinced but gives a single nod, still making sure to hold me lest my legs collapse under. Which admittedly is a concern of mine. I feel wobbly, probably a mixture of exhaustion, adrenaline, and oxygen deprivation,

"I'll be alright."

"My guards are taking them to the cells," Chione informs me. "What did they do to you?" She frowns.

My mind flits back to the pressure on my throat, my eyes, the panicked kicking of my legs, how my neck stung as desperate nails scratched the skin. I swallow, my eyes going hazy a moment. "They tried hanging me," I say as emotionlessly as possible, not wanting to reveal how shook up I feel. I clutch my dagger in my fist, so tight that I tell myself it's the tension that makes me shake. "From a tree in the woods. I suppose they wanted it to seem like a suicide."

"Do you think they know?"

I glance at her, sighing with exasperation. "About our thoughts?" I ask.

"Among other things," she replies, looking me over with furrowed brows.

"Perhaps. Although, only the surface is a motive for them to commit murder."

Chione gives a single nod, her eyes travelling over my neck again. "Would you like me to talk to them, see what I can get out?"

"We can both go," I say, and she opens her mouth to speak, most likely to tell me to rest or say another time but quickly clunks her teeth shut, apparently deciding it to be redundant—which it is.

"Alright. Certain you don't want the prince to look you over?" she checks one last time as the two of us begin wandering towards the door where Björn and Hui San have just been dragged.

"I'm certain, thank you," I croak, my eyes catching with Koen's. His face is pale with shock, eyes wide as he sees me after seemingly watching the scene unfold. He seems... betrayed. Of course, his new family tried their hands at killing his childhood friend. For a single moment, we stare at each other directly, but I snap my head forward, following Chione in. I don't have time for his feelings at the moment.

We go straight to the cells. Oni no longer resides there. She is back on her ship, most likely sailing between Prithan and Europa. The cell she was in is now occupied by our two guests.

Hui San sits in a corner, crouched, rocking back and forth as she silently cries. Björn has his fingers gripped around the bars, forehead rested against them as his eyes follow Princess El Sayed and I as the two of us step in, looking them over. Treason is punishable at the monarch's discretion under Prithan law. Historically, that punishment was beheading. For the assassin, it was drowning— although, that was spontaneous. For Prince Khan, it was a marriage proposal.

My mother had a few treasonous criminals in her time. They were all executed if memory serves. My grandmother had a few too. She was more... *creative* with her methods of retribution. I used to think some of them were barbaric, but now I understand—it's a sculpture of anger and betrayal. Painted in blood, bile and entrails.

"Your majesty, your highness," Björn mutters as a guard brings the stool over for me to sit. I perch down, keeping my eyes on his. Chione, instead of sitting, leans against the stone walls, arms crossed, glaring like an eagle ready to pounce on its prey.

"Titles," I mock. "Shame you didn't have such manners earlier when you were attempting to hang me from a tree."

"It's just business," he replies. "That's all politics is—business with manners."

"Maybe business is politics without them," I counter, and he gives a small chuckle.

"What do you want me to say, Queen Thornton? That I'm sorry?"

"Well... an apology would be a nice start," I joke with a small smirk. He doesn't find it amusing. Chione does at least. I peer over and the corner of her lips are lifted slightly. I give a small sigh, peering between the two in the cell. Hui San has stopped sobbing uncontrollably, only sniffling every now and again.

"What am I going to do with you two?" I ask, mostly myself and the room. I am angry, frustrated. I must make an example, but I know that killing them will be starting war with the Collective, and I'm not entirely sure I wish to do that just yet.

"You understand that I cannot let you two out and about the castle after this," I state plainly. "I can't trust you not to try and push me down the stairs or something."

"Oh, come now, Lorilynn. We are far more calculated than that," Björn says, then nods. "But yes, that is understandable."

"I'm not interested in a war with the Collective. You'll remain here until after my coronation." I peer behind me at Chione. She still has a cold look on her face but also gives a single nod of agreement.

Hui San finally looks up from where her eyes are buried in her skirts, a sense of hope in them as they glint in the torchlight. "We're going to live?"

"In exchange, you will release Koen from whatever contract you have him trapped in."

Björn scoffs. "Koen doesn't have what it takes for our line of *politics*. He is too weak to do what must be done."

"And by too weak do you mean that he refused to kill Queen Thornton?" Chione pipes up from where she leans against the wall.

"Exactly," Björn says casually, as if it were a regular conversation. "But we thank you for your *hospitality* and perhaps you could figure out some more comfortable accommodations?"

Chione raises a brow. "You're both lucky to have your heads."

"You'll stay here. Perhaps I can have some of your things brought," I suggest, and both members give a small smile of appreciation. A thank you would be nice, however, I am fortunate enough there are iron bars between us.

I debate saying something else, but there is only so much politeness I have to spare at this moment, so I stand, letting the two sit in the dank darkness. While I promised I'd have some things brought to them, I never said how quickly.

I turn to a guard as Chione and myself pass her, keeping my voice low. "Give them a few hours to think before bringing them their comforts."

"Of course, your majesty."

Chione and I stride out of the damp, decrepit cells and part ways, at least for the evening. She has prayer and studying. I have a headache and would like some time to reflect on today with the Entity.

The chapel greets me with the familiar warmth. It's ironic that some weeks ago, this place was my least favorite in the world, and now it's where I find the most comfort. Soft flames flicker at the side, filling the room with amber light. I slowly make my way to my usual pew at the front, but am surprised to see Koen there. Maybe I'm not the only one who needed time to think.

I silently take a seat next to him, placing my hand over his as it rests on the wooden seat. He moves it a moment and I worry he's angry with me and taking it away, but instead, he clasps his fingers through mine, squeezing. A tiny smile creeps on my lips and I squeeze back.

I peer over at him, at the concern in his face, and am surprised to find he's looking back at me. "I'm sorry I brought them here," He apologizes, his voice quiet.

I shake my head a little, still trying to give him comfort with my smile. "Don't worry. You can take me in your airplane next time as an apology."

Koen chuckles a little. "Anytime. Anytime." He pauses a moment. "Did they hurt you badly?"

I shake my head. "I'll survive."

"You always do, Lori." He casts me a charming smile. I notice he's not wearing the chain anymore. It's refreshing, seeing him as his own person.

"Thank you for not killing me, by the way." I chuckle. He shoots me a worried look, but relaxes when he sees I'm also relaxed about the situation.

"They told you about that?" he asks with a raised brow. "I thought about it. But when it came down to it, I couldn't. So, then they asked me to attack you, take your virtue. Then you'd have to marry me."

"Again, thank you for not raping me. However, to take someone's virtue, they'd need to actually have it."

He snaps his eyes to me in shock. "You aren't a virgin?" He looks forward, eyes still wide and mouth open a little.

"If you tell anyone, I'll deny it." I smirk. I don't mind telling Koen such things. We were close friends once. In fact, we still are. I trust him to keep that a secret. I also trust he will not see me ruined as a result.

"The secret will die with me, I promise," he says, sighing a little. "I don't want to marry you because you were forced into it." He clears his throat. "I want to marry you because you are the most amazing woman I've ever met."

My heart hammers in my chest.

"I can't give you the Southern Isle. I can't give you more power, or wealth." He continues, his voice beginning to shake as he speaks, "Beside the airplane." Koen gives me a nervous smile at that, and I manage to spare a chuckle. "But I can give you love and support. A shoulder to cry on, arms to hold you on your worst days. And maybe children in the future?" He stands nervously in the spot which I stood on only yesterday with Prince Khan in front of me, and sinks to one knee, gently holding my hand in his as if it were a tiny bird. "Queen Lorilynn Thornton—Lori. Will you do me the honor of becoming my wife and making me the happiest prince in this world?"

A tear falls down my cheek. I can see our life out in front of us. Stolen kisses and warm embraces. Making love under the stars, nursing young children as they run around our feet. Growing old and gray together. It would be perfect. He would be happy. I would be happy.

I scoot off the bench, going on my knees in front of him, taking his stubbled jaw in my hands, tracing my thumbs across his cheekbones. I bring his lips forward to mine in a simple kiss. His hand cups my cheek, the other stroking the hair at my shoulder. And after a beautiful moment of bliss when the whole world calls me back, we part and I look his face over, the last tendrils of our possible future together clinging to me like thread.

I have to cut them.

"It would have been a pleasure falling in love with you," I whisper as tears continue to trickle down my cheeks. "But I'm engaged to someone else. I'm so sorry."

Koen's face falls, but he gives a small nod of understanding, wrapping his arms around me and pulling me close as my tears continue. If I was selfish, I'd pick him, but I have to think of Prithan.

"Do you love them? The person you're going to marry?" he asks after a painful moment.

"Love has nothing to do with it," I mumble into his chest.

He kisses my forehead, keeping his arms around me as we sit on the cold stone floor. And after some time, he silently stands, helping me to my feet.

"You'll always have me as your friend," he promises and kisses my knuckles. "Always." And then he walks out of the chapel, casting me a quick glance before shutting the door behind him.

CHAPTER TWENTY-NINE

I was right. Bruises did make me look like a rainbow. While the two weeks have helped them fade, there are still tinges of yellow across parts of my face and neck. As well as a few patches on my legs and arms, but those are covered by my dress.

As per tradition, the night before coronation, the new ruling monarch must be bathed in the water of the earth to wash away past sins. Without this, they cannot ascend the throne. Of course, what my memory forgot is that I have to wear a white dress that's more like a potato sack than anything else. Worse is that I can wear nothing underneath, so I suspect that as soon as I rise from being submerged, the entire congregation will get a full view. I presume that is why the queen is allowed to choose who is in attendance at this event.

I chose those closest to me. Adora, Ed, Heather, Chione. Koen. Tariq. Apart from them, a few guards, and the priest to perform the ceremony, there is no one else. It's an intimate affair. Maybe picking complete strangers would have been better.

On the beach, where the group of us now standing, torches have been placed in the sand. Any sign of the blood spilled is gone. Only the memories of the pyres. The wind is surprisingly warm and gentle, tiny waves lapping at my bare feet as I stand in the sea, peering back at the small group of guests. They are quiet, watching respectfully.

I peer at the priest, who holds his hand out, framed by the rapidly setting sun. He has healed well, even has a beautiful smile. While he talks somewhat slurred, his soul is still pure and healed, which when it comes down to it, is all that matters.

"Ready?" he asks as I take his hand. We walk into the water, the coolness nipping at our skin. I get used to it soon enough, and we keep walking until it is at our waist, rippling as it moves.

"As I'll ever be," I say back with a small smile. His wrinkled hand comes and holds my cheek a moment before he places it on the back of my head. I relax and lean back so I am in his control.

"I baptize you, Lorilynn Thornton," he begins and lowers me into the water. "In the name of the Entity." And then he pushes me under. Memories of the assassin flash through my mind, of the Collective members straining me from the tree, of the night I thought I would die—yet I feel calm. I feel as if the ocean carries them away. It's peaceful.

Seconds later, he brings me out, water dripping from my hair. I take a breath and peer up at the amber of the sky.

"You are washed," he declares.

I smile at him, gently taking the man in my arms and hold him a moment. He is a friend, and while religious law means I can never address him by his name, hopefully he knows he has one in me.

And we will be alright. Because this is a new start, and new starts are healthy.

•

My coronation is today. After the ceremony last night, I came back to my chambers to rest. Sleep has been nice recently, and I've been enjoying not dreaming. It's as if the world stops for a little bit while I rest. I like it.

Heather woke me as the sun rose this morning, at my request. Chione is not able to train me as much now, and Magnús is dead so he cannot, but I still wake up at the same time each morning and ride to the beach, partly in memorial. Partly as a reminder of my sins. Always with a dagger though. When Snowflake and I return, I am served breakfast in my room. The castle is alive, preparing in the ballroom for the coronation. Maids carry flowers and finery. Guards are patrolling around with their armor gleaming. Officials wear their best clothes. Azra passes me as I make my way to back my chambers, and for a single second, fear does flash before her eyes. Neither of us stop— we don't even bow or nod. Good.

Once I'm back in my chambers, I'm immediately bustled to the bathroom by a variety of maids. Efa has brought on extra help for today. The past week I've had a seamstress come see me each day to fit a sleeve or tighten the waist of the dress.

The maids wash me, scrub my skin, dry me off, and then braid my hair once it has dried somewhat, painting rouge on my cheeks and a hint of rose balm on my lips, make-up around my eyes in such a way it is neat and elegant. I look like I demand respect. Afterwards, the seamstress enters, the dress in brown parchment. She lays it on the bed, unwrapping so that paper falls, revealing the satin fabric. It looks as if it is woven from the night sky. Dark blue, so dark it's as if the shadows sewed it themselves. The neckline is high, sleeves long, the skirt billows like a waterfall. It's sleek and amazing. She has sewn a leather chest plate that goes over the top, the skin dyed a deep gold.

Admittedly, I am a little breathless. It is divine. She, an older woman with blonde hair that is peppered in white, peers at me with a worried look.

"Do you not like it, your majesty?" she squeaks.

I reach down and carefully run my hand across the fabric of the skirt. "It's magnificent," I compliment, and a smile beams across her face, tension visibly leaving her shoulders. The maids give a small applaud to her, and blush creeps up her cheeks, particularly when I join in too.

"Let's put it on you then!" Heather declares with excitement, busying everyone as she physically drags me in front of the mirror, helping slip it on. It fits flawlessly, like a second skin. And with the leather bodice piece, it is faultless. My hair is tied out of my face, but the back is left loose so that it frames my face.

Heather comes forward with my dagger, then helps me lift the fabric as I secure it to my thigh.

A small knock sounds at my door, and the room of people all turn. A guard opens it, and the prince steps in, a little taken back by the many women looking at him.

He's scrubbed up well. Clean-shaven, wearing a white shirt and black trousers, a jacket around his shoulders sewn from black satin with embroidered gold leaves. His hair is slicked back, and he even has a little kohl around his eyes too. Perhaps I could even spare a compliment and admit he looks rather attractive.

"Is this a bad time, your majesty?" he asks, motioning to the various audience. Heather looks between the two of us with raised brows before turning to the maids.

"Let us give the two royals a moment. Perhaps you can all quickly see how preparations in the ballroom are going?" Heather directs, and they file out, muttering about the various things they must see to.

Soon it is only the prince and me. Adora would warn me it is improper, but seeing how we are betrothed, it doesn't matter. Besides, we have done far more improper things.

"I don't think I've ever seen so many maids in one room," he comments, standing awkwardly by the door, clearing his throat. "You look beautiful, your majesty."

I shoot him a warning glare. "Don't. What do you want, Prince Khan?"

"I come with an offer. I noticed before you would train with Magnús or Chione. But with Chione busy and Magnús..."

I raise a brow, trying not to show how his name still hurts to hear.

"I wanted to offer my services, to train with you in the mornings," he states plainly, shuffling on his feet a little.

"Want to hold a knife to my throat again?" I snap, taking my gaze away from him and instead to my reflection in the mirror. The high neckline hides the small purple scar that has formed on my neck, a reminder of what he did. Always on my skin.

I should tell him to leave, that I don't want to see him again. But I don't. The past weeks, past months, past years' worth of anger has all built up. I feel as if I'm so out of control, so anguished. I'm tired of people treating me as a malleable child. I'm tired of feeling so lonely when I am surrounded by people. I'm so exhausted with feeling angry.

I turn back to him, the train of the dress falling behind me, crinkling slightly at the floor. "I'd... appreciate it. Thank you."

A small hint of light enters his eyes, but he gives a firm nod. "You do look beautiful, Queen Thornton." A small string tugs at my heart.

"You look very dashing also," I compliment back, clearing my throat. "After they have placed the crown on my head, I need you to step forward and stand by my side. It'll be the official declaration of our engagement."

"An old Prithan tradition for the queen's partner to stand beside her at coronation," he states. I'm surprised he knows that. It is uncommon lore. But it is correct.

"Exactly," I murmur. "I'd like to wait two weeks before we marry. Just some time to settle into my role."

"Of course," he says. "How're you feeling? Any discomfort with your wound?" Ah, always the doctor.

The wound has been healing well. He'll occasionally check it, but there have been no issues since the night he took some fluid or something. No more headaches, although the hearing hasn't come back and the ringing in my ears still continues when I'm trying to sleep.

"It's fine. Nothing new."

"Good. Good." He bows a little. "I'll leave you to finish getting ready. Best of luck, Queen Thornton."

I peer back at him again, once more. "And you also, Prince Khan."

•

Music bellows as I walk down the ballroom, along a carpet that has been rolled out to a throne at the end. The priestess – a woman who oversees religious ceremonies for Prithan and Entity worshipping countries—waits at the end. She wears dark robes, a single black line pained horizontally across her nose. She has no hair and holds the new crown on a pillow in her hands.

I met her last night when she arrived. We walked through the ruined village together, and she blessed the land. Now she will place the crown upon my head.

I reach the throne, kneeling before the people who stand watching, bowing to them as a promised servant of the people.

"Do you vow to watch over your countries with your body?" the priestess says, her voice loud and clear.

"Tha mi," I reply just as loud so the congregation can hear.

"With your mind?" she then says.

"Tha mi."

"And with your soul?"

"Tha mi."

"Until your dying breath?"

"This I vow upon the Entity." My final words ring out, and she offers a hand to me, helping me stand, and then keeps a hold of it as I sit on the throne, a chair carved from dark wood, old symbols of Prithan etched within it and molten gold embossing the details. It is beautiful, crafted hundreds of years ago.

The priestess steps forward, the gold crown in her hand. It is fashioned like a vine to sit across my forehead, with sapphires and diamonds like small petals. Magnificent. All of this is glorious. I hope that I am worth it. I want to be worth it. I *will* be worth it.

The crown is placed carefully on my head. It fits perfectly. I shut my eyes, memories flitting over every person that has been lost, every life that I must make better. I reflect over my regrets. My goodbyes. The smiles and laughter I have shared.

The crowd cheers and applauds as I look over it. But then it settles, replaced with gasps when, as ordered, Prince Khan walks up the small stairs and gets on his knees in front of me, bowing his head low and planting a kiss on my knuckles.

I feel them watching with wide eyes. Even Azra is somewhat surprised but spares a genuine smile. Of course, this plan is working in her favor, and therefore mine.

"My queen," he murmurs, standing and taking the position behind me, his hand ending up on my shoulder. I lean into it a little admittedly. Because suddenly I don't feel so lonely.

My eyes shift over to where Chione stands beside Koen in a few rows. The two have become fast friends in the past few weeks since the Collective was imprisoned below. She looks somewhat surprised at the prince's actions. Koen does not—he simply stands there with a sad smile, giving a single nod in understanding.

Then again, the crowd breaks into cheers, shouts of joy and applause.

"Long live the queen, long may she reign! Long live the queen!"

The tinnitus takes over, and I let it. I'd rather hear the ringing right now than their joy.

Afterwards, when the prince and I have led out the procession and moved to the gardens where wine is being poured and food served, Chione comes and finds me. She holds a glass of apple juice in hand, her eyes moving over the people there as the two of us find a quiet corner. It is always about business between us.

"Congratulations, your majesty," she says and bows her head. "May I inquire about how our special guests are?"

Our special guests. I'd let Björn and Hui San reflect upon their time in the cell a little before their belongings were brought. But I kept my promise, and the two have been eating well and enjoy fineries and even were allowed to have small beds brought in so they didn't have to sleep on the wet floor.

Yet, knowing they're alive and untouchable is irritating. They tried hanging me from a tree and get to go home. But I need security before war. And if I am going to produce tea, having the Collective breathe down my neck because I had two of their members executed seems like a recipe for disaster.

"I heard the cook made them beef for dinner last night," I complain.

"My guards told me they've been sending letters and acting like the executioner is their personal postman," she adds, and I frown.

"I don't understand how they can act so nonchalant." I sigh. "It is insulting."

"You should have them whipped or something."

I give a low chuckle. "It would be too good for them." Hatred swirls inside me like darkness. "I cannot do anything without security. The Collective could total Prithan in this vulnerable time."

"Perhaps, but you seem to be forgetting that Prithan has a sister in Ptah, just as you have a sister in me. And soon a husband in Turkish Arabia."

"But killing them could possibly mess up our plans to produce tea," I argue.

"It won't. Unless the Collective burn the fields, they can't stop anything. Don't let them walk over you, Lorilynn. You're queen now. They mustn't forget."

I take a sip from my glass goblet of wine, letting it sit on my tongue a moment as I ponder her words. Of course, with the new day and the crown on my head, I don't have much silence before one of the rulers from Europa asks me some questions about trade and whisks me away.

And while the plump woman tells me about her plans for the Europa-Prithan relationship, which I wholeheartedly support, I just nod and murmur. Thank the Entity Adora stands beside me and is able to reply on my behalf.

Koen also comes over to myself and Prince Khan on the one occasion the two of us stand close together. It wasn't on purpose, we just so happened to be getting a bite to eat from the buffet table at the same time, and Koen came over, offering a small smile to us each.

"Congratulations, Lori," he says, clinking his drink with mine. "And congratulations to you too, Ender. Prithan's Queen is a special woman."

The prince gives him a charming smile, shaking his hand as he rests the other around my waist a moment. As would be expected by a couple. Even if it is political. "That she is," he says, his voice surprisingly steady. "I just hope I can be good enough for her."

"I don't doubt you are," Koen says and then leans forward, kissing my cheek. He lingers longer than should be allowed. But instead of pulling him away, I stay still so he can. Eventually, painfully, he parts. "A pleasure as always, Lorilynn," he says as he steps back and begins walking towards a group of officials.

The prince removes his arm from my waist, brown eyes watching Koen depart. I'm sure he wants to ask questions, but he doesn't. Thankfully. No words he can say will change what's happened, what's happening. And what I can't let happen again.

Maybe Chione is right. Maybe I do need to make an example.

Adora wanders towards the two of us, giving a small smile, but then drops it as he analyzes my face. "Everything alright?" he asks with a frown.

"Adora, the two Collective members in the cells," I begin.

He raises a brow. "Yes?"

"I want them hanged. Today."

CHAPTER THIRTY

It was done quickly. And a week later, the execution doesn't even cross my mind. The first few days officially being queen were... underwhelming. Nothing changed. I signed forms, greeted people, and met with the council. The best part of my day was admittedly my training with the prince in the morning before the world was awake. We would meet by the stables, ride to the beach, and fight until sweat and blood were running down our bodies.

Today is no different. Sand flicks in my eye as he pounces, striking his sword forward. He knocks mine from my hand, flinging it away near the sea. He uses his foot to knock me down, my ass landing in the sand as he rests the tip of the sword over my heart. He does it every time he wins these training battles of ours. Which doesn't happen often, but honestly more than I would like to admit.

The prince moves his weapon away, instead replacing it with an open hand. I grasp it, and he hauls me onto my feet, more sand flying about. I shake the last of the grains from my sleeves and hair, reaching at the ground to where my sword is, the sea trying to claim it. I quickly sheath it away.

"You hurt, your majesty?" he asks, his doctor's eyes wandering over me. Your majesty. Queen Thornton. Prince Khan.

His highness.

"Stop," I breathe, ragged from training and from anger. "Please stop calling me by my titles. It's exhausting."

"But you said—"

"I know what I said," I interrupt with an irritated sigh, "but if we are to be married then the least we can do is call each other by our first names."

The prince. Ender. Tariq.

Tariq steps from one foot to the other, then simply says, "Are you hurt, Lorilynn?"

It has been weeks since the name was upon his lips. Hearing it now is like the morning bird song. Or the sing of a knife. Like the one he held to my throat.

"I am unhurt, Tariq," I reply and peer back at the top of the castle that peeks above the treeline. "I should head back. Get ready for today."

"Wait," he says, holding his hands out, "I have something for you."

"A gift?" I ask skeptically.

He runs the few meters to where his horse is tied and reaches in the saddlebag, pulling something out wrapped in fabric and a ribbon. Tariq then strides over again, making sure to keep a small distance between us as he always did now, and held out the small package.

I curiously reach and take it from him, feeling the weight in my hands and wondering what it is.

"I noticed, since the night I tried to kill you, you've been wearing a dagger on your thigh," he begins, and my eyes travel to where it indeed still sits, ready for me to grasp at any given moment. "And if I'm the reason you wear it, then it should at least be the finest dagger in Prithan."

I pull the ribbon, watching it fall to the sand, and then the fabric too. The dagger isn't too large, and the blade is thin. On the hilt is a blood-red ruby at the top, set in gold, a serpent curling up in such a way my fingers slip into place perfectly. I pull it from the leather sheath, the silver blade glinting in the sun. It has writing inscribed, in two languages. The first is Ghaldeig, my mother tongue.

You have the protection of my sword, until my last breath. The script turns into what I believe to be a mixture of Turkish script and Levantine. It's beautiful.

"'But for when it is my sword you need protecting against.'" He states, and I peer up. It truly is beautiful. "That's what it says."

"Thank you," I breathe and immediately attach it to the holster on my thigh. It feels good there, easy to get to and perfectly balanced for my hand. It feels like protection, my own protection. I look his face over, into those dark eyes I am rather fond of. "After the wedding... I'd like it if you stayed a while," I say, shocked by even my own forwardness. Because while my mind remembers the knife at my throat, my heart remembers his lips instead. He doesn't say anything, just frowns a little with confusion. "I really should leave, Tariq. Big day after all."

"Ah yes, of course. It's unlucky for the bride and groom to see each other before the ceremony." He smiles, kicking at the sand with his shined boot.

"An old superstition," I comment and step back to where Snowflake is, untying him from the tree and clambering on. "The one in white?" I tease lightly, even sparing a small smirk.

"The one in white," he says with a small, casual, salute before I guide my horse into a canter back to the castle.

Much like the morning of my coronation, the building is alive. And again, like my coronation, various maids and Heather rush me into the bath, washing my hair and quickly getting me out, drying every inch of my limbs.

She wraps me in a white robe, brushing my mane and priming it in such a way so that it curls. She seems excited by today. I wonder what her wedding to Mags would have been like. I wonder if they were even that serious.

"I've got some of your mother's roses to put in your hair." She smiles as she begins putting tendrils up on a small bun at the base of my neck and slides a single rose in there. I can't see it, as it is on the back of my head, but the fragrance is beautiful. Sweet like Màthair and Papa were with me.

I look at the ceiling as if I were gazing up at them in the heavens. I hope they're proud, I hope they're happy and with my brother.

Her eyes travel to the new knife on my thigh, which peeks out from the opening of the robe. She gives a small smile. Heather has never questioned why I don't take it off when someone else is in the room, or why I keep it beside my bed at night. But this is a new knife, and she raises her brows.

"A gift?" she questions as she fits a diamond necklace to my throat, the clear gem hanging from a delicate chain, so it sits perfectly in the divot of my clavicle.

"Yes. From the prince." I clear my throat nervously. "A wedding gift."

"It looks beautiful. Deadly," she says, and I peer up and offer a small smile. *If only she knew.* Afterwards, once the necklace is attached and she has put diamonds in my ears, I stand and remove the robe, her fetching the wedding underclothes. Special pieces that are meant to be enticing for my new husband. I'm surprised by myself when I look in the mirror, how the lace frames my breasts and helps me look... womanly. It is like armor. I feel empowered, as if I could take the world.

Time is not our friend, and while I could have looked at myself for admittedly longer, the dress must be put on. It's slipped over my head, the corset at the back tied. The gown itself is rather extravagant. Off the shoulder to frame the necklace and pulling in at the waist, skirt flowing out into a train behind. I slip the white shoes on to match, and Heather clips a veil of delicate lace over my head, so it covers my face and the back of my hair, only a thin sheen. But a veil, nonetheless.

Adora comes in just as Heather is finishing the touches, placing the last few bits of hair where they need to be.

It is strange, looking at myself in the mirror. With the white, the veil, the gown, the flowers. I look like a bride. Like I always thought a bride would look. Of course, I learned at sixteen that you don't have to look like a one to be one.

"Oh my, Lorilynn," Adora says, and I peer over to find tears falling from his eyes. I have some too, but not because of the wedding. Because Papa and Magnús should be here. And instead, it is just the two of us. "You look beautiful."

Ed follows in after, giving me a warming smile. "You're the most beautiful bride I've ever seen." He comes forward and carefully wraps his arms around me, planting a kiss on my cheek over the veil, "Beside Adora, of course," he adds, winking at his husband. The group of us, Heather included, give a small laugh.

But the laughter dies down, and we all look at each other. Adora and Ed are in their best. Heather too.

I peer at myself again, at the perfect bride in front of me. I don't want to do this. I don't want to marry yet. I only just got my single life back. But it is for Prithan. It is always for Prithan. For the world. Because I cannot bring stability and power to my nations without this.

"I wish Papa was here," I say to Adora, crying a little. "And Mags."

"I know, I know," he says and gently takes my hands in his, cupping my fist as if it were a baby bird. "But they're watching. They're here, you just can't see them."

"Can you walk me? Down the aisle?" I ask in a quiet voice. It is an old tradition, but one I would have liked to have shared with Papa. And while I'm perfectly capable of giving myself away, I wouldn't like to walk alone to the altar.

Adora smiles, a sweet, fatherly smile. "I'd be honored," he says and presenting his arm. I take it, casting a nervous smile at him. "Can I offer some last minute marriage advice?" he asks softly as Ed, the maids, and Heather leave the chambers to go take their seats in the chapel. It has gone from feeling surprisingly full to empty.

"Please do," I say. Any advice would be appreciated. Ed and Adora are the only stable marriage examples I grew up with. I'll take any of his guidance.

"It's alright to be in love with him. It's alright to love, even if it's scary," he says kindly. My mind flits to the stolen moments we had together in each other's arms. As to what his kisses felt like. "Just because you're queen, doesn't mean you have to have a marriage like your parents."

"Do you think they loved each other?" I ask though I know the answer is no.

"As friends. They were friends. And he loved you. Being your father was the greatest love of his life. Your mother also fell in love. They were happier than they let on."

"You think he and I can be happy?" I ask fearfully, scared to live a life cursed with hate.

"I do," he says, "and I think the two of you are going to be the best queen and king the world has ever seen." Adora's voice is filled with passion, with a fire that lights the embers inside of me that I thought had become ash. "You ready?" he asks finally.

"I'm ready."

He keeps hold of my arm as we leave my chambers, a group of guards escorting us. Inside will be the royals, people I find I don't care about aside from a few. But outside the chapel, waiting with flowers and smiles are the servants. The maids who have raised me, the gardeners who helped me pick roses. The cooks who would sneak me extra servings and let me help cut vegetables on Sundays in the lead up to the winter solstice. My family. They clap as I walk, girls who do not yet work run up, collectively handing me a small bouquet of red roses to match the one in my hair, little bits of paper with the well-wishes tied to the stems of flowers. I crouch in front of a particularly young one. Her red hair is tied up, ringlets falling, framing her rosy cheeks.

"Happy Wedding Day!" She giggles happily, presenting a small piece of paper to slip into the flowers.

I place it right in the middle, taking a small petal from one of the roses and putting it in her little hand. "Thank you. Enjoy the festivities," I say. In the past two weeks, the village has slowly come together. And today it was decided to stop construction for celebrating. Where before there had been blood, there is now light and food and joy. Just for now. But the Prithan people take what happiness they can.

She takes the petal in her hand and runs to a woman I believe is her mother or older sister. They both have fire-colored hair. I'm jealous.

After shaking hands with a few more and thanking the guards who escorted us, the doors open to the chapel. It has been decorated specially. Flowers are everywhere. Roses, as that is all we have to provide in the Prithan gardens. Music swells as my eyes travel over people as we begin slowly walking, hundreds of eyes landing on me.

A blush rises in my cheeks, a flame in the pit of my stomach. I worry I'll fall or trip. But I don't. And when I approach the front, my eyes meet his—the prince.

Tariq.

He dresses similar to my coronation. White shirt, seamless black trousers. Boots polished. But his jacket— instead of being black, it is a deep blue. Prithan blue. With silver embroidered roses. His eyes are dark, searching my face, still lined in kohl like before. But closer, I can see how it brings out the galaxy within them.

Two years ago, I looked into those eyes and knew they felt fear like I did. But this is different. He was a prince then and I a princess. It was filled with violence—this is filled with flowers.

He offers a hand, and I take it, quickly embracing Adora a moment before he goes to his seat at the front next to Ed and Azra. Tariq guides me opposite him, to where we stand in front of everyone. The priest is with us, already the cup and knife ready.

Tariq looks me up and down. I wonder if he is comparing this day to our first wedding. He certainly looks better without blood dripping from his features.

"You look picturesque," he says, keeping his voice low so only I and the priest hear.

"Shhh," I whisper but cast him a small smile in thanks. The priest peers between the two of us, our hands still together. A small smile raises on his lips, a knowing nod before his eyes go up to the congregation. The familiar words leaving his lips.

"Under the sun, we make a union between these two souls. Binding them forevermore."

I peer at Tariq, squeezing his hand once. Our shared memories of those words have haunted us for years. To hear them again is... uncomfortably grounding. My lungs feel tight just thinking about the last time I heard them.

"With the blood, we bind."

He takes the knife and holds his hand out for my palm. I present it, and peer at the thin line of a scar that is already there from my first wedding. He slices the skin again, although slightly across the other scar so they'll both be seen. It's a gift in itself.

It'll be a reminder of what the world tried taking from me, and that I survived despite it. Because surviving is the hardest thing I have ever done, but I've done it.

He squeezes the blood from my finger, a few droplets falling into the goblet as before.

The priest then turns to Tariq and does the same. He doesn't even flinch. Our blood mixes in the metal cup.

"Please say your vows," the priest continues, placing the knife down and keeping the goblet in his hand. Ready for the next part.

"I, Prince Ender Tariq Khan of Turkish Arabia, vow under the sun, our blood combined, we are bound by the Entity. Bodies and hearts loyal, souls as one," he says, his eyes on mine the whole time he speaks. A promise to himself, and me.

"I, Queen Lorilynn Elizabeth Einarsdottir Thornton of Prithan, vow under the sun, our blood combined, we are bound by the Entity." I look his face over. "Bodies and hearts loyal, souls as one."

The room is still silent. I sneak a look over at the congregation. They all watch, some dabbing their eyes, most smiling. Azra has surprisingly kind eyes. Adora and Ed hold each other's hands as if reminiscing their wedding.

"Prince Khan, would you kindly raise Queen Thornton's veil?" the priest asks in a low voice.

Tariq steps forward, his fingers reaching for the lace in front of my face, and lifts it, placing it on my hair, his hand brushing my cheek as he pulls back.

The blood is brushed across our lips, the metallic taste already seeping onto my tongue. My heart begins hammering as I know what part happens next.

"By the joining of the blood, the binding is complete."

I look over his face, the red on his lips. His dark eyes search mine.

Everyone is watching. I move forward. He raises his hand to my cheek, cupping it as our heads move together. And then our mouths touch softly.

Cheers and applause erupt. I don't look, too distracted by how my chest feels as if it will cave in on itself as his lips move against mine, his fingers brushing the scar on my neck that he put there. I hate myself for admitting it, but the feeling of his touch still causes my heart to flutter.

In the room of sound, I hear only silence as we move away, my eyes fluttering open to look at him. Prince Khan. My husband.

King Thornton.

CHAPTER THIRTY-ONE

The ballroom is decorated much like the chapel. Roses and light music. Waiters offer wine and food as couples dance to the orchestra. After the kiss, Tariq and I walked out together and straight here where he's been whisked away by Adora to be congratulated. I think my uncle is also doing it to give me a moment.

A waiter comes over with a glass of sparkling red wine and offers it to me as I stand in a corner that is strategically near the food. I'm starving. I accept the wine happily, sipping the bubbly drink as I watch him.

He's been king for ten minutes and already he's making people smile. While the rich officials are already gasping for a word, he is instead crouching in front of the very same girl who gave me the favor before the ceremony. I have no idea what he's saying, but her cheeks are bright pink, and she happily giggles. It's sweet. She nods, and he stands, offering her a hand, and the two walk to the dance floor where he begins waltzing with her. Waltz is a loose word as it is more of him holding her hands as she jumps about, but they both smile brightly. It's lovely. Everyone adores it, watching with kind smiles. Including me.

"He loves children," a female voice says, and I frown as my new mother-in-law sashays over, sipping on some wine. "Always has. He holds a lot of love for his countries' children." *Countries.* Multiple. Because Prithan is now his too.

"Is that how you convinced him to do it? For Turkish Arabia?" I question. Azra and I haven't spoken since I left the little gift outside her chamber window. She takes a sip from the wine, looking over at Tariq as I keep my gaze on her, waiting for an answer.

"I did what I had to do for my crown. Ender did what he had to do for me. However, it turns out both of us were wrong. The two of you are married, and I for one am keen to move past the whole thing." She finally takes her eyes from where the young girl still jumps happily, holding onto my husband's hand.

I sip my own wine. "I agree."

"Nothing I said to you was a lie, Lorilynn," she follows up, moving her gaze from her son to me. "I really do care for you as a daughter."

"Yet you still tried to have me killed. Multiple times." I glare.

"It's just politics. All of it is just politics. Including this marriage."

I take my gaze away from her again, holding the cup to my lips in an aim to hide the front on my face. It's ironic, that weeks ago I kissed the prince because I didn't want it to be politics, then we fell into the trap. A political marriage.

"On that note, you should go and finalize it," she adds causally. My frown deepens. The priest seems as if he's awaiting by the door too, ready to take us to my chambers to begin the honeymoon proceedings.

"Keen much?" I say judgmentally to her before placing my glass on a side table and make eye contact with Tariq as I begin making my way to the priest who also silently nods. The three of us are not looking forward to this next part. Last time I lay with him, he held a knife to my throat. Seduced me, intending to kill me. And the priest has already witnessed us consummate once already.

We're silent as we walk to my chambers. Heather has prepared the room. Whiskey sits on the bedside table, ready to be drunk. The sheets are cleaned and ironed. She also left a note saying to ring the bell when we want food.

The priest shifts from foot to foot. I'm not too much better. He takes his spot by the door in the corner, ready to lower his head and do his duty. I reach for the whiskey, pouring one of the glasses. Instead of sipping it, I pass it to Tariq. He looks me over before taking it, nursing the drink in his hand. The two of us share a small, thankful smile before I wander to the vanity and perch down, slipping the shoes off and unclipping the veil from the back of my hair, taking the red rose out too.

"Do you need any assistance?" Tariq asks and he starts slipping off his jacket, resting it on a chair, wandering behind me and meeting my eyes in the mirror reflection.

"Could you untie the back?" I ask. He reaches for the ribbons holding the dress together like a corset and begins undoing them so that the fabric is loose and I can remove it.

"Thank you," I say and stand, making sure to hold the front so it doesn't fall from me yet. "I'm going to go take it off in the bathroom," I declare and walk in, taking the robe at the same time. I slip the mess of fabric off and wrap the silk and lace dressing gown around me instead, tying it but keeping the dagger on my thigh. It is not time to remove that yet.

When I go back in, the priest is standing in his corner, eyes down. Tariq is still fully dressed, thankfully. He leans on the wall by the window, looking over the gardens as the sun rises over the dusk in the distance.

I stride straight over to him, my heart hammering, and suddenly use my weight to pin him to the wall, my arm digging into his shoulders. I reach for the dagger, the very knife he gave me this morning, and hold it to the scar on his throat. The scar I put time and care into sewing up.

"Entity..." I hear the priest breathe. I snap my gaze to him, eyes burning with fury.

"Leave," I order. For a moment, I worry he'll hesitate, but he paces out, only the king and me in the room.

His chest heaves as he breathes, sweat already beginning to sheen his forehead. His eyes are wide, but to my surprise, he keeps calm. His voice is straightforward, and he doesn't fight.

"Are you going to kill me now?" he asks.

Memories flash in front of my eyes of him holding the knife to my throat, feeling the blood pool on my cheek, to the fear and betrayal and broken trust. Of giving myself to him, body and soul, and him using it.

My hand starts shaking as I press the knife harder into his neck. Tears well in my eyes.

Politics. This is just politics.

"If you ever," I begin, seething through my teeth, "*ever* hold a knife to me again, I will have your head put on a spike. Understood?"

Tariq slowly raises his hand to my cheek, his thumb grazing my jawline as he stays still, letting me hold the knife to his throat. "Understood." He swallows, and for a second, we remain unmoving. He lets me have control of the room, his fingers still stroking my cheek.

I don't want this. I don't want this feeling. I was to rip the hate from my skin. I want to feel good things. Adora's words come back to me. *It's alright to love, even if it's scary.*

"It's just politics," I say, still not moving the knife as I go on my tiptoes, crushing my lips onto his. My eyes shut and heat consumes us. The dagger clatters to the floor, hands raising to his face, his hair. His palms hook around my legs, lifting me to the vanity, placing me so we're sat at the same height, hips pressing eagerly together. His kisses move to my neck. Deep, intense, hot caresses that make my toes tingle and my heart flutter. He pulls at the robe around my shoulders, revealing the under things. His eyes travel up eagerly, his fingers gliding along my stomach. The touch makes me shiver.

"Are you going to let me call you beautiful, princess?" he mumbles as he plants soft kisses down my chest.

"I'm not a princess." I pleasantly sigh, leaning my head back against the mirror as he nips his way back up my skin.

"I know," he says as he plants one single kiss on my lips, "but I think I will keep calling you that." His eyes trace over my body again. "You're beautiful."

I shake my head, not able to let the compliment sit right. He takes my chin in his hand and lifts it, so our noses are touching.

"You're beautiful, Lorilynn."

I blush a little, pulling him close and putting his mouth on mine again so that he cannot see this flush in my cheeks. His hands travel down me once more, lifting me again. I have my eyes shut, lips still moving with his as he lays me carefully on the bed, planting soft puckers on my skin.

I start tugging at his belt, trying to get it undone, but he shakes his head, hovering over me, looking deep into my eyes.

"Do you trust me?" he whispers.

I swallow and frown, hesitating. Do I trust him? Not exactly. But I give a small nod, nonetheless. He notices and offers a small smile, kissing my lips so delicately before he creeps down the bed until he's between my thighs.

He kisses me there, in ways I hadn't realized I could be kissed.

My back arches, fingers finding his hair. He doesn't stop. And soon, I'm panting. Only then does he creep back up, eyes and lips glistening after watching me writhe under him. I'm breathless. He's breathless, until he murmurs something in Turkish.

"What does that mean?" I ask quietly.

"I'm in love with you, Lorilynn," he whispers. "I'm so in love with you it hurts." He swallows, looking over my face. I peer up at him, heart hammering in my chest. I didn't expect that. "And I want to be beside you always." He swallows. "You asked me to stay earlier, on the beach this morning. But you walked off before I could answer." He presses a light kiss on the tip of my nose. "It's a yes. Of course, it is a yes. I'll follow you anywhere."

No one has ever told me they love me before. I'm not sure what to say. The words can't quite form on my lips. So instead, I kiss him—everywhere. We meld together, a mix of bodies and sex and adoration and love.

Husband and wife.

•

I lie beside him on my front, supported by my elbows as I look at him. He gazes back with a lazy grin. Our clothes are somewhere—everywhere. My hair is no longer tied neatly, instead flayed out on my back.

The ballroom is a muffled noise. We should probably go back, but I don't want to move just yet. I'm enjoying the quiet, the sound of our breathing. His hand gently plays with a strand down the side of my face.

The knife is placed neatly on the side table of my bed.

"We should probably go back down soon." I smile, beginning to lean up, but he catches my wrist, pulling me towards him, holding me close so my bare chest is pressed against his.

"Let me hold you a moment longer," he mumbles, burying his face in the nape of my neck, keeping his arms around me firmly. I try pretending it irritates me, but in truth, I melt into his touch. He still smells like spice, like my Tariq. "Will you allow me to share your chambers?" he asks quietly, the sound vibrating against my neck.

I stiffen. The idea of sleeping beside him, completely at ease and unprepared. What if this is still a ploy? Soon he will hate me, and he needs space when that happens.

"I... I am not yet comfortable with that," I whisper shamefully.

He gives an understanding nod, guilt flashing in front of his eyes a second. "Of course," he says and presses a kiss to my cheek. "We best get you dressed. I don't think your uncle would appreciate you going down in your current attire."

"And by current attire you mean... absolutely nothing?" I chuckle.

He laughs in agreement. "Exactly." He stands, offering me a hand of help from the bed. I take it and clamber out, holding a sheet for decency. Admittedly, I am shy. He keeps hold of me as we walk to the wardrobe, selecting a dress which happens to be white but is more manageable than my wedding gown, though it is beautiful.

I slip it on as he puts his trousers and shirt around himself, not bothering to tuck it in. I wander to the vanity which is somewhat cluttered thanks to the kiss we shared while I was on it, and slip the necklace and earrings off, beginning to run a brush through my hair.

"Ready, princess?" he asks, and I peer behind me to where he stands with a palm out for me. I step over, hesitantly taking it in mine as we exit the double doors of the chambers, guards following us to the ballroom.

The wedding party is now in full swing. We must have been up there for two hours. Entity. Chione is happily talking to some officials. Adora dances with Ed. Koen looks as if he's had a few drinks and spills one on the floor as he waltzes with Azra—who admittedly looks to be having fun.

I hope that the two of us can quietly sneak in, say our goodbyes, and then I can go. But as soon as we're in view the whole room erupts in cheers. More blush creeps up my cheeks as I peer at Tariq with a sheepish smile. He squeezes my hand in support as we walk in, both quickly being offered drinks. He happily accepts. I don't and take a step back and let go of him.

The music enters full swing again and dancing starts. He peers back at me with a frown. "Where are you going? What's wrong?" he asks.

"I think I'm going to head to bed. We have the meeting tomorrow, and I'm not the biggest fan of balls," I speak.

He steps forward and places a sweeping hand around my waist, pulling me against him. I'm surprised by the intimacy, but as a married couple, social construct says it's alright now.

"Dance with me, please," he says. "Let me show you off as my wife."

"This marriage is political, King Thornton," I say and clear my throat as I step back. "Don't forget that."

He keeps a firm but gentle arm around me, leaning down to my ear and whispering, his breath making mine hitch, "Was it political when you undid yourself for me?"

I bite my lip and lean up again, pressing a gentle kiss to his cheek. Somewhat to hide the blush and somewhat because I can't deny it. It wasn't political then—not that I'm complaining. The crowd around us proceeds to *oh* and *awe*, and he smiles sweetly before letting me go. I'm somewhat reluctant, but do step back, giving one last smile before I turn and begin to leave, heading back to my chambers.

"Enjoy your night, husband," I call as I meander out. "Try not to have too bad of a hangover tomorrow."

Heather and my maids are enjoying the party—as they should—so I get the rare treat of readying myself for bed. I slip the dress off and recover the robe from the floor, trying and give the room somewhat of a clean, folding the clothes we threw around into a pile on a chair. I pick his jacket up—the one he wore today—and bring it to my nose, breathing the scent in—citrus and spice—before adding it to the pile.

After the room is tidy, I jump in the bath for a while, soaking in lavender oil before putting a clean nightgown on and climbing into my bed, not caring it isn't made, and lie down. Eventually, I sneak to the library and steal a book, managing to avoid people beside two intoxicated servants who bow before falling over in a fit of giggles and apologies. I don't mind. It makes me laugh.

I'm still chuckling when I arrive back at my rooms, climbing into the bedsheets and beginning the book. A storybook. I haven't picked up one in years. It's as if I'm a child again. And then I read until the sun is long set and the music downstairs has died down into nothing. It's only when I hear the drunken footsteps of guests stumbling back to their chambers that I finally place the pages on the side table and lie down, eyes shutting.

I enjoy the sound of the tinnitus, of the feeling of the darkness, of being alone. While I am queen when I don't wish to be, married to a man who has tried to kill me, bound with the Collective announcing war soon to avenge the death of two of their members—I am happy. Truly happy. And when sleep comes, I dream of the future.

CHAPTER THIRTY-TWO

I lay in a little. I doubt my husband is up for training and there is no rush. The rest of the castle is still sleeping, therefore the quietness is nice. Particularly as I find I do have a small headache from the excitement.

In the morning, a very tired Heather walks in. Her hair is somewhat disheveled, and she looks a little queasy but brings breakfast in on a tray.

"You didn't have to," I say, jumping up and taking the platter from her, setting it on the bed. "Come join me. Tell me about the party." I pat the spot beside me and pour the hot water for her, offering the cup. She nurses it close, taking small sips.

"I don't think I've ever drank that much." She groans as I start eating the stewed fruits the cooks sent up. "I had a lot of fun. Danced with many people I think it wasn't proper for me to dance with."

I chuckle. "And the prince—I mean the king. He got back to his chambers fine?"

Heather gives a small shrug. "I'm not sure. He and the prince from the Southern Isle decided to watch the sunrise along with a few of the people from the village. I was helping Ed take Adora back by then."

"Adora drank?" I raise a brow, not quite believing it.

"Adora got pissed," she confirms, and we both laugh. Magnús would have laughed too. Mags would have enjoyed the night. He would have danced with Heather and me, would have made the orchestra play some old Icelandic folk songs and sing along with them. Very loudly. Very badly.

After the two of us eat breakfast, most of which Heather does throw up two minutes later, we select a dress for the day. I have a meeting in two hours... *the* meeting. Chione, Koen, Azra, Tariq, and I are joining with the council to discuss our plans and sign contracts. Tonight, they all sail on the night tide. Admittedly, I am a little excited by the possibility of quiet and time with my husband.

Once I am fully dressed, hair braided, dagger on thigh, I help Heather into my bed so she can rest more, pouring her a glass of water to help when she wakes up. I pull the sheets which she snuggles into, then leave my chambers, enjoying how eerily quiet it is while the entire court sleeps in. I wander to the king's chambers and gently knock on the door.

A shuffle later Tariq opens it, his eyes going wide when he sees me, and he stands up straight. He's still wearing the same clothes he was last night, including his shoes. I peer him up and down with a small chuckle. "Did you and Koen manage to watch the sunrise, then?" I ask with a small smile, leaning on the door frame casually.

"Yeah, we did." He yawns. "I've only had an hour sleep. You'll have to forgive me."

"Don't stress. I just wanted to remind you we have the meeting very soon. So, it's probably best you eat something and..." I look him up and down. "Bathe. Change your clothes perhaps."

"Do I get a crown?" he jokes but nods and bows his head. "Anything for you, princess." He even casts me a small wink. A wink, which makes me ache deep in my pelvis.

"I'll find you a crown." I chuckle and step away, "Don't be late. The guards will show you to the council chambers when you're ready." I bow my head as I turn and leave him, making sure to briefly knock on Adora's door and Koen's, proceeding to the council chambers where Chione awaits.

The lords and ladies haven't arrived yet. She perches on a seat to the left of my chair. The chair on the right is for the king, the left for the queen's closest ally which due to the union between the two of us, is her.

"Best part of not drinking, no hangover," she says happily as I enter, then stands, bowing and pressing a kiss to the back of my hand. "And what a blushing bride you make, dear Lorilynn."

I roll my eyes. "Are you this much of an ass with everyone?" I tease.

"Absolutely everyone." She grins back, and the two of us sit. "Have you heard anything from the Collective?" Always to business, as it must be.

"Not yet. Although, I imagine it'll be a matter of weeks now at most. My *gift* will most likely cause a stir."

"When you say *gift*, you mean the coffins?"

"And my note explaining that they can kindly fuck themselves."

Chione chuckles. "Wow, very mature and queenlike."

"I was having a bad day," I say in my defense. Both of us know I did it because I was angry. I hadn't even watched the execution, just informed Adora that it was to be done and later handed him the note. I even supplied the ship and crew. "But in all seriousness, I expect another very strongly worded letter to be arriving any moment now. Or an assassination attempt."

Chione nods. "We best get on with this... If only the morons were here."

On cue, the doors open and Tariq and Koen stumble in together. Both have tried to not appear disheveled. They are dressed, hair brushed, walking straight. But both are pale look tired. Koen attempts a polite bow, but it's sort of half-assed, and he quickly sits in the chair. Perhaps arranging this meeting the day after the wedding was a bad idea.

Tariq shuffles over to the chair on the right side, but before sitting, leans forward and plants a kiss on my hair, "Looking radiant, Chione," he murmurs to her as he sits, bowing his head politely.

"You certainly still enjoy a party, don't you, Tariq?" She chuckles and turns to me. "When he was visiting Ptah once, he snuck a bottle of his father's wine in and proceeded to get incredibly intoxicated at a party. Unfortunately for him, everyone there wasn't drinking, so he was the only drunk moron."

"Hey! Stop making me look bad in front of my wife!"

"Oh, you do that all on your own." I smile up at him, and he shakes his head but smiles. Always smiling. An Entity-damned smile.

"And now you're stuck with me. No divorce this time."

Koen raises a brow from where he sits across the table. "This time?"

Just then, right on the bell, Azra and Adora walk in, along with the rest of the council. Everyone is seemingly feeling a little unwell, but all take their seats, and a maid begins bringing around water. Then we begin. I thank everyone for coming, for their well wishes regarding my marriage and coronation. They all offer congratulations again. We thank them once more. It is tempting to make a law that we are never offered congratulations again.

"I'd like to begin the proceedings for today, starting with announcing that Prithan has not only entered a marriage alliance with Turkish Arabia. Princess Chione El Sayed and I entered the union of allegiance." There is an audible gasp.

"This is going to guarantee Prithan protection over the coming years regarding our new business venture with Turkish Arabia," I explain and take a breath, bowing my head to Azra in a symbol of mutual respect. She does it back, even though I'm sure she wished I had informed her of Ptah's involvement. "On that note, since my rise to the throne, it became apparent to me that the previous queen and king of Prithan—" There's a mumble of *may they be with the Entity*, "—had an agreement with Queen Khan in unite the countries to help grow and farm camellia sinensis. The products will be supplied to the countries involved and the rest sold at cost," I announce.

Adora raises his hand. "How does this involve the Southern Isle?" He motions to Koen. "No offense, your highness."

"None taken," Koen replies and stands. "It doesn't. It, however, does involve me. King Thornton and I will be building the machinery that'll give us an edge over the Collective. Besides, it is no secret that I was involved in the corporation for a time. I have information that'll become useful when war comes."

"War?" a lord repeats, his frown as deep as his wrinkles. "With the Collective?"

"Yes, war is to be expected. For a variety of reasons. Some being that the Collective is seemingly aware of our inventory, and therefore, our intentions. The next being that two of their officials attempted to hang me from a tree, so I had them executed. As per Prithan law. Their caskets are currently on their way to the eastern side of the globe where they will most definitely not be taken lightly." Again, the room is eerily silent.

"Did they send the pirates?" another council member asks.

"No, however, it doesn't matter. Captain Oni now sails under the Prithan flag. Those who sent the pirates have been... dealt with." I cast a glance at Azra, and she pales a little. I can almost see the memory of the flaming head in her eyes. "We will not be disturbed by such assailants again." I peer up at Azra once more, offering a professional smile, a queenly smile that the room sees as a sign of our friendship. She sees it as a threat, swallowing nervously as she jitters a little. "Queen Khan, is there anything you'd like to add?"

"Only that the tea will be grown in Turkish Arabia. My son and I will be leaving this evening to begin preparations for Queen Thornton in bring the electricity and saplings."

"Actually," Tariq speaks and rests his hand over mine on the table. "I have duties here to fulfil."

Azra frowns. "But you're my son. You're the prince of Turkish Arabia still."

"And Lorilynn is technically its princess. But here we are queen and king," he says back, leaning into me.

Azra has a panicked expression as she looks over him, even opening her mouth to argue, but snaps it shut quickly. Tariq's hand still rests over mine. He makes no move to remove it, but I don't encourage the action either. With all eyes on us, she drops the matter, and the meeting continues. Everything is discussed, from timings, to who oversees what, to how we will respond to the war declaration at its arrival.

It is arranged that Koen will travel with Chione to Ptah and spend time helping discuss intelligence regarding the Collective. Azra will sail to Turkish Arabia to figure the details out there. Tariq and I will collect the plans here, and when the declaration comes, we will sail to Icelandic Prithan and then the botanical island before heading to Turkish Arabia. But that gives us some time together, here in Prithan castle, alone to enjoy being married, at least before the chaos starts.

By the time we are done, it is well past lunch, and everyone is unfortunately sober. Chione and Koen excuse themselves to pack. The council also leaves, Adora following them. I wish they didn't, because now only Tariq, myself, and Azra remain.

"Well... Lorilynn, you certainly have captured my son." She sighs as she stands, stalking her way over.

"*Ana*," he warns, but she keeps her intense gaze with mine which is just as harsh.

"You forced us together. This is a political marriage. Don't look down on us just because there is fondness within it too," I say coolly. "I'll leave you two a moment." I bow, then gently squeeze my husband's hand before making my way out.

Sometime later, Chione and Koen are already packing the carriage to take them to her ship. I'm going to miss them a lot. Watching Koen carry some bags with Chione's guards as she orders them about.

"Take care of my airplane for me, Lori," Koen calls, Chione chuckling.

"You better not be leaving without giving me a hug first," I say as I walk towards her. She stops ordering the guards a moment and immediately jogs over, wrapping both her arms around me tightly.

"Promise you'll visit me in Ptah when you can, when everything has settled down," she says into my shoulder.

"I promise," I say and give her a light squeeze. "You must introduce me to your wife and the sultan."

"He's going to love you," she says, but I don't exactly believe her. The sultan is a respected man of a powerful country, and I've gone and shaken the dice up. "You're going to change the world, Lorilynn."

"And you're going to rule it," I say as she steps back, lingering a moment before bowing and heading to her carriage, guards following.

Koen comes in front of me, bowing low and kissing the top of my hand. "Lori, you are a remarkable queen." He smiles. "I can't wait to see where this adventure takes you."

"You're part of it too. You can't give me all the credit," I say, and we embrace, holding each other tightly. I shut my eyes and lean into him. "I'm going to miss you."

"And I you." He pauses a moment. "I like Tariq. You two are good together. He was the right choice." Koen steps back as the King takes the place beside me, and even the two of them embrace, slapping their hands on each other's backs.

"Stay safe, Koen," Tariq says. "Best of luck in Ptah."

"And you too. I know how much of a nightmare your wife can be."

"Hey!" I protest comically with a smile.

"Queen Thornton, King Thornton." He gives his last bows and hurriedly goes to join Chione. Their carriage is fully packed, and soon they roll away with the guards on horses behind. I'm going to miss them terribly. I peer up at Tariq. I think he will too.

The maids begin bringing Azra's things as well. I will most certainly *not* miss her. As she fusses, lecturing a maid for dragging the train of a dress on the ground, I peer up at my husband, keeping my voice low.

"What happened to it?" I ask quietly.

"It?" He glances at me with a raised brow.

"The head," I clarify, "of our dear friend, the captain."

"I'm not entirely sure. I suspect my mother probably got someone to remove it eventually." He shrugs. "Next time you should sneak one in her luggage perhaps?"

I chuckle but shake my head. "Even I have my limits." I smile.

She seemingly is finished directing and trots over to us. We both offer stiff nods at each other. She holds Tariq close, kissing his cheek, and the two share words in Turkish as she pulls away, then focuses on me. "I am so pleased that we sorted out the little misunderstanding," she speaks, holding her hand out for me to kiss.

I take it, making sure my grip is tight. "If by misunderstanding you mean your multiple attempts to kill me which resulted in countless deaths, then yes, I'm glad it is sorted." I shake her hand. I will not be kissing it. "And I suppose if we ever have a disagreement, I can always leave you another head on a spike outside your window." I keep my smile up.

She looks over me cautiously. I am certainly not the young girl I was when we first met.

"May the Entity grant you safe passage back to Turkish Arabia. I hope your journey is uneventful, Azra." I say her first name as if it belongs to me, because it does. I have her son, and when she is dead, I will have her country. She will never use me again, never force me again. After today, I never have to shake her damned hand again or offer her a smile.

Fuck Azra Khan, fuck her for thinking she could use us.

"And thank you for your hospitality. Prithan is a beautiful country,

I can see a lot of healing in its future." She again offers the fake, polite grin all royals are taught at a young age. "Once more, congratulations on your wedding. The two of you make a wonderful couple. May you spend many long and happy years together. Filled with love, and hopefully many children."

I cringe at that. Children? We have been wed for less than twenty-four hours and already we're making talk about heirs.

"We will certainly enjoy trying," Tariq says, wrapping an arm around my waist. I raise my eyebrows and glare at the comment. "Goodbye, *Ana*," he finally says and kisses her cheek, but his hand stays wrapped around me.

Azra seems as displeased at the comment as I am and takes her depart, turning quickly and wandering to her carriage which will promptly take her from my land to the sea.

"*We will certainly enjoy trying*. Really?" I raise a brow once more to him when she is on her way down the drive.

"It got her away, didn't it?" He chuckles, and we turn back in towards the castle, walking from the foyer and now shut doors. In our castle, our home together. His hand still on my hip. A part of me wants to push him off, another wants him to stay there forever.

After a while, as we're approaching his chamber doors, he shoots me a smirk. "Is that a no to the sex then?"

I let out a burst of laugher and smile back at him. "It's still political," I say and take his hand, guiding him inside and shutting the door behind us.

EPILOGUE

The queen and her king look back at what happened between them often. As days go by, they find themselves not only finding each other's company because they are the only ones who know the other well enough, but because they begin to truly enjoy it. The queen even laughs occasionally. He loves making her laugh. Loves seeing her smile and throw her head back. Loves seeing her free, happy.

Loves *her.*

The two sit in the gardens among new white roses and beds of lavender, watching the bees. Now that the dusk is staring to go, wildlife has started to integrate into everyday life. The queen can't believe she is watching them buzz about everything normally, even after the long journey from the botanical island. Soon they'd have honey. *Honey*. Even more natural antibacterial properties. Even more flavor for food and drinks. A little part of history making a comeback.

"You seem happy." The king's voice is gentle, calm and intimate. She peers over at her husband to see kind eyes. The brown caramelizing in the sunlight. He sees the glimmer in his queen, the peach cheeks on her skin, and the shine in her hair that he hasn't seen before. And a dimple. She has a dimple—just under the outer corner of her eye that only dips when she truly smiles. He could spend forever looking at that dimple. It makes his chest melt and his heart pound.

"I am... Is that bad? I'm waiting for war, one I know could be filled with so much death. Yet I'm here watching wildlife. In the sunlight." The queen loves the feel of gentle heat gracing the tops of her arms. In summer, it will be much more intense. She'll need to tell her people to protect their skin. But now, she bathes in it. Loves it. Loves all it does. Sometimes rabbits cross the grass. Even deer have come out of the extensive forest north, sightings of the beauties reported to her. As soon as a rumor starts that they are being spotted, she instates a law protecting them, allowing the population to soar again over the next few years. Considers it a small, good deed in an attempt to balance the negative ones.

"I don't think it's bad. There is no point worrying until the official announcement. Besides, *Ana* will be arriving in Turkish Arabia over the next few days and everything will begin."

Queen Khan had left a week ago with her automaton ship. Plus, the wind is reported to be going well. The queen expects news shortly. So does her husband. Nothing yet though.

She does not worry. He does.

"I'm tired of waiting," she snaps, perhaps a little too harshly. The king is used to it now. Stress is a dangerous thing. She has been exposed to it more than people usually are. That isn't exactly surprising. But the king can feel something isn't quite right, like a veil was hung over her head, or a demon watching her from the corner. That's how she described her feelings in the past. He has his demons too. Ones that eat away at his stomach. He never goes a day without feeling that knife between his fingers, the look in her eyes of betrayal, of anger like a hot poker. Only the sight of her, alive, staring up at the sky, can burn those aces away. Like delicate snow cooling embers, turning them into ash on icy ground. Icy ground covered in flowers. Lavender. Her favorite. Every day he puts a fresh vase outside her chambers when they get back from training. An apology. A little one each day until she sees how he cares for her. How he will bend a knee, honor her. Love her.

"You'll regret saying that." He chuckles.

His manservant comes over, passing each of them a goblet of wine. The king is happy to take it and drink the rich, warm liquid. But is surprised when his wife doesn't and insists his servant drinks it instead. He thought it may relax her a little.

"I'm feeling a little nauseous. Alcohol probably isn't a great idea at the moment."

"Look." He places the wine down beside him on the stone bench and takes her hands, rubbing along each knuckle tenderly.

The queen melts into the touch, not that she'd admit it. Like she won't admit how she longs for the way he grazes her hands sometimes, or for him to cup her cheeks, the feel of his touch across her waist when they look out the window of the library after an afternoon of reading... or to see him wild and free under her like he was on their wedding night. She can't let herself feel this way, let herself trust him again. No matter the effort he puts in, the little favors he leaves her, the lavender she often finds outside her door wrapped in white satin ribbon. And she won't ever admit how she has them in a vase on her bedside table, the ribbons saved in a drawer.

"Please do not worry now. Carry on being happy." The king's words guide the queen. She doesn't move away, doesn't snatch her hands back. Holds on a little tighter.

He will hate her soon.

"Sometimes I consider myself very lucky that you're my husband," the queen tells him, and he is genuinely and pleasantly surprised. "Despite how we met. The horrors we both endured. I honestly don't think I'd rather anyone else."

"I'm pleased you think that. Very pleased."

The queen and king stay for a little longer until a small drizzle of rain replaces the golden sun. Then they both run in, still hand in hand. The queen cannot help herself, with them both covered in the shower, hair stuck to the sides of their faces and clothes dripping onto the stone floor, she kisses him quickly. Passionately. Holding his face, their lips moving together. He was burning, and she is the frost cooling him.

She can't understand why she'd does it, just that she needs to. Not wants to. *Needs* to.

It's only when Lord Tersoo clears his throat that they part. The queen goes from euphoria to tidal waves.

"Lorilynn, Tariq...." His voice is grave, his hands behind his back. There's a tight expression on his face.

"Has the official declaration been made?" the queen asks, her voice monotone. Always monotone when it's official business. It's the part of her the king thinks is most like her mother.

How quickly she changes. She was kissing him and now holds herself tall, angry only moments later.

The lord hesitates, eyes shifting anxiously between the two. Seemingly a little embarrassed at breaking the intimate moment between the royals.

"Perhaps... a more private room?" The king's suggestion brings peace to Lord Windsor it seems. They walk to the nearest door—the castle's formal dining room. Queen Thornton takes a seat, her king standing by her.

Lord Tersoo retains formalities, something unusual for him. "We received two coding's today. The first from Turkish Arabia," Tersoo says. The king's eyes brighten. It's the message he's been waiting for. "Queen Khan's ship was raided by pirates. I'm so sorry, Tariq. Your mother was killed."

The king can't breathe, can't think. His mother is dead. Killed by pirates. Pirates. But it's so unusual... pirates remain near Collective lands. They've only been away once before when—when his mother paid them to kill the last rulers of Prithan. Then his wife had taken them in as her people...

She hasn't said anything yet. He looks at her, at how her face hasn't changed with shock or surprise.

"What color were the sails?" he stutters. The king doesn't want to believe it. He wants to be wrong. Wants her to at least say something.

"They were blue," the queen says. So, she does have a tongue to speak with. Just not the words he wants to hear.

She admits it. She's a bad person. A spiteful person. A person who had this planned from the battle and hadn't even told her closest friends. Oni was the only soul to know—until the rest of the crew were killing the queen, that is.

"Everyone else made it to Turkish Arabia unharmed. I'm sorry for your loss, King Thornton." The lord shakes gravely. His queen turned out to be just like the one before. Exactly what he didn't want. She knew that.

"King Khan," he spits. "My name is King *Khan*. And I'm leaving. Get me a ship. Now."

The queen has little surprise in watching him leave. Not looking back. She won't see him for a while. That's for sure. Lord Tersoo watches him go too, shaking his head.

"How long have you had this planned, Lorilynn?"

"Since I found out that bitch had my parents slain. She deserved death."

"And you're queen of Turkish Arabia?"

"Yes, I am. What was the second code received?"

•

Lord Tersoo leaves after the news. It is as expected. War. The Collective is threatening to invade if the queen doesn't stand down and bend a knee. The bodies made it then.

That was expected. Everything is done.

She has more to think about. Queen of Turkish Arabia. Turkish Arabian Prithan now. Or maybe Prithan Turkish Arabia. Both sound like too much.

"Oh, Mother, how you underestimated me," the queen whispers to the reflection in her dresser mirror, crown upon her head. So much suffering for a sparkling piece of metal.

Royalty is stupid, the queen often thinks, so stupid. Fighting, politics, just for power over borders that people put down years ago. Everyone thinks about *their* country. About only the people who live in it. Just a silly concept. Yet a concept worthy of the death of innocents. We all share this planet. All people from different places. Why can humans not think of such? That's not how the world works though.

The queen looks at herself in the mirror. The bruises have faded, blood washed away. The cuts have healed. Scars line her skin. Pale white and pink. Even the bullet in her shoulder no longer stings.

Except there would always be things. Things people will not be able to see. In her mind. Her bones. Her blood. Her stomach. Her skin. Her muscles. Reminders of what has been endured. Good and bad.

It is all she has. The scars and the motivation to help her people. All of them. In Prithan, Iceland, and now Turkish Arabia. She clings to that as she cries. Sobbing to herself, saying the same words over and over.

"I don't want this."

•

The king is gone by the time The queen wakes at sunrise. She goes to their usual place like she does every morning when they meet to train. He isn't there. That was a sacrifice. *He* was the sacrifice. Her happiness and feelings for him, they aren't hers. Her feelings belong to her country. They must. Her job is to rule, to give herself to it completely. It is the most important lesson her mother taught her.

Our lives are not our own.

The queen goes to her husband's chambers when he isn't at training, hoping that magically he decided to stay. She knows she messed up, knows she is a murderer and doesn't deserve his friendship. Doesn't deserve anyone's friendship. She was stupid to think they could work together. Queens do not work with anyone. They have people who work *for* them. Kings are for helping create heirs, offering moral support, and uniting countries. Queens are the rulers. She is a ruler.

There is no answer when she knocks. The queen opens the door, hoping for the smell of incense, his shirt flung on the floor somewhere, the bed sheets tangled. They aren't.

Windows are wide open, fresh air lingering. Everything of his is cleared. The bed has fresh sheets, ironed flat. The floor is clean. There is no trace of her father either. The person she held dearest. These were his chambers, then her husbands. Now... it belongs to memories. Good and bad. Memories of stories when she was younger being read to from leather-bound books, or King Khan's smile when he opened the door to her in their time together.

His servant walks in on her standing in the center, looking around in her training gear. He isn't shocked to see her. Servants have ears. That's something always to remember.

"He left at sunlight, your majesty."

Gone.

It's just me. She thinks to herself. Well, her and Lord Tersoo. He always has her back. Although she knows he will never look at her the same. Never think of her the same.

Murderer.

Bitch.

Just like her mother.

Lord Tersoo hated her mother.

Dwelling isn't good. It wastes time. Prithan is now at war. It is also starting the biggest global business in modern day. She is the face and voice of that. If she is forced by birth to rule boundaries in imaginary borders, then she will do it to the best that she can.

Two steps need to be done before planting can begin. The queen knows she needs to go to the Eden archives. Collect the seeds. Then, with those and the plans, sail to Icelandic Prithan and supervise the finalizing of the electric transfer. Then Turkish Arabia.

She vows to herself she will not think, will not dwell, will not let any memory or emotion taint her. Her mind will be autonomous. She will just... grow... like the lavender she loves so much. Like the tea they will create.

She loves nothing. Not the things she has grown over the years. Not the memories she holds close. Not the belongings she has.

Her life is not her own.

It belongs to her countries, her borders filled with people.

That's it.

No one else. She will not love another being ever, not risk herself like that.

Every day she tells herself this. Every second in the carriage on the way to the Eden archives. She doesn't even stop at the place she grew up, that she called home. Then travels all the way back, not thinking once about how she is holding probably the most valuable things Prithan owns in a wooden box.

The wind isn't in favor of sailing, so the queen must stay in Prithan before Iceland. She does not read. She does not train. Only works. Studies paperwork. Communicates with her new business partners. Has meetings with the council. Lets her power grow. She had been fire. She had been snow. She is something else now.

Dangerous.

Unstoppable.

Powerful.

Untouchable.

And when the nightmares come—blood, nausea, the rope, the

rose—she tells herself this. Dangerous. Unstoppable. Unlimited. She is the descendant of Queen Elizabeth Thornton, the Ruthless. Daughter of Queen Catriona Thornton, the Uniting. She wonders what she will be known as. She started as the sickly princess. Transcribed into an unknown queen, one who many presumed dead. She knows what she hopes to be. Untouchable. Always untouchable. No one is untouchable. All it takes is a weapon flung, accidentally hitting the wrong person, a knife across the throat and then discarded in the water, or the orders for pirates to get you. No one is untouchable. Not a guard. Not a king. Not a queen.

It takes more time for her to decide. It takes the sailing to Iceland. Takes the walk to the scientific institution. It takes going down the stairs, took looking through the glass, seeing lightning dancing through a metal cage in front of her. Alive. More alive than anything. The queen wants it to charge her bones, charge her muscles. She had been fire. She had been snow. She isn't that anymore. She isn't ever going to be untouchable. Anyone who pretends they are is more at risk than usual. But she can be powerful. She can be alive. More alive than anything she's ever seen before. She doesn't want to be Queen Thornton, the Untouchable. She wants to be more. She knows who she is more than ever. She doesn't want to be fire. She doesn't want to be snow. She wants to be electrifying.

Electrifying.

ACKNOWLEDGMENTS

Ashen Rose started as a dream. Not in a mystical 'I always dreamed this' way but as I literal dream when I was sleeping off too much wine. I'd dreamt about two characters having a secret marriage and it sort of went from there. Whilst developing it, I started looking into forced marriage and the effects of that on people round the world. With that, I would like to say that nothing in this book is truly fiction. Everything the characters experience happens to someone somewhere. Just because its set four thousand years in the future doesn't mean we shouldn't try and stop the issues of today now.

Another aspect I included was 'acute hydrocephalus' which is also a very real thing I experienced. As is the tinnitus, balance problems, and hearing loss. Whilst these were caused by a head injury for Lorilynn, they were caused by something different for me. In my recovery I wanted to read about amazing heroes who didn't become less great just because of how their body was working after trauma.

There are many people to thank for this book. Jessi Elliott - who is an absolute star. Miss Powell from secondary school who was the most supportive, amazing English teacher. My beta reader Mim - who would also send me the memes she made after reading it. You will always be the OG AR Stan. To Rosie, who spent the better of an evening sat with me helping me with everything and sharing her knowledge.

And my love, Jack, who has listened to me talk about this since I was eighteen.

My parents who are very supportive and have probably indulged my book buying too much. Everyone else in my family too who are the most supportive (On that note… please just skip the sexy scenes guys)

And to me. Because I'm kind of proud of this one.

ABOUT THE AUTHOR

Tabitha was born in the south of England. She studied Film at Aberystwyth University and runs a small media company. She lives back in her hometown with her animal family and partner. If she isn't working or writing, she'll be reading, gaming, or accidentally killing her herb garden.

Printed in Great Britain
by Amazon

85775263R00260